Kingdom of Illusion

Kingdom of

Random House ▪ New York

ILLUSION

Edward R. F. Sheehan

FIRST PRINTING

Library of Congress Catalog Card Number: 64–11988

MANUFACTURED IN THE UNITED STATES OF AMERICA BY

H. Wolff Book Manufacturing Company, New York

DESIGN BY TERE LOPRETE

To My Parents

Author's Note

The country I have created in this book may at times seem to correspond with one particular place, and then with another; but it is primarily a country of the mind. Equally, certain aspects of some of my characters may occasionally seem reminiscent of real individuals, but in a contemporary novel, this is unavoidable. My men and women are composite fantasies, and it would be futile for the reader to try to identify anyone in the story with real people, living or dead, in America or the Middle East.

On the other hand, although I have taken some liberties with Middle Eastern history for the purposes of the plot, I have endeavored to be factual in referring to the prayers, beliefs and practices of Islam. Equally I have endeavored to be true to the spirit, though not to the facts, of the real period in time of which I write—some few years ago, perhaps during the latter part of the last decade.

E. S.

I

And they said: Come, let us make a city and a tower, the top whereof may reach to heaven: and let us make our name famous before we scatter abroad into all lands. And the Lord came down to see the city and the tower, which the children of Adam were building. And he said: Behold, it is one people, and all have one tongue: and they have begun to do this, neither will they leave off from their designs till they accomplish them in deed. Come ye, therefore, let us go down, and there confound their tongue, that they may not understand one another's speech. And so the Lord scattered them from that place into all lands, and they ceased to build the city.

Genesis, XI, 4-8

1

Languid, clamorous, contradictory, the rhythm of the Arab city enveloped the Ambassador's reverie at the dawn of the new day. He lay alone in bed, serene among the sounds he loved, insensible to diplomacy, duplicity and God.

From the involved streets below, the sweet cacophony came: the grating of cartwheels, the braying of donkeys, the mendicant musicians strumming on crude instruments. The melancholy chants of the peddlers: "O watermelon, sweet as honey!" "Gas! Gas for sale!" He let the pictures parade in his mind: he could see the poor pouring out of the desert and villages with their wares, in their flowing raiment, on camel-back and barefoot. "Odors of Paradise! Flowers of the henna! O maidens!" *"Lemongo, Orango, Co-Cola, Bebsi-Cola! Bebs! Bebs!"* The Ambassador tried to remember if he had ever seen anyone drinking Pepsi-Cola at six o'clock in the morning.

4

It was not until he got up that he realized he had a hangover, and then he cut himself shaving. At breakfast he spilt some fresh fish on a striped tie sent him for Christmas by the Secretary of State. Waiting on the front steps of the Residence for his limousine, he looked across the Corniche and saw two hoopoo birds collide in mid-air—a most unusual sight—above the sparkling waters of the broad Mabrouk. Zebra and rufous-colored feathers floated over the waters in the wind as the birds limped upwards on their wings. *Hoop-hoop-hoopoo!* The Ambassador had lived a long time in the Kingdom of Al Khadra, and he had learned to revere the veracity of portents. He wondered whether he was going to have an unlucky day.

Then the official Cadillac darted past the pair of municipality police at the gate of the Residence and crunched to a stop below him. Taking up the rear was the Land-Rover with his keepers: three Bedouin soldiers festooned with silver daggers and submachine guns. They followed him wherever he went, ostensibly to protect him, but also to report on his movements; he called them the Three Stooges. Fawzi, the Ambassador's chauffeur, and Abdel Kader, his fezzed, dapple-garmented footman, popped out of the Cadillac. Fawzi dashed around to hold open the rear door, and Abdel Kader puffed up the long steps to relieve his master of his attaché case. The Ambassador got into the limousine, settled back on the soft cushions, put on his horn-rimmed reading spectacles and glanced at some state papers while Fawzi unfurled the American flag and the ambassadorial pennant on the front fenders. Then they roared off for the Embassy.

"It's bloody hot today, *ya Fawzi.* Turn on the air conditioner."

"Sorry, Fitz Basha. It's broke again."

"Get it fixed."

"Man say no sbare barts."

"Have they nationalized spare parts too?"

Sean Sebastian Fitzgibbon grumbled and pressed a button. The window came down and let in the dusty July morning. Speeding along the Corniche he had helped build, he inhaled anew the special smells of Al Asima, the capital city. The Mabrouk, the Blessed River—broad, cerulean, splendid—flowed on. A white-sailed *filucca* tacked upriver, against the skyscrapers on the far shore. On the promenade, two young gentlemen strolled hand in hand, and a veiled woman slapped a child. The ambassadorial party passed Liberation Bridge (formerly Napoleon Troisième Bridge) and crossed Victory (formerly Victoria Regina) Bridge, gay with the green flags of Al Khadra and large, grinning photographs of the Prime Minister.

The American Embassy in Al Asima was a tall and not unattractive building, cream-colored; it stood in an immense, walled compound embroidered with geraniums and flame trees, five miles upstream from the Residence. When the Cadillac pulled into the compound and came to rest in front of the Chancery, two of the gardeners competed for the privilege of opening the Ambassador's door. Mixing ceremony with subservience, they bowed the Pasha onto the pavement; one of them tried to kiss his hand. These histrionics were typical of the frenzy which Fitz Pasha's presence inspired. The Embassy always seemed to stand up straighter when the Ambassador was there. He waved to the brown-skinned messenger boys, gardeners and menial laborers who had gathered, as they did every day, to hail his coming. They reciprocated his greeting with warmth, for he had been good to them.

"Good morning Mohammed, Ali, Mahmoud!"

"May your morning be full of light, Fitz Basha!"

The Ambassador's appearance in the lobby of the Chancery caused the same sort of commotion. His footman—or *kavass,* as he was called—ran ahead of him imperiously, and people dived in all directions to make straight Fitz Pasha's path. At the reception desk, the Marine sergeant was giggling with a stenographer from the motor pool; he snapped to attention when he saw the Chief of Mission. The Ambassador recognized him as the young man who had discovered a microphone in the Political Officer's hat rack. "Is it your habit, Sergeant," he asked in passing, "to giggle while standing the guard?"

As for the Ambassador's habits, waiting more than fifteen seconds for the elevator was not one of them. He pressed the button. One. *Two.* Three. *Four.* That was his personal signal; no one else dared use it. On the sixth floor the operator evicted the Director of Personnel and the Potable Water Attaché and crash-dived for the lobby; he made it this morning in almost record time. Sean Sebastian Fitzgibbon was whisked to the Tower. Miss Speed, his private secretary, was typing when he entered his suite. She looked up from her machine and smiled chastely—reflecting, so the Ambassador had often mused, a predicament not uncommon among expatriate American maidens.

"Good morning, Mr. Ambassador."

"Good morning, Hortense. How is the little fellow this morning?"

"Pretty chipper, I'd say. I haven't had a chance to give him his breakfast."

"Don't bother, I'll do it myself. Any news on that appointment?"

"They just called. The Prime Minister will see you at ten."

"Good show. Have you got the morning newspapers?"

"I can get them from Mr. Grundoon. Did they forget to deliver them to the Residence?"

"They delivered them, but after last week's editorials I gave up reading them at breakfast. Tell Grundoon to bring in the papers and last night's cables, if there are any."

The Ambassador entered his commodious paneled office. Miss Speed had already turned on the air conditioning. On the periphery of the Persian carpet, within a semicircle of red leather chairs, stood a Regency desk. He sat down behind it in his high-backed swivel, and contemplated for a moment the trinkets of travel on three continents: a petrified fish, a silver arrow, an inscribed photograph of the Secretary of State. *To Shawnie Fitzgibbon—contemporary and classmate—with affection and esteem, Calvin."*

His eyes shifted from the blandness of Calvin Hampshire's smile to the militancy of his ways. On the blotter before the Ambassador were the commercial wire reports; he invariably began each day by perusing them; the momentous news this Thursday morning was the Secretary's latest pronouncement on the Middle East. ". . . Soviet seduction . . . tireless tentacles . . . Mideast mischief . . . mystic minarets . . . boisterous blackmail . . . xylophonic xenophobia. . . ."

Miss Speed buzzed. "Mr. Grundoon."

"All right."

Christopher Grundoon came in. He was young, golden-haired, and like the Ambassador, Boston Irish. The Ambassador considered this irrelevant; Fitz Pasha did not work very hard at being

Boston Irish. He had hand-picked Grundoon as his personal assistant because he considered him intelligent—or so he told himself.

He kept his aide standing while they talked. "What dragon is the Ministry of National Enlightenment slaying this morning?"

"Do you want it straight, Mr. Ambassador—or in translation?"

"Never mind the translations. Let me see the newspapers. I thought you were learning Arabic."

"I'm learning to *speak* it, sir."

"Mostly with the lights out, I imagine?"

The Ambassador scanned *Sawt el Hurriyeh*—Voice of Freedom—the government newspaper. ". . . fishing in troubled waters . . . plots hatched in the dark . . . to the last drop of our blood . . . hunger . . . martyrdom . . . treachery . . . witchcraft . . ."

"A bit negative about Calvin's speech, aren't they?" he observed.

"They mystify me," Christopher Grundoon said. "They're very good-hearted, underneath. Why do they use such violent language?"

"My dear boy, you have certainly been here long enough to answer that question yourself. You are at large now in the strange dream world of Arab politics—and, I might add, in the even stranger dream world of American diplomacy. Any cables?"

"There's one here, Top Secret. I haven't opened it. Eyes Only."

"Good heavens, why didn't you tell me?"

TO FITZGIBBON FROM HAMPSHIRE. AMBASSADOR'S EYES ONLY. It was an unusual telegram. Absent were the rolling periods and pyrotechnic metaphors which had endeared the Secretary to stylists from Reykjavik to Pnom-Penh; today Calvin came right to the point. He was not a bit pleased with the DEFAMATORY ANTI-AMERICAN PROPAGANDA EMANATING AL KHADRA and the ABUNDANT INTELLIGENCE KHADRA CONTEMPLATING SUBSTANTIVE AID AGREEMENT MOSCOW. Instructions to COMMUNICATE MY KEEN CONCERN PRIMIN IBN MABROUK. And then, further down, after a paragraph devoted to young King Mohammed: REGARDING THAT AGREEMENT FOOD AND PHARMACEUTICALS IM BEGINNING WONDER WHETHER WE SHOULD DELIVER UNTIL DETERMINE WHICH WAY WINDS BLOWING. IM AS COMPASSIONATE NEXT FELLOW BUT COMPASSION PATIENCE COTERMINOUS.

Ambassador Fitzgibbon was even less prepared for the final paragraph: PAUL PULLMOTOR ARRIVING YOUR BAILIWICK MONDAY NEXT. ROUTINE VISIT. EXTEND ALL COURTESIES. HAMPSHIRE.

"Oh God," the Ambassador groaned. *"Pullmotor* is coming. They must be cooking up something in Washington. It's touching how they take me into their confidence. And on top of everything Hampshire is threatening to cancel the *wheat* shipment. Half a million metric tons! They'll starve. Christ."

He sighed, and looked up at his aide. "Calvin asks after the King. Have you seen him this week?"

"I'm going shooting with him after lunch," Christopher Grundoon said.

"I suppose I should call on him one of these days. Pass on the Secretary's greeting, and my own. Keep me posted on his *proclamations*. They are so entertaining."

"If I may suggest so, sir, His Majesty may not be quite the imbecile everybody supposes."

"Of course not. That's why I'm so pleased to have you there as the receptacle of his sagacity. See you at Staff Meeting."

When Grundoon had gone, the Ambassador got up from his desk, stuffed the Secretary's speech and the Top Secret telegram into his pocket, and went out onto the great open terrace adjoining his office. He had made it a greenhouse without glass. A succession of scents perfumed his progress to the balustrade: arum lily, ox-eye, lobelia and Sweet William. An oasis of blue, crimson and chrome yellow. In symmetrical pools, the romping of geysers and goldfish.

The view never failed to console him. Across the Corniche and beyond the broad Mabrouk, recumbent before him, reposed the city of his heart: dynasties, crumbling castles, tottering aqueducts and Roman ruins; streets snaking through souks, ramparts on the river and marvelous mosques. *While as far as sight can reach, beneath as clear . . . And blue a heaven as ever blest this sphere . . . Gardens and minarets and glittering domes . . . And high-built temples fit to be homes . . . Of mighty gods. . . .* Moore's lines returned effortlessly to the Ambassador. In splendor this was a vision to rival the golden plain of Vega viewed from the Alhambra, or the steeples of Venice aspiring from the hyacinthine waters of the Adriatic. Century upon century, millennium upon millennium, lay piled pell-mell on one another. The legions of Babylon, of Byzantium, of Rome; the chariots of the Persians, Phoenicians, Philistines, Greeks, Assyrians, Albanians, Hittites, Omayyads, Turks and Franks and Britons had, in their hour, passed over this valley. And now innovation was the concubine of antiquity: the skyscrapers of the new city stood like Narcissus revering themselves in the river: the broad Corniche below blinked with the reflected glory of chromium bumpers. The new city fell like a bright wave on the brownness of the old, depositing brilliant bubbles: incongruous but burgeoning squatters in the slums. And the unity of it all was like some splendid uncut stone supine in a setting of sand. For there was only sand where there was not city; it molded the contour of the city like clay in its shapeless hands, and its desert breath seemed to hover above the buildings like a specter.

But that presence could become tangible, too, and the Ambassador watched while suddenly, as if alienated by his awe, the desert breathed before his eyes. The desert drew an enormous breath, and exhaled. Its breath blew in over the barren hills looming above the old quarter; it blew in over the pagoda-like minarets and bulbous domes of the City of the Dead, over roofs and mosques, over the workers' housing development and the new fertilizer plant and through the skeleton of a fortress. The sky turned to the color of rusty copper. Now the city would begin to gird itself against the ill temper of *khamseen*. Nature was a comedian, because in the language of the Prophet, Al Khadra means the Green Land, so named in a moment of cruel and immemorial irony. There was no green, except in the ribbon of growth on either side of the river, and there was but trite treasure buried beneath the sands. A bit of phosphate here and there, a few figs, dates, mangoes and pomegranates for export, but no black gold, no hidden lakes of petrol; only a pipeline or two en route from geysers in other lands to refineries in foreign places.

But the Ambassador had not come outside simply to observe the view. He turned from the balustrade and walked to the far corner of the terrace. There, amongst a profusion of potted palm, stood the cage. He opened it, and addressed himself to the tenant.

"Bon jour, chéri. Est-ce que tu as faim pour le petit déjeuner?"

It was Eminence Grise, the Ambassador's angwantibo.

He had captured it two years previously, on a safari in the rain forest of Uganda, near the Mountains of the Moon. It was a darling creature, a lemuroid, cousin to the monkey, kin to the baboon, but far more patrician and handsome. More than anything else, with his fuzzy fur and his golden eyes, he resembled a tiny teddy bear. His hands were remarkably human, and they grasped for everything in sight. He had an ostrich's appetite and would eat anything, but most of all he liked bananas, mangoes, hard-boiled eggs, fresh fish, dead birds, live grasshoppers and pieces of paper. The Ambassador kept relays of underlings constantly on call to satisfy the little fellow's needs; indeed, it was a rare third secretary who had not been despatched on what had become known in Chancery parlance as "the grasshopper run" or "the pigeon pick-up." Everything by way of modern convenience had been installed to guarantee the creature's comfort. Eminence Grise did not take kindly to the dry heat of the Middle East; for this reason his cage was humidified and temperature-controlled by an appliance appended to the Embassy air-conditioning system.

The British Museum had several stuffed specimens of the angwantibo on display, but Eminence Grise was the only member of his species in live captivity. Fitzgibbon Pasha's feat in capturing the beast had aroused international comment; the zoo keepers of London, Vienna and New York hounded him with offers to pay any price for this rarest of mammals. At first, the Ambassador answered their letters with a terse disdain; now he did not bother to reply. Eminence Grise had become so much a part of his life that even the reproaches of his superiors could not prevail on him to give the beast up.

At one time the angwantibo had accompanied the Ambassador practically everywhere; he romped about the office in the presence of visitors, attended staff meetings, promenaded with him on the Corniche, even went with him in the Cadillac to the Foreign Office. Then, several months ago, the Ambassador had attended a military parade commemorating Khadrian independence. The parade was the cause of some anticipation; Al Khadra had contributed a token guerrilla force to the Algerian uprising, and in combat the unit had seized a respectable quantity of French—and American—arms. The booty was to be displayed in the parade before being remitted to the rebellion; Prime Minister Mustafa ibn Mabrouk was eager for extensive international publicity. The Ambassador arrived for the festivities a full twenty minutes late, and as he hastened from his Cadillac he failed to close his door behind him. Fawzi and Abdel Kader did not act in time to prevent Eminence Grise from bounding out of the limousine in pursuit of his master. The procession of Fitz Pasha and his party to the reviewing stand made a memorable impression: first his military attachés in their gold braid, scrambled eggs and swagger sticks, then Abdel Kader in fez and balloon trousers, then the Ambassador in top hat and morning clothes, then the Three Stooges in rippling headdress and gleaming daggers and Tommy guns, then Eminence Grise in a brilliant green ribbon. (It happened to be the feast of St. Patrick, the one day of the year on which the Ambassador publicly reverted to his roots.) The foreign news photographers were delighted.

Unseemly though it was, the incident might have been overlooked if once on the reviewing stand the angwantibo had reposed obediently by his master's knee. He did not do this; at the very moment when the French bazookas passed by, the little fellow began taking certain unmentionable liberties with Lady Chetwynd-Pott, the wife of Her Britannic Majesty's Ambassador.

The front-page accounts of the parade in the great newspapers of London, Washington and Moscow the next morning scarcely mentioned the captured arms, but they did dwell on the Angwantibo Affair in generous detail. The Prime Minister was almost as outraged as Sir Charles and Lady Chetwynd-Pott. Nor did the Department pass over the matter: Sean Sebastian Fitzgibbon was very nearly recalled, and averted this humiliation only by writing the Secretary a personal letter promising that henceforth Eminence Grise would be restricted to the premises of the Embassy and the Residence.

But that was months ago. "Now it's time for your breakfast," the Ambassador said, extracting the Secretary's speech from his pocket. He tossed it into the cage, and Eminence Grise gobbled up the nutritious rhetoric of Calvin Hampshire.

"C'est fini? You little rascal. Today I've got something *special* for your dessert. A nice, tasty telegram—Top Secret. Eat up . . . every bit. Haven't had an Eyes Only in months, eh? I think the last one was about you! No scraps, or the Marine guard will give you a

security violation! Chop-chop! All of it! Give a good chew on that paragraph about Paul Pullmotor, the bugger Calvin is sending out here to knife Fitz Pasha in the back. Gobble-gobble! Down the hatch! I can see the bastard now, trying to make a secret deal with the Prime Minister, singing siren songs in the ears of His Majesty, intriguing with the tribes, writing reports to Hampshire that I never see. *Oui, Eminence,* gobble-gobble! . . ."

2

The Political Police made it their business to know what went on behind the cream-colored façade of the American Embassy, and they knew about Staff Meeting every morning at eight o'clock. Foiled in their attempts to conceal a microphone in the conference room, they had improvised stratagems even more ingenious. In a skyscraper window on the opposite bank of the broad Mabrouk, they posted a photographer with a long-range lens and a lip-reader with a telescope. The method may not have been infallible, but its results seldom failed to be fascinating.

The conference room was in the Tower, across the corridor from the Ambassador's suite. All the senior American officers attended Staff Meeting, and despite the spaciousness of the chamber it was a tight squeeze; the Embassy was larger than the Foreign Ministry itself. The meeting invariably began on schedule; though not always punctual himself, the Ambassador did not tolerate tardiness in others.

Snatches of conversation as the conference room began to come alive at ten minutes to eight: ". . . for the tournament on Tuesday . . . if the King is deposed . . . looking for a new cook . . . these galloping rumors . . . chickening out on the wheat . . . Hampshire wouldn't dare . . . says he saw the old man last night, plastered . . . says the spooks are covering the Gazooza Club now . . . I still say Hampshire'd never go that far . . . Charlie, how about a chit for three more Johnny Walker? . . ."

At the center of the long table in the conference room stood the ambassadorial chair, of red damask and imperial proportions. On either side, and circumscribing the entire table, were a generous number of folding metal chairs. In these reposed the luminaries of the establishment according to rank. At the Ambassador's right would sit the taciturn but tireless Tobias Davenport, Minister-Counselor of Embassy and Deputy Chief of Mission. At the Ambassador's left, Q. Emmet Pidlaski, the fastidiously clad Counselor for Political Affairs; radiating outwards, the Counselor for Economic Affairs, the First Secretary for Administration, the Army, Navy and Air Force Attachés, the Commercial Attaché, the Consul and so on. Occupying a place of privilege directly opposite the Ambassador was the Director of the Point Four Mission. Clinging to the extremities of the table were a gaggle of lesser gentlemen: the Agrarian Reform Attaché, the Mineral Attaché, the Printing Plant Manager, the Protocol Officer, the Locust Control Officer, the Potable Water Attaché, and COCO (Contraband Opium Control Officer).

The room was bare of embellishment save for a telephone at the Ambassador's place, ash trays and pads of white paper for the convenience of the officers, a red carpet on the floor and a ship's clock on the wall. At one minute to eight, Dr. Cauldron Pantry, the Director of Mutual Understanding, arrived bearing a bundle of Representation Reimbursement forms. "Those mimeograph operators!" he exclaimed. "No concept of time!" Rather breathlessly, Dr. Pantry ran around the table distributing the mimeographed questionnaires as the second hand crept inexorably toward the hour.

Lip-reader: Get a picture of those documents.
Photographer: I'm doing my best. It's not easy in this sandstorm.
Lip-reader: Plans for rocket bases, probably.

. . .

The ship's clock chimed eight; a Marine opened the door, and saluted smartly. There was a great shuffling on the red carpet; chairs were pushed back and the assemblage ascended in unison to its feet. Murmuring good mornings, the envoy extraordinary and plenipotentiary—tall, gray-haired, elegant—strode briskly into the room, Eminence Grise taking up the rear. The Ambassador settled slowly into the damask throne, glanced at the questionnaire and said, "Gentlemen." The others seated themselves, the angwantibo took his appointed place beneath the Ambassador, and the meeting began.

First to speak was Q. Emmet Pidlaski, the Political Counselor, reporting scuttlebut from the Ministries. "And, sir, the Soviet Minister of Energetics and Electrification flew in from Moscow last night."

"So I heard," the Ambassador said. "I wonder what he's up to. Do you think the Russians are trying to pull another fast one?"

"I wouldn't be a bit surprised, sir."

"Maybe we'll find out something at the Soviet reception tonight. And, Grundoon, run a check on this bloke's movements and appointments today, will you?"

"Roger."

The Economic Counselor was next, assessing the progress of the Five-Year Plan. The Ambassador interrupted a turgid recitation of statistics to ask, "Yes, but how is the Plan going?"

"Much better than I expected. But they need foreign exchange."

"Badly?"

"Desperately."

"How is the agricultural part going?"

"With this drought—unless they get some wheat—I don't know how the Bedouins are going to survive the summer."

"Poor devils."

Photographer: What are they talking about now?

Lip-reader: It's obvious, you idiot. The Sixth Fleet.

The Director of Point Four was halfway through his somewhat incoherent account of problems in rural water supply when, very slowly, the door opened and the Motor Pool Attaché attempted to tiptoe into the meeting. The others watched him in apprehensive silence; crimson with embarrassment, he headed for his assigned place between Dr. Pantry and the Regional Petroleum Attaché.

"Relax, Chester," the Ambassador said. "Take off your coat. Loosen your tie. Unbutton your collar. Kick off your shoes. Smoke a cigarette. I am sure you have an unimpeachable reason for being late to this meeting."

"I was delayed on a matter having to do with your personal establishment, sir," the Motor Pool Attaché explained.

"Chester, you have given me the one excuse I can accept. I presume you refer to the air conditioning in my Cadillac."

"I went downtown with the car again this morning, but the company keeps saying it needs a spare part they never have."

"Do you think they are doing this on instructions, to harass me?"

"I wouldn't be a bit surprised, sir. Why don't you mention the matter to someone high up?"

"To complain to the Minister of the Interior might be counterproductive, for it would infer that he had something to do with impeding the repairs. The affair is too trivial to present to the Prime Minister, and too tremendous to refer to the King."

But then the Ambassador had an idea. "I wonder," he went on, "whether the Political Police boys, who are so efficient in wire tapping, office bugging and the sundry other intrigues, might not be equally resourceful in a matter as rudimentary as my air conditioning. I have half a mind to pick up the telephone and make representations to whatever nitwit happens to be listening."

"In this country, it might just work," the Motor Pool Attaché said.

The Ambassador was delighted that he had received this inspiration in the presence of his senior staff. "This is going to be great fun," he said, lifting the receiver in front of him. "Look here, old man," he declaimed into the telephone, "your country is unconscionably hot in July and the least I'm entitled to is air conditioning in my Cadillac. Now, I don't care how you do it, but I want the cooler *fixed* or I'm going to protest to Mustafa ibn Mabrouk, understand?" He repeated the message in Arabic and rang off.

That done, the Ambassador addressed himself to each officer individually, giving each a chance to speak. Fitzgibbon Pasha had long since learned to pay the price of his imperious ways: he read practically every scrap of paper coming in and out of the Embassy. There was very little going on that he did not know about—even in the paint shop or the motor pool. He never brought any notes to Staff Meeting, but he asked systematic and searching questions. "What exactly do you want me to tell the Pakistani Ambassador on this? . . . I think we ought to beef up our reporting on African exiles in Al Asima . . . Really? Well, if I have time I'll mention it to the Prime Minister when I see him this morning . . . What are the second quarter receipts on mangoes and pomegranates? . . . I'm nearly flat broke and I need more money for representation. Prepare a new justification for forwarding to the Department requesting emergency funds. Make the plea as depraved as possible and interlard it with thick layers of latinism . . ." He never dithered; he seldom spent more than a few seconds on any problem. He welcomed advice beforehand, but when his decision came it was terse and improbable of appeal. One of his favorite tricks in Staff Meeting was to dictate at high speed a lucid dispatch on some complicated matter, send it out for typing, and then sign it without having to change a comma. As a technician—as a craftsman—he had few equals in American diplomacy.

The next piece of business was a report from the Post Exchange Attaché on new items in the Embassy supermarket. This was received with keen interest by all present; the Khadrian government had recently imposed stringent controls on the importation of Western luxuries, and the PX was now, more than ever, the survival station for the displaced gentry of Arlington, Bethesda and Chevy Chase.

"We have made special arrangements to cope with the emergency," the Post Exchange Attaché announced. "Commencing next week, our standard stocks will be supplemented with canned kidney beans, pink Alaska salmon, ravioli, strawberry and cherry Jello, chili con carne, cream of wheat, fruit cocktail, clam chowder, jiffy cake mix, instant mashed potato, Blue Cheese Chip Dip . . ."

Photographer: What's happening?

Lip-reader: Stop interrupting, you half-wit. A new man is speaking. He is an American specialist in plots! He and the Ambassador are hatching an imperialist plot! Give me your pencil. I must take this down.

". . . horseradish powder, meat tenderizer, frozen orange juice, pickled pigs' feet, dog biscuit, and green-mint mouthwash. Kotex regulars, aluminum foil, spray deodorant, chlorophyll toothpaste, California claret, Niersteiner Demthol White Rhine, full-quart Guckenheimer—"

"Did we get that vodka yet?" the Ambassador interjected.

"We got the Tovarish, but we're still negotiating with the Soviet Embassy for the Samovar," the Post Exchange Attaché said.

"How are you coming on the Schenley for the Soviet Ambassador?"

"Still working on it, sir."

"Don't cough up until he comes through with the Samovar."

"Roger."

"How about the Slivovitz?"

"The Yugoslavs are dragging their feet."

"Light a little fire under them with some Old Grand-dad."

"I'll get on that today, sir."

"Good show."

The Ambassador turned to Dr. Pantry, the Mutual Understanding Director. "How goes the battle for the minds of men?" he asked condescendingly.

Dr. Pantry's lower lip responded in a nervous twitch, and his pale myopic eyes liquefied a little behind his rimless spectacles. He was terrified of the Ambassador, and with reason, for he knew that Fitzgibbon Pasha held him in slight esteem. "It's the Battle of the Budget we're waging d-down in the Mutual Understanding Department this week, Mr. Ambassador."

"Yes, I saw something come in on it. What are you pushing for the fiscal year?"

"We envisage a very efficacious anti-communist program, sir," Dr. Pantry said. "Pamphlets, illustrated lectures, comic books, newspaper ads—that sort of thing. But our big effort will be behind a little brainstorm of my own. It's called the Do-It-Yourself Anti-Communist *Kit*."

"Good gracious. What's in it? A plastic bomb?"

"We're trying to be a little more s-s-subtle, sir. The kit will contain printed matter, phonograph records, colored slides, and other visual aids. It will come in English, French and Arabic. It's portable, and is designed to meet any emergency. For example, at a cocktail party, if someone mentions Lenin's childhood, or attacks private enterprise—"

"I think I get the picture," the Ambassador said. "How many are you distributing?"

"That's the problem, sir. We're aiming at five thousand, but Washington isn't giving us nearly the funds we need."

"They do pennypinch, don't they? But you look unhappy, Doctor. Is it your fiscal tribulations—or your lumbago acting up?"

"N-neither, sir. Eminence Grise is chewing on my trousers."

The Ambassador summoned the beast to his side, chided him, and continued: "Anything else, Doctor?"

"We have a musical specialist arriving sometime today on a Department tour," Dr. Pantry said. "We didn't even know he was coming until yesterday, but we've managed to book him at the Botanical Gardens tomorrow night and the next, and we hope that all Embassy personnel will turn out to give Chuckles a good hand."

"Chuckles."

"Vespucci, Mr. Ambassador. Chuckles Vespucci."

"Piano player?"

"No, sir."

"Saxophonist?"

"No, sir."

"I give up."

"He's a lutist."

"I notice the Boston Symphony is in Moscow this month," the Ambassador said. "In Al Khadra we wage the Cold War with Chuckles Vespucci and his *lute*. Yes, Doctor, by all means, get the whole Embassy out there tomorrow night. Tell them I said so. Round up every American you can lay your hands on. Because I don't imagine you will find the indigenous populace very well represented."

"In that connection, sir, do you want me to invite Mr. Pullmotor?"

"Pullmotor? He's not due in till Monday! How the hell did you know he was coming?"

"I d-didn't. I must have been mistaken. I thought I saw him late last night, checking into the Sheraton-Zahra."

Staff Meeting ended shortly before nine. The Ambassador withdrew in evident bad temper to his suite, and then the others came popping out of the conference room: dacron peas from an air-conditioned pod. In a torrent of talk, they piled into the elevators and cascaded down the stairs to their departments. The Minister-Counselor called in his secretary and dictated a routine note to the Foreign Office. The Political Officer resumed a biographical dispatch on the new Minister of National Enlightenment. The Economic Officer returned to the composition of his long and labored assessment of the Five-Year Plan. The Consul went back to the Consulate, where he got on the telephone and persevered in a fruitless effort to liberate an itinerant Nebraskan rapist from the city jail.

Dr. Pantry returned to the Mutual Understanding headquarters, which were situated not in the Embassy compound, but in an old gingerbread building across the street. En route to his office he paid one of his surprise visits to the Translation Section, where the staff were at work rendering the entire text of the Secretary of State's interminable syntax into classical Arabic. Mr. Hamoush, the chief translator, sat staring out of the window, an expression of inscrutable agony on his face.

"Anything the matter, Mr. Hamoush?" Dr. Pantry asked.

The chief translator looked up at the Director of Mutual Understanding with melancholy eyes. He waved some teletype copy in his hand and said, "This speech of Mr. Hampshire's. I can't make it mean anything in Arabic."

"It means what it says," Dr. Pantry explained patiently. "I read it before Staff Meeting, and I found it very clear, a clarion call to combat against the common enemy. It's about time someone told you A-rabs the facts of life, Mr. Hamoush. And I must confess I'm a little astonished at *you,* Mr. Hamoush. I hope the Ambassador never hears you talking like that. He'd be very upset."

Dr. Pantry went into his office and closed the door. It was a pleasant office, neither as spacious nor as well appointed as the

Ambassador's but airy and tasteful. There were beige carpeting and green leather davenports, portraits of late American Presidents on the walls, anti-communist tomes in the abundant bookshelves. On the desk, an adding machine and a framed testament:

THE SEVEN PILLARS

1. *Life leaps like a geyser for those who drill through the rock of inertia!*
2. *Trouble, like the hill ahead, straightens out when you advance upon it!*
3. *Failure is the line of least persistence!*
4. *People are lonely because they build walls instead of bridges!*
5. *A man all wrapped up in himself makes a pretty small package!*
6. *Jumping to conclusions doesn't always make for happy landings!*
7. *True wealth is found not in your purse but in your personality!*

Dr. Pantry sat down at his typewriter and pecked out a classified telegram to the Mutual Understanding Commission in Washington. FIVE THOUSAND COPIES SECRETARYS SPEECH DISTRIBUTED HERE TODAY IN ENGLISH ARABIC FRENCH GREEK ARMENIAN. MAXIMUM IMPACT ANTICIPATED. PANTRY.

He called in his secretary and told her to send the telegram "Priority." Then he attacked the pile of papers in his *In* box. Included among these was a personal letter typical of many he received.

Dear brother Sir Pantry
Good luck.
I wish you good health, peace and all the
blessings of God on you. I wish you all kinds
of pleasure. I send this letter
with great hopes.

Dear Sir;
I recognize you that I have wife by means
of I married one month and I

want to be in good life
with my wife by means of I am in need of your great book
Good Housekeeping Guide to Successful Homemaking. Of
course it is the first demand and I am confessing
that you are great character and that is the fact
in the name of God.
I hope you to come to my house to watch my wife and spend
some day between us. Eventually I am one of the oldest clients
of your embassy.

Good greeting.

Your faithfulness
Fuad Ahmed Ibrahim
Street Al Malik 11
Kindly forward to me your good book *Home Management* which
leads to preparation and organization of houses.)

Dr. Pantry dashed off a quick memorandum to one of his numerous deputies: "Please reply to attached, specifying we do not provide gratis copies of the printed matter requested. Send him *The Rape of Budapest*." He stapled the memo to the letter, tossed it into his *Out* box, and went back to the Budget.

And preparing the Budget was a strenuous business indeed. Dr. Pantry had a very large staff; his prestige in Washington depended primarily on his dexterity in continuing to justify the expense required to maintain it. The Mutual Understanding building was a labyrinth of antechambers, offices, auditoria, film laboratories, sound studios, reading rooms, editorial rooms, mimeograph rooms, unexplored corridors and even secret passages. In room after dim, musty, rabbit-warren room, communities of Arab, Armenian, Greek and French translators hunched low over their desks struggling to reduce to intelligible local idiom mountains of typescript received from Washington. It was not an easy task. All night long the radio teletype gushed out rivers of words; in the morning the airline and steamship companies dispatched Mack trucks to the gingerbread building delivering still more mountains of Washingtonese. The material attempted to transmit the totality of the American experience—from the Declaration of Independence to the lipstick industry to the horrors of communism. When the translators had duly rendered the Washingtonese into equally tormented and obscure documents in their own language, more Mack trucks delivered the material in bulk to the newspapers, radio stations, publishing houses and high government offices of Al Asima, where it was found serviceable for scratch pads, toilet paper, and, not infrequently, for wrapping fish. Every evening after sunset the Mutual Understanding Department presented free film showings on the Embassy lawn across the street, where multitudes of ragged children too destitute to afford the commercial cinema assembled to watch short subjects on ice hockey, asparagus canning and the horrors of communism. All this was in pursuance of the official gospel of the Mutual Understanding Commission: "America's interests are identical with the legitimate interests of everybody everywhere. America loves everybody. Everybody loves America. Or they will when we get over there and *Give Them The Word.*"

Parkinson's Law had operated with particular exuberance in the Al Asima apostolate of the Mutual Understanding Commission. From a minuscule operation the staff in the gingerbread building had burgeoned over the years until now it numbered a full fifty Americans and several hundred local employees, if all the janitors, drivers, messengers, coffee boys and other miscellaneous hangers-on were included. Every few months rumors galloped throughout the building of the imminent dismissal of superfluous employees; tremors of fright erupted among the native staff when a septuagenarian mimeograph operator or a consumptive coffee boy was indeed discharged, and serenity returned only when four additional bodies were impressed as replacements.

In the attic of the gingerbread building was the Reference Room, the repository of yesterday's Washingtonese, a department entrusted to the care of an illiterate dwarf and Miss Thanatopsis, a Maltese madwoman. Neither of them spoke a word of English; under the madwoman's inspired supervision the files for the last ten years had waxed in a condition of Augean confusion; any document committed to her keeping she interred with a zeal so single-minded that neither she nor anyone else was able to exhume it. A number of heroic attempts had been made to dismiss this extraordinary person, but whenever she was tendered notice she habitually took refuge on the window ledge, threatening to leap off and releasing a series of screams and shrieks so bloodcurdling as to terrify even a neighborhood long conditioned to the turbulence of anti-American rioting. On more than one occasion Ambassador Fitzgibbon had telephoned from across the way to complain that the noise was disturbing Eminence Grise.

The Political Police were convinced that the Mutual Understanding Commission was in truth a clandestine intelligence operation and that the gingerbread building was a nest of spies. In consequence the walls were extensively wired, and the Arab staff liberally infiltrated with informers; at frequent intervals Dr. Pantry's native employees were summoned to the Ministry of the Interior, where they were subjected to various indignities and interrogated at length on the latest movements of the Sixth Fleet. Dr. Pantry himself maintained an intricate network of eavesdroppers among the native staff, though for different reasons. They kept him continuously abreast of what his American subordinates were whispering about him; the reports were not always complimentary. Nor was this the limit of his curiosity; he loved to snoop, and much of his time was consecrated to surprise inspections of his domain in search of slumbering bodies and administrative irregularities. There was an abundance of both. Only last week he had apprehended a messenger boy washing out a coffee pot in the gentlemen's urinals; the suppression of such outrages endowed Dr. Pantry with a serene sense of fulfillment.

Dr. Pantry was a native of Rhododendron, North Dakota, where he had distinguished himself in community affairs after receiving his doctorate in Modern Farm Management at the state agricultural institute. But he had always aspired to more Promethean surroundings; he embarked for Washington, where he worked in a funeral parlor before being hired as an accountant in the Bin Storage Division of the Department of Agriculture. From there he gravitated to the Mutual Understanding Commission and a succession of bookkeeping assignments in Bonn, Helsinki and Djakarta. His efficiency reports invariably reflected a reverence for his ability to do long division; in time he accumulated the seniority he needed to demand "something more challenging." His superiors were shuttlecocking his dossier when the Mutual Understanding Director in Al Asima ran away with a nanny. "Why not give the job to Cauldron Pantry?" one of the Washington types suggested. "He may not be very heavy in the double-doming department, but at least his morals meet required standards." Thus did the diplomat from Rhododendron, North Dakota, make good. Thus did Dr. Pantry confront the tormented complexity of the Arab equation with the sagacity of the adding machine.

3

Unlike Ambassador Fitzgibbon, Paul Pullmotor did not get up early in the morning, breakfast on fresh fish or pursue his mysterious ends in staff meetings. It was well after nine o'clock when he got out of bed and headed for the bathroom in his commodious suite at the Sheraton-Zahra. He splashed cold water on his face, and then—for he was not a tall man—stood tiptoe before the mirror as he ran a comb languidly through his thinning hair. He made funny faces in the glass and stuck his tongue out at his reflected image. He loved everything about himself but his looks.

The old school zip began to come to life. Much more briskly, Pullmotor repaired to his salon with the intention of calling down for breakfast. By temperament a most decisive man, he stopped short for a moment. Two additional telephones had been installed the night before, and they lay contiguous with the ordinary hotel line. He could not tell which was which.

He picked up the first phone and jiggled it. A familiar voice answered.

"Oh, Mustafa, I'm terribly sorry," he told the Prime Minister. "I picked up your direct line by error. Thanks for installing it so quickly! I was trying to call for breakfast. I'll be seeing you later, right?"

He rang off, and lifted the second receiver.

"Oh, I *am* sorry, Your Majesty," he said. "I'm very confused about my telephones this morning. That's right, I have two right here on my table—the hotel extension and Your Majesty's. Thanks for installing it so quickly! I'll be seeing you later, right?"

When Pullmotor finally reached room service, they were not very helpful.

"What do you mean you have no tapioca? But I *always* have tapioca for breakfast! You had it a year ago! Send up a cup of black coffee, then, and step on it."

He slammed the receiver down, and began to dress. The situation in Al Khadra was deteriorating even more rapidly than he had feared.

Slipping into his two-hundred-dollar suit before a full length mirror, he wondered why all the artifice of Savile Row could not contrive to clothe him gracefully. His suit did not quite fit; his head was too large, his shoulders too narrow; he looked entirely too much like the innocuous nobody he was not.

He had other compensations. He was from Boston, and immensely wealthy, and wellborn, descended on either side from a long and distinguished line of Back Bay principalities: Governors, Senators and Secretaries of State. His maternal genealogy included a Founder of the Republic and two nineteenth-century Presidents. His paternal grandfather was the swashbuckling Peter Pullmotor, who sailed with Admiral Dewey at Manila and went on to finish the China railroad; his father, the vegetarian and inventor, had served with distinction in the Coolidge cabinet and as Ambassador to Rome and the Weimar Republic.

Paul Pullmotor was not quite like any one of them. Notoriety he did not have, but only because he did not want it. Fame he certainly had—not among newspaper reporters, whom he loathed and avoided—but among the handful of men in this world who truly mattered. His self-esteem was fertilized by the whisperings of chancelleries, not by the vulgarities of the Sunday supplements. He had traveled widely since the war, armed only with an attaché case, conducting intrigues of cosmic ramification. A very privileged few knew that he had personally masterminded the overthrow of several pro-communist governments in Asia and Latin America. His peregrinations far transcended trivial intervention in the affairs of sovereign states; he rarely took interest in a country until it had passed beyond the hopes and artifices of lesser men, beyond redemption through the gymnastics of conventional diplomacy—until, as Calvin Hampshire would say, it was ripe for "Kremlin kleptomania." Paul Pullmotor was—so the Secretary himself had once whispered—the Fireman of Freedom.

"All right, Mohammed, just leave the coffee on the table. Never mind the sugar. Now go out and get me the morning papers. I want the *Times* of London, the *Herald Tribune* and the Al Asima *Trumpet.*"

Although his official status was, to say the least, imprecise, and his role in any given international crisis always mysterious, Pullmotor seldom found it necessary to work under cover or to slip in and out of incendiary situations sight unseen. (On the other hand there were occasional whispers that his clandestine henchmen were everywhere, and in the most unlikely disguises.) He lived ostentatiously in the best hotels, surrounded himself with "flunkies" whenever he felt like it, and supped with prime ministers, presidents and emperors. He traveled on an ordinary passport and described himself simply as a "businessman"—the overseas vice-president of a prominent American investment bank. But he was accepted among the mighty as one of themselves. He was generous with advice to his peers, and very good advice it was—sometimes. He did not hesitate to speak up in the name of American industry, the President of the United States, the Free World, or even Christianity itself. Nehru had once asked him if he knew the Pope. "Not *really,*" Paul Pullmotor replied.

The hotel telephone rang.

"Why Shawnie!" Paul Pullmotor exclaimed. "How terribly kind of you to call! What time is it anyhow? Do you know I just got up? Sean, this country is going to pot, and no doubt of that. I couldn't even get tapioca—yes, I'm terribly sorry about that, Fitzy boy. You got Calvin's cable, of course? Well, I changed my flight plans at the last minute. Sorry to be so premature! Oh, don't worry about *that*. The P.M. had a car at the airport and everything was duck soup. I hate this kind of dither but Mustafa always insists. So, I think I'll drink my coffee and read my newspapers. No, Shawnie, nothing to get alarmed about. Just a routine look-around. I'll get in your hair as little as possible, then be off like greased— Oh really? That's not the poop going around Washington, Shawnie. He *wanted* Madrid but he's getting Kuala Lumpur. Understand there are a *number* of switches coming up. I wouldn't lose any sleep—they shouldn't affect your personal position *too* much. Calvin isn't terribly pleased with some of the performances he's been getting. No, Shawnie, I'm speaking in *general* terms. Besides, I don't know all *that* much about it. By the way, the Hampshires send their best, especially Rebecca! Well, how are you these days, anyway, Sean? How's Eminence Grise? I was in your corner every inch of the way during the Lady Chetwynd-Pott flap, Shawnie! I hit the Harvard reunion last month—one or two people asked about you. Can't recall their names. You're leaving to see the P.M. right now? Good for you, Shawnie. I'm going to drink my coffee and read the newspapers. I can't see you this *morning,* Shawnie. Let me catch my breath before breakfast, eh? Terrific. Terrific. You'll be hearing from me later . . ."

Dr. Pantry did not tolerate interruptions when he was working on the Budget, but now his secretary buzzed again.

"There's a man wandering around in the corridor who says he wants to see you," she said. "He seems rather . . . odd, and he's—"

"I meet enough odd people in my *In* box," Dr. Pantry snapped. "Don't bother me again for the next hour." Glancing out the window, he could see the official Cadillac pulling out of the Embassy compound, flags flying. "Not even if it's the *Ambassador!*"

4

The conversation with Paul Pullmotor put the Ambassador in a hideous mood for his audience with the Prime Minister. Perhaps it was fortunate that, halfway to the palace, the Cadillac was intercepted on the radio telephone. "The P.M.'s office has just called," Miss Speed told the Ambassador. "He's running behind schedule and hasn't delivered his speech yet."

"Fine time they pick to tell me," the Ambassador growled.

"Can you postpone your appointment until eleven?"

So Fitz Pasha had an hour to while away. The *khamseen* had died down; there was no point in returning to the Embassy; he decided to linger in the old city, which he loved. He hoped it would take his mind off Pullmotor. He got out of the limousine near the Red Mosque, by the teeming Bab el Mandeb—the Gate of Lamentations. "Drive on to the Ministry," he told his chauffeur. "I'll walk the rest of the way."

"You think it's okay today, Basha?" Fawzi asked worriedly. "Remember all what have been in newsbaber against States is blenty. And blenty beoble know you."

"If Abdel Kader can't protect me, the Three Stooges can," the Ambassador said, nodding at his Bedouin bodyguard, who had pulled up behind the limousine.

The Red Mosque was one of the Ambassador's favorites. Once within the beautiful bronze doors he felt transported to another age—that was the Irish in him, no doubt. He removed his shoes and entrusted them to the porter, a friend of many years and a victim of elephantiasis: the man's toes peeped like little pimples from his grotesquely bloated flesh. In stocking feet, the Ambassador went down into the great open courtyard, where the scent of jasmine did battle with body odor. He remembered then that this was the feast day of a local saint, for the place was swarming with paupers: men, women and small children. They settled on the Ambassador like lice, howling for baksheesh.

"Raboona yikhaleek, ya hawaja, ana maskeen"—God give you prosperity, O gentleman, I am afflicted.

"Al Allah"—I commit you to God, the Ambassador replied.

"I have recited the chapter of Yasin for thee, O Basha!" cried another.

"Al Allah," the Ambassador repeated as Abdel Kader and the Three Stooges chased them off.

In the corner of the courtyard crouched a quintet of blind brothers, their eyeballs punctured at birth because it is blessed to be blind, to beg. They were bound together by crude hemp drawn in nooses at the neck. The elder brother throbbed a wooden spoon against a copper plate, and sang.

"Hast Thou resolved on strangling me, O God?
Loosen the noose!
No mother weeps for me
No wife
No sister!"

And then the chorus of them, calling God by His oldest names:

"Samkin, Samkin, Samkin
Sam'akin, Sam'akin, Sam'akin
Sam'ukin, Sam'ukin, Sam'ukin!"

In the center of the courtyard, beneath a gnarled and dying sycamore, was a magnificent marble fountain; the faithful were performing their ablutions. *"Bismillah ir-Rahman ir-Rahim"*—In the name of God, the Compassionate, the Merciful, an old man intoned. "Praise be to God," his companion continued, "Who hath sent down water for purification, and made al-Islam to be a light and a channel, and a guide to Thy gardens, the gardens of delight, and to Thy mansion, the mansion of Peace." The Ambassador was particularly fond of these prayers. "O God," he muttered with the old men, "make me to smell the odors of Paradise, and bless me with its delights. And make me not to smell the fires of the Inferno. Free my neck from the Fire, and keep me from the collars and the fetters and the chains."

Not far from the fountain, a small pushcart stood: inside, atop a heap of refuse, a young man lay fast asleep, curled like a foetus in a wooden womb. The sun shone malevolently on him. The Ambassador had always marveled at the talent of poor Arabs for sleep in the most unseemly places. He had seen them huddled together at night on the pavements of the Corniche, or in the gutters; standing straight against walls, balanced on balustrades, squatting among Pepsi-Cola cases, squeezed into trash barrels and cardboard boxes, snoring gloriously. In fact, sleeping bodies were scattered all over this courtyard. Many of them were students, mere boys, for the Red Mosque was the Islamic seminary of Al Khadra. Pupils, professors, paupers, peddlers and a colony of scrawny cats who seemed to belong to the place stepped over and around these recumbent forms, considerate of their slumber. Some of the students, thick needles and thread in hand, were mending their garments; others were washing them in small wooden tubs and then hanging them up to dry on string suspended between the crooked Corinthian columns. Here and there a berobed student held a transistor radio to his ear. Otherwise the scene was much as it had been seven hundred years before, when Islam was in its glory.

Fitzgibbon Pasha went into the enormous mosque. More of the same: men and boys sprawled everywhere on the threadbare carpets. Students in flowing robes and striped pajamas walked to and fro and hand in hand, chattering to their companions or studying their lessons as they strolled through this petrified forest of crooked pillars, under this sky of sycamore beams mooned with gilded cupolas, starred with lanterns of enameled glass and fluorescent-tube lighting. The mosque was a monument to all the compulsive, copy-cat syncretism of the Arabs down the long centuries of their decline and eclipse. Every architectural style seemed incorporated here: Byzantine, Saracenic, Moorish, Persian, Corinthian, Ottoman, Romanesque. Contemplated individually, many of the specimens were exquisite: red mosaics and dados, niches of turquoise faïence, glazed green bricks, bronze balustrades, stucco ornamentations, Koranic friezes, lacelike fretwork, Cufic inscriptions in lapis lazuli, cedarwood doors inlaid with ivory and ebony, murals marvelously crenelated. Forbidden by the Prophet to reproduce human or even animal pictures as savoring of idolatry, Moslem craftsmen had bequeathed to history an art form all their own: these ingenious geometric flowers, traceries and encrustations. Yet curiously the mosque's charm lay chiefly in its disorder—the recumbent sleepers, corroding colonnades, sagging arabesques—an apt symbol of Islam at large, so "awakened" Arabs had often said.

They would have been embarrassed by the spectacle which delighted the Ambassador most: the young students, clustered cross-legged on the carpets about their sheikhs, committing the Koran to memory. The boys rocked backward and forward, chanting their lessons aloud, their voices reverberating timorously in the gilded cupolas above. Occasionally a sheikh would reach out and slap a slow boy. Here, perhaps—in the memorizing of the entire scripture of the Prophet—might be found the root reason for the obsession with slogans which so frequently seemed to paralyze the Arab mind. The Koran, which the Ambassador considered the most beautiful book ever written, had been the almost exclusive source of Moslem education for thirteen hundred years; only very recently had the awakened Arabs begun to gaze on less mystical horizons. The ordeal of learning by heart all six thousand-odd of the Prophet's verses often stretched the sinews of the mind until they were too tight to reason. And thus words—beautiful words, repeated again and again, resonant language, soaring rhetoric—became for the Arabs the very water of life, far more important than meaning, and infinitely more precious than mere facts. Arab behavior became a succession of elegant slogans and formalisms, from morning till night. Set phrases were concocted for nearly every conceivable human act: exchanging presents, purchasing clothes, drinking coffee, rising from sleep, awakening from a nightmare, lighting a lamp, making love, seeing the new moon, bathing, sneezing, shaving, and even yawning ("I seek refuge with God from Satan the accursed"—for it was believed that the devil was fond of leaping into open mouths). But if the Arabs were poor in logic, they were rich in intuition, and it was intuition which saved them, and indeed made some of them—the present Prime Minister of Al Khadra for example—more intelligent than men really have a right to be.

Such were the Ambassador's reflections as he perambulated about the Red Mosque. To a group of older boys, a green-turbaned, white-bearded sheikh lectured on Islamic law. "Right is the negation of negation. Property is a counter-claim against a counter-claim. Truth is the refutation of refutation, the rebuttal of skepticism!" The Ambassador wandered from group to group, eavesdropping on the lectures, shoplifting slogans, stumbling occasionally on an idea that was new to him. He had dabbled in much of it: the theology of Abdul Hakim, the mysticism of Dardiry, the metaphysics of el Taftazany. The Correct Reformulation, the Maiden, the Dewdrop, the Proofs of the Miracle, the Stairway of Learning, the Pearls of the Rulers, the Treasury of Extracts, the Steps to Success from the Light of Clarity! He had spent two decades at it, only to tell an Arab friend in a moment of flippancy, "It took me twenty years to realize I had opened the door to an empty room." He did not really mean that, but the remark had been repeated everywhere. It had made him celebrated among the intellectuals, skeptics and modernists; a whited sepulcher to the ulemas, mullahs and traditionalists.

The Ambassador left them there, chanting and rocking, and went back into the street. Languid, clamorous, contradictory, the rhythm of Islam had begun to make him giddy again. He thought, It is as tantalizing today as it was in antiquity. He wanted to surrender himself a little while to the throbbing candor of the street, to be caught up, coddled by it. These narrow, knotted, tangled, twisted, devious, cobblestoned streets: every step forward seemed to correspond to the crank of a kaleidoscope, revealing new murmurations of humanity squeezed and writhing within these walls. He passed the public baths, the booksellers, the open shops selling pipes, perfumes, flower pots, Birmingham jewelry, bric-a-brac, sham curios, brass trays, embroidered leather, carved wood, old weapons, vases, lamps, cheap and nasty Japanese imitations. Venders of sweet bread, eggs, almonds, and sugar cane. *Make room, O my mother!* Pots of chicken jelly, bottles of rose water, barbaric yellow ornaments. Red earthenware jugs piled high in a corner; bright blue carpets suspended on walls. Donkey drivers crying, shouting, cracking their whips. *Praise the Prophet and get out of the way!* Incredible awnings. The claxon of protesting taxicabs, the clanging bells of distant tramcars. Medlies and mixtures of indescribable smells: attar of roses, scented tobacco, fried fish, filth, mutton rotting in the open sun, incense, sewage, camphor, hair tonic, roasting coffee, cooking oil, the whiff of perfumed women. Sallow Greeks and Levantines, plum-colored Ethiopians, bronze Syrians, Tunisians, Moors, Berbers, Bedouins. *O Sheikh, take care!*

Sean Sebastian Fitzgibbon went into one of the coffee houses, where the men were drinking tea, sucking on hubbly-bubblies and playing tric-trac in the dim alcoves, half hidden behind curtains of glass bamboo. This was the Madmen's Café, a mecca in the evening for the maimed and stunted and malformed, for buffoons, boy dancers, storytellers, snake charmers, sorcerers and soothsayers. The walls were mounted with immense arabesque mirrors and the cadavers of crocodiles. A gnome hunchback was shining shoes; a magician with a great, bulbous goiter on the back of his neck was selling cigarettes. From the wireless blared *"Ma barrif leesh bahibbak"*—I don't know why I love you. In the back of the place some noisy youths were hurling darts. The Ambassador and Abdel Kader sat down in the bone-backed chairs and watched them; the Ambassador was babbling away in Arabic now, and soon he had the Three Stooges in stitches of laughter. Darts was not an Arab game. Longing for their pubs, British soldiers had imposed it on Al Khadra during the occupation: it was one of those imperial legacies which lingered on, and grew. Fitz Pasha had frequented this café nearly twenty years ago, and he came here now because it had not changed. He remembered the night when some Tommies had beaten up an Arab boy, and how the boy's companions had avenged him by hurling darts at the fair-haired Britons. A Tommy had bled to death that night, and Sean had been caught in the line of fire; one of the shafts had pierced him in the side. He carried the scar to this day; not for nothing had he been named Sebastian.

Not for nothing had he been named Sebastian. Not for nothing had he been named Sean. "I named him after two great martyrs, Monsignor." That was what his mother had told the parish priest on the day of his First Communion, and until he was ten Sean was determined that when he grew up he was going to be a martyr. Then he changed his mind and decided to be a bishop; it was not until adolescence that he lowered his sights to diplomacy. Later in life he liked to think that he had not so much disowned his youthful piety as he had outgrown it—outgrown it in a wistful way, and bade it good-by as, on the eve of puberty, one might tearfully kiss good-by one's beloved toys and tin soldiers and teddy bears.

But it was at Harvard, as any self-respecting nun or conscientious Catholic novelist might have warned, that he actually lost his faith. His apostasy was the crowning blow to his parents, for they had never wanted him to go there in the first place. His mother, who had once dreamed of him becoming a priest, pleaded with him to attend the Jesuit university; his father, who was by no means a poor man, had offered to send him to Notre Dame as a compromise between Boston College and Harvard. But Sean had *notions*. He won a scholarship to Harvard. He roomed in Adams House. In his youthful anguish he came home one weekend rampaging against a clergy which could condemn lipstick as sinful and condone whatever politician happened to be sacking the city treasury at the moment—if he was a Catholic. Sean brandished a book by Bertrand Russell, and read out loud to his parents about "nuns who never take a bath without wearing a bathrobe all the time. When asked why, since no man can see them, they reply: 'Oh, but you forget the good God.' Apparently they conceive of the Deity as a Peeping Tom whose omnipotence enables him to see through bathroom walls, but who is foiled by bathrobes."

"That's the truest description I've ever read of my own parochial-school education," Sean said, and with that he cut away the umbilical cord that bound him to his beginnings—or he thought he did. He refused to attend Mass that Sunday, or any Sunday, he said. His mother had a heart attack a week later, and since she could no longer lay eyes on Sean without breaking into tears, his father sent him on a trip to Europe with Calvin Hampshire that summer.

On the high seas, Sean felt badly about it, because his memories of his religion were not all unpleasant. He remembered the cold winter mornings when he had bicycled to the brick church before dawn to serve the six o'clock Mass, clutching his cassock and surplice in a rumpled cardboard box. He remembered the starched odor of albs and amices and the smell of crackling beeswax on the high altar, and the furtive, forbidden taste of the sacramental wine in the vestry after the priest had gone, and the burning incense in the thuribles of peeling gold. He remembered the nuns, the catechism classes, the novenas, the pious pamphlets, the May processions. *Qui laetificat juventutem meam.* Had they given joy to his youth? He remembered the taunts of the other acolytes:

> Shawnie's got a snotty nose
> *Ora pro nobis!*
> And everywhere that Shawnie goes
> *Ora pro nobis!*

His closest friend among the altar boys was the Cardinal today. He was a darling man, everybody knew, and never seemed to hold Sean's defection against him, as so many others had. He wrote to Sean every year on the feast of Saint Sebastian. "I aim this arrow of tenderness at you." His Eminence had a weakness for mixed metaphors.

The noisy youths in the Madmen's Café tired of their darts, and disappeared. The back door of the café opened on the Fish Market, and the Ambassador went there next. Today, under Al Khadra's chaste Prime Minister Mustafa ibn Mabrouk, the Fish Market was for fish; in former times the tenements of this quarter were more famous for their painted whores and perfumed catamite boys displayed behind barred, ground-level windows like caged beasts of prey. Native ladies of the lowest class and European harridans who could no longer meet even the minimum requirements of Marseilles had made this a city within a city, memorable for its abandoned dancing, depraved exhibitions and primeval squalor, and ruled over by a bejeweled, patchouli-scented sodomite, black-skinned, weighing four hundred pounds and dressed, like an enormous Negress, in white samite and tinkling golden bracelets. No more! Hardly a day after becoming Prime Minister, Mustafa ibn Mabrouk had personally descended on this place—wild-eyed, waving a pistol—surrounded by squadrons of police, sweeping the hundreds of *filles et garçons de joie* away to jail. Those who had resisted rehabilitation were still languishing there; with a Victorian—even Savonarolian—vengeance the Prime Minister had turned Al Asima into the most straight-laced city in the Middle East. And so once again—ancient, ill-smelling, clamorous—the Fish Market was for fish and only fish; the fishmongers stood in their stalls haggling over their scales; cooks and scullery girls and veiled women and boys on bicycles came, made their purchases and went away, merry to be making so much noise; the air was thick with flies and heat and underfoot were fins and fish eyes and slop.

The Fish Market was as familiar to Fitz Pasha as the Madmen's Café or the Red Mosque or any other corner of the old city; he came here often to shop for his own fish. He enjoyed haggling with the fishmongers, and he was specially fond of the fish sent up from the Red Sea. The basslike arabi; the parrot-beaked pseudoscarus; shrimp; dolphin; devil fish.

Fish. The fish had, after all, played an important part in shaping the course of Sean's career, and even in predetermining the vicissitudes of his life. In Venice, during that summer abroad in the late Twenties, he and Calvin Hampshire had decided, on a lark, to sail eastward. But Calvin did not enjoy the Arabs; repulsed by their customs, their religion and their plumbing, he insisted on returning to Europe. Sean refused, and they quarreled violently one night in Al Asima. They had been quite close, but Calvin left him. Sean fell in with some Englishmen who invited him along on a camping trip to the Red Sea. It was on those warm sands that he walked alone one evening, while his companions prepared the campfire, to watch the sun dissolve in the waters once rent by the rod of Moses. He felt content; all was silence save for the crunching of his naked feet in the sands and the gentle licking of the ocean on the coral shoals. The waters at first were green and limpid; Sean marveled at the landscape of the madrepore reef just beneath the surface of the sea; at the meadows of imaginary flowers, brighter and more beautiful than those of earth; at the lacelike vaults and archways and rocky domes rising as a cathedral above the indigo depths; at the schools of phosphorescent fish gliding with long, feathery fins in and out of their cloisters leaving luminous trails behind them—they were like birds seen in a dream, like creatures of Paradise. Then, for the ceremony of sunset, the sea became a chameleon crawling over the cathedrals of coral, changing from translucent emerald to shimmering orange: the setting sun transfigured the cruel cliffs above the shore to the tender color of apricot.

The sun went down; there is no twilight in the Arab Orient; darkness came almost at once. Pelicans, gulls and flying fish skimmed over the black waters. And then, like a sudden sunrise, the afterglow of the Arab tropics—the miracle of Zodiacal light—restored the scene to what it had been before. Again the madrepore and meadows of imaginary flowers and phosphorescent fish glowed in all their glory; once more the sea was limpid and the ghastly cliffs were illumined, but now with a crimson-lavender light, altogether unreal and gradually growing in intensity until it was almost as brilliant as the sun itself. Sean half expected to see Aphrodite rising from the foam. Instead some fishermen slipped to the shore silently from the sea, and with a great weariness drew their dhow onto the sand. He watched them, their frail, biblical silhouettes in relief against the glow, spreading their nets out to dry. He had never witnessed anything so otherworldly as this, or as silent. It was as if he had waited this long in the wings of life, had crossed oceans and continents and come all this way, simply to taste this transient, even mystical, moment of peace. The fishermen called out to him. He approached them bashfully. They were clad only in loincloths; they had fine features and burning, black eyes and their long, tangled locks fell far below their shoulders; their bare bodies, the color of copper, were shriveled and consumptive. One of the men offered him a raw fish. Moved by the kindness, he accepted it, and a bit of unleavened bread. The others, clawing their fish into pieces, sat down beside him on the edge of the dhow and supped with him in the miraculous light of the Zodiac. Over and over, they repeated a word that he knew: *Raboona,* they repeated, *Raboona*—Our Lord. One must hear a poor Arab utter that word; it touched a very deep wound in Sean. Later, in a letter to Calvin Hampshire, he tried to transmit his vision in words. He should not have.

In their room at Adams House Sean had often confided his ambitions to Calvin, whose uncle happened to be the Undersecretary of State, and they had planned to enter the Foreign Service together. But when Sean returned home from that summer of wandering and went up for his final year at Harvard, Calvin had taken a new roommate—Paul Pullmotor. Calvin never repeated his previous offer of presenting Sean to the powers in the Department; in due course he even suggested that it might be better if Sean began thinking of another field. All this because of a silly argument in Al Asima over poor plumbing? Or did Calvin, even then, see in Sean an incipient rival to his own wishful grandeur? "Something more in your line, Shawnie. How about the lumber business?" (Sean was majoring in European history.) The Department of that day was a very Establishment sort of place; an entrée through the Undersecretary would have made matters much easier, opened doors otherwise closed, assured him of glamorous assignments from the start. They were a luxury Sean learned to do without. In the examinations, he received the fourth highest marks on record; for some reason Calvin was not required to sit.

When Sean's nomination for Congressional appointment was reviewed by Calvin's uncle, he recommended that a young man as promising as Fitzgibbon, who had visited the Orient, be assigned to specialize in it. A curious emphasis in those days—when the frontiers of American interest seemed to extend no farther east than Warsaw—but it became a permanent part of Sean's dossier, and it made him a marked man. Thus his golden years were consumed in a succession of somnolent, peripheral places: Al Asima, Tehran, Jidda, Aleppo, Benghazi, Baghdad. There were breathers in Buenos Aires and Madrid, and he became fluent in French, Spanish, Persian and three dialects of Arabic. Calvin Hampshire embarked on more dashing business; he was in Berlin for the rise of Hitler, in Vienna for the murder of Dollfuss, in Paris for the demise of the Third Republic. During one of their Washington reunions, Calvin had one martini too many, and referred in passing to "the humble part I played in making an orientalist out of you, Shawnie." Calvin's accumulated indiscretions, the innuendoes of informed friends, and indeed the whole pattern of Sean's career in the shadows pointed back to one beginning. Sean had assembled the fragments in his mind a thousand times, and he had reconstructed the crucial conversation which he knew must have taken place, on the eve of his appointment, between the Undersecretary and his nephew.

The actual conversation had transpired pretty much as Sean imagined it.

Undersecretary: Yes, here it is. Fitzgibbon. West Roxbury. Harvard. What's your interest in this fellow?

Calvin: He's a classmate, Uncle Henry.

Undersecretary: *Magna cum laude,* I see here. Club man?

Calvin: Not the type.

Undersecretary: Damn good marks in the examinations. Not even Hasty Pudding?

Calvin: I'm afraid he wanted it a bit too badly.

Undersecretary: Mackerel-snapper?

Calvin: He was born one, but he outgrew it at Harvard, or he thinks he did.

Undersecretary: My old constituents in South Boston used to say that Harvard Yard was the largest Catholic cemetery in the Commonwealth.

Calvin: I'm hopeful that Shawnie will get the right *sort* of assignment.

Undersecretary: I believe there are some openings in the Balkans.

Calvin: Yes, I imagine he'd be quite enterprising in some Balkan province. Does it say there that he's been in the Middle East? He sent me a letter last summer raving about the sunsets on the Red Sea.

Undersecretary: I'll think it over.

Right *sort* of assignment . . . openings in the Balkans . . . Middle East? . . . I'll think it over . . . Of course at that time Calvin could not have foreseen the future importance of the Arab Orient, or that through a combination of ability and specialization Sean would achieve the Ambassadorship to Al Khadra before Calvin himself became Secretary of State. Thus the scarcity of Arabists—certainly not Calvin's personal esteem—accounted for Sean's longevity as Ambassador Extraordinary and Plenipotentiary to the Kingdom of Al Khadra.

And *mackerel-snapper*. Calvin and others had often brandished that phrase in jest, but the meaning distressed Sean. Why had the poor biblical fishermen and their loaves and fishes satisfied him so? What hunger did they appease that he had imposed upon himself? Wasn't the fish the cryptograph in history of the faith which he had abjured? In God's good time it was to dawn on Sean that the dichotomy of faith and reason existed mostly in his own head; he was to discover that the jingoism of his parochial-school education was as schismatic after its fashion as the sophistries of H. G. Wells and Alfred North Whitehead were in theirs. But this revelation came too late, when he was too committed to turn back. And so until this day Sean sought to satisfy his Eucharistic hunger with fish, which he ate constantly, even for breakfast.

He was convinced he deserved that consolation. When Calvin Hampshire broke his promise to present him at court, Sean entered the service the hard way, and bided his time. But he was too sensible to aspire to an ambassadorship of consequence, or dream of higher station still, simply on his merits. His father possessed a modest fortune, the kind of lace-curtain fortune embodied by a ten-room stucco house in one of the more elegant Boston wards, two cars in the garage, a papal knighthood and a summer cottage on Cape Cod. Francis Xavier Fitzgibbon acquired his contracts like any other Irish builder who cultivated city councilmen and fawned on auxiliary bishops. It was the Irish Catholic sort of wealth that awed the Knights of Columbus and earned you a seat on the dais at Communion Breakfasts, but it was not the kind of wealth that, divided up among the four sons and two daughters of a fine Catholic family, could buy you an ambassadorship in Paris—or, for that matter, in Montevideo.

It was in Washington, early in his career, at a garden party in the Royal Belgian legation, that Sean met Winifred Pendleton. "She's one of the South Carolina Pendletons—the tobacco people, you know." Sean approached her and said, "I'll trade you this daiquiri for your telephone number." She found this charming. She had a certain robust beauty; she was quite rich and a little younger than he; she did most of the talking. He was tall and more than presentable; people said he was brilliant and bound to be an ambassador before he was forty. She had already outgrown South Carolina, and the idea of entertaining royalty in . . . Brussels would be a good start, and then maybe Madrid, and then Vienna and London . . . was very much to her taste. She had a nervous giggle and drank too many daiquiris. They became better acquainted and Sean could hardly bear to be with her. They were married in the Methodist Church. It was not until after the union was consummated that he could summon the courage to tell her that he had been appointed vice consul in Al Asima.

Winifred went with him, and she found rather a lot to complain about in the Al Khadra of that period. "It's so hot, Shawnie . . . These flies, Shawnie . . . The food, Shawnie . . . All these filthy little children, Shawnie . . ."

All these filthy little children, Shawnie. Now in the twisted lanes of the old city a child, all but naked in her rags, ran tagging at his heels. "Hello! Good-by! How are you? *Hasta la vista!* I love you! Hey, give me one piastre!" Impulsively, the Ambassador scooped the little bundle up and kissed her shorn, pock-marked head. More murmurations of humanity: young, veiled women crouching in long rows, hawking quinces, glass bangles and watermelons. Water-carriers with bloated goatskins; others bearing terra-cotta pots and huge glass bottles on their backs, vending greenish lemonade, prune juice and licorice water; clinking colored drinking bowls and little brass cups between their fingers. An old hag, all bent over beneath her grotesque burden of twigs and branches. Scavenging, hungry dogs. Turreted gates; parapeted archways. *You, good fellow, to your right!* Mosques without number: walls striped red and white; fretted, fawn-colored domes; mother-of-pearl minarets. And the *houses*. Immense paneled doors, caparisoned with knockers of bronze and inlaid silver; wrought-iron latticework windows woven of intricate Saracenic design; richly carved, decaying corbels groaning under gables and trellised balconies jutting so far outward they all but interlaced, all but built bridges over the gnarled lanes below. And how they sloped and sagged, as if a good gust of wind would send them tumbling down on the heaps of impoverished people who darted in and out of them. *By your favor, effendim!* Glimpses of inner courtyards: tesselated pavements, marble fountains, hanging lanterns, ferns, palms, acacias—all half hidden now beneath the debris of generations—intimations of glorious lives once lived. *Ai-wa! Co-cola! Co-cola! Bebsi-cola! Bebs! Bebs!* Sunlight streaming through the fractures of an opaque glass arcade now spanning the street, emblazoning a junk peddler lustily extolling the superiority of his wares: broken green bottles, dead radio tubes, crushed flowers, an American movie magazine, rusty scissors, brown gourds, crumbling charms and amulets, a hub cap. A man howling his head off in the middle of the street, apparently for the fun of it. A girl selling green tomatoes. A fat fellow puffing on his hubbly-bubbly. *Ya Ahmed! Ya M'hammed!* A policeman urinating on a wall beneath a fading photograph of the King. A radio blaring. The tune meshing the syncopations of the samba with the wail of Islam.

And the wail of Winifred. Winifred had always wailed a little in the apogee of the love-act, but Sean had never really satisfied her in bed. Eventually she stopped sleeping with him. She abused him at cocktail parties. Sean knew what people were saying; one night at the Gazooza Sporting Club he had entirely too much to drink, and he stood up and recited a line from a comedy he had written at Harvard. "I did not marry my wife for her wealth. She married me for my poverty."

Soon Winifred left on the first of her little trips. "I think I'll take a little trip," she would always say. As the years accumulated each absence was more prolonged, the time with Sean a bit less. Spending her own money, she drifted from one European capital to the next, collecting lovers like necklaces. Inexorably, the rumors drifted back to Sean of her affair in St. Moritz, her flame in Budapest. She bought a house in Paris; he wondered why she did not divorce him. His sainted mother would have said, "It's the price God made you pay for getting married by a Methodist minister."

Possibly, though Sean suspected things went deeper than that. His morganatic marriage—was it, he wondered, a mere fragment from a much larger mosaic, something vulgar and compulsive in himself? Like Madame Bovary, he wanted to be something he was not, and could never be; he aspired to eminences he knew he could never scale, not because he was unworthy but because he was not wellborn. The consuming flame in him was not pride, nor ambition, but embarrassment. To this day, he believed he was a little bit . . . shanty. He had visited Ireland once, and the place appalled him. The dreary cities. The dismal towns. His father's birthplace in Galway. He found his uncles living in thatched cottages, on earthen floors, without privies or electric light. The men were cloddish, the children dim-witted, the women in peonage to the priests. There was no running water: the boys went down and drew it from the bog.

That was what Sean could never get out of his mind: *the bog*. The boys smelled of it, and the girls, and the men and women, and he was afraid that he smelled of it too. It was on his parents, his brothers, it was smeared all over the memories of his childhood, imbedded in the sofas and settees of the stucco house. How do you wash away the bog in a generation? He had spent a lifetime trying, a lifetime learning how to cover up—his education, his marriage, his manners, his poses, the elegance of his speech and dress, the grace of his literary style, his big-game hunting, his taste for fine wines and paintings—but even all of that was not quite enough. Every now and then the shanty in him, the bog-trotter, showed through. A man like Calvin Hampshire could spot it in a second: impulsiveness in speech, the pretentious tie, the wrong sort of smutty story. And Sean could spot it in others—in young Christopher Grundoon, his personal assistant, for example. Grundoon tried to cover up, too, and did very well. He was golden-haired and good-looking, well dressed, well spoken; he delighted the King with his company. But still the bog peeped through. Grundoon's compulsive habit of turning every conversation around to religion was his betrayal. That was pure bog, the irremediable residue of incessant childhood exposure to Irish priests, devout mothers and saintly aunts, chums who went off to the seminary, insipid sermons on purity.

And now that he had cut the cord, what did Fitz Pasha have? The compensations of high and ineffective office, the consolations of protocol. All that and his opiate, Islam. For at the bottom of things he knew that his love of the Arab poor, his fascination with fishmongers, his reverence for muezzins and murmuring sheikhs, Sufi mystics and swaying dervishes, his delight in urchins, peasants, peddlers, street sweepers, beggars, bootblacks—there was nothing noble, nothing grand, nothing democratic in that at all. They were the cry of the bog. What he had disowned, they were giving back to him. He was one of them. He was an underdeveloped country, too. They were the bog-trotters of Islam, calling him home. His sainted mother would have said, "It's the price God made you pay for getting married by a Methodist minister."

"Dr. Pantry, I feel awful about interrupting your Budget again, but that funny-looking fellow is back. He won't go away. He's sitting on the stairs insisting you want to see him, and strumming on a banjo—or something."

"Strumming! Good heavens, why didn't you tell me?"

"I tried to."

"Send him in."

Dr. Pantry's secretary went out into the corridor, where she found a fascinated crowd of typists, translators, messengers and coffee boys clustered about a young man with a shaven head, shorn eyebrows, a brown Vandyke beard, an orange toga, jodhpurs, and tennis shoes; he was strumming on a stringed instrument and lustily intoning the lyrics of "I Go Ape." She extracted him from the throng of admirers and conducted him to the door of the Mutual Understanding Director. Dr. Pantry got up from his adding machine and greeted his guest with mixed emotions of curiosity and panic.

"Mr. Vespucci! I'm sorry about the mix-up. We've been in a bit of a flap over your ETA. Washington didn't even tell us you were coming until yesterday. But it's wonderful to have you here."

Chuckles Vespucci sat down on the floor, cross-legged.

"Yes, you must be tired, flying nonstop from Rangoon. Did you come on that dawn plane?"

"At dusk the cock announces dawn," Chuckles said. "At midnight, the bright sun."

"I don't think I've ever looked at it that way, Mr. Vespucci. May I see your travel orders?"

"Zen is travel orders."

"No, I mean your IA-thirty-four form."

"Form is precisely emptiness. Emptiness is precisely form."

"Yes. Well, I suppose we can attend to the formalities a little later. Now, as to publicity, you'll be pleased to learn that we've arranged full coverage for your concerts."

"The wild geese do not intend to cast their reflection. The water has no mind to receive their image."

"Are you ill, Mr. Vespucci?"

"Illness alone exists, none who are ill. Death there is, but none who die. The deed there is, but no doer. Nirvana there is, but no one seeking it. The Path there is, but none who travel it."

"I'm sure you'll feel all right when you get some sleep. You'll want a place to stay, of course. Now at the Sheraton-Zahra I've fixed—"

"Fix!" Chuckles Vespucci came alarmingly to life. "Dad, did you say *fix?"*

"Your lute needs to be fixed, Mr. Vespucci?"

"No, dad, I do."

"Oh dear. I've got the press—personal appearances—cocktail parties—the Ambassador. I don't know what I'm going to do. I must keep calm. I must s-sit down and think this one out."

"When sitting, just sit. When walking, just walk. Above all, dad, don't wobble . . ."

5

The labyrinthine splendor of the old city had, as always, cast a kind of spell on the Ambassador. It was not until he emerged into the great open square facing the Prime Minister's palace that his thoughts became quiescent and clear again. But now he lamented the discovery of what the spasmodic *khamseen* and the heat of day had done to him: sweat bathed his body and his shirt was sodden. He did not want to present himself to the Prime Minister in this condition; he resolved to exchange shirts with his chauffeur.

Suddenly a procession of open trucks invaded the square and headed for the palace. They were bulging with riffraff, chanting and clapping, brandishing bright banners and enormous portraits of the Prime Minister and Gary Cooper. In the courtyard of the palace, the Ambassador's Cadillac was waiting and a noisy crowd was collecting beneath the central balcony. The air was torn with the screech of sirens. Streetcars stopped, and the people piled out and clambered up on top of them. Women held their sucklings aloft, and blind beggars cried "Thanks be to God for him," and the lame ran with the swift to share witness of a hero's coming. Preceded by motorcycles, an old, open Rolls emerged into the square. The spontaneous mob enveloped the Rolls before the car could reach the palace, and within moments had their hands on the tall dark man in the back seat, hugging him, clawing at his khaki and kissing him. The bodyguards tried to push them out of the car, but in vain. The mob ripped him out of the Rolls, mounted him on their shoulders and bore him in triumph to the palace.

The dark man sat motionless atop the pulsations of the mob, and stared straight ahead. He did not smile, even slightly. When the mob reached the gates of the palace, they bottlenecked. Unable to move, they passed the hero forward from shoulder to shoulder through the gate. The Ambassador had been caught up in the crowd, and for an instant his eyes met those of the hero. Fleetingly the hero smiled the faintest smile and, unmistakably, he winked at the Ambassador.

When the dark man reached the rococo palace he needed no staircase to reach the balcony. A common drainpipe scaled the wall, and some young men used it to improvise a human ladder. With some difficulty the hero climbed them to his balcony. No sooner was he astride the balustrade than the drainpipe gave way and the young men tumbled into the crowd.

It was one of Brigadier Mustafa ibn Mabrouk's most memorable entrances.

"Torch of Arabism!" the mob thundered. "Warrior of Islam! Mus-ta-fa! *Mus-ta-fa!* MUS-TA-FA!"

A microphone was placed before the Prime Minister. He raised his hand, and eventually order was restored. He spoke:

"O Arabs!

"Arab brothers, Arab workers, Arab delegates of the Arab Syndicates:

"Your Arabism warms me. Weary of flesh, cold of soul, I come here to reinforce my flame before the fires of your Arabism. How splendid is your Arabism, how its lanterns illumine my darkness! Today I had anticipated greeting the Arab Syndicates, but now I marvel that their legions have been multiplied, through the telepathy of Arabism, by Arabs and Arabs and Arabs yet again. God watches these wonders.

"So also does your leader. With a new piety Mustafa, who is nothing, quickens to your conquests as you construct new highways of hope and build great bridges of Arabism. He exults in your victories as your Arabism, embattled but irreversible, slays the Harlot of Iniquity.

"O Arabs, hear me.

"The building of our new society is a consecrated task and indeed a difficult one. On all sides we are beleaguered by treachery and evil. It is written, 'If the gifts are the gifts of the good giver, then verily do we accept them. If the gifts are the gifts of the evil giver, then verily do we give them back.' In the days when the banners of Imperialism fluttered freely in the breezes of the broad Mabrouk, the Imperialists came bearing many gifts. First they brought the *ful* bean, sowing it far, reaping it wide, because they knew it would suck the vitality of the people and cloud their brains. Then, from their enslaved colonies in the East, the Imperialists imported the forbidden weed, the Indian hemp, conspiring to turn us into a nation of dope fiends. Yes.

"And then as she sipped her tea one afternoon in Windsor Castle, the Queen of England decided that *ful* and hashish were not enough. 'Let them drink tea,' she said. But it was not the tea the Queen of England drank that we were given to drink. It was the black tea, made of bean husks, dried leaves and sawdust. The black tea became the new opium of our people. It enslaved them anew, and they came to crave it more than bread itself. In my own birthplace of Wadi Mafish all the flocks were auctioned off for a few detestable bundles of the black tea. Throughout the countryside, the farmers began taking their teapots with them to the fields. When they had no money to buy tea, they were unfit for work and lay down on the ground. The black tea ruined their stomachs and enfeebled their character. It brought about apathy and forgetfulness, and made our beloved land a toy in the claws of Imperialism. *Ful,* hashish, and the black tea—the three scourges of our country to this day! But did this satisfy the Imperialists? I think not. They despatched their armies bearing new gifts. Malaria, trachoma, syphilis, tuberculosis, cholera and leprosy, for example. So much for British Imperialism.

"O Arabs, hear me.

"No sooner had we thrown off the thongs and fetters of British tyranny than the Americans arrived with their gifts. I mean their Coca-Cola and their filter-tip cigarettes. I have already revealed to you that concealed in the filter-tips was an ingenious drug intended to weaken our resistance to military pacts and atomic bases. Thanks be to God this plot was smoked out before any damage was done! Coca-Cola, as everybody knows, is colored with the blood of the pig. Now the Americans have offered us some grains and medicine. From the beginning, we were wary of their good faith, but in order to leave no corridor unexplored either for the improvement of relations between states or for the prosperity of Arabism, we consented to negotiations. But we must persevere in our vigilance, children of Arabism, lest Imperialism, clad in new clothes . . ."

By this time the Ambassador was inside the Cadillac changing his shirt. He reproached Fawzi for parking the car in the courtyard and for leaving the American flag unfurled on the fender during a demonstration. Fawzi's shirt fit well enough, and it was passably clean, but the cuffs were frayed. "Sorry, Basha. If I know you need it, I wear new one."

"Never mind," the Ambassador said. "I'll tuck the cuffs inside so the Prime Minister won't see them."

The Ambassador opened the door and squeezed out into the throng of Arabs. Many of them recognized him. The Three Stooges had been swallowed up in the mob, but their protection was not necessary. People made way for Fitz Pasha courteously. They punctuated their apoplectic approval of Mustafa ibn Mabrouk's anti-American rhetoric with greetings to the Ambassador.

"May your morning be full of jasmin, Fitz Basha!"

"God go with you, *ya Basha!*"

Some of them even began applauding when they saw the official envoy of the United States. The Prime Minister ranted on.

Entering the rococo palace, the Ambassador felt nostalgic for what it used to be. He remembered the first time he had come here years ago, when a septuagenarian porter who had never heard of Arab nationalism operated an elevator that never worked. Gone now were the familiar odors and the endearing pandemonium, the squalid functionaries scampering like termites in and out of the woodwork, the scruffy boys brandishing trays of muddy coffee. Today there was a new German elevator, the place was antiseptic and carpeted, and peopled only by starched and solemn army officers.

The Ambassador was conducted without delay into the spartan office of the Prime Minister. Mustafa ibn Mabrouk was still on the adjoining balcony haranguing the mob. The room was cluttered with books, in English, French and Arabic, but mostly in English: they bulged out of shelves, lay heaped high on tables, on the unpretentious steel desk, and on the floor. The works of Laski, Toynbee and von Clausewitz; back copies of the *Economist,* the Congressional *Record,* and the House of Commons *Hansard;* a scale model of a municipal hospital about to be built. On the wall hung an effusively inscribed photograph of the King. Absent-mindedly, the Ambassador began contemplating the sensuous Royal physiognomy. Mustafa ibn Mabrouk, wheeling his body to stress a point, caught Fitzgibbon Pasha in the corner of his eye. He did not like to keep the American Ambassador waiting, so he hurled a final brickbat at the United States and finished his speech.

The mob was still expostulating when the Prime Minister closed the glass doors of the balcony behind him and addressed himself to his visitor.

"You seem to like that picture."

His English was soft and pleasing to the ear, with only a slight British accent. He sat down on the davenport.

"Tfadl," he said, motioning the Ambassador into an armchair.

"I was just wondering," the Ambassador said, nodding at the Royal portrait, "how much longer you will allow it to hang there."

"History will decide such things. In the meantime, Mohammed must be humored."

"I should hope so. In Washington he is regarded as an element of stability."

They both laughed.

"How is Eminence Grise?" the Prime Minister asked.

"I wish you would tell your newspapers to lay off."

"Want a Pepsi?"

"Do you think the pig's blood would agree with me?"

"Oh that. That was the other brand."

"What have you got against Coca-Cola?" the Ambassador asked.

"I asked them to build me a couple of clinics. They refused. So I made a little deal with the Pepsi people."

"And all that business about Windsor Castle and—"

"Take it easy, *ya habibi*. I'm trying to get my Arabs to diversify their diet. How can I industrialize this bloody country if half the population is undernourished? I thought if I blamed the British they might listen. Incidentally, your chauffeur's shirt fits quite well."

"I didn't think you could see me from the balcony."

"Is there anything I don't see?"

The Prime Minister rang for refreshments.

"The wheat and medicine deal is rather up in the air," the Ambassador said.

"That's old news."

"I *thought* you went a little far in your speech."

"Paul Pullmotor told me—on the telephone last night."

"He did!" The Ambassador did not even attempt to conceal his pique. "Well, it's not definite yet, you know. Did he tell you that? What if Hampshire reconsiders? What will you tell the street?"

"I'll think of something."

"You're very clever, Mustafa—but you lack wisdom."

"I need that wheat, Fitz Pasha."

"You have a curious way of asking for it."

"La parole a été donnée à l'homme pour dissimuler sa pensée."

"Voltaire?"

"Talleyrand."

An orderly came in with the Pepsi, followed almost at once by Captain Anwar A'war, the Prime Minister's military aide and man Friday. Captain A'war wore a waxed mustache and a preposterously large black patch over his left eye, though it was common knowledge that he enjoyed perfect vision. The Ambassador had once asked the Prime Minister why he tolerated such a charade. "Tolerate it?" Mustafa ibn Mabrouk laughed. "I thought it up! It is Captain A'war who enforces most of my orders. The eyepatch makes people jump faster."

"His Majesty is on the line," Captain A'war announced now.

"Tell him I'll call him back," the Prime Minister said. "Better still—take the message."

Captain A'war withdrew; Ambassador Fitzgibbon suppressed a smile.

"Yes, I know what you're thinking," Mustafa ibn Mabrouk said. "You think I treat the King very shabbily."

"Well, you know how much it means to him," the Ambassador said. "You might at least talk to him when he rings you up."

"You're right, Fitz Pasha. I should. It's about the tenth time Mohammed has called me this week. Do you know I've neither seen nor talked to him in nearly a month? I'm so *busy*. And now all these rumors galloping through town—that I'm going to depose him or even have him bumped off—"

"Yes, I've heard them."

"Well, they're a lot of rot."

"I know that."

"How could I harm him after all he has done for me? Haven't I saved his life once already? I love him. But he's such a *bore*. And honestly, I don't know what I'm going to do with him. The Royal Question! The expense of keeping up the Royal Palace, for one thing. Time and again I've been on the point of telling him he must go away, resign, abdicate for his own good. I even had a villa all rented for him in San Remo."

"But you couldn't bring yourself to tell him," the Ambassador said.

"No. He wouldn't understand. He's so . . . innocent. But I've got to make a move pretty soon. Otherwise he will remain the unwitting cat's-paw for plots against the government—against me."

The telephone rang and the Prime Minister sprang from the davenport to answer it. His movements were lithe, athletic, nervous. Barking orders into the telephone, he ran a lean, manicured hand through his straight black hair. There was no air conditioning here; the sweat made his long eyelashes sparkle; as he glanced over at Fitzgibbon Pasha his eyes seemed somehow as capable of compassion as of mendacity. They were exceptionally interesting, those eyes; the whites of them were peculiarly arresting, providing an even greater depth and inscrutability to the jet-black pupils. They were the eyes of a gypsy—the Prime Minister was a Bedouin by birth—and when they turned on you, they looked deep within you for a moment; then, glazing over, they seemed to see through you and far beyond you. And always they were like that —alternately darting, distending, wandering far, far, from under the thick eyebrows which so luxuriantly framed them. The sweat ran down his short, straight nose, moistening a neat mustache; his mouth was sensitive, a bit brooding. He was handsome; not as handsome as the King, but then the King was exceptional. When he had finished talking on the telephone, he sat down behind his steel desk and lit an American cigarette.

"Smoke?"

"No, thanks," the Ambassador said. "I'm trying to break the habit. Besides, I'm afraid the filters would poison me."

"That silly speech—why do you bother about it? I know how absurd it will sound when you send the translation to Hampshire, but how do his speeches sound in Arabic?"

"Touché."

"Politics is a caravan of compromises. I wasn't talking to you, Fitz Pasha, I was talking to *them*. If I spoke to them your way I wouldn't be Prime Minister another five minutes. And may I remind you that falsehood was commended by the Prophet to advance any struggle against the enemies of Islam? Politics is a caravan of compromises. I speak to my Arabs not as I wish they were, or even as I intend one day to make them, but as they are—with all their complexes."

"And so instead of restraining those complexes, you fertilize them."

"Precisely! They are practically my only source of national energy. We don't have uranium in Al Khadra, Fitz Pasha. There is only one way to reach that rabble out there, and that is to tell them what they want to hear. If I can galvanize their complexes I can remake this nation. You harnessed your atoms, now let me harness mine."

"Hampshire—"

"May God protect him. He is my catalyst, my great galvanizer."

"Pullmotor—"

"Every night before I go to bed I look to see if Pullmotor is under it. But Paul and I are brothers in blood. He knows what he wants, decides what he has to do, and then does it. He's *strong*. He will do whatever he must to achieve his ends, and I admire that, because so will I. Pullmotor is probably plotting against me at this moment. As for myself, plotting against Pullmotor is the most sublime pleasure I have in life. I'm glad Paul is here. It will clear the air."

"These reports about Soviet—"

"Please, ya habibi. I'd like to keep your Mr. Hampshire guessing for a while."

The Ambassador sighed. "Have it your way," he said.

"Yes. It is well to beguile those who have shown themselves masters of treachery."

"Lenin?"

"Cesare Borgia."

They fenced for another few minutes, but it came to nothing. In his frustration, the Ambassador began speaking in Arabic. But he should have known better than to resort to so transparent and patronizing a device with Mustafa ibn Mabrouk.

When the Ambassador had gone, the Prime Minister approached the photograph of the King, gazed for a moment at the beautiful but blank black eyes, large and set far apart, and then removed the portrait from its place. He put it on the floor, and from a cavity in the wall he extracted a spool of magnetic tape. He reinstated the picture of the King, and returned to his desk. In Arabic he scribbled the date and *Conversations—American Ambassador* on a large manila envelope, inserted the spool, sealed the envelope and tossed it into his *Out* basket.

It was an ordinary, workaday act—it would not have surprised the Ambassador, nor offended him—quite in keeping with Mustafa ibn Mabrouk's systematic and conspiratorial nature. That nature had served him well. He was not where he was simply because in the beginning he had won the confidence of the King. Conspiracy is the chemistry of the Arab character; Mustafa ibn Mabrouk had out-conspired a score of rivals in a hundred subsequent wars of will. When he came to power three years ago he had aspired to statesmanship and had carefully cultivated the image of moderation in the poses he struck before the world. But he was an empiricist above all else; he soon discovered that the political equations and coefficients of other, more serene societies would not work in Al Khadra. He found that his power could be preserved only by the same tormented methods he had used to acquire it. So, out with persuasion. Away with reason. He would run his country the only way he knew how: the only way it could be run: by *plotting*. To this day he invariably visualized all of his domestic and foreign problems, no matter how trifling, in terms of intrigue. This applied particularly to his day-to-day dealings with his own subordinates; he juggled human emotions, personal rivalries, ambitions, hatreds and vendettas with intuitive skill. He played this minister off against that one, pitted the cunning of Colonel A against the pomposity of General B, and most of the time got what he wanted: a weakening of their positions and a reinforcement of his own. That he had rejected statesmanship did not mean that he had ceased to cherish a certain stately conception of himself, however. His dreams at night were as recurrent as they were varied, and his favorite fantasy was of himself, in ermine and coronet, delivering a learned address in the House of Lords.

The ubiquitous intelligence apparatus that he had assembled was the envy of every other Arab government. It was like a pumpkin, cut into several slices. Each piece was separate and self-sufficient, often unaware of the operations or even the existence of the other segments. There was considerable duplication; spies spied on spies; it was exactly as he wanted it. The heads of the separate intelligence services, forbidden contact with one another, reported to a single man: Mustafa ibn Mabrouk. Only in his head did all the pieces of pumpkin fit together. If this suggested caution on his part, he could be reckless too. "I love to take chances," he once confided to Taj Pasha, an elderly civilian adviser. "If I am sixty percent certain I can get away with something, no matter what it is, I go ahead and do it. This has always been my policy in dealing with the Americans." So far that policy had worked very well. The Americans had been generous to him in the past. If he was deliberately alienating them now, was it perhaps because in the end he hoped they would pay a higher price for his good behavior than they were prepared to pay at present? It was a long chance, but now he had made up his mind; he knew he would have to play the game to the end; it was too late to turn back. His Five-Year Plan was lagging, and he needed an enormous amount of money. He was confronted with problems of appalling complexity. He had no place to put his people, and they were multiplying like mice.

But these larger problems would have to wait until, in the middle of the night, Mustafa had time to ponder them. Now he had work to do. He surrendered himself to the correspondence on his desk. He did an inordinate amount of paper work, not because he disliked delegating authority, but because he had so few subordinates whose competence he trusted. He was bombarded with trivia; very little was done in Al Khadra without his personal permission. He scrutinized a dossier from his Minister of Planning, then an intelligence report stolen from the foreign ministry of a neighboring Arab state, and then some despatches from his delegation to the United Nations. Like Fitzgibbon Pasha, he made quick decisions, which he scribbled out, sometimes in terse English, in margins, on the backs of envelopes, or on scraps of yellow paper. He hummed softly to himself while he worked. Occasionally he would mark a document for the attention of Taj Pasha, his octogenarian adviser, requesting an opinion on a point of fiscal intricacy or international law. Or, angered by the poor preparation of a report, he would pick up the telephone and heap his cold contempt on the man who had written it. Near the bottom of the heap he came upon an envelope with a British postmark, and he opened it eagerly.

It was from Sandhurst, which he had attended for a year following his graduation from the Royal Military College in Al Asima. The letter was a disappointment—a mimeographed sheet soliciting donations to the Old Soldiers Benevolent Association, and a brochure labeled *Life at Sandhurst*. "The Committee are confident that as a loyal alumnus of the Academy you will wish to contribute to this exceptionally worthy cause," the mimeographed letter said. Mustafa ibn Mabrouk smiled and wrote out a generous check from his personal sterling account. He attached it to a note stipulating that under no circumstances was his contribution to be publicized, and sent it off posthaste to the United Kingdom. Leafing through the brochure, he was seized with a nostalgia which did violence to a disposition ordinarily so unsentimental.

The Sandhurst illustrations were less numerous than he would have wished. King's Walk, the Waterloo Guns, the Passing Out. The upper and lower lakes, ringed with rhododendron, serene with swans and little islands of pine. It had been the loneliest—and yet somehow the happiest—year of his life. For his courses in advanced tactics and artillery, the military jargon had come easily. But otherwise he was unsure of his English, and thus his already reticent nature sought security in solitude. Mistaking his shyness for hostility, few of his instructors or fellow officers made any effort to cultivate him; he mixed with them only at meals.

He could remember the single occasion when they seemed to accept him as one of themselves—and his refusal to be accepted. It was a rainy day; they were drinking before luncheon in the lounge bar of the New Building. Gin for the Englishmen, fruit juice for Mustafa. One of the majors was to be married, and there was a tradition which required a prospective bridegroom to run across the room and land with his bottom in a wicker wastepaper basket. Profanely, the major refused, but after another round or two he was prevailed upon. The wicker wastepaper basket was placed in the middle of the room and he performed the rite amid general merriment.

"You buggers!" cried the major. "There's a splinter up me arse."

With abandon, the others ran the course. New baskets had to be fetched. When the romp was done, someone turned to the Arab, standing silently by the bar and feeling quite out of place.

"How about it, Leftenant? Your turn."

Managing a smile, Mustafa put his orange juice on the bar, ran across the room and scored a bull's eye.

"Good show."

Mustafa sat there on the floor for a moment, looking miserable.

"Anything wrong, old man?"

"Yes," Mustafa said, rising painfully. "I-I've got a splinter up me arse."

They laughed until the tears came, and two of the men kissed him. They hoisted him to their shoulders, and singing songs they carried him in triumph into the crowded mess. How curious, he reflected some years later, that Englishmen should have been the first to pay him that honor.

From that day he could have made any one of them his friend, but he did not seem to want friends. He kept even more to his room, and perfected his English from the printed page. As his grasp of the language grew, so did his awareness of the grand affairs that lay beyond the rhododendron and swans and pine-peaked islets. On weekends and afternoons and free days he began to go down to London. His memory was as keen as his intuition, and even now he could reconstruct the particulars of that brief journey.

On at Camberley. A second-class compartment invariably smelling of cigar smoke. From Surrey through Berkshire, down through Bagshot, Ascot (of the races and the Royal Enclosure), Sunningdale, Longcross Halt, Virginia Water, Staines Central, on to Twickenham and Waterloo. Clean, wooded country . . . rolling, quilted meadows (so incredibly green to a son of the desert!) . . . fat, grazing cows and sheep . . . intermittent towns . . . identical Georgian red-brick houses in tidy rows . . . baronial and squirish estates just visible in the misty distance. Before and after every town, the playing fields: wombs of Good Sportsmanship. Men all in white on the Polytechnic cricket grounds. Golf course near Longcross Halt! Identical houses along the tracks, each with a tiny, neatly fenced garden all its own. Staines Central. *Walter Bros. Ltd. Coal & Coke. W. E. Sykes Ltd.—MACHINE TOOLS.* After Staines Central, the first of the storage tanks and the great smokestacks. The spaces between the houses became negligible, then nonexistent; the dwellings appeared to be an unbroken line of barracks. The domestic gardens became even tinier, though just as neat, more and more squeezed, and at Clapham Junction were gone for good. A sea of roofs and chimney clusters; the brick of jumbled, jammed-together houses no longer red but a squalid, soot-covered brown. Coal yards, slag heaps, immense storage tanks, hundreds of freight cars, railroad tracks which seemed to web everywhere at once. Waterloo: like a large shed; grimy, glass arcade overhead; ubiquitous billboards.

Mustafa would hire a cheap room in Earl's Court, take the tube to the British Museum, and immerse himself in the history of British rule in his own country. So tempestuous and melancholy an epoch! He haunted the Houses of Parliament, and marveled that a race so authoritarian abroad could be so democratic at home. He considered himself particularly lucky to be present during a number of debates in the Commons involving imperial policy in Al Khadra; he would enter the galleries with a ream of foolscap, and when he emerged, hours later, the paper would be covered with notes written in his large, runaway hand; to this day he could quote those debates almost verbatim. But if he found Commons fascinating, he fell wildly in love with Lords. He did not know why; he had been born a goatherd—perhaps that had something to do with it. He was enthralled with the elegance of the inconsequential discussion ("Is the Noble Viscount endeavoring to suggest that these perambulating saloons in the south of Scotland . . .") and the splendor of the gilt and crimson chamber. And what splendor: stained-glass windows, the Earls and Barons of Runnymede, Edward III giving the garter to the Black Prince, St. Ethelbert being baptized, the guilded opulence of the Throne—all these gazing so benignly down on Their Noble Lordships so sparsely scattered among the crimson sofas and mahogany-chocolate carvings, the bewigged scribes with the inkpots and the hourglass, the Gentleman Usher of the Black Rod, the Yeoman Usher of the Black Rod, and, of course, the Lord Chancellor on the Woolsack. On those few occasions when he had to queue for admittance, he found himself in the Royal Gallery, engrossed in Maclise's immense frescoes devoted to the victories of Nelson at Trafalgar and Wellington at Waterloo. How well Mustafa remembered the Wellington mural, and how very much he loved it. There, amid all that carnage, amid all those tattered, prostrate forms with faces writhing or calmed by death, his guard of honor feebly raising their caps and swords to salute his triumph, sat Wellington on his horse, his face haggard, solemn, resolute, radiating his awareness of the dreadful price of victory—and his acceptance of that price. Here was the quintessence of the Victorian ideal: duty, discipline, courage, *strength*—Mustafa made them his own.

He was disappointed that during debate the Lords did not wear their ermine and coronets, as he did in his dreams. After the debates he would lurk in the corridors, or among the Tudor roses and creamy granite archways of the Peers' Lobby, hoping that one of Their Noble Lordships would mistake him for someone else and speak to him. This never happened. But he learned to identify many of them. Monkswell, Templewood, Tweedsmuir.

Methuen, Chorley, Pethick-Lawrence. Fairfax of Cameron, Lindsay of Birker, Lucas of Chilworth. Viscount Bledisloe, Earl of Iddesleigh, Marquess of Aberdeen and Tewair, Duke of Devonshire, Lord Bishop of Sheffield. Snatches of overheard conversation kept coming back. ". . . fobbed off on Admiralty . . . won't pay his bloody bill . . . the man is mad . . . I've nothing against adultery, old boy, so long as it's *tidy* . . . not at White's they won't . . . shower, my dear chap, absolute *shower* . . ."

He sought out the grim black buildings of the Colonial Office in Great Smith Street, convinced that in fact his country was governed there, and in order to pursue his researches on the British bases in Al Khadra. The few minor officials who received him found his questions altogether too intelligent. He remembered their offices: desks which were all newspapers and dirty tea cups, dusty heaps of dossiers lying not at all neatly on the floor; on walls sooty from the steam heat, cuckoo clocks ticking inexorably on. Through the unwashed windows Mustafa could see the black corrugated roofs of Great Smith Street, and above them the winter sun. He had never seen that sort of sun at home; even at midday it was the color of blood, and in the haze it looked like a wound hemorrhaging through gray gauze.

Mustafa visited the gas works, the abattoir, food-processing plants, machine-tool factories and pharmaceutical firms in and around London; later on he went up to the Midlands to observe heavy industry. He asked endless questions, and devoured company reports as other men might devour pornography or science fiction. All of his visits were unannounced; and yet he was amazed at how courteous to him most Englishmen were. Once, as he left the assistant manager's office in an electrical-supply plant he overheard the remark, "Rather a clever young chap, that—for a wog." In the Tate Gallery, he doted on the fair Ophelia, drowned in a lily pond. At night when he had finished reading and had nothing to do and nowhere to go, he walked the streets of London.

He was constantly alone. During his entire year in England he was not once invited to dinner, or comforted by the company of a woman. He liked to stand outside the theaters in Haymarket and Leicester Square and watch rich people and Royalty arriving. Sometimes during the day he would go down to the financial district around Throckmorton and Threadneedle Streets and wander in and out of the Royal Exchange and the great, sooty Greek temples which were the banking houses. But most of his time in that quarter he spent simply standing on street corners, studying the prim faces of the bankers under their umbrellas and bowler hats. He thought if he loitered there long enough he might read in that collective physiognomy useful lessons in national discipline, ethnic enterprise, and the capacity to govern lesser peoples on frontiers far beyond. He remembered particularly a winter afternoon when he came upon a perfectly commonplace queue of people waiting for a bus in Threadneedle Street. The wind was raw and the rain was turning to sleet. The queue was very long: ordinary men and women in their caps and tweed coats, hatless messenger boys, a little girl holding a woman's hand, several gentlemen in bowlers, an old lady, a soldier in uniform, a pair of nuns. Silently, in the shivering cold, they waited. The autobuses were infrequent and overcrowded and accepted only a few passengers each time. But the queue persevered without word or grumble, and not once was there any pushing or disorder. Mustafa tried to transpose the situation to his native land: he could picture the pandemonium and hear the screams. The experience made a deep impression on him; so deep, in fact, that it was to affect the very future of his country. But then his whole year in England affected him deeply, and what a splendid year it was. The romp with the wicker wastepaper basket; the quilted meadows and squirish estates of Berkshire; Lords, Wellington at Waterloo, the blood-red sun above Great Smith Street, the Tate, the abattoir, the machine-tool factories, the Threadneedle bus stop—they were *his* England, and they had erected a monument in his heart which he never could, and never desired to, deface. And in this, no previous bitterness had been appeased, nor a single grievance wiped away. He hated Britain, and loved England.

Even then, there began to form in Mustafa's mind a vision which animated him to this day. Even then, there began to evolve within him an ambition of such magnitude that at times he felt paralyzed in its presence. It was not just a vision of himself as the inevitable and charismatic leader of his homeland; that was comparatively simple and—so far as he was concerned—settled. The vision involved as well the entire identity and personality of his people. If they were to rise from the squalor of the present and redeem a millennium of darkness, they must be remade. He knew now that so large a task meant something more than new fertilizers and agrarian reform. He knew now what he must do: he must *remake* the very character of his people. He had found his mold at last: a model of obedient, tenacious, prosperous creatures—he was going to remake his people in the image of the queue in Threadneedle Street.

It would not be easy, he knew. He would have to begin at the bottom, turning them inside out and upside down. All the artifices of the omnipotent state would have to be mobilized, all the dreary disciplines and detergents splashed generously about. Traditions would be discarded, wealth confiscated, and the prisons enlarged to accommodate the dissenters. Islam, if it could not keep up, would be altered or if necessary ignored. The intellectuals and liberals would not like it, and indignant editorials would appear in London and the *New York Times*. The first few years would be the worst of all, because everything would break down as the society stumbled to get in step with the new music. New hopes would have to be built on old hates, and during the unpleasant transition everything that went wrong would have to be blamed on the British—or the Americans. It would take years, perhaps decades, but he would do it, he would turn his Arabs into—Britons? Allah forbid!—he would turn his Arabs into English gentlemen. Such was Mustafa ibn Mabrouk's mind then—and now, as he sat at his steel desk leafing through *Life at Sandhurst*.

He had not quite completed his paper work when Captain A'war came in and told him that the Soviet Ambassador and Minister of Energetics and Electrification had arrived—at the same time as Paul Pullmotor. The Prime Minister giggled; he had, of course, planned it this way. "Give them a chance to get acquainted, Captain," he said. "In ten minutes, show in the Soviet gentlemen. Then bring Mr. Pullmotor a Pepsi and ask him to wait."

6

The Ambassador was expected that evening for drinks at Dr. Pantry's and afterward at the reception in the Soviet Embassy. Al Asima could claim few modern entertainments except the cinema and was by consequence a very social sort of place. A single ambassadorial day might include a luncheon, a tea, three cocktail parties and a tedious diplomatic dinner. Fitzgibbon Pasha rarely had an evening he could call his own. He hated cocktail parties; otherwise robust, he had fallen arches, and the rigors of remaining on his feet hour after hour were often more than he could endure. He appeased his boredom with dry martinis, and sat down in a corner whenever he could find one. He was notorious for falling asleep during dinner parties.

Dr. Pantry's party was intended to introduce Chuckles Vespucci to the cultural community of Al Asima. Many professional musicians, a myriad of academic luminaries, the Rector of the University of Al Asima, and the Papal Internuncio had been invited. The Internuncio, himself an accomplished guitarist, arrived promptly, but most of the others simply ignored the invitation. People were wary of the unkempt, ill-mannered young men from the Political Police who invariably gate-crashed American receptions posing as "society photographers." Having one's picture taken consorting with American Embassy officials was hardly the wisest or most fashionable way to ingratiate oneself with the regime. And there were special hazards in being photographed with the Director of Mutual Understanding, whose celebrated ineptness was considered the camouflage of occult enterprise; for it was widely believed that in real life Dr. Pantry was the chief of American intelligence in Al Khadra.

The Ambassador's arrival caused the customary commotion among the many Americans and the clique of society Arabs who had come to do honor to Chuckles Vespucci. The society Arabs, mostly Christian and *ancien régime,* were the only representatives of the local population who could be depended upon to show up at American cocktail parties. Wherever one went in the American community one found these same swarthy middle-aged faces, forever saying the same things in Cambridge English and Sorbonne French. They rarely spoke Arabic, even among themselves. It was upon the society Arabs that most of the Americans depended for their information about what was going on in Al Khadra. Their addiction to Americans was well known to the regime; deprived of power and their once enormous wealth, they were past the point of caring what the new order thought of their associations. They whiled away the afternoons at the Gazooza Sporting Club drinking warm lemonade and muttering against Mustafa ibn Mabrouk.

Now they clustered adoringly about Chuckles Vespucci, who regaled them with the inscrutable verities of Zen. The minstrel was more conventionally clad tonight, the jodhpurs his only outrage of costume. (Dr. Pantry had risen to the occasion and lectured him severely that afternoon.)

"Mais Zen! Qu'est-ce que c'est?"

"Zen est Zen est Zen."

"Oui, je sais, mais—"

"Le Buddha est le Buddha. Le Tao est le Tao. Zen est Zen."

"Evidemment, je sais, mais qu'est-ce que la définition? Les attributs, les qualités de Zen?"

"Zen—"

"Chuckles, *please,*" cried Mrs. Pantry. "We don't understand a word."

"Zen is an elephant walking in the tall grass, playing the lute under the moon, the sound of a single-handed clap. Zen is instant mashed potato. Instant mashed potato is Zen. Zen and toothpaste taste the same."

When Chuckles was presented to the Ambassador, Fitz Pasha made an heroic effort to engage him in rational conversation.

"Are you sure we haven't met before?" the Ambassador asked. "Except for your beard you seem to remind me of someone I can't quite place."

"This illusory, changeful, empty body is Dharmakaya."

"Quite. Have you ever been in Buenos Aires?"

"Have you ever been in bhodi?"

"Not that I recall. Have you ever been in Benghazi?"

"Have you ever been in Sambhogokaya?"

"I notice you speak fluent French. Do you know any other languages?"

"Language is the dialogue between brass and alabaster."

It was a lavish cocktail party; the Pantry apartment was one of the handsomest in the capital. A platoon of black servants in flowing red garments and turbans of gold—outdoing even the watered silk of the Internuncio—dashed about dispensing drinks and juices, crevettes in pink mayonnaise, and caviar on Graham crackers. In due course Chuckles was persuaded to sing. He retrieved his lute from the Internuncio, and unleased an athletic rendering of "I Go Ape."

"The moon is bright above
Oh, what a night for love!
And as I hold you near
I whisper in your ear—

I go APE every time I see you smile!
I'm a ding-dong gorilla and I carry on cave-man style!

I'm gonna bop you on the head and love you all the while!
WOOH!
Well, I'm a monkey's uncle who's a cousin to a chimpanzee!
Like I was reelin' and a-rockin' and a-swingin' from a co-
coanut tree! WOOH!
O honey, can't you see?
You bring OUT the monkey business in me? WOOH!"

Barricaded by the other guests, the Internuncio stood at Chuckles Vespucci's side, fidgeting with his pectoral cross.

Eager for the night air, the Ambassador went out onto the terrace, overlooking the Corniche not far below. He was joined almost at once by Mrs. Pantry, a frail, confused woman, but good-natured and anxious to please.

"Can I get you anything, Mr. Ambassador?"

"Let me finish this one first, Agnes."

The night wind fondled her gray hair, and the Ambassador felt a sudden compassion for this fragile creature. She gazed out over the shimmering Mabrouk and said, "Wasn't God good to put this pretty river right below my balcony? I don't care what they write about my husband in the newspapers or how much they hate Americans. I love it here. I don't ever want to go back to Rhododendron."

On the Corniche below, in an open Fiat, a young army officer was teaching his wife to drive. On the sidewalk, pajama-clad youths crouched beneath the fluorescent lamps, reading their lessons; it was too warm tonight to stay inside. Beneath one lamp, some women and small boys were catching grasshoppers with their bare hands as the insects fell stupified from the incandescence.

"Have they no other meat?" Mrs. Pantry asked.

"Only vegetables," the Ambassador said.

Then he sent a second secretary down to tell Fawzi to bring around the Cadillac, and he left for the Soviet Ambassador's.

The gin had made him perspire. "That bloody cooler, ya Fawzi. I thought the phone call would fix it."

The Soviet Embassy in Al Asima was a strawberry-pink palace perched on the lip of the broad Mabrouk, gloomy inside with ill-lit electric candelabra and jaundiced lithographs of Marxist mystics—but otherwise well suited to the dual function of Chancery and Residence which the thrifty Slavs had imposed upon it, and to the reception honoring Moscow's visiting Minister of Energetics and Electrification. The flower of Al Asima officialdom was there. Joining the long reception line, Ambassador Fitzgibbon found himself sandwiched between a presumptuous *Life* photographer and a bearded Armenian bishop in a goblinesque black hood. The *Life* man kept snapping his picture and the bishop had body odor, so Fitz Pasha was not in his best humor when finally presented to the Soviet Minister.

"I hope you will enjoy your visit with us," Ambassador Fitzgibbon said.

"Da."

"Will you be staying long?"

"Da."

"Oh really? Here on business, I suppose?"

"Da."

"His Excellency does not speak very well English," interjected Comrade Bagolevsky, the Soviet Ambassador to Al Khadra, attempting to steer the American toward the refreshments. "The vodka is over there, Fitz Pasha."

"I was only trying to be sociable."

"Wait a minute," Ambassador Bagolevsky said. "Did you got the Schenley?"

"I'm still working on it."

"Your Samovar arrived last night. Ten cases. The Minister brought it."

"Good Lord! You didn't tell him."

"Keep your voice down. Of course not. He thinks it's for Mustafa ibn Mabrouk."

The Minister of Energetics and Electrification suddenly began expostulating in Russian.

"What does he say?" Fitz Pasha asked.

"His Excellency wants you to know that he likes individual Americans. He says they are like green leaves on a dead tree."

"Please thank the Minister for his gracious remark, and tell him that I like individual communists. They are like green trees—in a petrified forest."

Before he could reach the bar, Fitz Pasha was intercepted by K. J. Mohandas Gupta, the Indian Ambassador. A brown little bit of a thing, an Oxonian who looked down his nose at Americans because they do not happen to be British. But a born gossip.

"And the place is fairly ripping with rumor that something is afoot between the guest of honor and our man Mustafa," the Indian whispered.

"Oh, really?"

"No details from your side, Fitz Pasha? The Russians haven't been a bit helpful. I've been after the P.M. for an audience all day but he won't answer his telephone. You saw him this morning?"

"For a few minutes. Routine nuts and bolts."

"Rumor has it that Hampshire and Mustafa are bracing for a donnybrook."

"Utter rot."

"Well, what is Paul Pullmotor doing in town then? I understand he's delivered some sort of ultimatum."

"K.J., you are permitting your Bengali imagination to run away with your Oxonian perspicacity. Pullmotor is an investment banker."

Grunting, the Indian turned away from Fitz Pasha in quest of greener pasture. Out-obfuscated, out-fibbed, he decided he badly needed a cigarette. He turned brusquely to one of his aides and told him to fetch some.

"Plain or filter, Excellency?"

"Plain, you numbskull. And pay more attention to the P.M.'s speeches."

If the Indian Ambassador needed a smoke, the American Ambassador needed something stronger. Making short order of his first vodka martini, Fitz Pasha lamented that even the neutrals knew more of what was going on than he did. "Pullmotor is sure to show up here tonight," he thought. "I must buttonhole him and *make him tell me.*"

Paul Pullmotor did indeed show up, fifteen minutes later—and in the company of an emancipated Moslem woman, uncommonly beautiful, wearing her black hair in the latest French fashion and dressed in shimmering green organza. She was the daughter of a former foreign minister, and was at one time an intimate companion of the present King. Her name was Solafa; men of all ages competed for her favor. She and Pullmotor passed the hive of foreign correspondents swarming about the bar, none of whom noticed Pullmotor. For the moment all eyes were on Solafa, and more than one admirer marveled that the King could have allowed so exquisite a woman to slip from his grasp.

"By the way," everyone wondered, "where *is* His Majesty?" Royal courtesy required that no one leave until King Mohammed had come and gone.

"He is expected moment by moment," Ambassador Bagolevsky assured them.

"I hope so," Ambassador Fitzgibbon said, his eyes in pursuit of Pullmotor. "My feet hurt."

The Prime Minister and Sir Charles Chetwynd-Pott, the British Ambassador, drove up by chance at the same time and met in the driveway of the strawberry-pink palace; they chatted on the way in.

"I see from the newspapers that the Duchess of Gloucester is in West Africa," Mustafa ibn Mabrouk said as casually as he could. In spite of himself, he held Sir Charles in awe—and Sir Charles knew it.

"Is she really? I hadn't even noticed, Prime Minister."

"Yes. It's a pity you people never put me in jail, when you had the chance."

"I'm afraid I don't quite follow you."

"I mean those African politicians. They were all in jail, and now the Queen is entertaining them at luncheon at Windsor Castle. If I were an ex-convict I suppose my credentials would be considered in order. It's a shame, really."

"I doubt that HMG would consider inviting you to London at present, Prime Minister. Really, you do print bloody awful things about us in your newspapers."

"We have a saying, 'Strike with your sword, and draw honey.' But you disappoint me, Sir Charles. It's the Americans we're attacking this month. I was hoping you'd notice."

"And next month?"

"We shall see."

They parted company in the vestibule; the Prime Minister had no intention of making his entrance on the arm of the British Ambassador. Sir Charles went in first. A minute later Mustafa followed him, attended by Anwar A'war, his military aide, Hassan Walahadan, his serviceable but powerless Foreign Minister, and Taj Pasha, his octogenarian adviser. There was a shrill clamor and the popping of flashbulbs as Mustafa embraced the Soviet Minister.

The foreign correspondents—most of them Americans or British—pounced on the Prime Minister like wild animals. At first he refused to speak in English, but when they began insulting him he lost his temper and lashed them back with acid epigrams, mocking metaphors. Then, almost ostentatiously, he retired to a private room with the Soviet Minister, an interpreter, and Taj Pasha. The Foreign Minister went to fetch a fruit juice. Ambassador Bagolevsky was left alone to appease the reporters.

He could not; they descended on Ambassador Fitzgibbon before he could reach Paul Pullmotor and persuade him into a privacy of their own.

"Mr. Ambassador, there is a report out of Washington tonight . . ."

Pullmotor and Solafa on the mezzanine:

"Look, Solafa, they've trapped poor Shawnie."

"Are they such bad people, journalists?"

"None worse, my dear. I avoid them like lepers. I can't decide which are worse—the British or the Americans. The British lie more imaginatively, but at least the Americans *bathe*. Those creeps down there are all staying at my hotel. Smell up the place. Sit in the bar all day telling dirty stories, drinking Bloody Marys and interviewing each other. That one talking to Shawnie now—do you know him?"

"Doesn't everybody? He'd be cute, if he had hair."

"Cute? Yes, I suppose you could call his column that. Not to mention his phony British accent. His new book—*The Pied Piper of Marxism and the Inscrutable East*—have you read it? Gave Mustafa apoplexy. Calvin loved it."

"Paul, you know the Prime Minister. Couldn't you talk to him about my passport?"

"It would not be opportune right now, my dear. Perhaps I can do something later. Now stop tickling me . . ."

Dr. and Mrs. Pantry:

" . . . and we apologize for being so late. We had our own party. We'd like to present a distinguished American musician. Chuckles Vespucci, the Soviet Ambassador."

The gentlemen of the press and Ambassador Fitzgibbon:

" . . . and that you officially notified him of the Secretary's decision to withdraw the offer of wheat and medicine. Would you care to comment on that, Mr. Ambassador?"

"No—except to deny it."

"Can we quote that?"

"Yes, I suppose you can."

"In other words, you informed the Prime Minister that American aid will *not* be withdrawn?"

"My dear fellow—whom do you work for, by the way?—I don't care to have words put in my mouth."

"What about Soviet aid to Al Khadra?"

"Well, what about it? Why don't you ask the Soviet Ambassador?"

"We have. He says he doesn't know."

"Then how do you expect me to?"

"Your Excellency, what action will the United States Government take in the event that King Mohammed is deposed or assassinated?"

"This is the first time I have heard either possibility suggested, and I consider both of them inconceivable. His Majesty is loved by everyone in this country. As for the view of my government, we regard the Monarchy as an element of stability."

"Oh for Chrissake. Give us some news. The Department said that last week."

"You can hardly take exception if my statements are parallel to the Department's. They happen to employ me."

"Shawnie, it's an open secret that you and Calvin are at loggerheads over Department policy in this country."

"I categorically deny that."

"Then we can quote you as saying that the Secretary's views and your own are absolutely identical? . . ."

Sir Charles Chetwynd-Pott and the Minister of Education:
"And your children, General?"
"All grown up, Sir Charlie. Three adults, one adultress."

The Soviet Minister of Energetics and Electrification in camera with Mustafa ibn Mabrouk:
". . . barter and ruble credits."
"No. No. I want at least half of it in convertible currencies . . ."

The Indian Ambassador to the Foreign Minister:
"Doesn't *anybody* know anything?"

Two of the Moslem bartenders:
"Allah is mocked. All these infidel women with bare arms."
"I thought only the Americans served ham sandwiches."
"This vodka is delicious."

Sir Charles Chetwynd-Pott to the Canadian Ambassador:
". . . and then he had the *cheek* to ask why we haven't invited him to Windsor Castle . . ."

Christopher Grundoon, Fitzgibbon Pasha's personal assistant, loitered by the buffet with Sami Abdel Rahman, an employee of the Political Police whose job was spying on the American Embassy, and Stanislav Kotchakov, an attaché of the Soviet Embassy whose job was spying on the Political Police. They were all good friends.

The buffet, its centerpiece an explosion of tropical pink flowers, catered to every international taste: Beluga caviar, *shish kebab,* legs of mutton, ham sandwiches, sardines, *pilaf, homus,* roast beef, *baklava, guava,* dates, mangoes, avocados, peanuts, pomegranates, vine leaves stuffed with wild rice, Russian fish dishes smothered in onion and saffron sauce.

"Mr. Christopher, you Americans make much better *shish kebab,*" Sami said. "Please don't be offend, Mr. Stanislav."

"By 1970, Socialist *shish kebab* will be twice as tasty as Capitalist *shish kebab,"* Comrade Kotchakov said.

Ambassador Fitzgibbon came over and had a sardine. "Have you seen Paul Pullmotor?" he asked Christopher Grundoon.

"Not during the last few minutes, sir."

"And what happened to the King? I want to go home." He drifted off.

"His Majesty should certainly be here soon," Sami said.

"What costume do you think the King will wear tonight?" Christopher Grundoon wondered aloud.

"He will come in his Field Marshall uniform, surrounded by security police," Comrade Kotchakov said.

"No," Sami said, "he will come in the robes of a Prince of Mecca, surrounded by his Bedouin bodyguard."

"No," Christopher Grundoon said, "he will come in a Dacron suit, surrounded by chambermaids from the Sheraton-Zahra."

As time passed it became obvious that the King was not going to show up. At last the Prime Minister emerged from his secret conference with the guest of honor, and his departure from the premises, pursued by aides, bodyguards, foreign correspondents and photographers, caused considerable pandemonium. Everyone else began to leave. The Minister of Education pumped Ambassador Bagolevsky's hand and said, "Thank you for your gracious hospitalization."

At last Ambassador Fitzgibbon cornered Paul Pullmotor. "Care to come home for a nightcap, Paul?"

"I'm terribly sorry, Shawnie, but I'm with a lady."

"You *were* with a lady. She just ran off with Chuckles Vespucci."

"Oh, all right, Shawnie. But let's make it short."

7

To the Ambassador's dismay and Pullmotor's pique, Fawzi ran out of gas several blocks from the Residence. The Three Stooges were prevailed upon to push the limousine with their Land-Rover the rest of the way. The Ambassador told Fawzi to leave the car in the courtyard for the night, and took Pullmotor inside.

The Residence was an enormous place—a palace actually—formerly the home of the King's uncle, Emir Wasfi, a notorious pederast now living in exile on the Italian Riviera. The Ambassador had found it desirable to renovate the interior almost entirely, repainting pink walls, removing the gross Second Empire imitations of Louis Quinze furniture, draperies of startling color, and figurines of preposterous pose. He had spent money he could ill afford on tapestries of respectable quality, and had salvaged from his tenuous marriage a number of Boudins and Daumiers, and a single Cézanne. In the great hall he had hung an excellent copy of Mantegna's *Martyrdom of Saint Sebastian.* Pullmotor's brittle footfall on the marble floors reverberated to the rafters, as if to mock the loneliness of a tenant who, attended only by his hired help, could inhabit such a house. They went into the library, and the Ambassador rang for Gassem, his houseboy.

"Would you like anything to eat, Paul? Some shrimp salad, perhaps?"

"Not really. I might have a cup of coffee."

"Finjan ahwa minshayn el hawaja, wa minshayni jibli el cognac," Fitz Pasha told the boy.

"Pity I never learned Arabic," Pullmotor said. "Still, I manage. By the way, where is Eminence Grise?"

"I'm keeping him at the Embassy during this heat wave. He seems to prefer the altitude of the Tower. I captured him at five thousand feet, you know."

"I didn't. Have you heard from your wife lately?"

"Winifred? No, not lately. I understand she's in Madrid."

Pullmotor yawned.

"Come clean, Paul. You're a walking poop sheet. Besides, I'd like to know."

"She left Madrid. She's in Tangier."

"What is she doing?"

"The last I heard, she was having an affair with the Police Commissioner."

"Well, that's an improvement, isn't it? At least she's off the viscount kick, learning to like Arabs. Maybe it will bring her back here one day."

"I hope so, Shawnie. I mean that. I know it hasn't been easy for you."

"Paul, give it to me straight. What are you up to here?"

"Simply what Calvin told you in his telegram. Picking up a few impressions, sorting out a few facts, coming to a few conclusions."

"Would you care to share any of them with me? I'm only the Ambassador here."

"Do you think Mustafa is a communist, Shawnie?"

"Of course he's not, and you know it."

"Do I? I don't like the look of things. This insane campaign he's waging against us—Calvin has every reason to be upset. Now all this praise for the Russians in the newspapers."

"I'm less interested in that than in what you intend to do about it."

"Why, nothing of which you would not be fully informed, Shawnie."

Gassem came in with the coffee and cognac.

"Sure you won't have some of this Courvoisier, Paul? All right, Mustafa is laying it on a bit thick. But have you ever stopped to consider what would happen to this country without him? Do you realize he is probably the best ruler Al Khadra ever had? Have you ever bothered to visit any of his co-operatives or these new industries he's building?"

"Don't get sentimental on me, Shawnie. It doesn't become you."

"Listen to me. Has it ever occurred to you that a man could be both anti-American and a good ruler at the same time?"

"No, Shawnie, I have never permitted such a notion to enter my head. Nor has it ever occurred to me that a man who is pro-American could be a bad ruler."

"Have you considered offering Mustafa more money—perhaps if we offered to underwrite the entire development plan?"

"We couldn't possibly bid that high. For your information, I did quote him a very generous figure when I saw him today, but he said it wasn't nearly enough. I'm just as glad. It will save us a lot of unnecessary expense. There are other ways of dealing with the problem."

"We've come a long way in three years, haven't we, Paul? I mean the three of us. Mustafa wouldn't even be Prime Minister today if it weren't for you—and me."

"Please, Shawnie. That is one of the more melancholy miscalculations of my career. I'd rather not be reminded of it."

It was not until the Ambassador put his guest in a taxi that Pullmotor told him he was returning to Washington in the morning.

"I assume you'll be back."

"You can count on it."

The Ambassador went up to his bedroom, undressed, bathed, and put on a pair of silken pajamas. Then he rummaged in his Chippendale desk (another remnant of his marriage) and extracted some Residence stationery and a ball-point pen. He put on his horn-rimmed reading spectacles, got into bed, and began writing a letter to his wife.

Darling Winifred, he began, but no sooner were the words on paper than he knew they would not do. *Dearest Winifred,* he wrote, but he crumpled the second sheet in his hand, and threw it on the floor. The telephone on his night table rang.

It was the Prime Minister.

"Fitz Pasha, the Soviet Union is going to help me to fight communism."

The Ambassador sighed. "Then it's definite? You're accepting Soviet aid?"

"Yes. I made up my mind this morning, after I saw you, and we hammered out the terms tonight at the Soviet Embassy. I told Paul what I was going to do. He didn't say anything?"

"He was just here, but apparently it slipped his mind."

"I was afraid it might. I told him to tell you."

"Thanks for remembering me, Mustafa. Can you tell me what the deal involves?"

"I'd rather not go into detail just now. Some heavy machinery. Several factories. A few hundred technicians."

"Any foreign exchange?"

"Not nearly as much as I need. Mostly rubles."

"Any arms?"

"Not at the moment. Later, perhaps."

"When are you going to announce it?"

"Within a couple of days, probably. I'd still like to have that food and medicine, by the way. The famine is getting worse in the Bedouin areas—they're getting pretty restless. The Russians can't spare any wheat, and besides I'd like to keep a balance."

"I doubt if Hampshire will come through—now," the Ambassador said.

"We shall see. You'll continue buying our figs and pomegranates, of course?"

"Will we?"

"And your dollar aid, of course."

"Will we?"

"We shall see," the Prime Minister said. "I understand you've been having trouble getting your air-conditioner fixed."

"You mean in my Cadillac? It's nothing. I just picked up the telephone on a lark and complained to whichever of your spies happened to be listening. You heard about it?"

"Is there anything I don't hear about? I was very cross. I am surrounded by nincompoops. I ordered immediate action. Good night, Fitz Pasha."

For a moment, the Ambassador debated whether to go to the Embassy and dictate an urgent telegram. But he was certain that Pullmotor had already notified the Secretary of State, and he had no wish to have his own velocity compared with Paul's. He decided on an interpretative message in the morning. He knew it would be ignored. In his mind he contemplated the wreckage of the policy which, during these last three years, he had toiled so patiently and painstakingly to advance. It had been a policy based on a very simple proposition: keeping Mustafa ibn Mabrouk happy. He had failed; Mustafa wanted much more than lay within his or any Ambassador's capacity to bestow. And now, Fitz Pasha knew, the matter had passed from his own hands; the battle between Calvin Hampshire and Mustafa ibn Mabrouk was joined; and it would be decided in a war of wits between Mustafa and Paul Pullmotor. The Ambassador had a very great respect for the Borgian abilities of both of these remarkable men, but as he brooded in bed in his neo-classical palace, Fitz Pasha knew one thing with an iron certitude: *Mustafa would win.* He wanted to tell Hampshire this, pleading with him to come to terms now before it was too late—but what good would it do? He knew that he would be ignored. He went back to his letter.

Winifred,

I have been told that you are in Tangier. I hope this letter will reach you. I regret that neither of us has corresponded for so long, but there we are. I really do not know why I am writing or what I shall say. How do you like Tangier? Do you go over to Tetuan? Do you take the boat over to Gibraltar or Algeciras? I climbed the Rock one evening and its was splendid to see the jagged mountains of Africa in the sunset, but I prefer the Algeciras side. Gibraltar town reminded me of Marble Arch, or even State Street. Would things have been different if we had had a child?

Life is getting a bit sticky here, but I'll spare you the details. If you ever want to pay a visit, there is plenty of room in this house and I have taught Gassem how to mix a decent martini.

Shawnie

He wrote *Mrs. Sean Sebastian Fitzgibbon, c/o American Express, Tangier* on an air-mail envelope, inserted the letter, sealed the envelope, and put it with his spectacles on the night table. He turned out the light. In the darkness he said his prayers. . . . *benedicta tu in mulieribus, et benedictus fructus ventris tui* . . . *nunc et in hora mortis nostrae* . . . Seat of Wisdom . . . Mystical Rose . . . Tower of Ivory . . . House of Gold. . . .

He rolled over. A delicious numbness in his loins.

"Oh God, even my wife would do tonight."

But it was not Winifred who came. Soon the centurions came, and lashed him to a tree. From afar, the Archer aimed arrows of silver at him. His quiver spent, he hovered over His anvil and flame, forging new arrows. Tap. Tap. Tap.

The Ambassador woke.

Tap. Tap. Tap.

He got out of bed, threw a robe over his shoulders and went downstairs in the dark palace. In the grand salon, he found Gassem standing in his underdrawers by an open window.

"What is it, ya Gassem?"

"Shh."

TAP. TAP. TAP.

The Ambassador looked out into the courtyard, spectral in street light. The doors of his limousine were open. Two men with flashlights were inside.

"Are they planting another microphone, Gassem?"

"*Shh.* I hear them talking. They make fix air-condition."

II

Ixion . . . designed to enjoy Juno, the goddess of Power; and instead of her had copulation with a cloud, of which mixture were begotten centaurs and chimeras. So whosoever shall entertain high and vaporous imaginations, instead of a laborious and sober inquiry of truth, shall beget hopes and beliefs of strange and impossible shapes.

Sir Francis Bacon
Advancement of Learning

8

Christopher Grundoon was a rather wild Irish boy from Boston who had gone to all the wrong schools. *A young Apollo, golden-haired . . . Stands dreaming on the verge of strife . . . Magnificently unprepared . . . For the long littleness of life.* Christopher Grundoon was perhaps a little like that, except for the Apollo part; though golden-haired and not at all bad-looking, he was hardly in the category of a Greek god. His intimate friendship with the King was the cause of keen envy among most of his colleagues in the Embassy, not to mention the undisguised displeasure occasioned by his other qualities. He was unmarried, and his private life was the subject of grave speculation; the Embassy stenographers resented him because of his open preference for younger ladies with more local color and fewer inhibitions; the Embassy wives were outraged by his opinions, not the least odious of which was his frequent pronouncement that, like Mohammedan women, they should confine themselves to "keeping house, bearing children, and being obedient to their husbands." He cared little for the refinements of diplomatic courtesy, and went out of his way to ignore invitations from the Potable Water Adviser and the Contraband Opium Control Officer. Christopher's own cocktail parties appeared to be inspired by Mrs. Murphy's chowder, mixing together such contradictory ingredients as society Arabs, Soviet attachés, illiterate Bedouins and beautiful women. He surrounded himself with characters, and worked rather hard at being one himself. No one could figure out why he was working for the United States Government.

Neither could Christopher. He had led an uncommonly cloistered life until selective service liberated him from his Boston beginnings, and deposited him in Berlin as a private in the American garrison. The encounter of his parochial-school inhibitions with the real world—the impact of his simultaneous exposure to the promiscuity of martial behavior and the complexity of European culture—had disoriented him totally; he had never been the same since. When his term of compulsory service in the army ended, he found he could not bear the prospect of returning to Boston; he arranged to be discharged in Germany, and for the next two years wandered the face of Europe on his meager savings, haunting museums, concert halls and libraries, struggling to learn languages, doing menial work and sleeping in fields when he had to; living, during the last year, little better than a bum. He had never been so happy.

In Montmartre one evening he mingled with a young woman who surreptitiously relieved him of his passport; in quest of a new one in the American Embassy next morning he walked inadvertently through the wrong door, into a classroom-like chamber full of young compatriots, was handed some papers and asked to take a seat. He was a bit hung over; it was not until he had completed the first page that he realized he was engaged not in filling out a form for a new passport, but in a competitive examination for entry into the American foreign service. Out of curiosity he decided to see the thing through; he made short order of the sheaf of questions, finished before anyone else, and then went out to make inquiries about his passport. He was amused, a fortnight later, to find a letter at the American Express informing him of his high marks. Did he wish to proceed to Washington for an interview and an oral examination? He mentioned the matter in a letter to his mother; almost by return post he received a bank draft paying for his passage home, and a note imploring him not to ignore this singular opportunity.

Six months later Christopher was posted from Washington to the American Embassy in Madrid, where he was designated Assistant Tourist Entertainment Attaché and entrusted with the care and feeding of itinerant Congressmen. "My mornings," he wrote to his mother, "are spent with the wives, whom I chaperon on shopping expeditions. My afternoons are taken up with teas, and my evenings devoted to cocktail parties. I sleep in night clubs and at Barajas Airport, where it is my privilege to greet the debarking legislators with a stainless-steel ice bucket, full of Counterpart pesetas, inviting them to help themselves."

He was on the point of submitting his resignation when Ambassador Fitzgibbon happened through Madrid on business; he and Christopher met at a cocktail party in the Castellana palace of the Duke of Montellano. Fitz Pasha liked him instinctively. Christopher was everything the Ambassador had been in his youth: a misty-eyed romantic, full of ingenuous questions, parochial-school overstatement, and a self-conscious effort to disguise his Boston accent by stressing all his *r*'s—and yet at the same time an uncommonly intelligent and charming young man. They had not been talking twenty minutes when someone came over and told Christopher it was time to take tonight's Congressmen to another cocktail party. The Ambassador was leaving Madrid that evening; he made an impulsive decision.

"Look, Grundoon, would you like to work for me? As my personal assistant? I think I could arrange it."

As impulsively as the Ambassador had made the offer, Christopher accepted it. Within three weeks he was in Al Asima. He had never regretted his decision. Fitzgibbon Pasha was a demanding but indulgent patron; the Arabs fascinated Christopher; Islam betwitched him; he wanted to go on living here forever. And yet precious little in his previous experience had conditioned him for his confrontation with the Arab Orient. To an even greater degree than Ambassador Fitzgibbon, Christopher Grundoon was an embodiment of Boston-Irish innocence unmoored on the misty lake of Arab indirection. To be sure, the two cultures had many qualities, in common, not the least of which were an almost comic xenophobia and a constant awareness of Divine involvement in the affairs of men. The Arabs—the poor ones anyway, and most of them were poor—were *obsessed* with God, as was Christopher Grundoon; it was probably for this reason that he found them so interesting. The obsession did not always ennoble their behavior, any more than it did Christopher Grundoon's. He doted on the writings of St. Augustine and St. John of the Cross; his favorite indoor entertainments were talking about God, and fornicating.

No one was more conscious of the discrepancy than was Christopher Grundoon himself. He assessed his inner contradictions in terms of sacred history; he was well read in this, and knowledgeable about early Christian schisms and heresies. The heresy which particularly intrigued him and which he found most to mirror the cleavages in his own nature was the Manichaean, that third-century eruption which preached a dualist vision of man and vaunted the existence of two contradictory deities: the God of Good—Spirit—and the God of Evil—Matter and Flesh. In Boston, Yankee Calvinism and Irish Jansenism, both of them diluted descendants of Manichaeism, had long since amalgamated into a single neoManichaean culture. Among the Irish Manichees, a bemused tolerance of shenanigans with the public exchequer was absolved by an unremitting crusade against carnal desire. Thus the scenes of Irish nuns screaming against little girls with short skirts and little boys with bare knees and against kissing parties and lipstick; thus the scenes of Irish priests ranting about burlesque shows and masturbation—incessant scenes which had been so much a part of Christopher Grundoon's youth that they gave him guilt-haunted nightmares to this day. Guilt-haunted nightmares and, he was convinced, his Manichaean personality. Christopher knew many Manichees besides himself. Ambassador Fitzgibbon, torn between his beginnings and his ambitions, was a Manichee. Mustafa ibn Mabrouk, asunder between East and West, was a Manichee. Young King Mohammed, with one foot on the gas pedal of his crimson racer and the other mired in the black magic of his ancestral past, was a Manichee. Calvin Hampshire collected chastity belts, and that made *him* a Manichee. The irony of it all was that Manichaeism was a Middle Eastern heresy to begin with. And thus Christopher Grundoon saw his sojourn in the deserts of the East as a homecoming—not only to the birthplace of his faith but to the cradle of his complexes.

Such were Christopher's metaphysical speculations, on the day after the eventful reception at the Soviet Embassy, as he sat on his rambling terrace overlooking the broad Mabrouk, waiting to watch the sun go down. His flat, which occupied the entire second story of an old Ottoman palace, had high ceilings, gilded mirrors, Second Empire furniture—rather a grandiose dwelling for so junior a diplomatist, and hardly the sort of place where one would be likely to look for a Manichee. He called out for a cool drink; in a moment his berobed, one-thumbed servant, Ahmed abu 'Sba, wheeled a mobile bar onto the terrace.

Christopher mixed himself a gin and tonic, and then opened his journal. He was a compulsive scribbler in addition to all else, and now he aspired to commit the approaching sunset to paper. How many moments on this magical river had he already endeavored to describe! He had observed the broad Mabrouk in a hundred different moods . . . In the early morning, when the thistles and acacias were cobwebbed with dew, and a white mist hovered everywhere over the waters, and wild geese and pelican were the couriers of sunrise . . . During the day, when the palm trees and mimosa were whipped in the wind, and the lateen sails of the boats were wide arcs, and the river reflected an amethyst sky and tormented, groping formations of cloud . . . In the evening, just before sunset, when lithe and graceful girls with water pots on their heads ambled on the banks, and lateen sails hung limp and lavender from their masts, and tired men dipped their oars upstream to the weird, otherworldly throb of a darabooka tom-tom . . . Moonrise on the river; ashen palm trees; hoopoo birds gamboling like ghosts.

Christopher's journal brimmed over with this sort of thing. And now it was the best part of the day. In a few moments the tangerine sun would set; from the river's opposite shore a muezzin on his pencil minaret chanted the Angelus of Islam. *Hayi illa as sala.*

Hayi illa as sala. Come to prayer. Come to prayer. The world hung inanimate like an oil painting, suddenly silent and still in the gallery of God. The shadows on the Moorish villa to one side of Christopher's terrace seemed to him El Greco-like in their elongation. Then one of them came to life. It was the shadow of a young woman in tight trousers, stretching herself, languidly, as if just summoned from a deep sleep. The shadow lit a long cigarette. A breeze came up and tossed the shadow hair. In a little while the shadow was seized by another's El Greco hands, and the cigarette was cast on the wind, and the two torsos became a single shadow. Christopher Grundoon ran his hand through his golden hair, and hiccuped. Faint laughter from the balcony above.

"Christopher! Christopher! Are you down there? Michel says you are spying on us!"

Christopher leaned over the balustrade, looked up, and saw Solafa. "Yes, I'm here. But I'm not spying."

"Come up for a drink."

"I already have one."

She threw a box of matches down at him, hitting him on the lip. "Don't sulk," she said.

"All right. I'm coming."

"A tout à l'heure."

When the maid admitted him Christopher found Solafa on the sofa amid her leather-bound books and potted palms and gramophone records. Michel, that shy little fellow with the shaggy hair, was prostrate on the Persian carpet reciting to himself selections from a volume of *poésie.*

Solafa leaped up and embraced Christopher; he tried to be casual.

"Do you want your whiskey with water or on the rocks?" she asked in her hoarse French accent, which Christopher still found tantalizing.

"Can I have a banana?" he asked.

"Here. Do you want me to peel it?"

"I'll peel it myself, thanks."

"You didn't bring any books. You used to bring me such nice books."

"You never read them. And you have so many of your own."

"Yes, but all in French, and I haven't read half of them, either. People come and say, 'Solafa, you haven't even cut the pages!' With yours—you mark them so—I can pretend I devoured them."

"What a little liar you are, Solafa. You have read all your books, and what is worse, you have lived them. The Proust and the Stendhal and the Colette. Especially the Colette. Hey, this banana is *mushy*."

"Not the Proust! I'm going to have a book-burning party and invite all my friends and show them what I think of Proust. I've been bored lately with cocktail parties. I'm not going out any more."

"I saw you at one last night—with Paul Pullmotor."

"Oh, that horrible little man. That was special. I thought he might help me with my passport."

Michel, buried in his Baudelaire, had not acknowledged Christopher's presence.

"Bon soir, Michel," Christopher said.

"Son teint est pâle et chaud; la brune enchanteresse," Michel replied, without looking up,

> *"A dans le cou des airs noblement maniérés;*
> *Grande et svelte en marchant comme une chasseresse,*
> *Son sourire est tranquille et ses yeux assurés."*

"C'est moi?" asked Christopher.

"No, *chéri,*" Solafa said. "Michel means me. Ignore him. He's in one of his moods. How is Mohammed?"

"His Majesty? I was with him yesterday, and he asked for you. I'll see him again tomorrow evening. Why don't you come?"

"I'd rather not. That's all over, and besides he can't do anything about my passport."

"Solafa, they'll never give it to you."

"They *must*. I must get to Switzerland, and Paris. I can't live in this country a day longer. Look what they've done to me. I've been thinking. Your Ambassador—I mean, how is he?"

"He was fine when I saw him off at the airport this morning."

"Poor dear, he deserves a holiday."

"He wasn't going on holiday. He was called very suddenly to Washington. Urgent consultations."

"Oh dear. I hope there isn't going to be any trouble. It will only make things more difficult for me."

"It's funny, isn't it, Solafa? All you want in life is to leave this country. All I want is to stay."

"Ô le pauvre amoureux des pays chimériques!" intoned Michel.

> *"Faut-il le mettre aux fers, le jeter à la mer? . . .*
> *"Son oeil ensorcelé découvre une Capoue*
> *"Partout où la chandelle illumine un taudis."*

"C'est Solafa?"

"No, Christopher, this time he means you."

She put on a gramophone record and made Christopher dance with her. Happy Birthday to you cha cha cha. Michel stayed where he was, on the floor. Solafa tossed her hair in a slightly exaggerated way, as Michel had suggested; to Christopher it was irresistible. He resolved to pinch her bottom, but the doorbell rang. It was Pride Lyon, the *Time* magazine man. She was mixing Pride's drink when the doorbell rang again and in drifted Sami the Snooper, the chap from the Political Police who spied on the American Embassy, and Stanislav Kotchakov, the chap from the Soviet Embassy who spied on the Political Police. Then Chuckles Vespucci, en route to his concert. She put on more music and mixed more drinks and everybody stepped over Michel.

"I didn't know you were having a party," Christopher whispered.

"Neither did I."

But it was now as it had always been, and, he knew, as she always wanted it to be: she was the only woman among men. Christopher had never seen her with a female friend, but he had attended dozens of parties such as this. Tonight it was Solafa and Michel and Christopher and Pride and Sami and Stanislav and Chuckles; tomorrow it would be Solafa and Michel and half a dozen others. He got up to go.

"Stick around," Solafa said.

"Too many guys. Besides, I've got to get back to my novel."

"That silly novel. You'll never finish it."

Sami pursued him to the door. "Can I come down for a talk, Mr. Christopher?"

"Tormorrow, Sami. Or next week."

As he closed the door in Sami's face, he could hear Chuckles Vespucci and the frenetic refrain of "I Go Ape."

Christopher told the one-thumbed Ahmed to put on the fish; when he had finished supper he went into his study and began writing again in his journal.

Friday. The party is over. I can hear them laughing and bidding good-by to Solafa at her door; I can hear them coming down the stairs and passing my door, Chuckles strumming on his lute, Pride and Sami and Stanislav harmonizing. So they are alone again, she and Michel, among the potted palms and the Baudelaire and the gramophone records. She has shut off the music, and he has closed the Baudelaire. I hear her now in the room above me—her room. Michel's shy shuffle. The clink of earrings and bracelets being dropped on the crystal-topped night table. Michel is a boor and lets his suede footwear fall with a—thump! Another clink on the table. Is she being noisy on purpose? Is she saying, *Christopher, tu es là? Viens voir, chéri!* Silence. Michel rises and shuffles to the corner of the room. The chair is there. He has forgotten his contraceptives and is fumbling in his pants pocket. (I refused to use them. I told her, Let it be Catholic fornication.) Silence . . .

Silence still! Now all I can hear is the one-thumbed Ahmed cackling with his cronies on the back stairs. I have told him time and again to keep his friends away from here; he brings them into the kitchen and they eat me out of house and home. All Arabs have a sweet tooth; Ahmed's cronies consume prodigious quantities of my Embassy tea and sugar. (The local tea is like sawdust, and the sugar granulated like gravel.) Ahmed is very pious. He prays five times a day, performs all his ablutions, observes the Ramadan fast, and goes to the mosque regularly. (He went today.) I brought home a ham once and asked him to cook it; he refused. I told him to use a knife; he would not have to touch the meat. "It makes no difference," he protested. "The blasphemy of the pork will pass through the knife and contaminate me."

He is nearly as bad about alcohol. When he pours me a whiskey he holds the bottle and glass at arm's length, as if Iblis or Beelzebub, en route from the one to the other, might somehow leap out and take possession of him. For some obscure though no doubt sublime reason, he won't even eat *watermelons.* Regrettably, his piety does not preclude the smoking of hashish, nor has it endowed him with any tangible reverence for the institution of private property. Some time ago Ahmed heard over the radio that the Prophet was the first socialist, and ever since then he has enthusiastically been sharing my modest belongings with me. He has a particular fondness for razor blades, underwear, handkerchiefs, silk ties, cuff links, paper clips (!), mechanical pencils, toilet paper (!), filter-tip cigarettes (very valuable on the black market), and grocery money. Let me say it more simply: the one-thumbed Ahmed is a thief.

Ah! Now I hear the water running up in Solafa's flat. Time for bath. She and Michel will take it together. She had said to me: "This damn government! There has been no water all day. This never happened when Grandfather was Prime Minister. We must lie here, and you will read to me while we wait." She adored my atrocious French, and how she laughed and teased when I recited the verse of de Musset from that peeling leather volume of her grandfather's. But she was well pleased with me that night, for once. "I'll say one thing. You give a girl her money's worth." And then, when there was water, we bathed together, and the pipes vomited the brown, rusty water on us, until it ran warm and clear on our bodies . . .

This rite was a commemoration of their first meeting, for it was in the swimming pool at the Gazooza Sporting Club that Christopher had discovered her. She had on a very brief bathing suit, not quite a bikini, but one sufficiently provocative even for so cosmopolitan a place as the Gazooza Club; even the beatnik Arabs were making remarks. She was slightly tanned and rather tall, and from the way she squinted when hailed from afar a trifle near-sighted, Christopher surmised; she was lovely. Dark hair; exquisite black eyes; a complexion naturally fair; fine, patrician features; her nose was just barely turned to one side, but this imperfection somehow made her more beautiful.

"Who is she?" Christopher asked.

"You don't know Solafa, His Majesty's former . . . friend?"

She had been climbing up to the high-diving board and somersaulting off into the swimming pool. Christopher mounted to that eminence himself, resolving to wait until she came up again and catch her in conversation before she flew away. She did not come at once; as he lingered on the high-diving board he looked everywhere about him and marveled for the first time at the splendor, from that perspective, of the Gazooza Sporting Club. He could see all of the immense place: the cricket grounds and soccer fields; the courts for tennis, squash, badminton and volleyball; the splendid brown bodies of upper-class Arab youths glistening in the sun; the level golf course and the race track and the manicured croquet lawns and bowling greens; he could see the two enormous swimming pools, the lido, the piebald umbrellas, the stucco clubhouse and the domed and pillared bandstand, around which on Sunday evenings Al Asima's *ancien régime* convened to hear the café concerts, sip cool drinks and commiserate with one another. Some young army officers were playing polo, and he could hear the hoofs of their horses on the hard turf and the chink of long mallets against wooden balls. All of this green was ringed round with flame trees. The club had been built by the British as an oasis for themselves. Times change! The membership now was more egalitarian and less opulent. Mustafa ibn Mabrouk had confiscated half of the golf course as the site for a new fertilizer plant, and the Club was not the best place to be when the wind blew from that direction; the society Arabs said that Mustafa had done it deliberately.

When Solafa finally came up the ladder Christopher lay prostrate on the high-diving board in his rather brief bathing trunks. She had to step over him. He waited until she was poised to leap, and then he said, "Excuse me, mademoiselle, but are you the high-dive instructress?

Without turning, she replied, *"Je ne parle pas les langues, monsieur. Et je ne suis pas instructrice!"*

"Je m'excuse, mademoiselle," Christopher said. *"Puis-je me présenter? Je suis M. Grundoon de l'ambassade des Etats-Unis. Je suis ami de Sa Majesté, le Roi Mohammed."*

She turned to him, and laughed. "Oh, if you're a friend of Mohammed's then I suppose I've nothing to worry about, have I?" Christopher did not understand what she meant. She dived into the pool; he dived after her. He came down upon her, gently, cushioned by the waters, and before they surfaced they knew. They went to the cinema together that evening. He was looking for a place to live; she suggested the empty flat in her own building. The Embassy wives were unanimously scandalized when the word got out, but Christopher was too infatuated to care. Solafa was mad about him, for a little while. His hours with Solafa: walking together on the teeming Corniche; dining with friends in jasmin-scented gardens, she in satin, he in a white jacket; sailing down the broad Mabrouk in moonlight. Reading Sir Richard Burton aloud to one another on his terrace: *and now we are sitting silent and still, listening to the monotonous melody of the East—the soft night-breeze wandering through starlit skies and tufted trees, with a voice of melancholy meaning.*

In the pages of his journal Christopher had preserved practically every morsel of his experiences with Solafa. There was one entry, written many months ago, to which he was particularly attached.

> Last night the moon was full; Solafa and I hired horses and galloped out into the desert in the pure evening air, to a crumbling Omayyad castle, where we removed our clothes and reposed together between the paws of a wingéd lion. From afar, deep in the silver wilderness, we heard the baying of a hound. Eucharistic moon.
>
> "Americans don't know how to love," Solafa said.
>
> "They do! They do!"
>
> "Bostonians, then."
>
> When we were done, she did not want to dress. As unclothed and carefree as children, we played tag, hide and seek, cops and robbers, romping round the wingéd lion, beneath the haunches, behind the ears, between the paws. And

then, when she had tired of our sport, she stood there, stark against the ruins in the mendacious moonlight, lifted her limbs to heaven and—stretched. *S-t-r-e-t-c-h-e-d.* I ran to her, fell to my knees, and encompassed her with kisses. "Solafa," I cried, "I will cross a hundred deserts, climb all the mountains of the moon, endure all the torment of this world and the next, but you must recapture for me the beatitude of that moment."

"Will you give up your religion if I do it again?"

"Anything!"

She giggled, and stretched again, but it was gone: it was not the same.

"Give me back my religion," I said.

"I can't. I've thrown it away. It is out there now, in the desert, scattered in the sand and stars. Gone, irretrievable, with all your sense of sin."

"I wish I could believe that," I said, kissing her again. "I'm angry at God for making me an Irish Catholic."

"So am I. Doesn't He ever make allowances?"

"I'm afraid not," I said. "He is very possessive. He doesn't want us ever to grow up—remember He said something about becoming like little children? And when we have grown up, He cannot reconcile Himself to our growing away from Him and going our own way. I wonder if He really understands why we must do as we do. He is vindictive and vengeful because we want to be ourselves and not as He designed or destined or intended us to be. I can hear Him saying, 'You shall pay for every hour you have spent in Solafa's arms.' "

"Let's get dressed. I'm getting cold. You have been mutilated and emasculated by laws."

"I don't find your metaphors very flattering," I said, climbing into my underclothes. "Somehow you make the laws more real to me at this moment than they have ever been. As true as the alphabet or the equilateral triangle. That's the trouble with triangles: they wear you out. It's not that you don't believe or even that you don't want to believe—you get exhausted knowing He won't let you stop believing, not even for an evening or an afternoon. And you hate Him a little more each time, because He won't stop being Himself, He won't let his hair down, He won't let His triangle hatch a fourth angle or father a fifth side."

"Hand me my sweater," Solafa said.

We mounted our steeds and galloped back to the city, without speaking.

I should never have said those things. Even as I spoke, I knew how possessive Solafa was herself. I wonder, how long will it be before she asserts the primacy of her claim on me? . . .

She did so sooner than Christopher expected. The following evening they went to the new cafeteria in the Sheraton-Zahra and had a banana split. Out of a blue sky Solafa began saying nasty things about the Pope. Christopher humored her, and then lost his temper.

"You sound very common," he said.

"Oh yes," she laughed bitterly, "I'm just a tart you met in the street."

"Not in the street, my sweet—in the swimming pool."

She got up from the table, and walked out. The door of the cafeteria was open, and Christopher could hear the anger of her high heels on the marble floors. His eyes, but not his legs, pursued her; she passed the gurgling fountain in front of the flower shop, the sparkling display in the jeweler's window, the tangle of elderly American tourists in the lobby. She went out into the street swarming with dragomen and Diesel taxis and beggars and baksheesh boys, and she did not come back. What puzzled Christopher was that little Michel, her next lover, had spent three years in a Greek seminary.

Christopher learned later that Solafa had abandoned the King for roughly the same reasons—a dispute over Islam in his case. There were many entries about King Mohammed in Christopher's journal. Last week's, for example:

> His Majesty is not only more oversexed than I, he is more religious. He is very keenly conscious of the mystical associations of his high office and talks constantly of them; they are practically all he has left, besides his motorcars and his year

at Harvard and that huge, hideous palace he lives in. Poor innocent handsome Mohammed . . .

And as Christopher continued tonight's compulsive scribbling, it was about Mohammed that he scribbled.

We had a strenuous afternoon together yesterday, the King and I, driving in the desert in his Land-Rover. Yahutha, his deaf-mute batman, was at the wheel because His Majesty intended to shoot later on; the three of us rode in the front seat, and we headed for Wadi Mafish. What a remarkable place the desert is; the sun was never so fierce as yesterday, in its merciless metallic sky, and its reflection on the trackless wasteland was dazzling beyond endurance. We passed mirage after mirage, and were it not for the drought neither of us could have known that the luminous lakes we saw were all illusion. Away from the broad Mabrouk, this country is incredible in its desolation, like the landscape of a lifeless planet. All blanched desert in this drought: not even analogous to the Sahara or the Holy Hejaz, which at least are luxuriant with sand. The plain was a leprous white, a crystalline madness redeemed only at random by an anemic shrub, a tuft of gray grass. The distant prospect seemed less menacing because the atmosphere in between bathed it in a brilliant blue fog, but we knew that those jagged peaks on the horizon were no less barren than the land beneath us. What overwhelms me is the wasteland's scope. A dagger of rock which seems near enough to touch becomes an hour's drive away; an apricot cliff whose every pockmark you can scrutinize is half a day's journey distant. Mohammed had his rifle, and we raced up one wadi and down another in quest of desert grouse, but now the pools are all dry and where there is no water there are no birds. Only a single hoopoo circled relentlessly above our Land-Rover—crying occasionally *hoop-hoop-hoopoo!*—and marksman though he is, the King is dreadfully superstitious and refused to shoot it down; he attributes to the hoopoo some sort of magical power. It seemed curious to me that a bird normally only of the river should pursue us so deep into the thirsty desert.

At last we sighted the black tents and mud hovels of Wadi Mafish, like lumps of sickly meat shriveling on a sheet of brimstone. When the Bedouins saw us they came charging toward us on their camels, firing their flintlocks in frenzied greeting. They love the King. (They should; the blood Royal is Bedu too.) They escorted us to the tent of Hassan, Sheikh of the Beni Talal tribe, who from all appearances had been roused hurriedly from his siesta. (His Majesty never tells anyone when he is coming; he doesn't know himself.) The Sheikh insisted on slaughtering a sheep, but Mohammed knows how badly the famine has ravaged these people, and he begged off, inventing an appointment in the capital that evening. We drank endless cups of muddy coffee instead; it was flavored with *hal*—cardamom seed—and had an exciting taste; your cup is filled and refilled until you wiggle it a little in your hand, indicating to the boy that you have had enough. Mohammed had some cigarettes and a carton of tinned vegetables for Sheikh Hassan, and the old man was overjoyed to get them. There was the customary exchange of compliments; otherwise the Sheikh talked of nothing but the famine. He pointed down into the deep of the wadi, where the Point Four has built an immense reservoir for the flocks of the Beni Talal. "Last year two hundred families were encamped there," he lamented, "but it has not rained since then, and the American lake has gone dry, and the flocks are dying, and my people are dispersing like dead flowers in the desert wind."

He spoke bitterly of Mustafa ibn Mabrouk, a Bedu himself and born in Wadi Mafish. "What has he given us, blood of his blood?" the Sheikh asked. Mohammed reminded him of the clinic and school. "Yes, yes, but now we are starving!" the Sheikh said wrathfully. "Mustafa constructs factories and beautiful new buildings for his capital, but he forgets his own people. What are factories to us? We need wheat." I follow Bedouin Arabic only with great difficulty, but from what I understood of Mohammed's replies, he kept changing the subject. I thought this due not to indifference but to loyalty; it causes the King an almost physical anguish to hear Mustafa criticized. He did promise to speak to the Prime Minister, and at that point we prepared to leave. In the crowd that pressed about our Land-Rover, the Sheikh pointed to a consumptive child, adding casually that she had been coughing up blood that morning. Characteristically, Mohammed seized the little girl and put her in the back of the Land-Rover. "She will receive good care in Liberation Hospital," he said. The Bedouin women ululated and invoked the manifold blessings of the Prophet on him, and about thirty of the men mounted their camels and escorted us to the rim of the neighboring wadi. The child remained quietly on the back seat, but as night descended she began vomiting blood again.

Enough of His Majesty for the moment; I shall see him again tomorrow. Now I must cease this haphazard composition and get down to my novel before bed.

Christopher's novel had been inspired accidentally. Late one evening several months ago he had noticed some documents peeping from beneath his garbage can on the back stairs. He looked at them: letters from his mother, fragments from his personal correspondence, newspaper clippings, old laundry bills. He left them where he found them, and the next day they turned up among the pile of periodicals in his study. He knew then what he had half suspected for some time: the one-thumbed Ahmed was smuggling out his personal papers, piece by piece, to the Political Police for photostating. His ensuing vigilance revealed that Ahmed would leave the documents underneath the receptacle in the morning, while his master was at the office, and that normally they were returned there the same night. Since Ahmed could not read, he was indiscriminate in his scavengings; hence the laundry bills. Christopher said not a word to him, knowing full well that the poor fellow had no choice but to cooperate in the intrigue. Besides, the Political Police could not have uncovered anything very compromising; Christopher was not permitted to take classified papers home from the Embassy, and his journal he had always kept in his study under combination lock. But it was at this time that he began work on his horror novel, *Perfidious Albion.*

Christopher considered himself eminently qualified in this subject. After all, he had been systematically reared in the suspicion of the Lion and Lloyd George, and the abominations of Oliver Cromwell and the Black and Tans were as familiar to him as the prayers of childhood. But it would serve a more immediate purpose, he thought, if he endeavored to tell his tale with a local flair. So he set it in Al Khadra, and made Mustafa ibn Mabrouk the hero, embattled on all sides by the skulduggery of the Sceptered Islanders. He made Mustafa a sort of Arab de Valera. After all, what were Arabs but circumcised Irishmen? Each chapter unmasked Britain in a new enormity: foundlings garroted in their cradles, pregnant mothers bayoneted, defenseless cities blitzed . . . Mustafa is captured, escapes, is captured and escapes again . . . a man hunt is mounted . . . Mustafa rallies the guerrillas under his banner . . . the battle is joined. What will happen?—will good prevail over evil, freedom over enslavement, truth over treachery?—will Mustafa be martyred or emerge triumphant? Tune in tomorrow!

Christopher had been leaving whole episodes lying about the flat; the one-thumbed Ahmed seized upon them and passed them on to the Political Police. This was precisely what Christopher wanted. It was not simply that he was enamored of this country and anxious to remain in its good graces; he was confident that by giving a good odor to his dossier in the Ministry of the Interior *Perfidious Albion* would assist his work, ease his associations and facilitate his freedom of movement. Already, Sami the Snooper had confided to him that each new episode of the clandestine opus was awaited with such intense interest by the Political Police that now he must hasten to the finale because they found the suspense unbearable. Christopher was gratified. Who said these devious Arabs could not be hoodwinked? Wasn't he hoodwinking them? *Ha!*

While Christopher Grundoon labored over *Perfidious Albion,* the Prime Minister was enjoying one of his relatively rare evenings of leisure. He had decided to announce his new economic pact with the Soviet Union at noon the next day, and he knew that from that moment—what with the angry American reaction he anticipated, and in fact counted on—not many hours of conventional recreation would ensue. In addition to his reading he had a fondness for the cinema, especially when seen in solitude. He no more enjoyed watching a good picture in the company of others than he would have enjoyed reading Keynes or hearing Vivaldi during a street riot. Indeed, if there was one thing Mustafa loved more than good books and films and gramophone records it was loneliness itself. Nothing gave him more pleasure than the late evening hours when he could putter about his shabby apartment in the attic of his Ministry, all by himself. Tonight, as so often in the past, he chased away his cook and batmen and prepared his own supper, a simple meal of brownish *ful* beans and ice cream, washed down by warm Pepsi. As he ate he hummed softly to himself. Then he repaired to his private theater. This room was equipped with a cinemascope projector and stereophonic loudspeakers, which he was paying for, out of his own modest salary, on the installment plan. But he left this new equipment lying idle most of the time. His real weakness was for old pictures: forgotten westerns, Charlie Chaplin, Ronald Colman, Greta Garbo and Gary Cooper—especially Gary Cooper. Like Lord Wellington—and Paul Pullmotor—Gary was *strong*.

There was a particular film which Mustafa invariably watched on the eve of any momentous occasion; one which, for no reason he could fathom, infused him with the energy he needed to endure any trial. It was an antiquated melodrama set in French North Africa, starring Gary and Marlene Dietrich: he a lowly private in the Foreign Legion, she a jaded chanteuse, both of them in glorious youth, Gary and Marlene fell bashfully and impossibly in love. The Prime Minister ran the film through again tonight, on his old projector.

Two scenes moved him more than all the others. In the first, Marlene is seated at dinner in a grand Moorish palace with a dashing Adolphe Menjou and some stuck-up French people. It is her engagement party; she consents to Adolphe's proposal of marriage. But then, from the street outside, the drums of the returning Foreign Legion patrol begin faintly to be heard. Marlene leaps up from the table, her painted face a poem of panic and compulsion; as she whirls, her pearls catch the back of her chair and splatter on the floor. She runs out into the street to find Gary. Adolphe says, "Pick up the pearls, Mohammed, and put them in my room."

The other sequence was the last in the film. With a shy, wistful smile, Gary waves good-by to Marlene and marches out again into the desert on another perilous mission. Marlene stands with Adolphe by Adolphe's elegant limousine, and waves back at Gary. She has on a broad-brimmed hat, a flimsy dress and high heels. Then she sees the women camp-followers and their donkeys and goats trudge into the desert after the patrol. "They *love* their men," Adolphe had said earlier. Marlene's moment of truth. Desperately she looks from Adolphe to the patrol and the camp-followers, fading away now into the dunes. She embraces Adolphe, throws away her fancy hat and high-heeled shoes, and runs out into the desert. As she overtakes the camp-followers, a sandstorm begins to rage. Gary on his patrol, Marlene among the camp-followers, disappear over a hill, into the infinite desert. The End.

Mustafa ran the projector backward and forward several times, repeating the final scene, fondling it in his mind. "Lovely! Lovely!" he repeated aloud. "I can even forgive him killing all those Arabs!" Then he rewound the machine to the part about the pearls, playing it over and over at least a dozen times. Tears of pleasure and sorrow streamed down his dark face. "She's gone to find Gary," he sobbed quietly. "Pick up the pearls, Mohammed, and put them in my room."

It was four o'clock in the morning when the Prime Minister shut off the machine. He was not at all tired. He went out onto a balcony, smoked a filter-tip cigarette, and contemplated his capital, snoring softly at his feet. "I will do it," he whispered in English. "I will make it," he whispered into the stillness. "Do you hear me, my noble lords? Mustafa will do it!"

A cock crew, and the Prime Minister went off to bed for a few hours, humming softly to himself.

9

The offices of the Al Asima Municipality and the Ministry of the Interior were housed together in a huge building on the Sharia Baad Saa', in the modern quarter not far from the American Embassy. The edifice—identified in popular parlance simply as *el-Baladiyeh*, the Municipality—was a triumph of post-Rooseveltian craftsmanship, unsymmetrical of structure and trapezoid of line, but otherwise very much an Arab Pentagon. In the hectic street outside, Mustafa ibn Mabrouk had erected a pair of traffic lights; jaywalking foreigners were now politely reprimanded, indigenous offenders fined. The lights did not always function, but when they did they flicked from red to green without warning; then the poor pedestrian, caught in the middle of the wide concourse, would have to dash for it—and in the Arab East haste was still considered the most unbecoming manner of human progression.

Under patchwork parasols on the pavement outside the Municipality squatted dozens of shriveled little men scribbling on tiny, portable tables. These were the scribes, who kept body and soul together by filling out forms for illiterate patrons of the Municipality. The scribes were in ill humor this Saturday morning, for their commerce had been disturbed by a pair of inquiring reporters from *Sawt el Hurriyeh,* the government newspaper, obstreperously conducting "citizen interviews." A curious crowd had collected.

Reporter: What is your name?

Street Arab: Wasfi Ramadan Mohammed.

Reporter: Age?

Street Arab: Nineteen.

Reporter: I want to ask you a few questions. How much do you earn?

Street Arab: Fifteen to twenty piastres a day, if I'm lucky.

Reporter: Do you live by yourself?

Street Arab: No, with my mother, father, wife and two sons, and we all eat on the money I earn.

Reporter: Do you have your own flat?

Street Arab: My brother, you are joking. We are lucky to have one room.

Reporter: Whom do you admire most in this world?

Street Arab: Mustafa ibn Mabrouk and Gary Coober.

Reporter: What is nationalization?

Street Arab: Isn't she Mustafa's mother?

Reporter: What is democracy?

Street Arab: My brother, you are wasting my time. Leave me alone. I never paid any attention to that monkey business.

Reporter: What is capitalism?

Street Arab: I don't know.

Reporter: What is socialism?

Street Arab: Ah, this I know very well. Socialism means that I live in the same room with my mother and father and feed them.

Reporter: Who are the enemies of the people?

Street Arab: The Municipality.

Reporter: You are mistaken. The correct answer is the capitalists and the imperialists.

Street Arab: Aren't they the Municipality?

Reporter: And you, sir—what is your name?

Street Arab: Zaki Mahmoud Zaki.

Reporter: How old are you?

Street Arab: Thirty-five.

Reporter: Where do you live?

Street Arab: In the Bab el Mandeb.

Reporter: That's pretty far. Why don't you stay there?

Street Arab: You can't buy or sell anything there.

Reporter: How much do you make a day?

Street Arab: Sometimes thirty piastres. Sometimes nothing.

Reporter: Do you know anything about imperialism?

Street Arab: Imperialism *what?*

Reporter: What is feudalism?

Street Arab: Feudalism *what?*

Voice in the Crowd: Why don't you tell him the truth, ya Zaki, since he's just a journalist?

Street Arab: All right. Feudalism is the Municipality.

Reporter: Do you know what capitalism is?

Voice in the Crowd: God bless the Prophet! I'll give you an example. This boy here takes twenty chickens from the wholesaler in order to sell them and pay his debts to the merchant. The Municipality comes and takes the chickens, the wholesaler never gets his money and after that he gives no more chickens to the boy. This is capitalism.

Reporter: Who are the enemies of the people?

Voice in the Crowd: The traitor, the thief, the feudalists, the capitalists, the imperialists and the British.

Reporter: You forgot the Americans.

Voice in the Crowd: All right, but let's keep the cowboys.

Reporter: You there. What is your name?

Street Arab: Ismail Abdul Hakim.

Reporter: Married?

Street Arab: By God, I'm looking for a wife now.

Reporter: Where do you work?

Street Arab: I'm looking for work, too.

Reporter: I notice one of your ears is missing.

Street Arab: God is generous.

Reporter: What is socialism?

Street Arab: It means that you and I are both employed. It

means that we should both wear the same clothes. It means that I should have a cigarette holder—give me a cigarette, please—and a wife like you do.

Reporter: But I'm not married.

Street Arab: Then permit me to tell you that you are making a mistake. If my appearance were as clean as yours and I had as much money as you do I would certainly get married and stop asking people silly questions on street corners.

Reporter (a bit rattled): What is feudalism?

Street Arab: It is the rich, may they never return.

Reporter: And capitalism?

Street Arab: The rich also. It was because of them that I lost my ear.

Reporter (encouraged): At least you are an intelligent citizen. Tell me, who are the three greatest men in the world today?

Street Arab: Mustafa ibn Mabrouk, Brigitte Bardot and Gary Coober.

Reporter: And who is the greatest of these?

Street Arab: God forgive me. Gary Coober.

Reporter (to the crowd, weakly): Who are the enemies of the people?

The Crowd (in unison): The Municipality!

The assemblage was dispersed by a battered Peugeot honking its way into a parking place alongside the pavement. A beautiful woman, in bright bandana, sunglasses and an orange frock, got out of the car. It was Solafa. "I'll be as quick as I can, *chéri!*" she called to Michel, sitting behind the wheel; she dashed past the ogling scribes and street Arabs and up the long steps into the trapezoid building.

Solafa's business was not with the Municipality. She was here, as usual, to see about her passport. This meant scaling several flights of stairs to the Ministry of the Interior on the upper half-dozen floors; it was a mystery why elevators had never been installed in so tall a building. Gingerly, she managed her way upward through the throng of men, women and children reclining and mingling clamorously on every level of the immense spiral staircase, and arrived out of breath at the familiar office on the seventh floor.

She entered without knocking. Behind a wobbly wooden desk

piled high with newspapers sat a fat man in gold-rimmed spectacles and a red fez. The middle drawer of the desk was open, revealing a breakfast of beans swimming in a saucer of green oil. Head down, he was scooping the meal into his mouth with a crust of unleavened bread and a mechanical pencil.

"May your morning be blessed, ya Mish Mish Effendi," Solafa said.

Mister Mish Mish looked up languidly, the grease running in tiny rivers down his chin. To be disturbed during so gratifying an interlude was obviously not to his taste, but he summoned a tired smile as he replied, "And may your morning be full of light, ya Anissa Solafa. Welcome, and good greeting." He put the mechanical pencil in the plate of beans, rose from his desk, and waddled over to the long counter where she stood.

"Do you want your coffee sweet, or half and half?" he asked.

"No coffee today, thank you," Solafa said, opening her rather large handbag. "I trust your grandmother is well?"

"Thank God, she's well," said Mr. Mish Mish. "She gets cranky, but she's well."

"I brought along this box of *marrons glacés* from the new sweet shop in the Sheraton-Zahra. I thought she might enjoy them."

"That is very kind of you, ya Anissa Solafa. But my grandmother could not consider accepting such generosity."

"Ya Mish Mish Effendi, the value of the gift betrays the value of the giver. But if I were to give your grandmother a gift worthy of her value, it is the whole world I would give your grandmother. Besides, it is my great pleasure."

"The Prophet forbid that I spoil your pleasure, ya Anissa. Yes! Are they from Paris?"

"Of course."

"In that case I think I shall nibble on one," Mr. Mish Mish said, ripping the box open with his stubby fingers. "Just one, mind you, before I bring them home to my grandmother. A sweet always goes well with breakfast."

"I have something else here," Solafa said, extracting some documents from her bag.

The smile on Mr. Mish Mish's face evaporated even more rapidly than the confection in his mouth. "Ah, yes," he said.

"It's the affidavit certifying my education in this country," Solafa explained. "It took me three months to get it. The government closed the school a year ago and turned the building into a bus station. The Mother Superior had returned to Brussels, and when I wrote her there I found out she was dead. But I wrote to another nun, and she sent back this affidavit. Please note the official stamp of the order. I hope it will do."

"I will submit it to my superiors."

"I hate to put you to so much trouble."

"Not at all, ya Anissa. It is my duty to help you."

"Do you think the approval will take long? I've been waiting over a year for my passport."

"If you will excuse me for a minute, I will go and fetch your file. I want to be certain there are no further . . . formalities."

Mr. Mish Mish popped another *marron glacé* into his mouth, locked the box of sweets carefully away in his desk, and disappeared into some adjoining rooms. Solafa sat down on a steel bench, took out a cigarette, lit it with a silver lighter Christopher Grundoon had given her, and waited. After several minutes a boy came in with a tray of warm soda pop chanting "Aiwa! Orango, Lemongo, Co-Cola, Bebsi-Cola, Bebs! Bebs!," tapping his bottle opener in monotonous tempo against the tray. He was decidedly sinister in appearance, horribly thin and with the shriveled face of an old man, like a baked potato. She waved him away, but he persisted; finally she gave him a bit of baksheesh and he wandered off. She wished she could bribe the flies to go away; the air was thick with them. It was deathly hot.

For fifteen months it had been like this, since the day Solafa decided she could no longer live in her own country and had filled out the first form for her new passport. In the beginning they had only required a five-piastre stamp, a birth certificate, and a clearance from the tax collector. Then there were the absurd questions about her family—the religion, birth dates, and marital status of her maternal aunts, for example—all verified by affidavit. When she produced one document she was asked for another: a ten-year record of her banking transactions abroad; separate affidavits from the police attesting that she had never plotted against the security of the state, blasphemed in public, earned her bread by begging, smuggled hashish or been employed in a brothel; certificates from her doctor absolving her of trachoma, alcoholism, leprosy, syphilis, and insanity. When she despaired of acquiring evidence legally, she had had it forged, often at considerable cost. And she had been obliged to pay for many of the authentic documents as well; a box of sweets or a bottle of whiskey would do for Mr. Mish Mish, but they would hardly suffice for a police colonel or the private secretary to an Undersecretary. For she was at large now in the dark world of the baksheesh Arabs. A few of her prominent friends had made obscure, guarded suggestions that her name was on the black list, but she stubbornly refused to believe this. For their part, the men in the Ministry of the Interior remained blindly loyal to their oriental birthright of Never Saying No, particularly to a woman so beautiful.

Nearly an hour later Mr. Mish Mish returned. "Please accept my apologies for detaining you, ya Anissa," he said. "Your dossier was not in our files here, and I was obliged to send a man down to the basement. Our system is . . . uh . . . being *reorganized* down there, and he had some slight difficulty in . . . uh . . . *identifying* it. Now let me see."

He opened the dossier—half the size of an encyclopedia—brushing away the dust with a porcine palm. The upper layers of paper had disintegrated in several places, and a dry, grayish substance, exuding a curious smell, flaked off the pages as he turned them over.

"Now let me see. Yes! Everything seems to be in order. Birth certificate. Tax clearances. Bank statements. Municipality affidavits. Police affidavits. Medical certificates. Immunization certificates. School certificates. Yes! Everything seems to be in order."

Solafa's heart leaped.

"But wait—"

Mr. Mish Mish flipped over a few more pages. "What has become of your paternal nationality certificate, ya Anissa?"

"I'm afraid I don't understand."

"Surely you were informed of the regulation requiring evidence of your father's citizenship?"

"My father is dead. He was Foreign Minister of this country four times. Surely that is sufficient evidence."

"I am sorry, ya Anissa. You must prove it."

"How? Whom do I ask for such an insane document?"

"I am a poor public servant, ya Anissa. Such a matter lies outside my competence."

"Look here, you fat little fool. I demand to see Khalil Bey."

"I am sorry, ya Anissa. The Bey is in Beirut."

"Take me to Hussein Pasha!"

"I am sorry. He is not here. He will return after one hour."

"Then I'll *wait.*"

"As you like."

Solafa stormed into the teeming corridor, where she paced rapidly up and down, stabbing the air distractedly with her cigarette. In a few minutes her mood relapsed to one of mere melancholy, and she leaned more calmly against the balustrade of the immense circular staircase, infused with a new compassion for the hundreds of poor encamped on the steps; she wondered what would become of them, and of herself. They never seemed to move; how long had they been there—hours? days?—waiting without protest for the identity cards and work permits and licenses and myraid other papers the Municipality required them to possess. She leaned out over the balustrade and looked down the stairwell to the bottom: she remembered all the tales told of those who had despaired of their papers and had leaped to death below. Her own brother, an Ambassador once, had been driven to that—but he had dived down the light well instead, only to land on a cushion of crumpled application forms and discarded correspondence two stories high. So he had picked himself up, brushed off his Savile Row lounge suit, and gone home to blow his brains out.

Solafa was, as her brother had been, the embodiment of a disintegrating way of life. Her family, and a few others, had ruled Al Khadra once. She had been born in an eighty-room rococo palace, educated by Belgian nuns, refined in Swiss schools and finished in French academies. French was her first language; her English was now nearly as flawless; though weak in her native Arabic, she spoke it better than most of her friends. She would turn thirty in a few weeks and would probably celebrate her birthday in the swimming pool at the Gazooza Sporting Club; in happier summers the scene would have been her grandfather's villa at St.-Jean-Cap-Ferrat, with princelings of Europe dancing in attendance. But all that was vanished now, thanks to the egalitarian zeal of Mustafa ibn Mabrouk. Cautiously at first, then systematically and inexorably, he had pillaged the aristocracy of prerogative and vast estate, and put its politicians out to pasture. He had made *ancien régime* an epithet as unclean in connotation as Imperialism or Albion. In fact, Mustafa had been less harsh with the former Establishment than he might have been; though he had confiscated their palaces and converted them into ministries and museums, he was at least allowing the aristocracy to live out a parody of their old lives in respectable apartment houses and sporting clubs, and he had put many of them on modest pensions. From her resplendent past, Solafa had managed to salvage a secret Swiss bank account (which she could not get at), some leather-bound books, and two or three of the monumental gilded chairs from her grandfather's palace; today the chairs reposed in her shabby rooms quite out of proportion, like pineapples squeezed into flower pots, the last evidence of a garish but not forgotten grandeur. But Mustafa ibn Mabrouk's generosity, such as it was, was powerless to appease the malice his rapacity had aroused. The aristocrats had always been given to recrimination and vendetta among themselves, but now in adversity they were homogeneous in their hatred of *him*. Irreconcilable fathers and prodigal sons, incompatible marriages—husbands and wives who had not shared the same bed for ten or twenty years—all were reunited now in their adhesive hatred of *him*. For Solafa, simply to be thrown to the mercy of the bureaucracy—whose squalid methods her own family had done much to encourage—was quite enough to earn her unfathomable hatred of *him*. "Come tomorrow, ya Anissa. . . . You will need another affidavit, ya Anissa . . . The Bey is in Beirut, ya Anissa . . . The Pasha is not here, ya Anissa. He will come after one hour, ya Anissa . . ."

The irony of it—that the aristocrats should become victim to a venality of their own making—amused Mustafa ibn Mabrouk. But as for the bureaucracy itself, Solafa's disdain was bland in comparison to his own. The baksheesh Arabs, fat-bottomed, ill-shaven, coffee-slurping, ensconced like starling hordes in the ministries, were to him the undoing of all his aspirations. One day not long after becoming Prime Minister he had slipped unnoticed into the Municipality in search of the men's room, lost his way, and ended up in the cellar. There he confronted the files of the last fifty years: they lay heaped in chaos, cocooned with cobwebs, overrun with rodents, encrusted with the excrement of bats. He stormed upstairs and charged up and down the endless, labyrinthine corridors, darting in and out of offices, dumping dossiers and wastepaper baskets and coffee cups on the cement floors, overturning tables and desks, hurling inkpots out of windows and at the fly-spattered walls, screaming, "I will crush you! I will crush you!" The baksheesh Arabs observed this spectacle with their customary torpor—it had occurred under previous reformers—though when caught directly in the line of fire they made depraved promises to mend their ways. That week, Mustafa shook the ministries from top to bottom. But it was little more than a game of musical chairs, nor could it have been much else. The baksheesh Arabs were durable, indispensable, indestructible. When the Prime Minister's attention had turned elsewhere—to his new factories, his Five-Year Plan, his foreign policy—they unlocked their wobbly desks again, liberating their bean breakfast, booty of bon-bons and Scotch whiskey, newspapers and picture magazines, dossiers adorned with bat dung.

Seated on the balustrade, Solafa waited another hour. Then Mr. Mish Mish came down the corridor and told her that Hussein Pasha, the director of the passport department, would not be coming to the office at all that day. "It's his hemorrhoids again, ya Anissa."

Solafa turned away without speaking and descended the spiral staircase. The sinister boy with the warm soda pop spotted her and ran after her crying "Bebsi-Cola! Bebs! Bebs!," now tapping his bottle opener against the tin tray, now clawing at her orange dress. She pushed him aside; he spat on her. A hairy hand appeared, seized the boy by the scruff of the neck and shook him violently; the tray went crashing on the stone steps. The hairy hand was Hussein Pasha's. "Piles Pasha!" Solafa shouted at him in English. He blinked, uncomprehendingly. She left him there, in a pool of soda pop, and ran down the stairs, out of the dark building into the dazzling noon.

Michel was waiting, patient in his Peugeot. He had the radio on, and they were announcing the new economic pact with the Russians. The afternoon newspapers were on the street with great headlines in green ink. Patriotic hymns blared from loudspeakers mounted on the Municipality. *There will be water . . . There will be grain . . . The dawn of dignity . . . The end of pain.* Down the street came a procession of school children, blowing on toy trumpets, beating on tin drums, bearing banners and slogans of their own. *Mustafa, Warrior of Islam! Mustafa, Torch of Arabism! Long Live Khrushchev! Hambshire to the Hangman!*

"Recueille-toi mon âme, en ce grave moment," Michel intoned.

> *"Et ferme ton oreille à ce rugissement.*
> *C'est l'heure où les douleurs des malades s'aigrissent!*
> *La sombre Nuit les prend à la gorge—"*

"Oh Michel, darling, shut up," Solafa said wearily. "I behaved very badly in there. I'll never get my passport now! Come on, let's go to the Gazooza Club."

At the Embassy, Dr. Pantry was immersed in the morning's classified cables from Washington. They were devoted for the most part to routine, mechanical matters. A special pleasure sparkled in the rimless spectacles of the Director of Mutual Understanding when he came upon the message marked *Secret;* only a handful of Embassy officers were permitted access to these, and owing to the eminence of his position, Dr. Pantry was one of them. SECRETARY HAS SUMMONED URGENT MEETING ADVISERS ALL AGENCIES CONSIDER POLICY CHANGES KHADRA WAKE MABROUK-SOVIET AID PACT. URGE EXTREME DISCRETION ALL EMBASSY CONTACT KHADRIAN GOVT PENDING FURTHER DIRECTIVES. HAMPSHIRE.

In the upper right-hand corner of the message Dr. Pantry was distressed to find the initials of one of his numerous deputies. He turned to his typewriter and pecked out an untypically terse memorandum: *You were not intended to see the attached telegram. Please erase your initials and initial your erasure.*

10

That evening, right after supper, Christopher Grundoon went to see the King.

Their meeting had no particular purpose, other than their desire to enjoy one another's company. In the beginning, their association had been merely a matter of official convenience; Ambassador Fitzgibbon had delegated Christopher to serve as the pipeline between the Embassy and the Royal Palace in order to dispense with the need of serving in that capacity himself. Though chief of state, His Majesty's impact on the operations of government was symbolical at best; the Ambassador limited his calls on the King to two or three a year, and left to Christopher whatever reportage was necessary on the intrigues of the Royal household. Christopher's formal contacts with the King quickly ripened into friendship. Intellectually they had little in common, but Mohammed more than made up for this by his undisguised delight in having a companion in Christopher; as for Christopher, he could not get over having a King for a companion. Christopher was an entertaining talker, an excellent sportsman, and convivial company; moreover, he too was a discarded lover of Solafa, and this shared sense of loss was not the least of the bonds between them. Whatever the reasons, His Majesty could not seem to get enough of the American; he showered him with invitations and called him on the telephone at all hours of the day and night.

An Embassy Chevrolet chauffeured Christopher to this evening's appointment; as the car climbed the Jebel al Malouk, the Mount of Kings, the embarking sun splashed waves of pastel radiance on the ramparts of the Royal Palace. The bartizans and battlements loomed high above the city; for a millennium they had been the first sentinels to see the Galleon of Fire invade the morning sky, and the last to witness her westering oars. The Palace was encircled by a high and toothy wall, within which orchards and neglected gardens and a driveway of white gravel led upward to the Palace proper. Beneath the porcelain portals of the ancestral seat of the House of Hamad, some Bedouin soldiers were playing tric-trac and sucking on watermelon. They recognized Christopher and greeted him mechanically as he strode into the Royal diwan.

It was deserted. Christopher did not bother to search for any of the royal retainers, of whom there were precious few remaining in any case. Unescorted, he descended the interminable tesselated corridors to the King's private apartments in the rear of the royal compound. This was not a terribly large palace as royal palaces go—less than three hundred rooms—but all save a few of these were now unoccupied. The most splendid feature here was not the interior but the courtyards and gardens, neglected though they were, interlacing and hyphenating the entire edifice. The courtyards were rich in arabesque arches and chipped marble fountains from which water no longer flowed. In the gardens the crumbling statuary and vagrant bougainvillaea, the unkempt sycamore and orange trees, gave melancholy but beautiful evidence of erstwhile grandeur. Perforated plaster windows, designed with delicate geometric traceries and stained glass, looked down from harems no longer inhabited, and when at night the electricity was turned on behind them they projected exquisite patterns of colored light on the corroding pavements of the courtyards below.

Twice Christopher lost himself in the maze of corridors and

courtyards, and had to retrace his steps. He had begun to despair of ever seeing Mohammed that night when he heard a quick, throbbing sound palpitating down the mosaic arteries—as if to suggest that the Palace had heart trouble—and he pursued it until it brought him into the royal gymnasium. It was an enormous room, full of bar bells, parallel bars, and other body-building equipment. In the far corner, in the middle of a raised boxing ring, danced the King of Al Khadra, his back to Christopher, sparring with Yahutha, his deaf-mute batman.

Christopher did not wish to interrupt the King's sport, so he lingered silently for a little while in the shadows. At the Soviet reception he had speculated with Stanislav and Sami what raiment His Majesty would wear: Dacron, Field Marshal, or Prince of Mecca? No: Mohammed was naked, but for a pair of brown boxing gloves. These beat pitilessly about the head of Yahutha, whose loins retained their mystery beneath balloon-like Bedouin drawers. The Bedu—and the blood Royal was Bedu—are like the Irish a prim and reticent race, but the King's nakedness was no accident. He reveled in revealing himself to concubine and companion alike. Such narcissism, if it could be called that, was understandable. His brown Arab body was perhaps six feet tall. He had an ingenuous, wistful, boyish face, thick black hair, flashing teeth, luxuriant eyelashes. His torso was smooth and sculpted, his waist slim, his buttocks prominent, his legs long and fawnlike. He was almost mythically handsome. Indeed, whenever Christopher contemplated the King without his clothes he remembered statues he had seen in the Uffizi Gallery and the Vatican Museum. Even to the eyes. For like those demigods, Mohammed's eyes were without expression.

And now His Majesty shouted furiously at Yahutha, who was making a very bad show of defending himself. *"Idrubni, ya Yahutha, idrubni!"* the King cried. "Strike me, O Yahutha, strike me!" But the batman's blows were perfunctory and poorly aimed. This aroused the King's pugnacity all the more, and Yahutha responded with a spasmic, throaty honk, as deaf-mutes do, like a wounded goose. At this point Christopher took pity on Yahutha, and called out to the King.

"Your Majesty?"

Mohammed whirled around. "Christopher!" He came leaping out over the ropes toward his friend. Putting his gloved hands up, crying "Hit me, ya habibi! Hit me," he danced around the American full circle. Christopher sparred for a few seconds, but like Yahutha his jabs were perfunctory.

"You boxed in college! You won silver cups and blue ribbons! You told me, Christopher, don't you remember? Show me your right cut-upper cha cha cha!"

"I can't, Your Majesty," Christopher said, putting his fists down.

"Why not?"

"Because you're the King. I can't hit a King."

"Oh, that's what all my guards say," Mohammed protested. With his teeth he unlaced his gloves and threw them on the floor; Yahutha scampered to pick them up. "Why can't I ever get anyone to play rough with me? When I was at Harvard people weren't such—such poop-parties!"

"You mean party-poops? Anyway, you were only Crown Prince then."

The King did some push-ups on the floor and then a few flips on the parallel bars. "Perhaps so," he said, "but that year was the happiest in my life cha cha cha. Okay. Enough exercise for today. I'm going to take a shower. Do you want to get wet?"

"No thank you, Your Majesty. I bathed before coming here. May I wait for you in your rooms?"

"As you like. I shan't be long. You know the way?"

"I think so."

The King's rooms were in startling contrast to the antiquity of the rest of the Royal Palace. Or rather, they were a curious mixture of that antiquity with certain daring modernities of design and experiments of style. The decoration was by turns Turkish, Italian and arabesque. The stairways and balustrades sagged with lumpy, disproportionate classical columns. Haphazardly the ceilings sprouted crystal chandeliers, stalactites of teakwood, and naked electric light bulbs. Walls and ceilings alike were lined with plumbing pipe—like varicose veins—painted pink. Faïence tile floors, porcelain archways, Gothic windows. Vases everywhere filled with wilting hyacinth flowers. Chests and tables of heavy mahogany

—carved bananas, grapes and gargoyles. Louis Quinze couches and puce-colored Victorian davenports reposed in cluttered coexistence with modern plastic bucket chairs. In the royal library, where Christopher Grundoon went to wait for the King, pin-ups of French nudes and American football players had been pasted on the immense, yellowing mirrors suspended in rococo frames.

Quite apart from considerations of taste, there was something about the royal apartments, and particularly about this library, which made Christopher uncomfortable. There was an atmosphere of decline, even of decay, which the robust evidence of the King's youth made only more bizarre. Christopher sat down before a round copper table of fine Damascene design, heaped with copies of *Life* and *Look* and *Hot Rod* magazines. Perched precariously atop these was a large cardboard carton advertising an American brand of instant mashed potato. Out of curiosity Christopher opened the flaps to see what the carton contained.

On top lay a sheep's horn, red tassels, blue glazed beads. Then a human jawbone, strands of camel hair and sachets of jasmin petal.

Christopher plunged his hand deeper into the cardboard carton and rummaged among the mysteries. Fragments of masonry and mosaic; miniature Korans enclosed in velvet and embroidered leather. Magic squares and incantations scrawled on crumbling parchment; combinations of numerals and diagrams scribbled on scraps of brown paper. A donkey's ear, a blue bottle, stubs of candle, the double tooth of a camel. Snapshots of Mustafa ibn Mabrouk in his youth. Paper cutouts of men and women inscribed with charms and magic spells. A live chameleon. Locks of human hair; dried lotus leaves. Potions in sealed vials; a book on alchemy; a rock-and-roll gramophone record. Inside a sealed bottle, the pickled head of a puppy.

"It seems you've discovered my charms."

Startled, Christopher turned to find the King standing at the door of the study. He wore a lounge suit of light blue Dacron and a white shirt with a button-down collar; his hair was still moist from his shower.

The American extracted a leather sachet of particular elaboration from the carton, held it up, and asked, "What's inside this, Your Majesty?"

"My umbilical cord cha cha cha."

"Have the nightmares come back?"

"I'm afraid so. Dreadful ones, in fact."

"Is there any particular recurrent dream?"

"Recurrent?"

"I mean a dream which keeps coming back."

"No, each one seems to be different," the King said. "But they all end in treachery, and betrayal, and death. Sometimes I hear a strange, whirring sound—like the chopping of great swords in the air—and the cries of men, in the distance."

"And you think these charms protect you?"

"I know they do, ya habibi! Every night when I retire I hang some of them on my bed. Sometimes I tie one or two around my neck. They don't always stop the dreams but they do make them less nasty cha cha cha. And then when I awake, the sweat running like ice over my body, I say, 'O God, bless our Lord Mohammed!' and—"

"And you spit over your left shoulder three times."

"How did you know?"

Christopher suppressed a smile. "You told me, don't you remember?"

"Yes, you smile," the King continued. "You're just like Mustafa—he used to tease me about these things when we were boys. You can afford to smile—you never saw your family butchered before your eyes. But my late father— oh, God bless him!—he knew the power of magic and charms and potions—and his fathers before him—and so do I."

"You don't have to convince me, Your Majesty. I do think you exaggerate it a bit, but I must admit I've seen things in this country which no man of science could ever explain."

"Do you want a cup of coffee, Christopher?"

On panther feet Yahutha had slipped silently into the room with a tray of refreshments. He laid out some pastilles and potato chips, and into tiny porcelain cups he poured that fragrant Bedouin beverage, flavored with cardamom seed, which Christopher found so tasty. As he filled and refilled the King's cup, the deaf-mute's twisted face assumed, in the contemplation of His Majesty, an attitude of almost tormented adoration.

"Where did you find Yahutha?" Christopher asked.

"Mustafa gave him to me, as a birthday present, nearly three years ago—shortly after I appointed him Prime Minister."

"But why a deaf-mute, of all things?"

"God bless Mustafa! He wanted me to have someone whose loyalty and discretion I could completely trust."

"I should think you'd find it difficult to communicate," Christopher said.

"Not at all. We've worked out a sign language, and if it's anything complicated I write it down."

"He can read and write?"

"Oh yes. He may be quite ugly, but he's surprisingly well educated. I even caught him reading a book in English once."

"He is obviously very devoted to you."

"I've been very good to him, you see."

As silently as he had come, Yahutha withdrew. The King was seated now in one of the garish bucket chairs, his leg dangling over the side; he nibbled thoughtfully on a potato chip and then said suddenly, "You know, about Mustafa, sometimes I wonder what he is trying to do. All this praise for the Russians in the newspapers. And now this new economic agreement."

"He didn't even tell you about it?"

"No, the first I heard of it was on the radio, this afternoon. I'm not sure I like the idea awfully much. Aren't all Russians atheists? I read in *Life* the other day that they are against Islam. I must remind Mustafa of that one day soon. That's the trouble—I've seen him so seldom lately. Every time I ring him up, his aide—you know, the one with the eye patch—his aide says he's not there, or he's tied up in a cabinet meeting or something and he'll call right back. But he never does. I know Mustafa wants to talk to me. It's those people around him—do you suppose they are jealous of our friendship? You remember the Bedouins the other day? I called Mustafa to tell him of the Sheikh's complaint they are not getting enough to eat, but I couldn't reach him. So I wrote him a letter. I hope they'll show it to him—the Sheikh seemed rather upset. I do miss Mustafa, I'll tell you that. When I appointed him Prime Minister he used to seek my advice every day. But now I hardly see him—just these long documents he sends me to sign. They're so confusing—so technical."

"There is one document which I hope Your Majesty will never sign," Christopher said impulsively.

"Which one is that, ya habibi?"

"Your ab—the one which would authorize him to enact laws without your consent."

"Strange you should say that. That's exactly what Mr. Pullmotor told me the other day."

"Yes, I heard he called on you."

"Twice, as a matter of fact. He was very charming, and he brought me a letter from your Secretary of State. He made me a little bit cross."

"Mr. Hampshire made you cross?"

"No, Mr. Pullmotor did, a bit. He suggested I take a greater interest in affairs of state. I told him I take a great deal of interest in affairs of state. I showed him my most recent proclamation! 'But,' I said, 'I have entrusted the day-to-day government of my kingdom to Mustafa, in whom I have complete confidence.' It was then that he made me cross. He said some things about Mustafa I could not accept. He even questioned Mustafa's loyalty to me. Can you imagine?"

"I'll try not to."

"Oh, I was very firm with him. I said, 'Do you realize, Mr. Paul, that my throne would be empty today but for Mustafa?' I said, 'Do you forget the night when the mob stormed the Palace, butchered my family one by one—and that only Mustafa, standing in this very room with his submachine gun blazing, prevented them from killing me? Mustafa saved my life! Do you think I could ever forget a loyalty like that? And how about yourself, Mr. Paul? Do you forget that it was you who first advised me to appoint Mustafa Prime Minister?' That's what I said. Poor Mr. Pullmotor, I'm afraid I offended him. You know, Christopher, I'm really not very fond of politics. It's so complicated. And *confusing*."

The King fell silent for a few moments, and then brightened. "Did you know I've had my throne room redecorated? Come along, I want you to see it. Then we'll go down to the city cha cha cha."

The cerement of night had fallen over Al Asima and the ramparts of the Royal Palace; the King led Christopher down darkened corridors, flicking on electric lights as he went. The throne room was even more startling than the rest of the imperial apartments, its aspect a mishmash of Moorish, Tudor and neo-Renaissance. A massive sun motif shone everywhere, from the candelabra, the chandeliers, and the great gilded chairs. Suspended on the walls were muskets, cutlasses and oil portraits of the King's ancestors. Above these were engraved the ninety-nine names of God, and a number of pious precepts. *Heaven Will Fortify Thy Throne. O God, O Saint, Sanctify Our Reign.* It was in this chamber that Mohammed received the credentials of new Ambassadors; it was here that, perched on his damask throne in the luminous white uniform of a Field Marshal, he had addressed the last inaugural of the now extinct Khadrian parliament. Christopher contemplated the immense portrait of the King's late father, festooned in medals, military tunic and a wide sash of watered silk; behind him cascaded a vernal English landscape. The face was fat and bearded and middle-aged, but there was the son's elusiveness of expression in the eyes, the same sensuousness in the mouth, and a slightly satanic quality as well.

"Do you like our throne room?" the King asked. (He was slipping into the royal plural now; it was the chamber, the memories.)

"It's quite overwhelming, Your Majesty."

"We derived some of our ideas for decoration during our year at Harvard. Unfortunately in applying them we had to cut a few corners. We're not a wealthy monarchy, you know."

On the dais, beneath a tasseled canopy and the sun motif, stood the throne of the House of Hamad, its threadbare damask and peeling gold paint exuding a sort of regal jaundice. His Majesty sat down. *"Ouch!"* he cried. "We've got to get those springs fixed. What a pity we don't have a Queen to sit here beside us. We must get married one of these days. We are very concerned with the question of dynastic succession. Have you a pen, Christopher?"

"I seem to have forgotten it. Do you want to write something?"

"Here, use ours. Will you take this down? We want to make a proclamation."

"I'm afraid I haven't any paper."

The King fished in his pocket. "Here, use the back of Mr. Hampshire's letter." As he took the crumpled piece of paper from the King, familiar phrases flashed before Christopher's eye. ". . . Free World . . . compassionate concern . . . Soviet seduction . . ."

"It's a shame you don't write Arabic," the King continued, "but I'll—we'll—have it translated in the morning."

"Your Majesty, why do you burden yourself with proclamations?"

"They are printed in the Royal Gazette. They are the chronicle of our reign. A Sovereign's first duty, to his subjects no less than to himself, is to be remembered."

Christopher sat down on the edge of the dais. "All right," he said. "Shoot."

"In the name of God, the Compassionate, the Merciful. We, Mohammed Seven, Ahmed Abdullah ibn Hamad, by the Grace of God King of the Kingdom of Al Khadra, Scion of the House of Hamad, Sheikh of the Sheikhs of Mecca and Medina, Direct Descendant of the Prophet in the line of Khadijah, Imam of Islam, Promoter of Piety and Captain of the Caravan of Arab Martyrs, being in this the thirteen hundred and seventy-fifth year of the Hejira and the third year of our reign, responding to the summons of Almighty God and summoned by the sagacity of our sacred heritage, do hereby proclaim—"

The King hesitated. "Help me, ya habibi," he said, "I need something new, timely, significant cha cha cha."

"How about public health?"

"I covered that last week."

"Tourism? Antiquities?"

"Too specialized."

"Royal camel races?"

"Undignified."

"What does Your Majesty wish most for his people?"

"Their happiness."

"How would you bring that about?"

The King hesitated. "Economic development!"

"Well yes, but what kind?"

"We must develop the economy. Isn't that enough?"

"If Your Majesty will continue."

"—do hereby proclaim a State of Economic Development in the Kingdom of Al Khadra, embracing fringe benefits, pension plans, comprehensive coverage, escalator clauses . . ."

. . .

In his own palace, the Prime Minister hovered over the teletype, scrutinizing the Associated Press despatches as the machine chopped them out. "So Hampshire's called a meeting to deal with the ibn Mabrouk menace, has he?" he remarked to Captain Anwar A'war, his military aide. "Call up the radio station, Anwar, and tell them I want to make a broadcast."

When they had finished with affairs of state, Christopher and the King got into Mohammed's crimson Ferrari and went down to the city in search of excitement. "I've just had a new engine installed," Mohammed said, as they roared from beneath the outer battlements of his ancestral home. "It's the latest GT—twelve-cylinder, three hundred horsepower, seven hundred forty r.p.m.! The curb weight is eight hundred eighty kilograms, and the gearbox five-speed. Maximum speed one hundred seventy-five miles per. Dry-sump lube system!"

They negotiated a curve on two wheels, and Christopher cried out to the King to slow down.

"I want to get away before my bodyguard knows I'm gone!" Mohammed shouted. "Besides, it pleases us to apply our foot to the accelerator!"

The descending road dashed in and out of sandstone gorges. When the city appeared in full view again, the King braked the Ferrari to a screeching stop. "Look, Christopher, at my capital!" he exclaimed. "I come here often at night, to gaze upon my capital."

The city's lamps beckoned like a golden lake in the black wasteland, their radiance rendering barely visible the tumbling tomb-mosques outlying the walls of the oriental quarter. "My God, it's an old city," Christopher said.

They zoomed off again, careening down, down. "Yes, it's old," Mohammed said, "but no older than my family or my throne. Remember, I'm a direct descendant of the Prophet cha cha cha."

Sir Charles Chetwynd-Pott and his young daughter were out for a drive on the Corniche when the royal Ferrari roared past them, Mohammed laughing behind the wheel, Christopher Grundoon's golden hair awry in the wind.

"Coo, Daddy, what a couple of corkers."

"Yes, they're splendid-looking chaps, all right," Sir Charles said. "But that young Grundoon had better watch out, spending so much time with His Majesty. Find himself in the line of fire when the bullet comes."

11

"Or the Sheraton-Zahra? I know that new pair of Spanish dancing girls. They're pretty sociable!"

"Gosh, I'd love that, Your Majesty, but the Political Police watch me in all those fancy places."

"Then what will we do tonight? Where will we go?"

Christopher reflected for a moment. "How about the Madmen's Café? There's always something going on there. We might even see Solafa."

The King turned the Ferrari away from the new city and in the direction of the old. They passed the municipal zoo, where the banter of baboon and hippopotamus was muted among the murmuring eucalyptus and the ululating expostulation of Chuckles Vespucci. For as if to confound Fitz Pasha, the minstrel's first concert the previous evening had been an astounding success; overnight, the name of Mister Chuckles had become celebrated among the youth of Al Asima. And now a mob of blue-denimed beatnik Arabs, overflowing the botanical gardens into the street beyond, punctuated his lyrics with explosions of demented applause. "Rangle-tangle-ring-ting-tong," pealed the lutist from the loudspeakers.

"I'm related to old King Kong, WOOH!
Baby, won't you say you're mine
With a honkey-donkey monkey shine?
When you hold my hand I'm a prehistoric man
I go APE!"

"That fellow has talent," the King said, slowing down. "I'd like to meet him sometime."

"Oh, I can easily arrange that," Christopher said.

The blaring, electronic lyrics pursued them into the Greek quarter; and here, on the periphery of the old city, began the ghettoes. Roaring down the cobblestoned streets, Christopher saw half the history of Christian schism and Mediterranean migration fly by in a blur. The Byzantine basilica of the Greeks galloped into the graveyard of the Gregorian Armenians, the Gregorian ghetto tumbled into the Italian, the Italian entangled the Chaldean, the Chaldean careened on the Melchite, and the Melchite enmeshed the Maronite. Then, like mercury, the crimson racer spurted among the minarets and timeless tenements of the old Islamic city and screeched to rest at last in the courtyard of the Madmen's Café.

Actually it was not a courtyard so much as a narrow, cobblestoned *cul de sac,* where wobbly tables and chairs and long wooden benches reposed beneath bowers of black foliage and fluorescent-tube lighting, suspended (so it seemed) from the nothingness of night. The King put on a pair of dark glasses and tossed a checkered *kaffiyeh* around his head before he and Christopher entered the café. They came upon a long corridor lit with sputtering primus stoves and lined with carpet-covered benches; they descended a dim stairway to dark alcoves lurking behind lattice and curtains of glass bamboo. Filthy flagstoned floor, kittens and bitch-cats everywhere underfoot, bone-backed wooden chairs, marble-topped tables, ubiquitous brass and copper crockery. Overhead the cooing of doves, dozens of dirty green flags, stars (constellations of tarnished tinsel), unlit lanterns, bare electric light bulbs casting not incandescence but gloom. Scowling from the walls were a stopped clock, immense mirrors (almost opaque), and whole crocodiles (talismans against the Evil Eye) impaled on spikes.

Unnoticed, the King and his American companion sat down at one of the tables and ordered glasses of *tamr hindi,* a cool and amber-colored beverage. In the other alcoves, the sparse clientele (it was early yet) were playing tric-trac, sucking on hubbly-bubblies, and drinking tea. Al Asima had lately been plagued with polluted water; when the boy brought the drinks, he handed Christopher an announcement in several languages; in English it read, *Please to be inform that all drinking water in this café has been passed by the Manager.* Christopher's American laughter attracted attention, and it was then that the King was recognized. A hag came and put peanuts—her offering—on the table before His Majesty. An obese gnome-hunchback, a cigarette peddler by profession, and an old man with a great bulbous goiter on the back of his neck—he was a bootblack, and the resident magician as well—came forward with boisterous greetings. The King discarded his disguise and greeted them with reciprocal warmth. *"Ya ustaz Abdul Aziz! ya Sheikh Soliman!"* he bubbled, embracing them.

Sure enough, Solafa drifted in. She wore a white bandana and a black dress, luminous and sleeveless. In her backwash were little Michel, Sami the Snooper, and Pride Lyon, the *Time* magazine man. The King called out his greetings and invited them to his table. "We've all been to Chuckles Vespucci's concert," Solafa told Christopher when they had seated themselves. "It was a bit wild, I'll tell you. Sami had the bright idea of looking for you and Mohammed over here, and Chuckles said he'd like to meet the King. He'll be along any minute."

"This joint looks like a communist cell," Pride Lyon said.

Enter Chuckles Vespucci, escorted by a band of blue-denimed beatnik Arabs and a smattering of emancipated young women in print dresses. Chuckles brandished his lute; the beatnik Arabs were armed with transistor radios bobbing from plastic straps about their bodies. The minstrel joined the royal party, and the King at once moved to another chair so as to sit beside him; they fell into an animated conversation on way-out American music. Then from the adjoining alcoves the transistors of the beatnik Arabs blared out a samba which particularly pleased Solafa; she took Mohammed by the hand and said, "Come on, let's dance."

"This is not the place for that," the King laughed.

"They can't see us from the other tables. Besides, what do we care?"

Solafa and Mohammed were born dancers. Christopher admired the grace of them together; now they were torso to torso, now away from one another, now side to side, now pivoting and bending their knees a bit, now back to back. Solafa kicked off her sandals, and once or twice she touched Mohammed's leg with the side of her bare foot. Mohammed began improvising his movements, mixing in rhumba and some other rhythms and crying out joyously "cha cha cha!" Solafa threw her body back and laughed. They were—*youth.* And that was fitting; the only things which seemed really to concern the King were death, and being young.

When they sat down again Chuckles passed around an unfamiliar brand of oriental cigarette.

"This tobacco has a peculiar taste," Christopher observed.

"That's the hashish," Chuckles said.

"Ya salaam!" the King exclaimed. "Mustafa would be very cross." But Mohammed made no motion to snuff out his cigarette, nor did the others.

"I think I'll try one after all," Pride Lyon said.

"Take two," Chuckles said. "The State Department is paying for it."

Christopher Grundoon was delighted. He inhaled deeply, slumped down in his chair and closed his eyes, expecting to experience the laudanum hallucinations of Coleridge and the apocalyptic pipe dreams of Aldous Huxley's metaphysical mushrooms. He kept his eyes shut, eager to be enmeshed in kaleidoscopic geometries and animated architectures. He anticipated the perpetual present, the primal state of innocence, fabulous antelopes, landscapes inhabited by seraphim. He aspired to glimpse Ezekiel's Garden of God; to plunge into the sacred Alph; to marvel at the marble grottoes and domed treasuries of incandescent diadems and blazing scepters; to romp in fields of poppy with lovely, live, naked caryatids singing songs of purest gold looping like charmed serpents among the enchanted rhododendron. He yearned to be transported, to navigate all the cavernous intricacy of the mystic voyage, to teeter on the precipice of the Void, to grasp Grace—and Transfiguration!

Instead, he got sick to his stomach. He saw nothing but commonplace red spots, multiplied somewhat by his queasiness and a sudden, throbbing headache. Minutes passed. Reluctantly he realized there would be no apocalypse. And yet he felt that the forbidden weed entitled him at the least to Sir Richard Burton's voluptuous tranquillity, to the street Arab's delicious stupor, untroubled by the "displeasures of memory and the vanity of thought." These also were withheld from him. His headache and nausea ebbed, only to be followed by an aphrodisiac longing for Solafa and mushy intimations of disaster, a goofy certitude that somehow the little cosmos he had fashioned for himself in this country—the country he had learned to love not in spite of its faults but because of them—was about to come crashing down. The magic hemp had failed. Christopher opened his eyes.

It was better this way. In the real world, there were diversions of a different sort, and they were as entertaining. For the word had flown rapidly throughout the quarter of the King's presence in the Madmen's Café. This was the neighborhood of the scent-vendors and circumcising barbers, of the maimed and stunted and malformed, of the blood-letters, buffoons, story-tellers and snake charmers, of the cataleptics, alchemists, magicians and witch-doctors. And now many of them scampered like merry mice for their headquarters, the *Ahwa el Megazib,* the Madmen's Café. The place was beginning to fill with these enchanters and freaks, all contesting to be jesters to the King. The café occupied the former premises of an ancient monastery of the Sufi dervishes, those Mohammedan mystics who had found in locomotion and frenzy what the Christian visionaries had fulfilled in flagellation, levitation and stigmata. The stupor of their whirling dances had not been their only path to Paradise. The Sufis had also subjected themselves to incomprehensible privations and torments. They exercised dominion over the kingdom of snakes, and the power to enchant and converse with them; they devoured these venomous creatures for breakfast, and nibbled on scorpions as luncheon appetizers. They lacerated their own flesh with knives, broke bricks on their chests, passed packing needles through their cheeks, thrust swords through their bowels, and iron spikes into their eyes; they chewed on glass like celery and on live coals like lettuce. They prostrated themselves before the hoofs of charging horses; they shouted *Hu!*—He!—at half-minute intervals for years and decades at a time. Some of them became quite mad, went around stark naked, and were venerated as living saints. Few of them would have found the telephone of value; so articulate were their powers they communicated telepathically with one another across deserts and mountains. The target of their torments was, of course, direct congress with the Divine—or rather, through the derangement of the reason and the ecstatic transfiguration of the self, the annihilation of their own identities in the infinity of the Godhead.

The magicians who patronized the Madmen's Café claimed direct spiritual descent from the Sufi dervishes. This was debatable; the Sufis were genuine mystics, the modern magicians for the most part mere conjurers. Still, many of them commanded remarkable powers, and of these men none was more renowned than Sheikh Soliman, the bootblack sorcerer with the great bulbous goiter on the back of his neck. Mustafa ibn Mabrouk had personally instructed the police to prevent Sheikh Soliman and his disciples from engaging in their occult craft, on the grounds that such practices did violence to the dignity of a modern state. But Mustafa's edict depended for enforcement on policemen who were often as superstitious as the Sheikh himself and in no hurry to incur one of his evil spells; to this day the magician did pretty much as he pleased. The King had a particular reverence for his skill, and now he summoned him to the table to meet Chuckles Vespucci. He attributed to the Sheikh the power to detect thieves, converse with the dead, and evoke visions of unquestionable veracity. Chuckles seemed fascinated. "Do you want to watch Bismarck at Waterloo?" the King asked. "Shall we learn how Caesar made love to Cleopatra cha cha cha?"

"I'd rather learn how Mustafa plans to turn this country into a communist satellite," Pride Lyon said.

"Sheikh Soliman can see the past and present—not the future," the King replied, altogether mystified by the *Time* fellow.

The beatnik Arabs still had their transistors turned on; several stations blared simultaneously; suddenly the competing cacophonies stopped all at once and a single voice announced, "His Excellency the Prime Minister will speak." Silence descended on the Madmen's Café. There was a slight rustling sound from the loudspeakers and then the voice, sonorous and faintly amused, of Mustafa ibn Mabrouk. ". . . treachery in the air . . . Hampshire meeting at this moment with his henchmen to hatch new plots . . . a meeting of my own at midnight to consider countermeasures . . . Hampshire's spies lurking in the most unsuspecting places . . . extreme vigilance . . . emergency measures . . . your Arabism will crush them . . ."

When the brief broadcast was over and the music came on again the King said, "Mustafa sounds very cross. Perhaps I had better return to the Palace. If there is a crisis, he may want to ring me up for advice."

Christopher was equally concerned, but he could not resist a sudden impulse to make mischief. "I have a better idea, Your Majesty," he said. "You claim this old Sheikh here can conjure up visions. Ask him to describe Mr. Hampshire's meeting."

"What wonderful fun!" Solafa exclaimed.

"Yes," Pride Lyon laughed. "Then Your Majesty can call Mustafa and give him all the details."

In Arabic, the King explained Christopher's request to Sheikh Soliman. The magician nodded and promised he would do his best. He seated himself cross-legged on the floor and ordered a pot of incense to be placed at his feet. He called for a cup, a bottle of black ink, and some common cooking oil. Then he directed Christopher to select a boy—any boy, provided he had not yet reached puberty—to assist in the magic exercise.

"The lad will be our eyes and ears," the Sheikh said, "but beware. If he is not pure, and uncorrupted by lust, we shall fail."

From the patrons now pressing around the royal alcove, Christopher chose at random a neatly dressed and angelic-looking youth of about twelve. The magician beckoned the boy to sit facing him, cross-legged; he poured ink into the cup, added a few drops of oil, and gave the cup to the boy. Then he drew a few fragments of paper from beneath his copious garments, scribbled some magic squares and invocations on them, and fed them to the fire of the incense pot.

"What is your name?" he asked his apprentice.

"By God, my name is Mahmoud," the youth answered.

"Stare into the cup," the wizard told him. "Do not lift your eyes."

The old man recited some sacred verses. Christopher could not understand all of them, but he did grasp those prayers which were constantly repeated. *"Malak al yom, Malak al yom*—Angel of the day, Angel of the day . . . Come down! Be present! Remove the veil!"

The magician addressed himself again to the boy, bent low now over the cup. "Ya Mahmoud," he asked, "do you see anything?"

"Yes!" the youth answered. "It isn't clear."

"Stop shaking the cup. Is that better?"

"Yes!"

"What do you see?"

"A face."

"That is a good beginning. What sort of face? A man?"

"No."

"A woman?"

"No."

"An American?"

"No."

"Not a man, not a woman, and not an American. Hmm. Stop shaking the cup."

It took ten minutes of further questioning to establish that the face the boy saw was the reflection of his own. The wizard leaned over and boxed him hard on the ear; the magic mixture went crashing to the floor. "This boy is worthless!" the magician protested. "One look at him and you know he is not pure. He could never see Hampshire or anybody else. We must have some other lad."

Another cup was fetched, and the ritual repeated with a second pre-pubescent boy, again without success. By now thoroughly embarrassed, Christopher chose for the final attempt an urchin of startling appearance. Here was the Artful Dodger of Islam. He wore a cap marked B STON RED SOX; his torn shirt and tattered trousers were a rainbow of splattered paint, and he was without shoes. "My name is Wasfi," he replied gravely to the magician's questions. "I work in the sign shop around the corner."

Again the Sheikh inscribed some magic squares and invocations on scraps of paper, fed them to the fire of the incense pot, and muttered over and over, *"Malak al yom, Malak al yom!* Angel of the day, Angel of the day! Come down! Be present! Remove the veil!" The urchin Wasfi's response to the wizard's enchantments was immediately more promising than the performance of the other two boys. Squatting cross-legged and bareheaded opposite the Sheikh, he bent very low over the cup, his little hand forming a bridge between his dappled forehead and the mystic porridge. "Yes, I see something," he said after a few minutes.

"Perhaps it is your own face, ya Wasfi?" the wizard asked.

"No. It is not a face, not a person. It's like a garden."

"A garden?"

"Yes, a garden full of beautiful birds and flowers. There is water shooting from a white rock, and the birds are flying into the water, and the birds are flying into the air. It isn't clear."

"Go on," the Sheikh said. "Go on. Look harder."

"Above the garden there is a red wall, I think. High in the wall there is a window. An old gentleman is looking out the window into the garden. A black man is coming into the garden. The black man is a doctor."

"A doctor?"

"Yes! He is dressed all in white. The black doctor has something in his hand. It is a chair, I think, made all of silver. There are birds and flowers everywhere. A man with red skin comes through the wall."

"Ah," said the Sheikh. "A Red Indian."

"No, he is a prisoner."

"A prisoner?"

"Yes! His suit is all striped, like the one they gave my uncle Ahmed when they put him in jail for stealing vegetables."

"What is the prisoner doing?"

"He is wearing black spectacles and he has a large bag in his hand," the urchin Wasfi said. "He sits down in the chair. He opens the bag. He has laundry in the bag, and lots of papers. He wipes his spectacles. He comes through the door in the wall again."

"The same man—the prisoner?"

"Yes!"

"What is he doing now, ya Wasfi?"

"He is sitting down."

"In the same chair?"

"No, in another chair, next to himself. He opens the bag. He has laundry in his bag, and lots of papers. He cleans his spectacles. He comes through the door again."

"The same man?" the magician asked.

"Yes!"

"What is he doing?"

"He is sitting down beside his two selves, and opening his bag of laundry in his bag, and lots of papers. He cleans his spectacles. He through the door again, and again. Now there are some other men. They are all in blue, and they are wearing big black spectacles, and their skulls are very white, like ghosts. Now some other men, like police officers. Some wear brown, some wear white, and they all carry small whips. Now an old lady comes. I think she is an old lady, but she is dressed like a young man. She is giving something to the men."

"What is she giving them?"

"Bebsi and pieces of dry mud, I think. They are eating it, and laughing. Another man comes through the door. He is very tall. The old lady throws her arms around him. It isn't clear."

"Look harder, ya Wasfi!"

"I see the old gentleman again, standing at the window, shaking his head. He turns, and sits down at a table, and reads some papers. He reads and reads. There are very many papers, and the room is full of books. The old gentleman takes off his spectacles and rubs his eyes. He is very tired. He gets up from the table and goes to the wall with a great big book in his hand. There are rusty chains and great big locks and little spikes and spears, all close together, in a cabinet near the wall. Oh, those spikes are black and sharp and so very, very ugly! The old gentleman takes some of the spikes in his hand. He has cut his hand. There is blood. He drinks the blood. He binds the wound. He goes back to his table and puts on his spectacles and looks out the window again and shakes his head. He takes some books and papers from the table and walks away—it is not clear."

"Where does he go?"

"He comes through the door. He is in the garden with the other men. The other men get up from their chairs. The old gentleman sits down. The other men sit down. The old gentleman is talking. The other men are not talking."

"What is the old gentleman saying?"

"I cannot hear anything. Now another man is coming through the door. He is very small and ugly, and he is almost naked. He has a big club in his hand."

"A club!"

"Yes. He swings the club and hits the old gentleman on the head."

"On the head! Is the old gentleman dead?"

"No, he is talking."

"Tell us what he says, ya Wasfi!"

"I can see him. I cannot hear him."

At this point the wizard leaned over and slapped the boy. "Of course you can hear him, you little weasel!" he cried, his goiter shaking like jelly. "That is Hampshire! He is hatching an imperialist plot!"

The King asked the magician to compose himself and to continue questioning the boy. But now little Wasfi would only say, "It is not clear. I see a garden with beautiful birds and flowers. It is not clear. I see nothing." The Sheikh's outburst had broken the spell.

Solafa had provided a running translation for Chuckles Vespucci and Pride Lyon. The *Time* man could barely control himself. "Imperialist plots!" he roared. "Red Indians, jailbirds, naked midgets swinging clubs at the Secretary of State! What a comedy!"

Christopher Grundoon ran his hand through his golden hair, and hiccuped. "I had hoped the hashish would show me Ezekiel's Garden of God," he said. "Instead I get Calvin Hampshire's cabbage patch in Georgetown. The boy had everything all wrong, of course. To begin with, the Secretary's staff meetings are held in his private conference room on the fourth floor of the Department. Still, there is something about this boy . . ."

"He is in cahoots with the old man," Pride Lyon said.

"I wouldn't be so sure," Sami the Snooper said.

"Neither would I," Solafa said.

"I have never known Sheikh Soliman to tell lies," the King said passionately, "and it was Christopher who picked the boy."

The urchin Wasfi, sensing disbelief, put on his B STON RED SOX cap and stuck to his story. *"Shuft kulshi ulto, shuft kulshi ulto,"* he kept repeating, his black eyes flashing. "I saw everything I said!"

There were no more visions that evening. As quickly as they had come, the colorful patrons of the Madmen's Café began to drift away. Chuckles Vespucci ran out of happy tobacco; boredom descended on the royal party.

Mohammed tried to engage little Michel, who had been silent all evening, in polite conversation. "We understand you enjoy poetry," the King said.

Michel looked up at His Majesty with those poodle eyes. *"C'est la Mort qui console, hélas!"* he answered, *"et qui fait vivre*

"C'est le but de la vie, et c'est le seul espoir—"

"I wish you would not speak French in my presence," the King said. "You know I don't understand it."

> *"—Qui, comme un élixir, nous monte et nous enivre,*
> *Et nous donne le coeur de marcher jusqu'au soir . . ."*

"But I do not want to go home!" Mohammed protested when they were all out in the street, wondering where to go now and what to do with themselves. "I do not want to go back to that empty palace with its horrible memories and the restless spirit of my father!" In the end he dragged all of them—Christopher and Solafa and Michel and Sami and Pride Lyon and Chuckles Vespucci—back to the Palace for a nightcap. When they had consumed his only bottle of Scotch, he ran through his private rooms pulling out drawers and rummaging in chests in search of souvenirs for his friends. How luminous the green watered silk, how sparkling the gold medallions under the gloomy chandeliers as the King of Al Khadra invested each of his guests with the Grand Cordon of the Broad Mabrouk! It had been, until that night, a decoration reserved for visiting Heads of State.

"Your Majesty is much too generous," Solafa protested.

"Good works cast out bad dreams," Mohammed said.

When Christopher Grundoon went to bed that night, it was with the Royal decoration pinned to his pajamas.

12

The clocks of Washington ran seven hours behind those of the Arab Orient; it was midafternoon in the American capital at the time of the curious events in the Madmen's Café. A heat wave enveloped the city; in the Department of State, the air-conditioning system had broken down. Since it was Saturday, and so hot, and because he was a considerate person in any case, the Secretary of State had decided to convene his conference on the Middle Eastern crisis in the more congenial environment of Georgetown. He stood at the window of his study on the second floor of his rambling red brick house, anticipating the arrival of his advisers and contemplating the quiet loveliness of his garden, where willows wept on flagstone walks embroidered by bright clusters of zinnia and rhododendron. In the center stood a bird bath of purest marble, gushing tiny geysers of resplendent water. Long a devoted birdwatcher, Calvin Hampshire could identify today a cinnamon-breasted roller and a wood nymph.

Now he watched while Roscoe, his black butler, all spotless in white, began arranging shiny aluminum garden furniture around a long glass-topped table. Then he heard the doors of automobiles being slammed shut; a slim, sunburned fellow, slightly gray about the temples, came into the garden and sat down in one of the aluminum chairs, followed almost at once by half a dozen other slim, sunburned fellows, slightly gray about the temples. These were the Secretary's Junior Bright Young Men, Special Assistants to the Assistant Secretaries; they were invariably the first to arrive at any meeting, ten minutes before the appointed time, precisely. The Secretary marveled at how similar—even identical—they seemed. They all wore seersucker suits and carried bulging attaché cases; whenever they sat down they unconsciously and compulsively removed their horn-rimmed spectacles and cleaned them. They opened their attaché cases, and from his vantage point the Secretary could see their soiled rowing togs peeping from beneath the batches of position papers. The Secretary knew they had been most of the morning on the Potomac, heroically striving to master a sport for which, on television some few weeks ago, he had volunteered a bemused admiration.

Four more men came into the garden, bearing the same general impedimenta, but distinguishable from the others in several respects. Their suits were of dark blue Dacron, their horn-rims were heavier, and they were all bald. None of them was sunburned. ("Not a chance this weekend, Charlie. The Secretary's just tossed me another Mashed Potato.") These were the Senior Bright Young Men, Assistant Secretaries of State and Defense. They were joined by several generals and admirals, whipping their palms with swagger sticks. Rebecca Hampshire, the Secretary's wife, clad gregariously in a pair of turquoise trousers, stepped into the scene with a tray of soda pop and brownies. "Dig in, boys!" she exhorted, "I made these myself!" The men made short order of the refreshments and laughed at her little jokes.

Rebecca turned to find a tall, elegant man standing behind her. "Shawnie Fitzgibbon!" she cried. "It's been *years!* When did you get in?"

"Late last night," Shawnie said. A trifle annoyed at the warmth with which his wife embraced his old classmate, the Secretary shook his head. He wondered what had happened to Paul Pullmotor. Paul was notoriously unpunctual, even for the most important appointments. But there was no purpose in starting the meeting without him. The Secretary decided not to go down into the garden until Pullmotor had come; the others would just have to wait. He turned away from the window and sat down at his desk.

The desk was cluttered with cablegrams and position papers, many of them devoted to the situation in Al Khadra and the Byzantine diplomacy of Mustafa ibn Mabrouk. Calvin Hampshire never conducted business of any kind without meticulous preparation, and today was no exception. There was an especially stimulating report from Paul Pullmotor, and the Secretary perused this once more. There were other reports and alarums from elsewhere in the Arab world, from Southeast Asia, from Pakistan, Uruguay and Somaliland. President X threatens us with Y if we do not do Z. Emperor N will fly to Moscow if we do not give him O, P and Q. They were all, the Secretary reflected, like locusts, the swarm of them. And none was more tiresome than Mustafa ibn Mabrouk—this brash Bedouin whose only assets were an empty desert and a debilitated population; this noisy ingrate who had entrenched himself with American support, built himself a radio station with American money, and who now was threatening to drag half the Middle East into the enemy camp. Conversation continued to drift up from the garden, and the Secretary could hear the schoolgirlish laughter of his wife. "Shawnie Fitzgibbon, will you *stop pulling my leg!*" The Secretary doubted whether his old classmate would approve of the measures he intended to take against the Prime Minister of Al Khadra. But then, the Ambassador did not have the Secretary's global responsibilities, or the perspective that went with them.

Curiously, the temperament and working habits of the Secretary were similar in many respects to those of Mustafa ibn Mabrouk. Like the Khadrian Prime Minister, Calvin Hampshire hungered for solitude and was really happy only when he was alone. Like Mustafa, he was an insomniac, and most of his heavy thinking was done during the small hours. Like Mustafa, he did an appalling amount of paper work, scribbling out his decisions in margins and on backs of envelopes in a hand that was notoriously undecipherable. Like Mustafa, he was a gifted in-fighter, suspicious, strait-laced, and cunning. Like Mustafa, he trusted no one (or hardly anyone) and found it painful to delegate authority; the most routine decisions were often delayed until he found time to consider them. He differed from the Arab in one very important particular. Calvin Hampshire was a devout Unitarian; Mustafa ibn Mabrouk's devotion to Islam was considerably less intense. They were both, of course, prodigious workers. The youthful Arab was tireless; the Secretary was no longer as fortunate—in fact, the burden of his problems and the accumulation of so many nineteen-hour days over so many years had taxed his rather frail frame to the limits of endurance. Although the same age as Ambassador Fitzgibbon, the Secretary looked at least fifteen years older. And he felt it, too, today; he removed his spectacles and rubbed his eyes. Through the open window, he heard General Obfuster wondering out loud where the Secretary and Paul Pullmotor were, and when the meeting would begin. That Pullmotor! What in heaven's name was keeping him?

The Secretary took a book from his desk and returned it to the shelves along the wall. It was Spengler's *Decline of the West,* and he inserted it between Asquith's *Addresses* and Langer's *Diplomacy of Imperialism.* Ordinarily the Spengler would go between the Gibbon and the Toynbee, but the Secretary was rather farsighted, and he had left his spectacles on the desk. This was an excellent library, and as he lingered among his books Calvin Hampshire could congratulate himself on having read at least half of them, surely a commendable accomplishment for a man so active. He could—and often did—quote knowledgeably and at length from Lord Acton, Admiral Mahan, Karl Marx, Metternich, Gladstone, Tawney, Wheeler-Bennett, and from Bismarck's *Gedanken und Erinnerungen.* Carlyle's *History of the French Revolution,* Talleyrand's *Memoires,* Plutarch's *Lives,* Belloc's *Richelieu,* and Churchill's *Life of Marlborough* were among his favorites. He was less at home with Herodotus, Plato, Bacon, Descartes, and Hegel, but even among these his dabbling had been, as with everything else he chose to touch, extremely systematic.

For there was in Calvin Hampshire very little left of the shallow and flippant youth whom Shawnie Fitzgibbon remembered from their years together at Harvard. Even today, Shawnie's opinion of the Secretary failed to do him justice. True, Calvin had been an indifferent student; true, he had from the start exploited his exalted connections and gained glamorous assignments in the choicest capitals of Europe. But favoritism of that sort was commonplace, and it could hardly have carried him as high as he had come. Calvin's brilliance was of the kind which is born of experience and which ripens in the middle years. In the beginning, his written reports were merely pompous; with time and tenacity, they were penetrating as well. He had been one of the first American diplomats to recognize the menace of Hitler and to predict with chilling accuracy the direction his rule would take. Calvin's tour in Berlin was followed by equally indefatigable service in Vienna, Paris, London, and Washington. He learned to speak good German and passable French. By the end of the war he had earned, at the age of forty, and only partially as the result of his inherited wealth, the ambassadorship to Paris; he became Secretary of State less than a decade later. Since then it had been occasionally suggested that his firm grasp of European problems did not always extend to the complexities of the world beyond—that he attempted to deal with Orientals as if they were Scandinavians, expecting them to behave according to the accepted conventions of continental diplomacy. "Mr. Hampshire cares only for Europe—that is all he understands," the President of Pakistan once publicly complained. This kind of criticism offended and puzzled the Secretary. He considered himself, with some reason, the custodian of Western civilization. He interpreted his mandate largely as one of pedagogy and edification; he had been chosen to instruct the brown and black and yellow races in the responsibilities of statecraft and the defense of Christendom.

Every man who aspires to the mountain peaks of Power is animated by a vision, a glimpse of the purpose which Destiny has appointed him to pursue. Such visions are very often revealed in symbolic and unfamiliar forms, and their meaning may at first elude the recipient. For Mustafa ibn Mabrouk, the apocalypse had been a common queue of Londoners waiting for a bus, but he realized at once that in this image he must remake the personality of his own people. For Sean Sebastian Fitzgibbon, the apocalypse had come on the shores of the Red Sea, when he sat in the afterglow of the Zodiac and supped with some biblical fishermen on loaves and fishes; but it had been several years before Sean recognized in that experience the foreshadowing of the career he would squander in the deserts of Moses, expiating the apostasy of his youth. Calvin Hampshire's apocalypse had been even more elliptical, and it was half a lifetime before he fathomed its depth of meaning. It had come when he was very young, still a student at Harvard, during that summer of the grand tour with Shawnie, after he had abandoned Sean in the Middle East and returned alone to Italy. It had happened in Venice, in the Palace of the Doges. There, in one of the exhibition rooms overlooking the Square of St. Mark, was the most extraordinary collection of chastity belts.

Calvin had been caught up in a group of elderly British ladies, and he stood there in the midst of them, as horrified and enthralled as they, while a guide recalled in broken English the history of these ingenious appliances. Pride of place was given to a fourteenth-century model from the castle of Francesco di Carrara, the Tyrant of Padua; in it had been imprisoned not only the Tyrant's spouse but a succession of his concubines—and what an incredible piece of craftsmanship it was, with its porcupine exterior and dangling rusty chains. Before leaving Venice Calvin came across another chastity belt, inexpensive in price but odious in aspect, for sale in a curiosity shop. Purely as a prank, he bought it, and brought it home to Boston. His father—a patron of the Watch and Ward Society—was fascinated; his mother would not have it in the house. So he hung it up on the wall of his room at Harvard. It quickly became standard equipment at all Hasty Pudding parties.

When Calvin returned to Europe as a young diplomat, he continued from time to time to purchase additional specimens of this macabre contraption. Rebecca, his wife, was aghast; he persevered. By the end of his tenure as Ambassador to Paris, Calvin Hampshire owned one of the finest collections of chastity belts in Europe. He had acquired them from impoverished museums in Cluny and Brussels, from the Paris Flea Market and the Madrid Rastro, from the junk dealers of Genoa and the jaded eccentrics of Riviera society. They were of every style and decoration, and in terms of antiquity they spanned the Third Crusade to the Storming of the Bastille. There were Italian models made of leathern pouches and bristling armor shields. There were French *pergamesques,* fashioned of flexible metal and upholstered in velvet. One which had been worn by the Marquise de Verneuil, paramour of Henri IV, had no fewer than six locks, all of purest silver. Another, the raiment of Catherine de' Medici, was a mixture of perforated ivory and impenetrable steel, engraved with arabesques. The paragon of Calvin's collection was a belt from the harem of the Tyrant of Padua himself. It was a sort of bloomer, woven of black iron wire, its outer surface garnished with gargoyles, gothic inscriptions, and innumerable claws and spikes twisting upward in tormented patterns; in the rear was a padlock, diabolically large.

But as he had so often explained to bewildered friends and dumbfounded strangers, Calvin considered the belts nothing more than comic conversation pieces—his way, he jested, of keeping his wife in harness. It was not until he became Secretary of State that the more metaphysical importance of his youthful experience in Venice became clear to him. Now, as Secretary, he was confronted with the pitiless complexity of containing international communism. The Moloch was poised to devour what remained of the Far East, and already the outer ramparts of Europe's bastion were beginning to crumble. In his very purposeful and methodical mind, Calvin Hampshire pondered the problem for three nearly sleepless nights. He thought, "We are going to be destroyed unless I stop them." Lying alone in bed, he slipped occasionally into anguished fantasy: and always the same vision returned to him, the vision of that room in the Palace of the Doges. He awoke trembling, realized what he had to do, and then wrote an article about it for the *Saturday Evening Post*. It was entitled "For the Free World, a Chastity Belt," and was at once recognized as a classic document of the Cold War. The Secretary opened by recalling the genesis and growth of his private collection, and went on to suggest how cogently his little hobby symbolized what he wished to achieve in foreign policy. In a crescendo of metaphors, he proposed to construct, from Casablanca to Singapore, a ring of fortifications impenetrable as padlocks, of rockets spike-shaped, of air forces gargoyle-fierce, "preserving virgin and inviolate the non-Marxist nations from the rapacity of concupiscent communism."

The new policy was applauded in America and in wide sectors of European opinion; elsewhere it was not as enthusiastically received. Moscow responded with a torrent of threats. The non-European capitals expressed open misgivings. The liberal weeklies of London lampooned the Secretary for what they hastened to label his "chastity-beltmanship"—a phrase which became a part of the living language, but which did not deter Calvin Hampshire. Unpopularity, caricature, ridicule—what did it matter so long as he did what had to be done? He had long since abandoned the myopia of mere ambition, of seeking esteem among men, for a stewardship which was not entirely of this world. And that stewardship had a life of its own, antennae of its own, which however intangible far outreached those of less consecrated men. *We are going to be destroyed unless I stop them.* The sleepless nights, the infested days, the venom of his critics—they had become the adrenalin of deeds which it had been given him to do. For the most amazing thing about Calvin Hampshire's strategy was that it had succeeded. It had not been easy; he had been obliged to be as generous with money as with guns; governments that could not be persuaded sometimes had to be cajoled; but within three years he had what he wanted: a chastity belt of bases, trussing up the world. The advance of communism had been arrested. At a dinner one evening in Windsor Castle, the Duke of Norfolk congratulated the Secretary on the vindication of his global doctrine. "Don't thank me, Your Grace," Calvin Hampshire chuckled. "Thank the Tyrant of Padua."

Now the Secretary stood before the open glass cabinet in his study, absent-mindedly fidgeting with his collection, wondering how far he would be compelled to go in rebuking the upstart in Al Khadra. (Preoccupied, and clumsy without his spectacles, he cuts a finger on the Tyrant of Padua's jagged claws. Blood. He puts his finger to his mouth for a moment, and then slowly wraps a white handkerchief around the wound.) He remembered the one occasion, more than two years ago, when he had met Mustafa ibn Mabrouk. It had not happened under the most ideal circumstances. The Secretary, en route to Bangkok, landed for an hour in Al Asima to refuel, and Mustafa came out to the airport to meet him. Calvin Hampshire was prepared to be impressed; in fact he had supported the youthful Prime Minister from the start, mostly on Paul Pullmotor's recommendation. Mustafa arrived ten minutes late, and they sat down alone together in the threadbare VIP lounge. The Arab seemed to be everything Paul had promised: dashing, intelligent, incorruptible—the sort of fellow you instinctively want to have on your side.

And yet for some reason they did not get on; somehow these two brilliant men could not find a common language. It was not Mustafa's English; he was perfectly at home in that respect, with a faint British accent musical to the ear, and syntax less rambling than the Secretary's own. No, the difficulty had been in points of view: a disparity of personal visions, of apocalypse. Despite a splitting headache, Calvin Hampshire had tried very hard not to seem schoolmasterish as he set out to explain the compulsions of global strategy. Communism, he began, was the great enemy, not only of America but of all mankind, and in collective defense lay the world's one hope. The Prime Minister listened respectfully for a few minutes, and then interrupted with a question about chemical fertilizers. Fertilizers were on Mustafa's mind that week; he needed them quickly and in great quantity. "That is the sort of thing you should take up with Ambassador Fitzgibbon." The Secretary smiled, turning the conversation back to the horrors of Sovietism. The Prime Minister interrupted again with a discourse on his agricultural problems, embellishing practically every paragraph with quotations from Gibbon and Carlyle. Apparently he believed these might sway the Secretary, but Calvin Hampshire found them merely pretentious and tiresome, and irrelevant to the more important matters he wished to discuss. And so they continued for nearly an hour, the American talking about communism, the Arab about fertilizers, until it was time for the Secretary to go to Bangkok. On the way to the plane, Calvin Hampshire remarked, "Your Excellency seems to be well acquainted with Western culture."

"Oh, I've dabbled a bit," the Prime Minister replied. "Best of both worlds and all that. And you, Mr. Secretary?"

"You mean your literature? I'm afraid I don't know very much about it. I read the *Arabian Nights* once. In translation, of course."

"Of course."

Such had been their single confrontation. The relations between the two governments deteriorated from that day. The Secretary read carefully most of Ambassador Fitzgibbon's subsequent despatches, and he was made well aware of Mustafa ibn Mabrouk's continuing and far-reaching domestic reforms. But laudable as they were, how much had they contributed to the greater struggle? And now the Khadrian Prime Minister had committed the greatest of crimes: he had broken the strategic chastity belt, or rather he had helped the Russians to leap over it, establishing themselves in the very womb of the Middle East. That sort of political promiscuity could not—at any cost—be allowed to spread. *We are going to be destroyed unless I stop them.* The Secretary regretted now that he had called this afternoon's meeting, for it did not really matter: his mind was made up: he knew what had to be done. He had no choice; while the world watched and drew the lesson, Mustafa ibn Mabrouk must be chastened—drastically. But how to do that decently, and with honor?

Calvin Hampshire returned to his desk, put on his spectacles, and looked out again into the garden. Pullmotor had not come. It would be discourteous to the others to delay the meeting any longer. A batch of documents and position papers under his arm, the Secretary of State went downstairs to determine the destiny of the Arabs.

Everyone stood when the Secretary came into the garden. When he had exhausted his little hellos, he chose a chair at random and sat down at the glass-topped table. The others, despite the informality of the occasion, arranged themselves around him according to rank; the Junior Bright Young Men automatically formed an outer circle. To his dismay, the Secretary found himself sandwiched between the Acting Chief of Naval Operations and General Obfuster.

"I see some new faces here today," Calvin Hampshire began pleasantly. "Or should I rather say I see some fine old faces—some fine old friends—home from the wars? They don't look any the worse for wear and tear!" (Pause. Faint laughter.) "General Obfuster, I know I needn't tell you how much we all appreciate the devoted work you have done in Paris. Welcome back. We hope you enjoy your new assignment."

"Mr. Secretary," General Obfuster replied, "I—"

"And to Ambassador Fitzgibbon, may I also extend a—uh —*sincere* welcome home? I need hardly embarrass you, Shawnie, by belaboring the *sort* of esteem in which this distinguished company holds you."

"Thank you, Mr. Secretary, I—"

"I regret of course that due to the dinner for Prime Minister Papadopoulos last night and a number of equally urgent matters this morning, I have not yet had the opportunity to chat with you, but I'm confident we can steal a few minutes before I leave for La Paz. Now, as to all these reports here, I've been reading them, and I must say that I found them fascinating, so fascinating in fact that I forgot what time it was, and now I'm late to my own shooting match—or rather, rowing race!" (Pause. Hearty laughter.) "But I do want to congratulate all of you gentlemen for adhering to your habitual standards of excellence in preparing these penetrating position papers. As a result of these assessments, and, if I may say so, of my own experience in previous matters of this sort, I find that I cannot conceal from you gentlemen my very real distress over the exacerbated direction of events in Al Khadra. I have very carefully reviewed the chronology of our relations with the Khadrian government during the last several years, and I am persuaded that the trend there which is becoming progressively in evidence is due to no obduracy or delinquency on our part. We have, after all, contributed nearly one hundred million dollars to Al Khadra since the present regime came to power three years ago, and we have been more than forbearing in the face of its unprovoked and increasingly virulent criticism. Ambassador Fitzgibbon has done a—uh—*painstaking* and *earnest* job under extremely trying conditions, and I appreciate how very painful the present picture must be to him, especially in view of the very strenuous labor he has expended in the past in behalf of—with a view to—securing the friendship and good faith of the Government of Al Khadra. The challenge we face in Al Khadra today reminds me very much of the intransigence which Viscount Castlereagh confronted vis-a-vis the Government of Norway following the Congress of Vienna. There are some striking parallels, in this context, that—"

"NEVER MIND, ROSCOE, I'M IN HOME WATERS!" From within the Georgian house the jolly, shameless voice invaded the garden. The gentlemen at the table sat up with a start. The Secretary, who was not in the habit of being interrupted, continued talking. "In this context, that—"

The screen door sprang open. Paul Pullmotor, clad only in white sneakers and tan Bermuda shorts, toddled into the garden brandishing a tennis racket. "Four-six, six-four, seven-five against the Vice President!" he exulted, playfully bouncing his racket off Calvin Hampshire's stately gray head. "The V.P. insisted on a rematch. Creamed him!"

"Outrageous!" General Obfuster protested. It was indeed, especially in view of the Secretary's notorious aversion to the Vice President.

Outwardly serene, the Secretary finished his sentence. Without looking up, he added, "I wish you would try to come to these meetings on time."

"It won't happen again, Calvin," Paul Pullmotor promised with mock gravity. Like a scolded child, he retreated to a lonely aluminum chair by the zinnia patch.

There was a respectful silence again as the Secretary tried to retrieve his train of thought. The words would not come; he looked up, his grumpy countenance suddenly benign as he smiled at Pullmotor. "You rascal!" he said.

But the Pullmotor strategy now was to sulk, to pretend ignorance, to delay committing himself until he knew more precisely how everyone else stood on the issues at hand. "What's this clambake all about?" he grumbled.

"Yes," the Secretary resumed, "I believe I had just established the very clear analogy between the crisis which the British Government faced vis-a-vis the Government of Norway in 1815, and the situation as it obtains today between ourselves and the Government of Al Khadra. As I believe I demonstrated, the Norwegian Government was clearly pursuing an obstructive policy with regard to the Napoleonic menace, and Lord Castlereagh had no alternative but to rescind certain tentative commitments His Majesty's Government had made to Norway, to cancel some prospective purchases of Norwegian timber, and to threaten certain other economic sanctions of a more general character. Now there exist a number of other precedents for this distasteful but perfectly proper international practice, and I wonder, Clarence, whether you would care to refresh my memory."

"I'm trying to think of some," the Secretary's legal counselor said. "We took a similar position against Tamasese, the Usurper of Samoa, in 1887, when he encouraged German incursions to the detriment of American interests in the islands, but it wasn't quite the same thing."

"Yes, I remember that," the Secretary said. "I also seem to recall that we applied sanctions to Mexico in 1925 when the Calles Government repudiated the Bucareli Agreement, revived the confiscatory clauses of 1917, and encouraged the pro-communist insurrectionists in Nicaragua. Any workable parallel there, Clarence?"

"It would be a bit fudgy, Mr. Secretary. The ibn Mabrouk Government hasn't expropriated any of the American companies in Al Khadra, at least not yet. Let me think. The Zelaya regime was suspected of conspiring with Japan for the construction of an alternate isthmian canal linking the San Juan River to the Pacific Ocean. That, together with the harassment of American concessionaires, led us to sever diplomatic relations in 1909 and to support an insurrectionist faction—but I don't believe you intend to go that far in Al Khadra, do you?"

"How about the crisis of 1901—excuse me, 1902—with Venezuela?" volunteered one of the Senior Bright Young Men.

"Wouldn't you say the Khadrian situation corresponds more to our difficulties with the Marroquín regime in Colombia in 1903?" interjected one of the Junior Bright Young Men.

"Of course, there's the embargo on scrap iron to Japan—"

"And the 1938 blockade against the Reich—"

And so it went, around the table, until the legal counselor interrupted with an irritable, "Yes, yes, but each of them deals with a different problem."

"I suggest you do a little more homework on it, Clarence," the

Secretary said. "I don't want to get caught off base with regard to the legalities."

General Obfuster started to speak, but at that moment the black men brought more brownies and iced beverages, reducing to total chaos the already confused point the General wished to make. (This looked accidental, but was not. The Secretary's servants were under standing orders to make as much commotion as possible whenever a Pentagon official was talking.) The Secretary asked for a map of the Middle East; a pair of the Junior Bright Young Men collided in the frenzy to find one; an Assistant Secretary came to the rescue with a crude drawing on a very small piece of paper. Everyone except Ambassador Fitzgibbon and Paul Pullmotor clustered around the Secretary, straining to look over his shoulder while he marked up the drawing and delivered a little lecture on geopolitics. He asked a number of questions. The answers he received were quick and well-informed; it did not matter; he did not interrupt his lecture long enough to listen. But by the time he had discarded the drawing and the others had returned to their chairs, the Secretary's intentions toward Al Khadra were clear enough. Among his advisers, a blurred but decipherable division of view began to emerge. The Pentagon people and others, eager to meet the Soviet challenge head on, welcomed the prospect of stern economic measures against the government of Mustafa ibn Mabrouk. The State people were not as enthusiastic. The idea of sanctions seemed to distress the Middle East specialists in particular, although they took care to veil their misgivings in verbiage and indirection.

Ambassador Fitzgibbon, who had remained silent throughout the meeting, decided it was now or never. "I don't want to be a party poop," he said, "but I wonder whether I might make a comment?"

"Why of course, Shawnie," the Secretary said. "After all, that's why I called you back—so that you might assist us in coming to a decision."

"I haven't got a degree in international jurisprudence," the Ambassador began, "so I'm afraid most of today's meeting has gone over my head. But unless I've misunderstood, we are canceling our agreement to give the people of Al Khadra the bread and medicine we promised them. Unless I've misunderstood, we intend to halt all other aid to Al Khadra and to suspend our purchases of Khadrian figs and pomegranates. Apparently we also plan to line up a number of other nations to impose some sort of economic blockade on Al Khadra as a reprisal for Mustafa's—Prime Minister ibn Mabrouk's—decision to accept Soviet aid. The geopolitical argument, as I understand it, is that ibn Mabrouk has jeopardized Western global strategy and the local balance of power by introducing the Soviet presence into his country, and that the infection must be isolated before it contaminates his neighbors."

"That's about it, Shawnie—more or less," the Secretary said.

"Thank you. Will I be out of order if I express some reservations about this policy? I regret as much as anyone the fact that Brigadier ibn Mabrouk has signed an agreement with the Russians. I did everything I could to prevent it. At the same time I'm convinced that sooner or later it was bound to happen. For one thing, we were simply not willing to give him as much money as he needed for his development plan. I do not share the view that by accepting Soviet aid he will become a tool of atheistic communism—did our aid make him an apostle of American materialism? I am under no illusions about this man. He's an opportunist, a demagogue, and, I suppose, a dictator—not exactly the type who appeals to Lord Beaverbrook and Harry Luce, although God knows I'd like to see *them* go into that chaotic country and run it as well as he has. Unfortunately this is an imperfect world, and the paradox of Mustafa ibn Mabrouk is that he is a deplorable statesman and a good ruler—probably the best ruler Al Khadra ever had, in fact. If he's not as sensitive as we are to the perils of Soviet imperialism, it could be that Soviet imperialism doesn't have all that much to do with the great problems—poverty, superstition, disease—he is struggling to overcome."

"Same old Shawnie," the Secretary smiled. "Full of Gaelic eloquence."

"I consider that a compliment, of course. As for this scheme to bring Al Khadra to her senses, I am not, I hope, naïve enough to object to it on moral grounds, or because it may make millions of people even hungrier than they are already. I have never thought that sentiment had any pride of place in relations between governments. I trust also that I am as capable as the next fellow of making the ethical compromises required by the national interest. My misgivings are not moral, ethical, sentimental, or for that matter even humane. I dissent from the policy for a much simpler and more cynical reason—it won't work."

"Hear! Hear!" exclaimed Paul Pullmotor.

"Balls!" exclaimed General Obfuster. "They'll fold in a week."

"You don't seem to have much respect for my determination to make it work," the Secretary observed quietly. "Frankly, I find your views rather partisan."

Exhilarated by the unexpected support from Pullmotor—or was Paul simply teasing him, baiting him on?—the Ambassador leaned forward earnestly on the glass-topped table, and continued. "On the contrary, Mr. Secretary, Mustafa has set a trap for us, and that we should step into it is the very thing I'm trying to prevent. We're not dealing with Rebecca of Sunnybrook Farm, you know. As a student of power politics, the Prime Minister of Al Khadra is probably as well read as anyone at this table. There is hardly a trick from Nebuchadnezzar to Rasputin that he hasn't analyzed in terms of his own needs. But it's not so much his intellect which frightens me—it's his intuitive talent for intrigue, the cunning which came with his mother's milk and his Bedouin blood. He seems to have inherited every artifice ever practiced by a people who have lived on guile since the dawn of history. Nothing gives him greater pleasure than to play games of chance—the more risky and tangled they are, the more they amuse him. The fact that his is a weak nation, and ours a great one, simply intensifies in his mind the temptation to make mischief—"to be nimble like the gnat on the carcass of the clumsy elephant," if I may quote one of his more graphic figures of speech. As you said, we've been quite generous to him in the past. Why do you suppose he has now unleashed against us this barrage of slander and signed a pact with our enemies? It is because he is counting on the very crisis which this new policy of ours promises to give him. He *wants* us to condemn him to the four corners of the earth. He *wants* us to wage economic war on him. It will give him the justification he needs to make life in the Middle East a living nightmare for us. It will raise the stakes that much higher—it will double or even triple the price he is gambling he can make us pay to get him to stop."

The expression on the Secretary's face was not very encouraging. He asked, "I presume you have an alternative policy to suggest?"

"Give him the wheat and medicine. Deny him the starvation argument. Accept the Soviet incursion as a fact of life for the moment. Sit tight until the Russians and Mustafa tire of one another. They will, you know—and when he has gotten what he wants out of them he'll begin abusing them as he has abused us. Above all, we should *keep quiet*. Serenity wouldn't change our objectives, only our tactics. There doesn't have to be a crisis unless we want one. Later on, perhaps in six months or so, when Mustafa sees that we haven't swallowed his bait, we can probably come to some sort of arrangement on price. I'm confident it will be a lot more reasonable than the one we'll pay if we pursue this policy of reprisal. Now, as to specific steps—"

Ambassador Fitzgibbon had much more to say, but he stopped in mid-sentence. The Secretary had signaled to the servants to bring more refreshments, and now they were making another commotion at the table, rattling glassware, banging ash trays empty, asking loudly what everyone wanted. The Ambassador knew exactly what this meant: he was being publicly reduced to the nuisance category of General Obfuster. He felt a stab of anger. His face reddened. All eyes were on him. In an instant he relived all the real and imagined humiliations, all the snide telegrams and condescending bombast he had endured, down the years, from Calvin Hampshire. But he could not endure this. He hesitated. He decided. He rose awkwardly from his chair, bowed very slightly toward his host and said, "Mr. Secretary." He turned to the others and said, "Gentlemen."

Then he walked out of the meeting.

Behind him, he left a delicious silence. Paul Pullmotor was the first to speak. "I think we'd all be making a mistake if we sold Shawnie short," he said. "Shawnie is an extremely dedicated man."

"I quite agree with you," the Secretary said.

"Shawnie is a dedicated man," Pullmotor continued. "Second-guessing a fox like Mustafa ibn Mabrouk is no picnic, and I think that all things considered Shawnie has done his best. Shawnie's been working under tremendous pressure, remember, and yet in spite of that and all his personal problems he seems to have cut down on his drinking. I will confess that at times I've wondered whether this Khadrian situation was quite Shawnie's sort of thing, but give him a job he can do and he'll never let you down."

The Secretary grunted and asked, "Now, where were we?"

The conference ran its course. "I want all agencies to coordinate closely, an effective effort on all fronts," Calvin Hampshire said. "I think we had better research some of the more lurid aspects of Prime Minister ibn Mabrouk's record, and leak it to the *Times*. Special emphasis on his leftist connections when he was in London, and on those Marxist advisers he has been appointing to his Ministry of Planning. Compile all his pro-Soviet statements of the past year and put that out, too. You might also suggest that, in exchange for all that heavy machinery, he's mortgaged his economy to Moscow—that sort of thing. What else can we do on the psychological side?"

"Quite a bit, Mr. Secretary," the man from the Mutual Understanding Commission said. "We've got some sizzling radio scripts all ready to go, and a comic book on Mabrouk that should knock 'em dead."

A butterfly alighted on General Obfuster's ear. "They'll fold in a week," the General said, his hand poised to crush the little creature. "In a *week*."

When the others had gone, and he was alone with Pullmotor, the Secretary said, "Fitzgibbon's argument is not entirely without merit. I'm no more anxious for a crisis than he is, and I don't enjoy making people hungry any more than he does. What he fails to understand is that ibn Mabrouk's reaction, as troublesome as it may prove to be, isn't all that important. It's the Russians I'm worried about. If they see me sitting by twiddling my thumbs, looking the other way while they move into Al Khadra, the next thing we know they'll be moving into the rest of the Middle East. And what of all the other countries howling like wolves at the gate? Threatening to go to Moscow if we don't double and triple our present generosity? If I allowed ibn Mabrouk to get away with all his blackmail—that would be a lovely lesson for them, wouldn't it? Too bad Shawnie doesn't read the cables that bombard me every morning from ninety different capitals. That would cure him of his parochialism in a jiffy! But you mystify me, Paul. Why in heaven's name did you cry 'Hear! Hear!' when he said my policy wouldn't work?"

"Because," Pullmotor replied, "he was right."

"Right?"

"Dead right. Come off it, Calvin, this dainty little sanctions plan of yours hasn't a Chinaman's chance of succeeding, and you know it. It will only drive Mustafa to insane reprisals, make him more popular with his own people, and entrench him more deeply in power than ever before. We'll be worse off than when we started. You've read my report?"

"Yes."

"Then you know we've got to act quickly. Mustafa is playing for keeps, shooting the whole pot—just as Fitzgibbon said."

"The blockade should trim his sails."

"Come off it, Calvin."

The Secretary grunted again. "What are you getting at?" he asked.

"It shouldn't be too difficult to pull off. I've already done the spadework, and I'm returning to Al Khadra tonight to iron out the details. Of course, when Mustafa is behind bars, I'll have to find someone to take his place, but I can cross that bridge when I come to it. The main stumbling block at the moment is the King. The poor boy is still stuck on Mustafa. But when we confront him with an accomplished—"

"I haven't heard a word you said, Paul," Calvin Hampshire interrupted wearily.

"—fact, I think he'll come around. It's all too bad, in a way. I'll never forgive Mustafa for double-crossing me after all I did for him, but I still love the guy. We're peas of a pod, you know. It shouldn't be too difficult. I've been in contact with the Bedouin tribes. They're starving and desperate and ready to go along. Now, as soon as I get back, I'm sending my best man, a fellow called—"

"Paul. After all, what are we fighting for? What does America mean? Does the end justify the means? Of course, in the context of the global struggle, there *is* the principle of legitimate self-defense, but that could be invoked only under the most extraordinary circumstances. I'm leaving on Monday for La Paz. From

there to Bonn, and then on to Manila for the conference. I'm going to be gone a good two weeks, Paul, and when I get back I'm not anxious to find my *In* box cluttered with a lot of nasty business about Al Khadra. In the meantime, the economic blockade will go forward. You know I think highly of your ability, Paul. I'm confident that on your end you can find a way of dealing with this problem in an honorable, tidy, and effective fashion. More effectively than Shawnie Fitzgibbon, I'm sure."

"By the way, Calvin, what are you going to do with Fitzgibbon?"

"Let him return to Al Asima, I suppose."

"After that little scene he just made?"

"I was going to keep him here, change his assignment. But if I did that now—after he walked out—it would look vindictive. I'm not a vindictive man, Paul. He'll have trouble living this incident down. Let's leave it at that, for the time being. What does the desert do to these Irishmen, anyway?"

Rebecca Hampshire came out into the garden again. "You boys!" she laughed. "Always talking shop! Paul, don't you look darling in your Bermuda shorts! What happened to Shawnie?"

"I think he had another appointment," Pullmotor said.

"Oh, Calvin, you know how *much* I wanted him to stay for a chat. I've always liked Shawnie! Well, we'll just have to do it another time. Paul, I'm going to kick you out now! Calvin is going to lie down for his nap, and then I'm taking him for a nice drive in the country . . ."

Ambassador Fitzgibbon wrote out his resignation in the margin of an old newspaper he found on the floor of his taxi. He had the driver drop him several blocks from Foggy Bottom. He resolved to walk the rest of the way to the Department, type out the terse statement, and sign it. It was better to walk, to walk out the rage he had only barely managed to control in Calvin Hampshire's garden. He wanted to enter the Department and announce his decision with cool malevolence. Cool? He was beside himself. *Why did I let them lead me on? Have I ever been so clumsy? So unprofessional?*

He found himself in a shopping district, zippered by chromium bumpers, picketed with parking meters, garish with gasoline stations, supermarkets and beauty parlors. He looked around him, and longed for the bog-trotters of Islam—the grating cart wheels, the braying donkeys, the barefoot baksheesh boys, the junk peddlers, the mendicant musicians, the bootblacks, the howling women, the policemen pissing on walls, the medley of smells. *No. You will have to give up all that. All that and your palace in Al Asima and your entourage of servants and third secretaries and bodyguards and everything else. You will take an efficiency flat in Chevy Chase and after a while they will invite you to join a Foundation and on weekends you will go up to Boston to visit your sister.*

He passed an appliance shop where they were displaying electric home shoe-shiners and television sets, all of them turned on. An aspirin commercial flashed from one screen, and against the inside of a man's skull a great black hammer pounded without pity. On another channel an effeminate comedian tossed his playmate into an immense lemon meringue pie. The playmate emerged from the pie, slipping, squishing, lunging his way toward the Ambassador. *You will take an efficiency flat in Chevy Chase and on weekends you will go up to Boston to visit your sister.*

KEEP WASHINGTON CLEAN. He fumbled in his pocket for the fragment of newspaper, tore it with methodical violence into tiny pieces, and threw them into the receptacle. *I am still an Ambassador . . . I hope.* He needed a drink. And some fresh fish. He wanted to see Eminence Grise. He hastened to a telephone and made inquiries about the first flight to Al Asima.

13

Mustafa ibn Mabrouk was not being outdone in the matter of meetings. At midnight, in his spartan chambers on the second floor of his Ministry, he convened thirty or so of his advisers to consider countermeasures against the Americans. He conducted most of his conferences in the late evening, when it was normally somewhat cooler; but Al Asima, like Washington, was in the grip of a heat wave, and there was not even a breeze on the broad Mabrouk tonight.

Mustafa opened the meeting by telling his associates, very matter-of-factly and without his usual embellishments, "My brothers, it is now clear from American press despatches, and from warnings I have received from our Ambassador in Washington, that Mr. Hampshire intends to bring Al Khadra to her knees. We are not going to get that American wheat—at least not for the moment. And I expect that all other American aid will be cut off—at least for the moment. Hampshire will probably attempt as well to impose all kinds of criminal pressures against us—perhaps even worse. Fine! If it's a fight he wants, I intend to give him a good one." Now he sat impassively behind his steel desk while, one by one, army officers in the room leaped up from their wooden chairs and unleashed impassioned little diatribes against the United States. ". . . we will annihilate them, O Mustafa! . . . you are the refuge of the oppressed, O Mustafa! . . . God give you victory, O Mustafa! . . ." This was a kind of catharsis, a ballet of the emotions that had to be danced out before any serious business could be considered. The Prime Minister would have preferred not to waste the time, but he knew the innate needs of the Arab psyche. It was part of his genius that from the mercurial chemistry at his disposal he could concoct a cult of blind obedience, and convert hyperbole into action. This wild castle-building rhetoric was simply the Arabic analogy of the juridical gymnastics that had gone on in Calvin Hampshire's garden. At the present stage of their political development, Mustafa's men felt no compulsion to festoon decisions already arrived at with the frills of legalism; they were immune to precocious precedents and to all the sublime clichés of European diplomacy. As for the Congress of Vienna, half of them had never heard of it.

The group assembled in the Prime Minister's office would have made an interesting study in sociological contrast. Most of Mustafa's confreres—he had no intimates—were army officers. He depended on the officers mainly to enforce decisions rather than to make them. Still, much of his personal strength rested on his willingness to listen to a lot of unnecessary advice and to sustain these men in the conviction that their opinions were important —which indeed they sometimes were. He had carefully chosen the ablest and most loyal of the young officer class, made them ministers and directors-general, presidents of banks and boards and corporations. They were energetic and generally honest, but their performances did not always please him. Unlike their leader, they were not addicted to sitting up most of the night devouring books on European history, Keynesian economics, and agrarian reform. Some of them were outright boobs, and retained their posts only because more talented replacements were in short supply.

Just last week, the incompetence of his Water Commissioner had resulted in a ruptured pipeline and a day-long drought in the capital. The Prime Minister privately docked the man a month's pay, and publicly blamed the mishap on "imperialist sabotage"—a shibboleth which no one found more tiresome than Mustafa did himself. Tiresome, and—during this tormented stage of national development—utterly indispensable.

Not all of Mustafa's advisers were soldiers. He depended almost as much on his civilian specialists, that select community of technicians who kept his economy going and his Five-Year Plan from falling apart. About a dozen of these specialists were here now, from various ministries. He surmised they disapproved of the more daring policies which he handed them to carry out; like their opposite numbers in the American Department of State, they took care to veil their misgivings in verbiage and indirection. The older technicians were generally Oxonians, the younger ones often Harvard men. The Harvard Arabs despised the soldiers (the feeling was mutual), wore American-cut suits, horn-rimmed spectacles, and carried attaché cases. They were the Bright Young Men of Islam, the vanguard of that mushrooming middle class which Mustafa was struggling to strengthen and expand. Most of Mustafa's specialists were competent; some were brilliant. Slowly, it was these machine-tooled technicians who were replacing the corrupt, coffee-slurping Mish Mish Effendis of the bureaucracy. Mustafa knew that as time passed, as the country industrialized and as the machinery of government became ever more complicated, real power would begin to pass more and more from the officers—and even from himself—into the hands of the Harvard Arabs. He was resigned to this; indeed he was planning the constitutional progress of the country to coincide with it; but he also knew that in the *meantime* only the iron and omnipotent force of his own personality could hold the country together and impose order where chaos would otherwise prevail.

Thus, as of this moment, for this midnight meeting in Mustafa's austere office, it was the soldiers rather than the technicians who had pride of place and did most of the talking; it was the soldiers who sat up front nearest Mustafa; the Harvard Arabs kept their own counsel in the back of the room, and regarded the histrionics of the officers with a bemused silence. ". . . we will burn down the American Embassy, O Mustafa! . . . we will scuttle the Sixth Fleet, O Mustafa! . . ." Sitting on either side of the Prime Minister were the two men upon whose services he depended most. To his right was Captain Anwar A'war, his military aide and man Friday, and the most efficient—though hardly the most intelligent—of his immediate entourage. Captain A'war had also attended Sandhurst and spoke English with a British accent markedly more pronounced than Mustafa's own. With his light skin, waxed mustache and preposterous eye patch, he could easily have posed for a Grenadier Guards recruitment poster. Beauty is skin deep; the liberal press of London and New York habitually identified Captain A'war as "Brigadier ibn Mabrouk's hatchet man." Captain A'war was probably the second most powerful person in Al Khadra, and certainly the most disliked. He attended to a great many of those tasks, distasteful but necessary, which the Prime Minister found unsuited to his own temperament. Captain A'war headed military intelligence, personally conducted the interrogation of important political prisoners and supervised the administration of the notorious desert penitentiaries (where, curiously, at least half the inmates were communists). He had a reputation for cruelty; in fact he was only ruthless.

To the Prime Minister's left sat Rifaat Taj, the octogenarian ex-Vizier. No one loved Taj Pasha either. Indeed everyone—and Mustafa most of all—despised him. He was corrupt, ill-tempered, and dissolute. His advanced age (he was eighty-six) had not diminished his manly vigor, his harem, or his fabled predilection for very young virgins; only last week he had exchanged conjugal vows with a fourteen-year-old. He was believed to dabble in black magic. Taj Pasha had no ideology, no scruples, and no heart; his only reverence was for power, and his loyalty belonged only to whomever happened to wield power at the moment; his genius, as they say, was for survival. He had been Prime Minister of Al Khadra nearly twenty times; he had served King and conqueror, colonial and xenophobe; he had pandered to the Sublime Porte and collaborated with the British; he had outlasted reactionaries and reformers alike. He was the von Papen of Islam. He would quickly have gone the way of all the other *ancien régime* politicians—either into exile abroad or into obscurity at home on an extremely modest pension—were it not for his exceptional gifts. He could manipulate Al Khadra's nightmarish finances with a dexterity which no Harvard Arab could hope to surpass; both in Arab politics and in power diplomacy he combined an unparalleled tactical adroitness with an almost satanic ability to read the minds and anticipate the movements of his adversaries. His long years of association with the British and his innumerable trips to London had given him an insight into the machinery of the Anglo-Saxon mind which Mustafa found priceless, not only in matching wits with Whitehall but with Washington as well. There was a body of opinion among the Western embassies in Al Asima which maintained that Taj Pasha was Mustafa's Mazarin. This was a gross exaggeration; Mustafa did his own thinking; but in emergencies such as this, when he was risking the very existence of his regime in taking on opponents as formidable as Calvin Hampshire and Paul Pullmotor, he found Taj Pasha's experience and counsel more valuable than ever. So there sat Taj Pasha, at the left hand of the revolutionary, white-bearded, bespectacled, a bit deaf, mumbling amongst his garments of green and crimson and interwoven gold, an exquisite antiquity among the men in khaki and the Harvard Arabs in their Dacron. He leaned forward and whispered gently into the Prime Minister's ear. The others, straining to hear, asked themselves why, since he was deaf, did he not shout out loud like the deaf? (There was a theory, defended warmly by some of Mustafa's own associates, that Taj Pasha's hearing was as sound as his appetite for little girls—that he pretended to be deaf simply to encourage his enemies in inadvertencies and indiscretions, but this was absurd. Or was it?)

When the officers had completed their declamations, the Prime Minister rose to his feet and came quickly to the point. "I am interested in one thing," he said in his most resonant no-nonsense voice. "I want to pinpoint our exact capabilities in this crisis. What weapons can we count on to foil the Americans? First we must find some wheat and medicine to replace, for the time being, the shipments they promised us. We must do this very quickly. The Bedouins are starving. We've got to feed them, or the next thing we know the whole desert will be rising up in revolt. Perhaps we could obtain a commitment from the Italians or the Argentines before Hampshire gets to them. TAJ PASHA, WOULD YOU LOOK INTO THAT? Now, how about the American companies? I know nationalizing them wouldn't be worth the fuss, but a little systematic harassment shouldn't hurt. Would you gentlemen from the Ministry of Finance care to look into that? As for propaganda, I want a pitiless campaign against Hampshire and the United States on the radio and in the newspapers. Pull out all the stops. Say the worst things you can think of. Yes, Major, I realize that you exhausted all your superlatives last week, but Arabic is a very rich language and I am counting on your patriotic imagination to rise to the occasion. Have you called Hampshire a prostitute?"

"Last week," replied the Minister of National Enlightenment.

"Epileptic?"

"Yesterday."

"Dope fiend?"

"Tomorrow."

"Splendid. Ya Anwar, let's generate a little fraternal solidarity in the other Arab capitals. I want riots in front of every American Embassy in the Middle East within three days. Does the Mutual Understanding Commission have separate offices in any of those places?"

"In Beirut and Baghdad."

"Have them burned to the ground. Better burn down the British Council in Beirut too. That will make the British properly annoyed at the Americans for having started this. *Now hear me.* I want a good demonstration in front of our own American Embassy here in Al Asima—but no damage, understand? That would be pushing things too far. Fitz Pasha is a personal friend of mine, and besides I don't want to give Hampshire a pretext for breaking off relations. Ya Anwar, you had better quadruple the guard around the Embassy in case the enthusiasm gets out of hand. Dr. Pantry's offices are across the street from the Embassy, aren't they? You might have two or three rocks thrown through the windows there, but no fires! Now let me see. It's Sunday morning now. Start the demonstrations on Wednesday and run them through the rest of the week. That will give Hampshire's criminal new policy time to get announced, to sink in, and to justify our reaction in the eyes of world opinion. And, Anwar, before I forget, tell our men at the pumping station to stand by. We might want to tamper with the transit pipelines, or even blow them up—but we'll hold that as our last card. Now, have we thought of everything? Harassments, riots, propaganda, petrol pipelines. Have we thought of everything? . . ."

When the others had gone, Taj Pasha asked, "What are you going to do about the King? The Americans may try to turn him against you."

"Pullmotor has already tried," the Prime Minister said. "But there's no problem there. Besides, my special source tells me everything I need to know about Mohammed."

"Then what about Pullmotor?" Captain A'war pressed. Shouldn't he be kept out of the country?"

"On the contrary, Captain. I have already instructed the airport to roll out the red carpet when he returns. I expect him tomorrow, in fact. He'll be plotting all over the place. It should be great fun."

It was past three o'clock in the morning when Mustafa ibn Mabrouk retired to his private rooms in the attic of his Ministry. He bathed and got into bed wondering which he treasured more, his solitude or the celibacy that went with it. He did not say his prayers like a good Moslem, for he was not really a religious man. Instead he turned on his night lamp and opened up his Gibbon, hoping to find repose among the mossy ruins of distant majesty. *Cast your eyes on the Palatine hill, and seek among the shapeless and enormous fragments the marble theatre, the obelisks, the colossal statues, the porticoes of Nero's palace: survey the other hills of the city, the vacant space is interrupted only by ruins and gardens. The forum of the Roman people, where they assembled to enact their laws and elect their magistrates, is now enclosed for the cultivation of pot-herbs, or thrown open for the reception of swine and buffaloes. The public and private edifices, that were founded for eternity, lie prostrate, naked, and broken, like the limbs of a mighty giant; and the ruin is more visible, from the stupendous relics that have survived the injuries of time and for-*

tune. . . . "What a splendid passage!" Mustafa exclaimed aloud. "I must add that to my collection." Near dawn he grew drowsy, and was piped to pasture by his gramophone, softly singing the *Four Seasons,* of Vivaldi.

14

Calvin Hampshire's new policy of chastisement against the government of Mustafa ibn Mabrouk was immediately leaked to the *New York Times*. Radio Al Asima responded with a broadside of delirious abuse. Otherwise the next two days passed without major incident. Both Ambassador Fitzgibbon and Paul Pullmotor returned to Al Asima. On Monday evening Christopher Grundoon had an early supper at home, and then sat down to make an entry in his journal. One thought led to another, and another.

Monday. I finished the final episode of my novel, *Perfidious Albion,* last night, and left it lying about. This morning my one-thumbed Ahmed dutifully smuggled it out of the house, and now it is in the hands of the Political Police. The ending is almost unbearably gory—but all the bodies are British, and the final scene is of Mustafa, Warrior of Islam, Torch of

Arabism, stepping forward to accept the Nobel Peace Prize for his "services to humanity." I hope it will turn the trick and continue to keep my dossier in good odor down at the Ministry of the Interior, particularly in view of the developments over the weekend, which I find most disquieting. Something dreadful is going to happen. I could feel it the other night when I was smoking the hashish, and I can feel it now, in my bones. Is there any link between these intimations of imminent disaster and the sudden compulsion I feel to commit the remainder of *my* Middle East to the pages of this poor journal?

After finishing *Perfidious Albion* very late last night I went for a walk along the Corniche, and I met Ambassador Fitzgibbon. He was *smashed.* "I returned from Washington only an hour ago," he said. "I have been imbibing, above the clouds, on Air France." He had Eminence Grise along on a leash. His three Bedouin bodyguards were hovering behind him, giggling softly among the shadows. I could see at once that he wanted, very badly, to talk. We had one of those wild Irish conversations . . .

For a few minutes Christopher and the Ambassador had leaned with their elbows on the stone balustrade, smoking their cigarettes, watching the relentless voyage of the broad Mabrouk. From across the liquid stillness came the almost inaudible baying of a hound. "Do you know that men once worshiped these waters?" the Ambassador asked. "They made human sacrifices to it. Tonight I feel like one of those victims, born into the world to appease the appetite not of one river but of three. It took me half a lifetime to learn that the waters of the Mabrouk run deeper than those of the River Charles. This last weekend I discovered that the Potomac is deeper still, and more treacherous."

"I take it your trip was a disappointment," Christopher said.

"Not a disappointment, a disaster. I behaved very badly. I'm surprised Hampshire didn't decapitate me before I got away. Pullmotor would have been pleased."

"It's very strange. You're a Harvard man yourself, a classmate of them both."

"Are you trying to be funny? You know very well they consider me an intruder. An *arriviste*. A climber. A turncoat! But it's not my beginnings they resent so much as my . . . my brilliance. Brains belong to the aristocracy. No matter now, my days are numbered. I had my resignation all written out."

"What made you change your mind?"

"I saw some electric home shoe-shiners in a shop window."

"I don't follow you, Mr. Ambassador."

"How lovely, I thought. Half the people in Al Khadra don't even have shoes."

"Give them time. One day they'll have shoes and electric home shoe-shiners too. That's what America wants for the world."

"Really? Well, that's not what I want. I don't want the world to be Americanized."

"So it wasn't compassion that made you come back," Christopher said.

"No, it was avarice, and penury. I haven't got the proverbial pot to—"

"Nor a window to throw it out of?"

"Not in America, at any rate. Here in Al Khadra I have a palace, a cook, a Cadillac, a chauffeur, a footman, a gardener, a private secretary, a personal assistant, an angwantibo, three bodyguards, four houseboys, and more first, second, and third secretaries than I can shake a stick at. Do you know where I stayed when I was in Washington?"

"Park Sheraton? Shoreham?"

"At the Y.M.C.A. I'm broke. *Destitute*."

"I know what you mean. In Al Asima, I mingle with ambassadors, cabinet ministers and Kings. At home, I don't even know the fire chief."

"It's amusing, isn't it, Christopher? We had to come out to the desert to be princes. In Boston, we were just another couple of Mickies. We're a pair of underdeveloped countries, you and I. Hod-carriers. Pot-wallopers. Bog-trotters to the bone. Shanty Irish."

"I'm not sure I care for your choice of adjectives. Lace curtain, if you like."

"No, *shanty*."

"It's such an ugly word, Mr. Ambassador. So many unpleasant connotations. Shabby, shoddy, shame."

"Shack, shady, shiftless."

"Shallow, sham, shambles. Never mind. We do a pretty good job covering up."

"Do we? Do you want to know what Hampshire said to me on Saturday? 'Same old Shawnie,' he said, 'brimming with Hibernian eloquence.' "

"All right. The Establishment will never accept us. Why do you care that much?"

"Why does anybody? Why does Mustafa? Why do you think he has destroyed the Establishment in this country?"

"Because it was living off the backs of the people," Christopher said.

"Possibly, but I have my own theory. He destroyed it because he recognized it for what it was—a cheap, gimcrack imitation of European aristocracy. Better to have none at all than such a nasty reproduction. Have you ever noticed the glaze that comes into his eyes when he is talking with Sir Charles Chetwynd-Pott?"

"Yes, you've told me this before. Mustafa's greatest regret is that he wasn't born an English duke."

"Precisely," the Ambassador said. "He feels the same way about Pullmotor. He loves Pullmotor because he's an aristocrat. If he can out-fox Paul, he proves to himself—"

"That he's as good as Paul is?"

"Precisely. I have seen the same glaze come into your eye, Christopher, when you talk to Mohammed. Running after royalty is your way of covering up."

"You gave me the job! And you don't understand me at all. I'm very fond of His Majesty."

"His *Majesty*. Would you be as fond of him if he weren't a king?"

"I know that you consider him stupid, and that you'll never forgive him for flunking out of Harvard, but he and I are the same in many ways. *Cor ad cor loquitur.*"

"There you go again," the Ambassador laughed. "Which favorite priest are you quoting now?"

"Cardinal Newman. The inscription on his coat of arms."

"I suspected it was something like that. You see, Christopher, I've discovered your dark secret."

"I doubt it."

"You studied once for the priesthood, didn't you?"

"How did you find that out?" Christopher asked.

"When Solafa began going with you. She never has affairs with anyone but spoiled priests. It's one of her less celebrated but more memorable peculiarities. I suppose it's her way of getting back at God for all the dirty tricks He's played on her. Besides, *prêtre manqué* is written all over you. I sensed it the first day we met in Madrid."

"Is that why you wanted me as your assistant?"

"I've often asked myself that question," the Ambassador said.

"What about Mohammed? Solafa had an affair with him. He's not a priest, spoiled or otherwise."

"Isn't he? He's a direct descendant of the Prophet and an Imam of Islam. What more do you want?"

"Of course there's little Michel, her present lover. He studied to be a Byzantine monk. She's become very chummy with Chuckles Vespucci. But I can't quite imagine Chuckles as a theological student."

"Nothing would surprise me about that fellow," the Ambassador said. "There's something fishy about him. I feel I've met him before, but I can't quite place him. How long were you in the seminary?"

"Only a year. I wanted to go to Harvard too, you know. I used to take the streetcar over to Cambridge and peep through the wrought-iron gates. But the priests and nuns and my mother and father and all my maiden aunts told me it was a mortal sin to go to Harvard. I was very much afraid of mortal sin. When I was seven years old, a nun caught me kissing a little girl on the back stairs of the Immaculate Heart of Mary parochial school. She made a scene in front of the whole second grade and—"

"And said you had sinned against holy purity."

"Yes. I guess that's the story of your own boyhood, isn't it? What an experience for a child. I have nightmares. I can still hear that nun shrieking at me. Ever since then, in spite of myself, I've done my best to live up to my depraved reputation. If they had given us compulsory courses in Free Love I'm sure I'd be a chaster man today. Anyway, I went to the Jesuit college instead of Harvard. I hated the Jebbies, and I loved them. During my senior year I became convinced I had a vocation, and the following summer I entered their novitiate. I loved the cool mornings, walking through the moist grass to the chapel, chanting the Divine Office and hearing Mass. If the priesthood were only made up of mornings I'd be a priest today. Divine love was all I needed—in the morning. The evening was my undoing. In the evening, when I was in bed by myself, sacred love was not enough. I had to have human love, too, and that's why I came out. Now, outside those convent walls, I find I have neither. When I was in the seminary, all I wanted was to get out. Now that I'm out, all I want is to be back in. So sometimes I stay away from women for weeks or even months at a time, as I'm doing right now—since losing Solafa. It doesn't do any good. I've been abandoned between the frontiers of faith and lechery. I'm adrift on two oceans, suspended between two worlds. I'm a Manichee. Every night before I go to bed I pray, 'Here I come, God—half-priest, half-whoremonger.' "

"Why don't you just leave the Church, as I did?" the Ambassador asked.

"I tried that. For three months once. But He bound and gagged me by umbilical cord, and dragged me back. Even when I was free, I was wishing He would."

"Sometimes I find myself wishing the same thing."

"Maybe the reason you're so fond of these impoverished Moslems is because you envy them, too—I mean because they seem so close to God. Maybe He's chosen them to lead you back to your own beginnings. After all, what are Arabs but circumcised Irishmen?"

"What are Irishmen but uncircumcised Arabs? Same old Christopher—brimming with Hibernian eloquence. To hell with Ireland."

"To hell with Harvard," Christopher said.

"To hell with Rome."

"To hell with Boston."

"To hell with Hampshire," the Ambassador said. "To hell with *Pullmotor*."

. . . I suppose the Ambassador has every reason to feel as he does about that weird little man, but Pullmotor fascinates me. He arrived back here late yesterday. Why? What on earth is he up to? Has he come to make a deal with Mustafa, to deliver an ultimatum, or to overthrow the government? If he is as dangerous as the Ambassador claims, then why in heaven's name has Mustafa allowed him back in the country? The Ambassador is in a quandary, and last night, just before we parted on the Corniche, he waved his finger in my face and said, "I tell you, Christopher, Pullmotor will be the undoing of us all." If that be so (and I pray it isn't) then it is high time I confided to this journal my observations on the man. Let me think. Perhaps, from my conversations with the Ambassador, and on the basis of my own fragmentary reconnaissance, I can convey Pullmotor in terms of what Fitz Pasha once told me were Paul's personal operating principles. "Pullmotor's Five Pillars of Success," he called them. *Voilà.*

1. *Be a Name-dropper.* And Pullmotor has every right to be; there are few people of genuine importance in this world whom he hasn't cultivated. I dined once at his residence in Georgetown. I don't know why I was asked, because I suspect he does not particularly care for me, and an invitation from Pullmotor is supposed to be the supreme accolade. There are two reasons why dining *chez Pullmotor* is even more prestigious than dining *chez Hampshire*. First, one is immediately made to feel that one is now a member of an exclusive little club which surpasses in distinction any other body of human society, even the United States Senate; you are now "a friend of Paul's"; you are henceforth authorized to preface your pronouncements, ever so casually, with the sublime phrase, "When I was at Paul's the other night . . ." Secondly, the moment he is announced the guest can see that the common denominator of the evening is not the Social Register—though of course half the guests do happen to be listed in that publication. One has clearly been chosen because one is, like the others, "interesting people." Typically, there will be an eminent newspaper pundit; a missionary who has spent the last forty years on the Lower Zambesi ("Paul has at least *one* Albert Schweitzer on any guest list," Louise Pullmotor says); two or three members of the cabinet; a best-selling novelist; an impoverished poet; and, for salt and pepper, an anti-American celebrity of the Krishna Menon stripe, an unconventional actress, and a Miami Beach gangster.

Pullmotor has some very individual rules for Name-dropping. Here are some of them:

a) Refer to all heads of government—Adenauer, Nehru, U Nu, etc.—by their first names. Indicate that you reciprocate the privilege with such remarks as, "The last time we lunched in Rangoon, he said, 'Paul, I wish you . . .' " And I said, 'Nu, is it true . . .' "

b) Call all "characters"—big-game hunters, roller-skating champions, strip-tease artists, etc.—by their first names. Moreover, show them much more deference in the presence of others than you do ambassadors, prime ministers and royalty. Never appear even slightly impressed at meeting a maharajah, field marshal, British peerage, etc.

c) First names for all journalists of prominence: "Stew called me again this morning, and I told him, 'Stew, I've already given that story to Scotty . . .' " Exceptions are the minor ones (including Drew Pearson); with these you make a studied attempt to remember their names but you keep getting mixed up. All newspapermen are slobs, anyway.

d) Refer to persons of inferior importance as "Mr."—"Mr. Johnston," "Mr. Stassen," etc. Let this slip occasionally, in order to make the point that when you are with them they become "Eric" and "Harold." There is yet a lower order of inferiority. Refer to Ambassador Fitzgibbon as "Fitzgibbon"—but call him "Shawnie" to his face.

e) When dealing with someone on the Fitzgibbon level, do *not* say, "I saw Calvin when I was in Washington." Instead say, "I saw *the Hampshires* when I was in Washington." This suggests that you saw them *socially*, possibly that you spent the weekend with them in the country, and is guaranteed to make the victim twice as miserable. In some instances you can add, "Rebecca is a riot," but this gambit is usually overdoing it.

The Second Pillar:

2. *Be Mysterious*. The more obscure and inscrutable your authority, the more encompassing. No one has ever explained to me the legal foundations of Pullmotor's omnipotence; they don't exist. Ostensibly he is nothing more than an investment banker; the very vagueness of his charter is his chief ad-

vantage; it enables him to do things no one else would dare dream of. He is the object of extreme resentment, envy and outright fear, not only in the chancellories of the world, but, even more, among Washington officialdom. Ambassadors and cabinet members who care to tangle with him must be prepared to risk the wrath of Calvin Hampshire. Pullmotor's immense power depends almost totally on his unique personal and social intimacy with the Secretary of State. They are both immensely wealthy princelings of the Back Bay. They attended St. Mark's together; they roomed at Harvard together; they were admitted to the Hasty Pudding and Porcellian together; they graduated to their hereditary armchairs at the Somerset together. Their wives went to Radcliffe and are first cousins and as First Family as either of their husbands. Both Hampshire and Pullmotor are Unitarians. Pullmotor's offbeat, shameless exterior may be partly a reaction against all this, but it is also very deceiving. His green, pig-studded Porcellian necktie may protrude less frequently than does Hampshire's, but he flashes it whenever he wishes to strike terror into the hearts of townies like myself. For all his flamboyance, Pullmotor—like Hampshire (and Mustafa!)—is puritanical in his private life and shocks easily in matters of other people's morals or dishonesty over money; at the same time he would not hesitate to bribe anybody if he thought it would advance our cause in the Cold War. Hampshire—and now I am quoting the Ambassador verbatim—Hampshire dotes on Pullmotor because Paul is the old school playmate who in his own preposterous way remains withal as consecrated as Calvin himself to class, to caste, to club, to country, and to Harvard. I need hardly add where this leaves Ambassador Fitzgibbon.

3. *Be Reckless*. Or rather, pretend to be. Pullmotor has a genius for saying the right thing to the right person at the right time, despite his squeaky voice. But on certain occasions he becomes not only voluble but rash. Or so it seems. Actually, he is now wielding one of his favorite weapons, a device he calls "controlled indiscretion." Those who know him well swear that he has never uttered a genuinely impetuous word

in his life—that when he appears to be losing his temper or blurting out some dreadful state secret, it is always for a definite, if cryptic, purpose. Sometimes, I suspect, he plays this game for no other reason than to confuse his friends (not to speak of his enemies) or for the simple joy it gives him to make mischief. Like Mustafa ibn Mabrouk, he loves to take long chances in strategic and tactical matters. I would estimate that he gets away with ninety percent of his outrages.

4. *Be Devious.* Pullmotor is a past master at maneuvering other powerful men. He is at his most Borgian in high-level Washington conferences, particularly when there is a controversial problem to be resolved. First, he will study the problem just enough to grasp its bare essentials. This usually takes him about ten minutes; he avoids homework unless it is absolutely necessary. His ends are far more effectively served by human reconnaissance than by abstract scholarship. (He barely got passing grades at Harvard.) When he arrives at the meeting he remains silent until everyone else has taken a stand. When he does enter the discussion he is careful to pretend that his own point of view—which he rarely actually reveals—does not derive from hasty cramming, and that he speaks more from wisdom than from "World Almanac knowledge"; he affects ignorance of some important detail just to make the point that he is above details. He goes on to insinuate, ever so subtly, the incompatible character of the different positions the others have already adopted. "Your brainstorm is brilliant, Jim, but I wonder whether you have considered how it would affect *Fred's* plans?" Inevitably, the smoldering interdepartmental feuds and personal rivalries—Pentagon vs. State, Admiral Afterdeck vs. the Air Force, the Secretary vs. the Vice President, etc.—flare up anew. This is precisely what Pullmotor wants. "Gentlemen," he suggests, "why don't we all take another night to sleep on this thing?" With nothing decided, the meeting adjourns.

Then Pullmotor goes to work. He buttonholes people, gets on the telephone, visits various high officials individually. He flatters artfully; he whispers gossip and repeats subtle little slanders; he reinforces existing vendettas, revives old ones, and weaves new webs of umbrage, disgruntlement, and malice. When the meeting reconvenes in the morning, the rival factions are ready for blood. In the nick of time, Pullmotor enters the dispute in the role of the Great Peacemaker. "Gentlemen, may I have the floor for a moment? I don't think we're in as much disagreement as it appears." (This line is *obligatoire.*) "I think Fred is quite right to be concerned about Jim's Operation Musclebound, but I speak from experience when I say I appreciate what Jim's boys over in Musclebound are up against." Pullmotor then produces his own "compromise" scheme. It may not be the least bit superior to Jim's or Fred's or Admiral Afterdeck's scheme except for one major ingredient: it places everyone involved, including Pullmotor himself, exactly where he wants them. How does all of this minister to the needs of the Republic? For Pullmotor, the resolution of issues is secondary. The manipulation of men, for its own sake, is what matters.

This brings me to the last and most important pillar of all:

5. *Be a Bastard.* Pullmotor has made this principle a philosophy of life. There is so much evidence of this I hardly know where to begin. A sub-heading here might be, *Never attack a man until you have first firmly convinced everyone that you are his friend.* If you spend a month saying how much you like your victim, you will be taken much more seriously when the time comes to denounce him than if you were known as his enemy. There are variations of this. Prior to slandering an intended victim—Fitzgibbon, for example—Pullmotor will go out of his way to praise a number of other Ambassadors. "Too bad Sidney is tied up in Turkey. This is just his sort of thing." Or: "Of course Sylvester would be ideal for this, but the citrus-fruit lobby would crucify him." Or: "Throckmorton! Just the man! But wait a minute—I just remembered Throckmorton doesn't speak Arabic." This establishes Pullmotor as a "booster," so that when he is ready to attack Ambassador Fitzgibbon it won't seem to come from someone who never has a good word to say for anybody.

Pullmotor's Pillar No. 5 is even more indispensable to his doctrine for the global struggle than it is to his personal relations. Some years ago he wrote a number of controversial pamphlets for Top Secret circulation among high Washington officialdom. I know only a few of the titles—*How To Be a Boy Scout and Lose the Cold War . . . How To Overthrow a Pro-Soviet Government in Five Easy Steps . . . How To Prop Up a Wobbly Anti-Communist Regime on the Installment Plan.* Practically everybody thought he was trying to be funny; far-sighted friends like Calvin Hampshire knew better. I cannot say that I approve of Pullmotor's methods (I don't imagine that the governments he overthrew approved of them, either), but the man does get results. We have him and a handful of other cynical men to thank for thrashing the Russians at their own game of dirty tricks. So much for Pullmotor's Five Pillars.

As I piece the puzzle together, it seems to me that, more than anyone else, Pullmotor *invented* Mustafa ibn Mabrouk . . .

It was during a diplomatic reception—at the Royal Palace some three years before—that Pullmotor first met the Prime Minister. At that time a mere major, Mustafa was teaching tactics at the Royal Military College and serving as aide-de-camp to Mohammed, who was then Crown Prince. Mustafa's brilliance was already recognized—and feared—in government circles. He was notoriously anti-British and rumored to be a conspirator; and yet his good looks and literate conversation had made him the lion of the diplomatic community. He and Pullmotor took to each other as ducks take to water; they began to be seen often together.

Pullmotor had come to Al Khadra because the country was on the brink of anarchy over the British-bases question. Demonstrations, riots, and arson had become commonplace; the government could no longer maintain order; despite this the British were threatening to withdraw their subsidy unless the base agreement was renewed. The final explosion came a fortnight after Pullmotor's appearance on the scene. The old King, a morose and venal man, capitulated under pressure and put his signature to a pact extending the bases another fifteen years. The mob erupted in the old city; they broke the police barriers, charged up the Jebel al Malouk, stormed into the Palace and slaughtered the Royal Family. Only Mohammed was saved, and that thanks to the personal heroism of Mustafa. Mustafa's role, if any, in arranging the riot in the old city was never clearly established.

In any event, Mohammed suddenly found himself King, and as unsuited to that office as any young man could ever hope to be. Almost immediately Pullmotor was at his side, warning him that to appoint another of the old politicians Prime Minister would inflame the street still more and bring down on his own head the same fate which befell his father. There was only one man, Pullmotor argued, loyal enough to be trusted, radical enough to satisfy the street, and intelligent enough to rule well—and that man was Mustafa ibn Mabrouk. In his bereavement, it had not even occurred to Mohammed that he would be called upon to name a new government. He accepted Pullmotor's counsel at once; in fact he was delighted with it. He called in his young friend. "Would you like to be Prime Minister, Mustafa?" When Mustafa asked him whom he wanted in the cabinet, the King said, "The cabinet? Oh yes. The cabinet! Do you want to take care of that, too, ya habibi? Perhaps Mr. Paul can help with some names."

Indeed Mr. Paul could. In fact he remained in the country another three months helping the new Prime Minister to consolidate his power. Pullmotor established his own headquarters in a suite at the Sheraton-Zahra and was on a direct line to Mustafa twenty times a day; together the two of them ruled Al Khadra. Hardly anyone else knew of this liaison; for obvious reasons Mustafa kept it a secret from his own men.

To the gamut of Pullmotor's suggestions, Mustafa gave his quick assent and the music of his most ingenuous laughter; during those first fragile weeks of entrenchment, he needed all the American support he could get. Pullmotor drafted most of Mustafa's messages to foreign governments—spicing them with pot shots at Moscow—and even ghosted some of his speeches. He introduced the young ruler (Mustafa was only twenty-eight) to the latest gobbledegook of progressive government, provided him with elaborate graphs and organization charts, and mesmerized him with such notions as "cost analysis," "middle management," and "multiplier theory of economic development." He helped Mustafa to streamline the Political Police and taught him the most modern methods of spy detection. He provided him with the minuscule microphones, tape-recorders, wire-tapping devices, and other intelligence knick-knacks which the Prime Minister said were necessary to uncover the conspiracies of the local communist party; it was not until some time later that Mustafa started using this equipment against the American Embassy. Pullmotor even made a number of quick trips to London and bullied the British into evacuating their bases; then he persuaded Hampshire to replace the sterling subsidy with a generous injection of dollars.

But inevitably, the two men quarreled. Although Fitz Pasha was as favorably disposed to Mustafa as Pullmotor was, from the beginning the Ambassador had cautioned him against the Prime Minister's duplicity. Not that Pullmotor was ever under any illusion in that respect; for his heavy investment he expected to extract a high price, and his miscalculation was in thinking that he could convince the Prime Minister that the best interests of Al Khadra were identical with the best interests of the United States. In effect, he asked Mustafa to convert his country from a British satrapy into an American satellite. "So it's only a few landing strips you want?" Mustafa laughed. "Why don't you ask me to gouge out an eyeball or chop off a leg? My eyeballs and legs you may have—but not my landing strips."

Pullmotor returned to Washington in a rage. Mustafa's crucial encounter with Calvin Hampshire at the Al Asima airport took place a few weeks later.

> . . . And as I look back, I wonder whether Pullmotor's current maneuvering against the Prime Minister is because he really believes that Al Khadra is going communist or because he cannot forgive Mustafa for outfoxing him three years ago. I wish to heaven I knew what Pullmotor is up to at this moment.
>
> God, I've got to get to bed! It's nearly two o'clock in the morning. Flipping through these pages, perusing what I've already written, it's curious how much of my Middle East keeps pointing back to Boston. Well, I will examine the reasons for that some other time: I'm calling it a day and I'm going to put

down my garrulous pen and go to bed now. Funny thing about Boston. I hated it. I never want to see the place again. The King says, "Boston! That year in Boston was the happiest in my life cha cha cha . . ."

Was it? Like most Arabs, His Majesty Mohammed VII, Ahmed Abdullah ibn Hamad, Scion of the House of Hamad, Sheikh of the Sheikhs of Mecca and Medina, Direct Descendant of the Prophet in the line of Khadijah, was inclined to find the past a more amiable companion than the present. From infancy he had been the despair of his British and Arab tutors; his father insisted nonetheless that as Crown Prince and heir to the throne he must complete his education abroad. The British Embassy was arranging his entry into Brasenose, Oxford, when Ambassador Fitzgibbon volunteered the suggestion that Harvard might be more suitable. This outraged the British, impressed the old King, and delighted the Crown Prince, who greeted with childlike *élan* the prospect of living in America. At Harvard itself, there were misgivings about Mohammed's capacity as a scholar, but the State Department applied pressure, and he was reluctantly accepted. Ambassador Fitzgibbon personally arranged his lodging—not at Eliot House, the usual receptacle of royalty, but at Adams House, the alma mater of the Ambassador, Calvin Hampshire, Paul Pullmotor, and Franklin Delano Roosevelt.

Mohammed was given a private room on the third floor of Adams and enrolled in the most basic courses the College could offer: Ideas of Man, Modern Government, Principles of Economics, Public Speaking. Socially he was an immediate success. Men liked him. Women were mad about him. He was a marvelous dancer. On weekends there were wild, wondrous parties. He took up tag football, rowing, wrestling, boxing and bodybuilding; he was a superb athlete.

The Prince was fascinated with his new surroundings. To him New England seemed a single, vast oasis; early every morning he would stroll barefoot and alone along the banks of the Charles; he loved the profusion of green grass—so commonplace to an American, so charismatic to an Arab—and the arched footbridge of the four obelisks. Often he performed his ablutions with the waters of the Charles, spread out his gold-buttoned blazer on the misty grass, knelt down upon it, and, his face to Mecca and the rising sun, gave thanks to God for his good fortune. Of Adams House itself, he loved the Tudor exterior, clad in ivy, and the wrought-iron garnishments; the imitation Moorish mosaic in the stairwell ascending to the library; the Florentine opulence of the swimming pool—in fact, they were subsequently to inspire the Tudor and Moorish and Florentine mishmash in his throne room. He loved the oil landscapes and the Persian carpets and the warm, green glow of the leather sofas in the Upper Common Room. He loved having hot dogs while he watched Westerns on the television set in the basement; and he wondered whether John Adams and John Quincy Adams and Charles Francis Adams and all the other Adamses whose Christian names he couldn't remember, staring sternly down from their immense portraits in the cafeteria, would have welcomed a Mohammedan prince to dinner. He loved going with his new friends to tea at the Master's residence in Apthorp House every Friday afternoon at five o'clock. There—amid the white paneling and leather-bound books and the matronly benevolence of the Master's wife, her Graham crackers and her homemade gingersnaps and all the pedantic banter about Restoration poets and T. S. Eliot—there, amid all that, was the most unexpected part of Mohammed's America, and for that very reason the part he loved best. He attempted gallantly to contribute to the conversation.

Mohammed: This Mr. Sweeney. Is he a nice man? Is he a friend of yours?

Master: *Which* Mr. Sweeney, dear boy?

Mohammed: Mr. Apeneck Sweeney. Isn't that his name?

He loved the portrait above the fireplace in the main parlor of Apthorp House. It was of a gentleman in the crimson military costume of the Colonial epoch; his face was soft and epicene, rather like the Master's own.

Mohammed: Oh, what a beautiful picture!

Master: Yes, that is Lord Fauconberg, the grandson of Oliver Cromwell. Doesn't look a bit like old Cromwell, does he? No warts, anyway.

Mohammed: I think he knew my grandfather!

Master: I doubt that he would have known your *grandfather,* dear boy. He might have known your great-great-*great*-grandfather. But I don't recall that Lord Fauconberg ever journeyed to the Muslin East. And I don't imagine that your great-great-great-grandfather frequented London society, now, did he?

Mohammed even loved going to class. But he did not do much better with Immanuel Kant and Lord Keynes than he did with Lord Fauconberg and Apeneck Sweeney. His examination papers were considered collector's items of comic incoherence. His tutors began to warn him that he would have to improve his marks if he wished to remain in the College. He did not take these admonishments lightly; the prospect of failure, of his father's wrath, filled him with terror. He studied harder, and did worse. At mid-term, he received failing grades in every subject except Public Speaking, and was placed on probation. He realized then that his task was hopeless, that in June he would have to leave Harvard forever and return, defeated, to face his father. He had always been given to revolving spells of elation and anxiety, of exaltation and anguish, of wild energy and paralyzing lethargy, but now he surrendered himself to an almost constant indolence, to days full of fantasy and disorder. He began to miss Mustafa. He stopped studying, cut most of his classes, and remained most mornings in bed, reliving his halcyon boyhood with Mustafa. Occasionally his longing stimulated him to sit down and dash off distracted and impassioned letters to Mustafa. He haunted his mailbox for letters from Mustafa. He rarely heard from Mustafa. In the afternoons he would go by himself into Boston to a cinema or to see one of the strip-tease shows off Scollay Square. Or, lacking the energy to leave Adams House, he would lock himself in his room and listen endlessly to phonograph records of Doris Day. Or he would go downstairs, remove his clothes, and spend hour upon hour lolling dreamily and naked about the swimming pool. It was there, in that neo-pagan bath where bathing suits were forbidden, that the splendor of his body was first called to Mohammed's notice, and there that he acquired his taste for appearing unclad before his friends. It was there that he learned that if he could not be admired for his mind he might at least be envied for his physique.

Mohammed's room in Adams House looked out upon St. Paul's, a rusy brick Roman Catholic church across the street. Perhaps nowhere in the environs of Boston is the contrast of two worlds, of two diametrically distinct and discrepant states of mind, more articulately symbolized than in the confrontation of Adams House and St. Paul's. The one is Tudor and rather rambling, a bastion of urbanity, heterodoxy, and iconoclasm; the other is Romanesque and monolithic, a castle of compulsion, rubric, and saints in stained glass. As the weeks passed, and his despondency increased, Mohammed found himself drawn out of Adams House and into the more matriarchal embrace of the building below. (He had never known his mother; she had been a concubine, banished from the Royal harem soon after his birth.) There are no mosques in Massachusetts, but the *campanile* belfry of St. Paul's reminded Mohammed of a minaret. The nuns, popping in and out of the parochial school next to the church, reminded him at a distance of Bedouin women in their veils and black hubbra dresses. One morning he went down to cxamine the arched inscription over the portico. THE HOUSE OF THE LIVING GOD. THE PILLAR AND GROUND OF TRUTH. This reminded him of the Koran. At that moment a black cortege crept up to the church. Mohammed gathered his courage and entered the temple for the first time. He was at once disappointed; the place was not at all like a mosque inside; it was full of flickering candles, wooden benches, and holy pictures, all of them alien to Islam.

But the vision which began to unfold on the high altar held him enchanted. "There were three rather fat gentlemen," he recalled to Christopher once, "all dressed in black. They went walking and bowing very slowly all over the stage, mumbling over books and bells, singing some terribly sad songs, and over my head an old lady answered them. She sounded a lot like the wailing women I used to hear at home." *Dies irae, dies illa, Solvet saeclum in favilla: Teste David cum Sibylla.* Yes, Christopher could imagine an affinity between that timeless dirge and the classic lamentations of Islam. The melodies of Rome and Mecca might not rhyme in life, but they did in death. The King continued, "At the end, one of the priests put on a long black gown which reached down to his toes, and he walked slowly around the coffin, sprinkling it with water. Then he made a fire in a golden bowl with golden chains, and sprinkled spice upon the fire. He walked around the dead man again, singing a song and waving the golden bowl over the body. The burning spice had such a sweet smell. It was all like black magic cha cha cha." The archives of Al Khadra's Royal Family overflow with allusions to vendetta and violent death; Mohammed might find America mystifying and Harvard incomprehensible, but here at last, in this Irish tabernacle amongst these strange sacraments and graven images, was something he could understand. From that day, whenever he heard the doors of many motorcars being slammed shut, he would leap out of bed and hasten to his window. If it was a cortege, he would dress quickly and go down into the church. *Quantus tremor est futurus, Quando judex est venturus, Cuncta stricte discussurus!*

New England had an early spring that year. Often after lunch Mohammed would take the subway into Boston, get off at Charles Street and stroll over to the Public Gardens. There he would remain until dark, riding the Swan Boats, feeding bread crumbs to the pigeons, or simply sitting on a park bench watching people pass by. The Public Gardens became his favorite oasis. "Arabs like to daydream," Mohammed gravely informed Christopher. "On the Swan Boats, in the lovely lake with everything so green around, I used to dream I was drifting on a swan's back to Paradise." He bought his tickets in batches, taking ten or more rides in an afternoon, and considered himself unusually lucky when Charlie, the man in charge, would move over and let him pedal. "But it's very good for my legs, Mr. Charlie!" Mohammed surely became the world's leading expert on that park; even today he could describe every inch of it to Christopher. "The trees in the Gardens are not weeping willow, as Mr. Charlie told me. They are weeping *beech*. I helped the policeman nail on the labels." Or: "The Bavarian bird castle near the pond was donated by Mrs. Webster." Or, on the absorbing subject of pedestal inscriptions: "The statue of George Washington on a horse was done by Ames Foundry, Chicopee, Massachusetts. Edward Everett Hale was done by B. C. Pratt, 1919, and Wendell Phillips by Jake and Sally, 1947."

And then there was Miss Finnegan. Cecilia Finnegan, the young tap-dancing teacher he began talking to that afternoon in April on the Swan Boat, when she sat down by mistake on his bag of bread crumbs.

"Oh, excuse me! I'm sorry! Did I crush all your peanuts?"

"They're bread crumbs, Miss."

"Oh yes! I saw you last week, feeding the pigeons! Where do you buy your bread crumbs?"

"I'm at Harvard. Every night after supper I take some extra slices of bread, and bring them up to my room. I leave them outside on the window sill, and in the morning I crush them—up in my room."

"Are you a Spaniard?"

"No, I'm an Arab."

"Are you a Catholic?"

"No, and I'm not a Christian, either."

Miss Finnegan, of whom His Majesty had shown Christopher dozens of snapshots, was not exactly a raving beauty. She was carrot-haired, freckly and frail. Mohammed took her to see *Rock Around the Clock*. He had not possessed a woman since he left Al Khadra; after the picture, he touched her hand under the table at Thompson's Spa and asked her, very politely, "Would you like to go to bed with me, Cecilia?" Miss Finnegan said no, she'd rather not—and besides, she had an appointment that evening to give a tap-dancing lesson. "Do you want to come and watch?" Mohammed went and watched, and that night he began to take tap-dancing lessons himself.

Every day after that, until late in June when he ran out of money and could not delay his departure for Al Asima any longer, Mohammed met Miss Finnegan at the Mattapan Personality Dynamics Academy, where they retired to a private cubicle and spent hour upon hour together, tap dancing. Even outside the academy, they became inseparable. Mohammed was soon a familiar sight, dashing up and down the stairs of her horrid, three-decker house in Mattapan, and a smash hit with her grandmother and seven younger brothers and sisters. She taught him the lyrics to "Does Your Mother Know You're Out, Cecilia?" and whenever he sang them she percolated with joyous laughter. Her grandmother gave him a miraculous medal for his birthday. Nothing, in Mohammed's mind, was too good for the Finnegans. He brought them candy, comic books, and beer; on Saturday afternoons he took the children to the baseball game. Miss Finnegan began to follow the obituary notices in the newspapers, and whenever there was a funeral at St. Paul's she would take the tube over to Harvard Square, and sit holding Mohammed's hand in the back of the church.

. . . I remember roaring with laughter when Mohammed told me about holding hands during the "Dies Irae." "Actually it was very appropriate," I apologized. *"Finnegans Wake* and all that. 'Hohohoho, Mister Finn, you're going to be Mister Finnagain! Hahahaha, Mister Funn, you're going to be fined again!' And St. Cecilia was not only a virgin, but a martyr too. You met Miss Finnegan on a swan's back. Swans sing only at the moment of death. I agree with you, Your Majesty—Boston is a city of death." He hadn't the vaguest idea what I was talking about. (Need I add I was tipsy at the time?) "It amuses me," I said, "a Moslem prince going out with a girl called Finnegan."

"Oh, she didn't know I was a prince," Mohammed said.

"You mean you concealed it from her?"

"No, I guess I just forgot to mention it."

"I still can't understand why you found her so attractive."

"I can't either. I think maybe because she was the only woman I've ever known who didn't tell me I was beautiful."

I wonder why that pleased him so; it was one of those bemused and misty statements which Mohammed will toss at you every now and again, as if to prove he's not quite the dunce everyone supposes. For despite everything, Mohammed remains in many ways the most complex and paradoxical of my friends. It mocks any power of mine to explain how so guileless and allegorical a youth could spring from such a dynasty as his. Avarice, cruelty, treachery, lechery, lunacy, depravity and pederasty: such was the long and unholy history of the House of Hamad before Mohammed grasped the scepter. That he so utterly fails to uphold the traditions of his family is one reason why he will probably be the last King of Al Khadra. There is another more immediate reason, of course, and that is Mustafa ibn Mabrouk. Mohammed may be harmless, but even an innocuous monarchy is an obstacle to Mustafa's ambitions; the monarchy must go, and soon. And yet I cannot believe—as do others—that Mustafa will stoop to regicide. Surely he has left the throne intact till now because he remembers the immensity of past royal favors. Did I say that Pullmotor invented Mustafa ibn Mabrouk? I was mistaken; Mohammed did.

The other day I wrote in this journal that the King had taken me to visit Wadi Mafish. He returns constantly to that forlorn jumble of black tents in the heart of the desert because it was the scene of his first encounter with Mustafa: he is forever trying to retrieve that idyll of his lost boyhood . . .

Mohammed was twelve years old when his father first took him to Wadi Mafish during one of those royal tours intended to reinforce the bonds that bound the Bedu to the House of Hamad. While the old King feasted with Hassan, Sheikh of the Beni Talal, Mohammed wandered out alone into the desert, shotgun in hand, in quest of wild grouse. In one of the wadis he came upon a flock of goats munching on gray grass, tended by a boy a year or two older than himself. The boy was sitting cross-legged in the sand; he had an open book in his lap and was turning the pages tenderly with his coarse fingers; he looked up, and said nothing. Mohammed had on his soldier suit; the herd-boy's head was swathed in a red *kaffiyeh,* but the rags about his body could not conceal the ravages of hunger. The sun was going down; a soft breeze was blowing. Only the wind had words for that primeval stillness. Silently in the hyacinthine sunset, Prince and goatherd contemplated each other.

Mohammed was the first to speak. "May peace be upon you," he said.

"And upon you, peace," the boy replied.

"May your evening be blessed."

"May your evening be full of light."

"Are you happy?" the Crown Prince asked.

"Praise be to God. Are you happy?"

"Praise be to God. By God, I am Mohammed."

"By God, I am Mustafa."

"O Mustafa, why do you read with your book upside down?"

"Can you milk a goat?"

"Will you teach me, O Mustafa?"

"Perhaps—if you will teach me to read."

They milked a goat together and drank the warm milk: in Mohammed's mind the experience lingered as a sacred covenant. Mohammed went to his father and told him he wanted to take the goatherd home to the Royal Palace; the King refused. "Haven't you enough princes to play with?" From that day Mohammed gave his father no peace. He would not eat, and remained in bed much of the time, sobbing quietly. He had made a *promise;* he had *promised* the goatherd he would teach him to read. Eventually the King relented, and Mustafa was fetched from Wadi Mafish. For the next five years, Mohammed and his protégé were rarely anywhere but with each other. They rode horses together, hunted together, swam in the broad Mabrouk together, took their meals together, bathed together, and slept in the same room—a typically Arab friendship.

Mohammed more than kept the bargain they had made in the desert. Mustafa arrived in the royal household totally illiterate, but his keen natural intelligence asserted itself at once. The royal tutors were flabbergasted—within a year he had caught up to Mohammed and began badgering them for more advanced instruction in history, mathematics, and English. As his knowledge grew, so did his audacity. In the King's presence he fawned on the Crown Prince, but when they were alone his teasing often reduced Mohammed to tears. Mustafa did this more from monotony than from malice; the disparity of their tastes, not to mention that of their awareness, was very great. So the goatherd, bored by the Crown Prince, began to slip out of the Palace whenever he could, and before long he had joined a group of young men who amused themselves by throwing bombs through the windows of the British Embassy. But Mohammed could not endure even these brief separations; he could not endure the day without Mustafa's laughter, Mustafa's praise, Mustafa's mockery.

Reports of Mustafa's clandestine political outrages were eventually whispered into the ear of the old King. The King had been wary of the young Bedu from the first day he entered the Palace, and only tolerated him for his son's sake. Mustafa was entirely too clever; he asked too many questions; he read too many books; he resented the kingdom's British protectors with a zeal which became as embarrassing as it was brash. But he could not simply be sent back to the wilderness whence he came; he was now a ward of the Throne. It was decided to enroll him in the Royal Military College, where a closer eye could be kept on him and where he would have less leisure to make mischief. The appointment pleased Mustafa; an army commission was just what he wanted. He studied hard, conspired and agitated more than ever, and was sent on to Sandhurst—simply to get him out of the country. He returned from his year in England on fire with radical new notions; nor did he hesitate to exploit his privileged friendship with the Crown Prince as a platform for propagating them. Even then, his doctrines were—at least implicitly—anti-Royalist. Then as now, Mohammed could not bear to hear him criticized.

> . . . Solafa thinks that Mohammed's blind loyalty to Mustafa is rooted in erotic memory. "A woman can sense these things more easily than a man," she remarked once. "Whenever Mohammed made love to me, his heart was never in it. He always held something back. He was such a *gentleman.*" I disagree with Solafa. Mohammed was obsessed, yes; but he was the victim of an inherited appetite which even to this day he does not understand. We will never know, but I cannot believe that this friendship, perfectly normal in a Moslem culture, was ever consummated. To the machinery of the loins Mustafa has always been serenely indifferent. The Ambassador is convinced that Mustafa always was, is now, and forever shall be, a virgin. Personally I am convinced that the only favor His Majesty ever got out of Mustafa was that quick lesson in how to milk a goat—except of course for the favor of saving his life . . .

The night of terror came only a few years after Mohammed's return from his dreamy sojourn at Harvard. When the old King agreed to extend the British bases, the mob erupted in the old city, broke the police barriers, charged up the Jebel al Malouk, and stampeded into the Palace brandishing clubs, table legs, staves, scissors, scimitars, meat-choppers, lead pipes, pickaxes. They overcame the guards and found the Royal Family barricaded together in the harem. They disemboweled and emasculated the old King and impaled him on a stave; they hacked and clutched at the fragments of flesh; waving severed limbs like crimson flags, they ran giggling and shouting down the tesselated corridors, beneath the porcelain archways, under the crystal chandeliers and teakwood stalactites, out into the starry night.

Another part of the mob had trapped the Crown Prince in his private apartments in a separate wing of the Palace. He and Mustafa had barricaded themselves in a salon. When the mob battered down the door, Mustafa stood there and fired his submachine gun point-blank into their faces. They fell back, momentarily. Mustafa seized the dazed Mohammed by the arm, and, his finger pressed tightly to the trigger of his gun, cut a corridor through the cauldron of howling flesh. By sheer luck and youthful legs, the two of them managed to lose the mob in the labyrinth of courtyards, and to reach the gymnasium in the basement. There they hid together beneath the boxing ring until the army, some fifteen minutes too late, chugged up the Jebel al Malouk on its mission to rescue the Royal Family. A hundred or more rioters fell before the army's blazing guns; the rest ran screaming wildly down the mountain.

It was darkly whispered afterward that Mustafa not only arranged the riot, but that he cold-bloodedly planned the murder of the Royal Family, sparing only Mohammed, whom he needed. In his despatches to Washington, Ambassador Fitzgibbon was at pains to dispute the veracity of these rumors. Mustafa was not bloodthirsty by nature; his year abroad had endowed him with an English gentleman's distaste for murder as a political weapon; moreover he was very nearly butchered himself. The Ambassador suspected that he did have something to do with the demonstration down in the city, but that the march on the Palace was spontaneous. In any event, things turned out very conveniently for the erstwhile goatherd. *Would you like to be Prime Minister, Mustafa? Do you want to take care of the cabinet, too, ya habibi?* For some months after assuming office Mustafa paid a great deal of attention to the King; in fact he did not discontinue his daily visitations to the Royal Palace until a full fortnight after he had finally consolidated his power.

. . . and yet in spite of everything, His Majesty refuses to despair of the Prime Minister's devotion. He spends half his time sitting by himself in that huge, empty palace, by a telephone that never rings, waiting to sign documents he does not understand. It is all rather sad, really.

And so many of Mohammed's other friendships are sad, too. His latest enthusiasm is for Chuckles Vespucci, of all people. I am puzzled by the subtle change which has come over Chuckles since his lunatic arrival here last week. To be sure, he still delights in playing the buffoon whenever there are people about, but in the King's presence he is altogether too fawning. And not only does Mohammed enjoy his music, he likes Chuckles personally. Ever since that night the King decorated all of us with the Grand Cordon of the Broad Mabrouk, Chuckles seems to be spending most of his time at the Royal Palace amusing His Majesty. He has even requisitioned Yahutha, the King's deaf-mute batman; in fact yesterday I saw Yahutha at the wheel of the King's Ferrari, dropping Chuckles off at the Sheraton-Zahra. Now the King tells me that Chuckles has volunteered to go out to Wadi Mafish to serenade the Bedouins. Why to Wadi Mafish, of all places? I am beginning to agree with Fitz Pasha; there is something fishy about that fellow . . .

When Christopher finally got to bed, he slept badly. He rose at dawn, and went right back to his journal.

Tuesday. The sun is rising beyond the river; its first rays are beginning to invade my library; I can hear the call of the muezzin, beckoning believers to prayer. I must bathe, eat my breakfast, and go to the Embassy. From where I sit, I can see a host of hoopoo birds exalting on zebra wings above the blinking waters, their rich erectile crests fluttering like crimson fans in the new sunshine. They trumpet softly as they glide—*hoop-hoop-hoopoo!*—a beckoning music, like the muezzin's. Rustic children stalk this bird, believing that the middle feather of its crest possesses magic powers, and as they do they cry "Keep your charm! keep your charm!" And yet it is another of the treacheries of this strange kingdom that this most beautiful of birds, crowned as no other airborne creature ever was, sustains itself on excrement.

Hoop-hoop-hoopoo! What are they calling out to me? As I watch the weird poetry of their ascent, I know that they are harbingers. But of what?

III

As for lying . . . it was the worst gambit against players whose whole life had passed in a mist of deceits, and whose perceptions were of the finest. The Arab leaders showed a completeness of instinct, a reliance upon intuition, the unperceived foreknown, which left our centrifugal minds gasping. Like women, they understood and judged quickly, effortlessly, unreasonably. It almost seemed as though the Oriental exclusion of woman from politics had conferred her peculiar gifts upon the men.

T. E. Lawrence
Seven Pillars of Wisdom

15

The royal Land-Rover, adorned on either door with the crest of the House of Hamad, zoomed over the cinnamon wilderness.

At the wheel was Yahutha, the King's inscrutably ugly deaf-mute. At his side sat Chuckles Vespucci, serenely assimilating Pascal's *Pensées* in Urdu, and scribbling, whenever the going was smooth enough, marginal notes in Mandarin Chinese. Chuckles was a linguist. Chuckles was many things. Chuckles was on his way to Wadi Mafish, to serenade the Bedouins.

The Land-Rover hit a rock, and leaped; Chuckles put his Pascal aside and began to marvel at the landscape. He was at large now in the great and terrible wilderness. It was very early morning. They had left Al Asima and the green gardens of the broad Mabrouk at the first hint of dawn; by dead reckoning due East—there were no permanent roads—it was fifty miles to Wadi Mafish. The same sun which at that moment was illumining the library of Christopher Grundoon, shed a gentle piebald laughter on this silent desert. The sky was mottled with black, broken clouds: portents of rain which would never fall. Where the sun splashed through, the wasteland glowed with subtle tints suggesting lilac, lemon and tangerine. The air had an opalescent sparkle; the surface sand twinkled with onyx, cornelian, and other colored pebbles. In the splotches of cloud shadow, the desert was indigo, and, in places, ebony with gravel and volcanic clinker. The distant cliffs, looming larger now, were some castellated, some smooth and round as the humps of camels; the closer foothills were of sand, slightly fretted, as if God had reached down and stroked them, softly, with His fingers; all were aglow in the celestial light of this young sun.

Soon the Land-Rover was twisting and protesting a path in the gorges of those fantastic cliffs. Granite walls, their cracks and furrows as wide as rivers, soared vertically a thousand feet, gnashing toothy parapets against the cobalt sky. Boulders the size of buildings teetered on pedestals so frail it seemed a single startling echo might send them dashing down. Fantasy-formations of black lava. Malevolent pillars of bluish basalt. Chasms so desolate, so timeless, so full of silence. And then the tormented turns, hacked out of molten mountain, heading down, down, down: it made a man feel he was falling from grace.

He was. They emerged into a vast, endless valley, far below the level of the sea: and at once they knew that the morning sun, so benign before the cliffs, had risen rapidly in heaven, and gone giddy and tyrannous with its new powers. Gone were the dark and heavy clouds: now they were wisps of tattered gauze, motionless in the metallic firmament. The sun had dissolved every hint and tint of color: now the world was a shimmering crystal plain, so glacial in its whiteness it made the mind swim and dizzied the eye's endurance. So the eye clutched at the horizon: only to glimpse grim mountain tops veiled in the vapors of heat. And vegetation everywhere had vanished; only some wretched thorn and ashen stubble sizzled on this crystal skillet, garnished by the bare bones of ibex and gazelle.

The heat was unbearable. The plain began to dance with a chorus of mirages. Now a necklace of silver lakes, luminous and evanescent. Now a glade of fig trees, thickets of oleander, green groves of doom-palm. For a fugitive moment, in the most distant mist, the tips of minarets and the towers of a modern city. Three dromedaries splashed neck-deep in a new lake; the dromedaries, at least, were real. The Bedouins on their backs called out to the Land-Rover. Chuckles motioned the deaf-mute to stop.

Two young men and a boy, their faces swathed in head-cloths against the glare. They wanted water. From his thermos, Chuckles gave them Pepsi. They drank sparingly and thanked him extravagantly. He reciprocated their compliments in fluent Arabic.

"Are you British?" they asked.

"No, American."

"Ah. Are you a Red Indian?"

Under way again in the Land-Rover, Chuckles turned to Yahutha and said, "As a matter of fact, I masqueraded once as a Cherokee Chief. Fascinating that Bedouins should be so interested in Red Indians. Supports a theory of mine. The two races are very similar."

Yahutha stared straight ahead, and went on driving.

"*Remarkably* similar," Chuckles continued. "The Bedouin and the Indian are obsessed with the same things. Sun, moon, wind. Water, courage, honor. Love, hate, hospitality. Fate, freedom, tribe, God. The Bedouin lives in a tent, the Indian in a teepee, each taken from the hides of his animals. The Bedouin buys his wife with a camel, the Indian with a horse. Both love beads, trinkets, and bright objects. Both paint themselves before riding into battle. Their raiding habits are similar, their proverbs almost identical, and their folklore interchangeable. Both wander, endlessly. I intend to write a book one day proving that in pre-history the American Indian migrated from Arabia! You see, Yahutha, I'm interested in anthropology, too, and I could tell you a lot about Indians, and Bedouins, and other things. Pity you're deaf and dumb."

Chuckles glanced at his wrist watch and estimated they would reach Wadi Mafish in half an hour. The heat was stupefying.

It had stupefied more distinguished travelers—and more learned anthropologists—than Chuckles Vespucci. For more than a century, Englishmen had roamed over this wasteland. They were of two breeds. The first were adventurers and romantics, at once enchanted by the desolation and smitten by the desert race. The second, who came much later, were mostly soldiers—Tommies in tanks and armored cars who sweetened their homesickness with sour ballads . . .

> Don't let's be nasty to the A-rabs
> Don't let's be horrid to the wogs
> The King has sent instructions
> To avoid all kinds of ructions
> We mustn't call the sons of bitches dogs.

But they went back to be bank clerks in Manchester and hod-carriers in Liverpool, and didn't matter. The men who did matter, the Oxbridgian romantics, remained behind with their beloved Bedouins, struggling to build a bridge between Arab and Arabist. They failed; but not before the love affair, as unilateral as it was epochal, had embittered both parties.

Why did the desert cast so irresistible a spell on the well-bred Englishman? Some suggested that in the fierce and noble Bedouin way of life the Briton discovered the sublimest extension of public-school sportsmanship—and that among the idyllic Bedu warriors he found the most deserving beneficiaries of his erotic yearning. Didn't Lawrence make lyrical allusions to "exquisitely made" Arabs "quivering together in the yielding sand"? Didn't the Koran itself promise a Paradise overrun by "dark-eyed houris and beautiful youths"? If such was the nature of the English ardor, it went unrequited. For in fact, Arab buggery is a pastime not of the desert but of the towns; the godlike Bedu are known to disdain this melancholy entertainment.

What was it, then, that drew Englishmen into the desert? More lofty minds speculated that the reasons were eschatological: that in these burning sands, the birthplace of the great religions and the scene of most mystical experience, the Briton believed he might have visions of his own. Certainly the desert was more congenial to this quest than the cluttered marketplace of modern England. In the wilderness there were no Liverpools or telephones to obstruct man's conversation with God. In the wilderness one knew at once that the soft wind was God, sighing; the primeval stillness God, holding his breath; the whirlish storms only God again, sneezing. Moreover the wilderness was fairly crawling with eschatological characters—men and women in Old Testament costume, living lives of glad destitution in a language which leavened every commonplace act with the nourishment of His name.

Skeptics suggested that the British appetite for desolate places was nothing more or less than the pangs of imperial hunger. Compared to the spicy feast of India, the Arab deserts were at first only hors d'oeuvres to be nibbled at; but with time they became as tasty. They lay along the route to Asia, and that route had to be secured; they were the crossroads of three continents; they were found to contain bottomless lakes of petrol. So it became more and more necessary to keep the tribes out of mischief, or at least out of the way. The task of pacifying the desert was handed to the romantics, who embarked upon it with mixed emotions. Like Lawrence, they knew that the Bedu's strength was the strength of man geographically beyond temptation, and that if forced into civilized life "they would succumb like any savage race to its diseases, meanness, luxury, crooked dealing." The romantics recoiled in horror at the notion of the Bedu becoming like the rest of men—like Englishmen—estranged forever from their childlike, halcyon closeness to God. So the romantics resolved to wipe out Bedouin warfare, but not the Bedouin culture.

In destroying the one they unwittingly wrote the death warrant of the other. Since the dawn of history, the Bedu had survived by a curious counterbalancing of hospitality and raiding. When in transit across another's wilderness, a Bedouin received feast and shelter under the marvelously reciprocal laws of tribal hospitality. Or, when his tribe grew even more impoverished than usual, he and his fellow warriors simply mounted their camels and galloped down into the next wadi, where they relieved their neighbors of their superfluous belongings. It was a harsh code, but an upright one: women and children were never violated, and it was the unquestioned right of the victims to mount a reprisal raid at the first opportunity. Life went on much as it had for a thousand years, and the Bedouin remained, as he had always been, a being destitute but glad. The British repression of raiding disrupted the rhythm and indeed demolished the very foundations of Bedouin society; it transferred the machinery of justice from the tribes to national governments and threw the Bedu on the mercies of the town Arabs, their historic—and often crooked-dealing—enemies. But for decades the romantics could not force themselves to face the consequences of their good intentions: the Bedouin way of life was dying. And from the Rif mountains to the Indian Kush, out of a millennium of trancelike slumber, the rest of Islam was awakening; in the towns, intellectuals and revolutionaries were clamoring for their share of the modern world. The romantics, still smitten by the noble Bedu, heard hardly a word. They reformed a bit here, innovated a smidgen there; the results only made them more certain than ever that the place for all Arabs was not in the twentieth century but in the Old Testament. This lyrical policy made inevitable a tragic and noisy collision between Britain and the awakened Arabs.

Such as Mustafa ibn Mabrouk. Whatever had drawn Britons into the desert—public-school fantasies, mystical longings, imperial avarice, or a mixture of all three—the Prime Minister had really ceased to care. The British were no longer running things, anyway. What Mustafa could never forgive the romantics was the image of the Arab they had enshrined in the Western world: the biblical Bedouin in flowing robes and wind-whipped head-cloth, riding a quaint camel across a sea of sand. This was precisely the image which, from the first hour of his public life, Mustafa had been most determined to destroy. There had been his famous interview over the BBC: "I'm getting tired of all those British and American trippers going out into the desert as if it were some sort of zoo, gawking at the Bedouins as if they were giraffes, or something! I should like to offer the British public a few facts. First, eighty percent of my people are not Bedouins. Second . . ." A month after he took office he declared the Bedouin areas off limits to cinema companies and picture magazines.

By blood, the Prime Minister was a Bedouin himself: that was the trouble. As in Ambassador Fitzgibbon, the consuming flame in Mustafa was not pride, not ambition, but embarrassment. He believed he was a little bit *jabali*—shanty. He was obsessed by the memory of his Bedouin boyhood. The exotic meals: gobbets of sheep fat, scraps of unleavened bread, husks and leavings from the Sheikh's tent. The quaint proverbs: "A head well populated by lice is the sign of a generous mind." The picturesque practices: camel urine for hair wash. His father had died of consumption, his mother in childbirth, and in infancy the Sheikh of the Beni Talal had taken him into his tents and made him a goatherd. That was what Mustafa could never get out of his mind: the goats. The Sheikh smelled of them, so did his wives and his retainers, and Mustafa was afraid that he still smelled of them himself. How do you scrub away the smell of goats in little more than a decade? He had spent every conscious moment of that time trying, teaching himself how to cover up—his Sandhurst education, his force-fed taste for Vivaldi and Mozart, his voracious reading, his torrential quotations—but he knew that it would never be enough. Every now and then the goatherd in him showed through. A man like Sir Charles Chetwynd-Pott could spot it in a second. Privately Mustafa was bitterly embarrassed by the methods he felt forced to use to retain his power: not the cunning and intrigue—that game he would always love—but the fawning, vulgar, mendacious rhetoric which filled his newspapers and his own speeches. In the acclamation of the mob he heard the cry of his brother goatherds calling him home. And for that he could never quite forgive them, or himself: he knew that he was an underdeveloped country, too.

And yet, for all Mustafa's resolve to exterminate the backward Bedouin way of life, it was not in his mind to maltreat the Bedouins themselves. They were, after all, his people. The more bloodthirsty of his aides urged brutal reforms. "No, no," Mustafa said. "The Bedu will rise up in revolt if they are forced. We will modernize them my way."

Mustafa's way was, at first, a grandiose and costly scheme to put all his Bedouins into pants. They wore them for a while, under their skirts. Then there was the crash program to discourage their nomadic habits and make them ranchers. All sorts of deeds and fertilizers were distributed, with the promise of piped water "as soon as we get the money." Schools and clinics were constructed—often without anyone to staff them. These and many other enterprising projects were mounted; most failed. Poor planning was not always the cause. The reforms had been openly resisted by the Bedouins themselves, particularly by their traditional leaders. It was not that the Bedu lacked intelligence or were incapable of civilized life; it was that, having seen civilization, they wanted no part of it. Their rare exposure to the neon-lit clamor of the modern city had sent them scampering in horror back to the beatitude of the wilderness.

But now there was drought, and famine, among the Bedu. The sun had laid their fragmentary crops to waste and decimated their flocks. Before, the Bedu had been fighting for their identity; now they were fighting for their lives. They bitterly blamed Mustafa ibn Mabrouk, flesh of their flesh, blood of their blood, for denying them the grain they could no longer grow themselves. But in fact, Mustafa had no grain to give them.

Such were the unhappy circumstances which prevailed in Wadi Mafish, the birthplace of Mustafa ibn Mabrouk, on the day of Chuckles Vespucci's visit.

> "We gathered our horses, got ready to fight,
> As the band of Sioux Indians just came into sight.
> They came down upon us with a whoop and a yell.
> At the crack of our rifles oh six of them fell."

The children pounded their desks with delight when Chuckles told them that the song was about Red Indians. The minstrel was holding forth in the rude stone schoolhouse at Wadi Mafish. Upon arrival he had gone directly to the tent of Hassan, Sheikh of the Beni Talal tribe, to present the King's letter and to pay his respects. Sheikh Hassan had not yet returned from the hunt; in the meantime, lute in hand, Chuckles was regaling the local population. His theater was this small classroom, crammed with the crudest of wooden desks and heaps of undernourished boys, their skulls all shaven to arrest the ravages of ringworm. Amid a pestilence of flies, still greater heaps of little girls, Bedouin soldiers and elderly toothless men pressed curiously about the open windows.

> "They made a bold dash and came near to our train,
> And the arrows fell down just like hail and like rain.
> But with our long rifles we fed them cold lead,
> 'Till many a brave warrior around us lay dead."

The schoolteacher, a town Arab in trousers, began to translate the American ballad into Arabic for the benefit of his pupils. Not that the boys were completely incapable of understanding the song themselves: Chuckles had interrupted them during their English lesson (one of Mustafa ibn Mabrouk's innovations). They were reading a simplified text of *Treasure Island.* Now, in gratitude for the minstrel's performance, the teacher called on his brighter boys to read some passages aloud. "I zaw zomeone d-draweeng zlowly neer along thee road. Hee was b-blainly blind, for hee tab-bed before heem weeth a steeck . . ." Chuckles began to smile, but then he wondered whether American children of the same age might do as well in Arabic. "But thee blind man bulled mee close ub to heem. 'Now, boy,' hee zaid, 'take me een to thee cabtain.' 'Zir,' zaid I, 'ub-bon my word I dare not.' . . ." Chuckles marveled at the discipline in this room, especially in such heat and human congestion. The romantics had been right about one thing: these people were close to God. "Heez left leg was cut off cloze by thee heeb, and un-der thee left shol-der hee car-reed a c-crotch, hob-beeng about ub-bon eet like a bird . . ." One boy, squeezed up tight against the window, particularly caught the minstrel's eye; his clothes were rags and his naked skull fairly bubbled with boils; he seemed slower than the others; the teacher did not call on him. " 'Meester Seelver, Zir?' I ask-ked. 'Yes, my lad,' zaid hee, 'such eez my name, to bee sure. And who may you bee?' . . ." The slow boy bent close over his book, his lips moving, his little hand racing across the page trying to keep up with Long John Silver's misdeeds. " 'No, not I,' zaid Seelver. 'Fleent was cab-tain. I was g-gward-der-maz-der, along of my teember leg. . . .' "

When Chuckles went outside again, the others followed, and there was the customary pandemonium as he proceeded to his Land-Rover. The Bedouin soldiers surrounded him and begged him to visit their fort on the hill overlooking the wadi. As Yahutha drove him away, he looked back. The crowd was scattering. Through the misty, lingering veil of their dust he perceived—only for an instant—the slow boy, alone by the window in the deserted classroom, still hunched over his *Treasure Island.*

. . .

The turreted limestone fort, built by the British, crouched high on an umber hill. Young Bedouin soldiers scrambled out of doorways and windows when Chuckles made his appearance in the courtyard. They spread goat-hair blankets and camel saddles on the gravel, sat him down and pressed glass after glass of hot, sickly-sweet tea upon him. They flaunted their marksmanship with pistols and made their gelded steeds and dromedaries dance. The romantics had been right about another thing: a great many of these warriors were outrageously handsome—sylphlike, a trifle vain, almost foppish. One of them produced a vial of cheap perfume, and they smeared their hands and faces in honor of the occasion. And yet they were completely masculine in manner, radiating a dignity quite beyond the dissembling of any Valentino Arab. They lived monastic, abstemious lives, visiting their women only rarely, and the rest of the time roamed the wilderness in quest of contraband and hashish smugglers. One of them fingered patience beads, his companion the dial of a transistor set.

Sergeant: You speak good Arabic.

Chuckles: Yes. I learned it in Libya. Please forgive my Benghazi dialect.

Soldier: Why aren't you drinking your tea?

Chuckles: The bottom of my glass is stuck to the blanket.

Sergeant: Ah. That means women love you. Ahmed, give Mr. Chuckles another glass. Did you like our school?

Chuckles: Very much.

Sergeant: The teacher said you were singing about Red Indians.

Chuckles: Yes.

Soldiers: Sing it for us, Mr. Chuckles!

Chuckles:

"We shot their bold Chief at the head of the band.
He died like a warrior with the gun in his hand.
When they saw their full Chief laying dead in his gore,
They whooped and they yelled and we saw them no more."

Sergeant: What a nice lute.

Chuckles: Please don't touch it! It's very . . . fragile.

Corporal: Do you know our King Mohammed?

Chuckles: He is my friend.

Soldiers: Oh, God bless him! He is our lord!
Chuckles: You must remain loyal to him—always.
Soldiers: We will die for him!
Chuckles (inaudibly): You may have to.
Sergeant: Eh?
Chuckles: I said it's terribly hot.
Sergeant: Do Red Indians wear clothes? Can they marry white women?

Chuckles had discarded his Zen outfit several days ago in Al Asima; now, as he looked around him, he felt that the exotic garments of his new friends put his own nondescript slacks and sport shirt to shame. He suggested as much, whereupon the soldiers presented him with a complete costume from their own stores. In the flowing skirts of the Bedu, and with his dark, brief beard framed by a checkered headcloth, he looked surprisingly Arab. As they festooned him with a red sash and a silver dagger, portentous, purplish clouds began to gather in the western sky. The air grew suddenly still, the camels apprehensive. *"Khamseen,"* the soldiers said. Chuckles looked at his wrist watch and then down into the deep of the wadi, where Sheikh Hassan's tents lay like long black caterpillars in the sand. He was confident the Sheikh had returned by now; it was nearly noon. Thus more decorously arrayed for his strange mission, Chuckles Vespucci borrowed the sergeant's horse and, still clutching his lute, cantered off into the wadi to be about his business.

But he had misjudged the proximity of the approaching storm. Hardly had he left the fort than the sun dissolved in a sulphurous soup of air, casting an uncanny, freakish pallor upon the face of the desert. As suddenly the wailing banshee wind became a thousand roaring, warring whirligigs of sand. A torrent of tiny daggers —slivers of thistle, pebble and rock—stabbed at his eyes. His horse, unable to endure the wind's distemper and an unfamiliar burden both at once, galloped wildly out of control. Though an experienced equestrian, Chuckles had all he could do to remain mounted as the steed charged pell-mell down one slope and up another. Then they careened around and around, chewed like chaff in the jaws of a vortex; Chuckles felt a snapping of the strap around his neck and his precious lute leaping from his grasp; he lurched, retrieving it in mid-air. The horse flew free of the whirlpool and in time grew tired enough to trot, as did the tempest, now a curtain of tawny dust whose dance grew lax, then languid. But the ebbing cast its own and even weirder spell, distorting size, perspective, distance. Rocks became mountains; shrubs loomed like trees. Chuckles at last reined in his beast and dismounted to regain his bearings, only to see an old man, tall as a giant, stalking toward him. He carried a staff; his flowing robes were as white as his beard, and he looked for all the world like a prophet emerging from the mists of antiquity. Chuckles wanted to cry out, "Are you Abraham? are you Isaias?"—but then the hallucination passed as quickly as it had come. The prophet shriveled to quite ordinary proportions as he grew closer; behind him in the dispersing dust were goats and Arabs and tents. Chuckles knew where he was, and he knew who the old man was, but still he could not resist the mischief of calling out, "Are you Abraham? Are you Isaias?"

"I am Hassan, Sheikh of the Beni Talal," the old man said. "Are you the American gentleman?"

"I am, my lord."

"May peace be upon you. I have been expecting you. Your disguise is preposterous, but suitable."

A large, oval copper tray, heaped with coarse rice, pieces of mutton, onion, and tomato. Garnishments of grease, intestine, and ostrich egg. In the center, the sheep's skull . . . and the Sheikh's hoary fingers plucking the eyeballs from their sockets.

He popped one of them into his mouth, like a grape, and offered the other to Chuckles. The eye was the delicacy. Chuckles was too sporting to gulp it whole and let it go at that; instead he chewed on it noisily, stuck out his tongue to show the little pieces, and then slurped them down one by one. The old man was impressed. He unsheathed his dagger, chopped out the sheep's brains and gave them to his guest, who managed them well, though with less flair. Then the final tidbit, the tongue. "Serves me right," Chuckles mumbled.

They were in the Sheikh's tent, squatting cross-legged with several of the old man's sons on a threadbare Persian carpet, devouring the day's manna with their bare hands. Above the food hovered a raucous conclave of flies. Tattered servants shuffled in and out attending to the various errands of the feast. The hearthside nearby was cluttered with wooden crates, blackened coffee pots, and an empty bottle of Heinz ketchup. Chuckles glimpsed a galaxy of silent, shining eyes peeping over the goat-hair partition; they were the women, watching. From behind them came the sound of someone braying coffee beans in a bowl, and the squealing of hungry children.

The Sheikh kept muttering wretched apologies for the unworthiness of the cuisine: ". . . drought . . . famine . . . not a scrap of bread . . . our dying flocks . . . hunted all morning for a gazelle . . . slaughtered our last lamb to feed you . . . the feasts we used to have . . ." In manner, the Sheikh was autocratic but kindly; his simplest gesture bespoke a lifetime of being obeyed; he had hardly to raise his voice but everyone around him, and particularly his own sons, stumbled over themselves in the execution of his wishes. His face was fascinating. Its deep, melancholy furrows would have defined the nuances of any artist's palette. The lines hinted, all at once, of wisdom, heartbreak, resignation; of piety, stubbornness, stern justice and, above all, of love of the old ways. But his feet were traitors: from beneath his timeless robes protruded a pair of fading Argyle socks, shod in shiny tan moccasins.

When they were done eating, Chuckles uttered the traditional "May God requite you, O Patriarch," a boy came in with a basin and a beaked ewer, and they washed their hands. The remains of the feast were taken outside, and Chuckles watched while the Sheikh's younger sons and servants, squatting in the naked sand, tore rapaciously into the leavings, disputing like wild dogs over every scrap of meat. The Sheikh dozed, sitting up; Chuckles lay down on a corroding mattress, and slept.

He was awakened an hour later by a clapping of hands; it was the Sheikh calling for refreshments. The servants came in with bowls of warm goat's milk, and over a primus stove they began to brew large pots of thick, black coffee flavored with cardamom. The deaf-mute Yahutha appeared, deposited himself at the American's feet, and jealously took upon himself the task of serving the minstrel. Chuckles waved him away, but the Sheikh put out a restraining hand. "Leave him," the patriarch said. "He is the devoted slave of His Majesty. He has come here with the King more times than I can remember. I trust him as I trust my own son. What a pity his ears are dead to sound, and he cannot hear the saga."

The saga? Chuckles wondered when the old man was going to dismiss the others and get down to business. But he knew there was no hastening the protocol of the wilderness, so he lay back on the pillows to enjoy the recitation. Most Bedu tribes had official poets, but the Sheikh of the Beni Talal fancied himself a better bard than any of his retainers. Slowly at first, in a rich, musical voice, he began to recount the genealogy and history of his tribe. He spoke of its conversion from paganism and idolatry to the true creed, of its fidelity to the Prophet, of its subsequent migrations from Mecca up through El Hajar, Wadi Safra, Wasta, Wadi Yenbo, Umm Lejj, Ras Gara, Dar el Nasara, Jebel Rufeiya, Abu Ajaj, holding high the green standard of the House of Hamad, propagating with fire and sword the glorious gospel of Islam. He told of victories in Mesopotamia, of conquests in Cyrenaica, of triumphal entries into Tunis. He evoked the cadences of horses' hoofs, the thunder of invading hordes, the roar of palaces put to the torch, the piercing cries of devastated populations. He relived the hardships of a hundred desert marches: heat, thirst, hunger, pestilence, famine, starvation; the joys of equestrian sport, javelin play, and festivals of circumcision; the waxing and waning of moons; the celestial stillness of starlit nights, broken only by the howling of wolves far, far away.

On a crude lyre, a boy began to accompany the breathless singsong of the patriarch's narration. Everyone in the camp had gathered round to hear this epic they had already heard a hundred times before. When the old man uttered a phrase which especially pleased them, they took it up, repeating it again and again as in a chorus, and then adding spontaneous embroideries and variations of their own. In turn the women, in purdah behind the goat-hair partition, seized on these variations and trilled them in spasms until the tent seemed to tremble with their keening.

Gradually the patriarch advanced from centuries past to the present epoch. He sang of the tribe's last great migration, to this desert in Al Khadra—and of the tribe's unvanquishable devotion to the House of Hamad, under whose banner it had first emerged from the sanctuaries of Arabia. He bore witness to the bonds which bound the Beni Talal to the present King's ancestors, and to his grandfather, and to his father—touching circumspectly on the flow of gold which had passed from Palace to patriarch in happier days. When he uttered the name of the reigning Mohammed the others cried "Oh, God bless him! He is our lord!" He testified to the Beni Talal's primacy among the multiple Bedu tribes of the nation, and unraveled the web of intermarriage and lateral alliance which established his personal pre-eminence over all other desert chieftains, and indeed over every Bedu officer in the army. He vowed the vengeance of the Bedu and of heaven on all perfidy to the House of Hamad, and cried out "Long live our King!" The others roared, "God give him victory! We will die for him!"

So ended the saga. It had lasted four hours. Chuckles was very weary. The Sheikh dismissed his entourage, and at last they were alone save for the deaf-mute Yahutha, who lay in a bundle at the American's feet, his eyes closed, snoring gently, like a good puppy. Chuckles was certain the moment had come: the Sheikh would put aside his parables and begin a serious discussion. He was mistaken; the old man glanced at his gold watch, reached for his transistor, and flicked on the dial. On came Radio al Asima, sputtering cha cha cha; then a voice, rasping with invective against Calvin Hampshire's criminal policies and exhorting Arabs everywhere to rise up against American imperialism. The Sheikh listened attentively for some minutes, and turned it off. He frowned inscrutably.

"We Bedu are not as ignorant of the world as everyone supposes," he said. "We hear other broadcasts—Radio Baghdad, Radio Beirut, Radio London—which tell other tales."

"They often speak more truth, my lord," Chuckles answered.

"Our own young men venture from time to time into the great city, and return to tell us that all is not well in the government of Mustafa ibn Mabrouk."

"Your young men have keen ears, my lord."

"Mustafa ibn Mabrouk does not practice his religion . . . they say."

"I have heard the same, my lord."

"Mustafa ibn Mabrouk allows young women to walk with bare arms in the streets of his capital . . . they say."

"I have seen them, my lord."

"Mustafa ibn Mabrouk has brought unbelievers, atheists, communists into his ministries . . . they say."

"I fear he has, my lord."

"Mustafa ibn Mabrouk erects factories and new buildings to adorn his capital, but will not send wheat to his own people . . . they say."

"The legends of his ingratitude could fill libraries, my lord."

"Mustafa ibn Mabrouk is plotting to dethrone our King Mohammed . . . they say."

"He must be stopped, my lord."

The patriarch paused. He seemed reluctant to pursue the points he had raised. There was a silence of several minutes, made only more exasperating by the gentle wailing of the wind outside. Finally the American took the initiative.

"My lord," he said, "your hospitality today has been extravagant—considering your present circumstances, prodigal. I feel I cannot leave you without in my own way attempting to reciprocate it. I believe it is the custom of your people, is it not, to accept some token of a guest's gratitude?"

The Sheikh sighed. "They say."

Chuckles reached for his lute, groped with his fingers about its bottom, and released a tiny latch. There was a springing sound; a rectangular section of the belly clicked open. A stream of sand hissed out onto the threadbare Persian carpet. From within the bowels of the instrument the minstrel extracted a small bundle of crisp, tightly-bound paper currency, and placed it before the old man. The patriarch contemplated it for a moment. Then he sighed again—rather sadly, the American thought—and, without speaking, deposited the money deep within the privacy of his inner garments.

Another long pause. The old man seemed very muddled.

"We are a poor people," he said at last. "But our memories are rich. We shall remember your generosity."

"Not my generosity, my lord, but the inexhaustible abundance of my Benefactor. My Benefactor—and yours."

"Then we shall remember him as well. In our prayers, and in our deeds. May I know his name?"

The sun was setting. Its beams streamed through the opening of the tent, bathing the old man's profile in a titian radiance. The American hesitated. He looked out into the desert. In the distance, a herd-boy was chasing two goats with a stick. Beyond him moved the solitary black silhouette of a woman, like a lost nun in such a vastness. On the horizon, the last glimmering of sun splashed a spray of jade mist over the landscape, suggesting a vegetation that was not there. Illusion, illusion; everything in this wretched kingdom was illusion. But the Sheikh had to be answered. The American leaned forward, and whispered a single word—a name so awesome among the mighty it had, at various times and places, sent tremors of fright through timid chancelleries, toppled insubordinate parliaments, chastened emperors. But the old man did not hear; just at that moment, a gust of desert wind blew furiously into the tent, raising little tantrums of dust and rattling the coffee pots. The patriarch repeated his question. "May I know his name?"

"My lord, his name is . . . Pullmotor."

16

"Bullmotor?"

"The Benefactor, my lord."

"Ah yes. The name comes back to me now." The old man smiled mischievously. "You were wondering when I was going to come to the point, eh?"

"I was as determined as you, my lord, to observe the proprieties."

"It has not been an easy decision for me to make. When my son came to me last week and told me of his meeting with you in Al Asima, and of your Mr. Bullmotor's proposals, I was alarmed. I am seventy years old. For forty years British agents have come into this tent, sat where you sit, and offered me their gold. I did not touch it. This is the first time I have ever accepted money from a foreigner, and I am not proud. But now my people are starving, dispersing like dead flowers before the desert wind, so, as God wills —" He trailed off into another daydream.

Chuckles plunged his hand again into his lute, pulled out a compact roll of paper, and spread it on the carpet. It was a map. "Now," he said, "if I may have your attention, my lord, these three red marks represent the places in the mountains where your men will find the small arms. Here, here and *here*. There will be pistols, automatic rifles, submachine guns, explosives, and plenty of ammunition. Also more money, if any of them have second thoughts at the last moment. The helicopters will cross the border—we're lucky it's so near—and deposit the treasure between midnight tonight and dawn. Your men will be able to recover it on their way into the city, after sundown tomorrow evening. I assume they can conceal the arms easily enough in their camel baggage. You're certain the movement of so many men will not arouse suspicion?"

"There is no problem. We have already informed the government we are sending a large delegation to join in the demonstrations against American imperialism."

"Excellent. Now it is important to remind your men that they are to be auxiliaries only. The burden of the work will be done by the Bedouin units in the army. You have conferred with their commanders?"

"Only with the ones I am sure can be trusted," the Sheikh replied. "Two of them came here secretly last night. They have accepted Mr. Bullmotor's plan. Everything is ready. Seven Bedouin battalions will be encamped near the capital tomorrow evening. Four of them are privy to our plan. At midnight they will surround the Prime Minister's palace, army headquarters and—I forget the others."

"The radio station, the telephone exchange and the Ministry of the Interior. Your men are to assist the regulars in capturing army headquarters and the Prime Minister's palace. Remember, everything depends on the element of surprise, and on timing. They must be as inconspicuous as possible in the streets around army headquarters until the regulars arrive. Also they must refrain unless absolutely necessary from firing on the civil population. The Prime Minister must be taken alive and treated with respect. He is a personal friend of Mr. Pullmotor's, and despite their political differences Mr. Pullmotor is extremely fond of him. Besides, Mr. Pullmotor detests bloodshed."

"What about His Majesty?"

"I was coming to that, my lord. I have probed the King's feelings as candidly as I dared during the last two days. He will not hear a word spoken against Mustafa. As far as I can see it has not even occurred to him that his throne is in danger. Mr. Pullmotor and I both agree that it would be extremely unwise to inform him of our plans beforehand. We must confront him with an accomplished fact. Accordingly, it is our plan to send a combined unit of Bedouin regulars and your own men up to the Royal Palace as soon as the operation in the city has been completed. They will present their grievances as a body, inform His Majesty of what they have done, and call on him to appoint a new Prime Minister."

The patriarch nodded. "Who will be the new Prime Minister?"

"I don't think Mr. Pullmotor has made up his mind yet. Perhaps Hassan Walahadan, the Foreign Minister. Perhaps, if he can be persuaded, old Taj Pasha."

"He is an evil man."

"It would only be until someone more suitable can be found. Remember, Mustafa has exiled most of the old politicians."

"I don't suppose it matters," the Sheikh said wearily. "All politicians are scoundrels. As long as it's someone who will send us some food, and then leave us in peace."

"My lord, on both points you have Mr. Pullmotor's word of honor."

"There is something which troubles me."

"My lord?"

"A full moon shines tomorrow. That is not a happy portent. We have a saying—*Let not the sun smite thee by day, nor the moon by night.*"

"Fascinating. Our own scripture contains almost the same words. Hundred and twenty-first Psalm, sixth verse. But it must be tomorrow night, or never. I will leave you now, my lord. Come on, Yahutha, time to drive me back—wake up!"

"He cannot hear you, poor lad. Give him a little kick."

In the open Land-Rover, beneath a sky blazing with stars, Chuckles and Yahutha began their journey back to Al Asima. Racing across the opaque wilderness, Chuckles felt both amused and satisfied by the events of the last several hours. He thought about the saga, the runaway horse, the hallucinations, the desert warriors and the keening women; they had made a memorable day—but hardly an exceptional one by the standards of Chuckles Vespucci.

For in truth, Chuckles Vespucci was not Chuckles Vespucci. He had been born Cornelius MacFlicker, and his beginnings were in the Bible-belt highlands of Tennessee. His Pentecostalist parents had named him after Cornelius the Centurion, in whose house in biblical Caesarea the elect of the Gentiles had been given the gift of tongues. Chuckles fancied himself to have inherited this very charisma, and judging by his Arabic—of which he spoke two dialects close to perfection—this was not a hollow supposition. Charismatic or not, Chuckles had an enchanted ear; exposed to a language for a fortnight, he could speak it as if it were his own. Both in his private peregrinations and on missions for Paul Pullmotor, he had had occasion to become fluent not only in Arabic and many of the European tongues, but in Osmanli, Urdu, Khmer, East Lao, Mandarin Chinese, Hausa, Fon, Twi-Fante and Efik-Ibibo. And with good reason had Solafa found him attractive, even to the point of attempting—not very successfully—to seduce him. For in his tender years Chuckles had studied to become a Pentecostal preacher; he had spent eleven months in the Smoky Mountain Institute of the Bible, and indeed might have graduated a full-fledged evangelist had it not been for his unhappy habit of bringing his water pistol with him to evening Hymn Sing. "The Lord's vineyard," the dean informed him, "is not a playpen for hobgoblins."

Thereafter Chuckles—or rather Cornelius—had embarked on a career of chameleonism and quest, excelling in odd jobs and impersonations. He became, at various times and in various countries, a sanitary engineer, a psychiatrist, an American Express guide, a male nurse in a leprosarium, a chiropractor, an artificial-flower maker, a mortician, a bookie, and a talking sausage on Italian television. As a salesman, he had peddled wastepaper baskets, electric blankets, spark plugs, vacuum cleaners, tulip bulbs, beer, fertilizers, hair spray, lawn mowers, greeting cards, marmalade, parakeets, sweet potatoes, Zippo lighters, and linoleum. From time to time he encountered people who told him he was grotesque. "Am I any more grotesque," he asked them, "than modern life itself?"

He wandered very far from the Smoky Mountains. In Tanganyika he was keeping body and soul together as a Swahili interpreter when he met Paul Pullmotor rhinoceros hunting on the plains of Serengeti. They became friendly, and Pullmotor knew a good man when he saw one. He put Chuckles on a plane to Washington, where he was met at the airport and whisked to Pullmotor's headquarters, fingerprinted, plugged into a lie detector and asked three questions: Are you a one hundred percent red-blooded patriotic American? Are you a communist? Are you a fairy? Chuckles answered "I suppose so" to the first and "I hope not" to the other two, and the machine passed him. Thereafter he became Pullmotor's favorite field man in the Impersonation Department. House detective at the United Nations, chorus boy in Saigon, physiotherapist in Conakry! He had infiltrated the communist parties of five countries and the households of nearly a dozen ambassadors, cabinet ministers and heads of government; he had bribed key officials in fourteen different languages and assisted Pullmotor in the overthrow of anti-American regimes on every continent except Australia. "Cornelius," Pullmotor told him once, "recruiting you onto my team is the most imaginative thing I've ever done—the crowning proof, if proof were needed, that I am a genius."

The present plot to overthrow the government of Mustafa ibn Mabrouk was quite simple. In Washington a fortnight ago, Pullmotor had got wind of Mustafa's secret negotiations with the Soviets. It was then that he decided to get rid of Mustafa. He called in Chuckles and asked for suggestions on ways and means. "Your disguise this time will have to be pretty ingenious," Pullmotor told him. "Mustafa can smell a rat through a brick wall, and he'll be watching me like a hawk. I'll mastermind, but you'll have to make the contacts. We're damned lucky you've never been in Al Khadra before."

Chuckles came up with some ideas for impersonations which he thought were rather clever. "How about a Happy Matrimony Consultant or a Doctor of Homeopathy?" he asked.

"No, no," Pullmotor said, "that's much too intellectual. I want something good and funny. You've not only got to get around town without causing suspicion, you've got to ingratiate yourself with the King."

Chuckles thought for a moment. "Isn't the King kind of a hep-cat? Couldn't I play the guitar?"

Pullmotor frowned. "Too commonplace."

"How about a rock-and-roll singer?"

"Now you're talking!" Pullmotor exclaimed. "But not with just a guitar."

"It would be a perfect place to put the loot."

"Loot? That's it! You'll carry a *lute*."

Enter Chuckles Vespucci. The more outrageous his disguises the more they pleased Pullmotor, because for Pullmotor overthrowing governments was a game, and a good game was always very, very *funny*. The gamesman drew up his master plan and flew off to Al Khadra by the direct route; Chuckles came around the long way, through the Far East, in order to deceive the enemy, not to mention the American Embassy in Al Asima. In Rangoon he purchased a pair of paperbacks on Buddhism, and it was from these that he derived the inspiration for his Zen costume. Pullmotor was delighted. Of course he could not tell Chuckles this—he wrote it on a piece of paper and passed it to him in the gentlemen's room at the Sheraton-Zahra. They could not risk being seen together; Pullmotor's room was wired, his telephone tapped, and he was shadowed wherever he went. But every day at a different prearranged time he had gone into the Sheraton-Zahra gentlemen's room and locked himself in the last cubicle. Chuckles would be waiting in the one contiguous to his, and without uttering a word they had passed notes to one another under the cubicle wall, flushing them down the toilet when they finished.

It worked magnificently. Pullmotor masterminded; the minstrel made the contacts. Chuckles was never shadowed, and he had only one close shave—the night at Dr. Pantry's cocktail party when Ambassador Fitzgibbon asked him if he had ever been in Benghazi. Indeed Chuckles had met the Ambassador in Benghazi two years previously, though under rather different circumstances—he was impersonating a dowager poetess at the time.

Now Chuckles nudged Yahutha and pointed to the lights of Al Asima just beginning to twinkle on the horizon; the King's batman nodded. The minstrel reflected that Mustafa might have saved himself a great deal of trouble simply by keeping Pullmotor out of the country—but as Paul had pointed out, Mustafa was much too sporting to do so cowardly a thing as that. Plotting against Pullmotor was Mustafa's favorite form of recreation; he thought it was *funny*. The Land-Rover crunched toward the city lights. Chuckles thought, *I wonder how funny he'll find it tomorrow at midnight when he is behind bars and Al Khadra has a new Prime Minister?*

Later that evening, Solafa, Ambassador Fitzgibbon, and Prime Minister ibn Mabrouk received messages of the highest importance to themselves.

Solafa's message was in the form of an unexpected visit from Mr. Mish Mish, the fat little man from the Ministry of the Interior.

"I apologize for calling on you at such an hour, ya Anissa Solafa," he began. "But it would not have been wise to come earlier. The Political Police are so . . . watchful."

"What is it, Mish Mish Effendi? Is anything wrong?"

"On the contrary, ya Anissa. I have come to tell you that I have finally made some progress in the matter of your passport. But there are certain steps . . ."

"If you mean another box or two of *marrons glacés* for your grandmother—"

"It will require more than *marrons glacés,* ya Anissa. And it will not be for my grandmother."

"But Mish Mish Effendi, I am no longer a rich woman. The government has confiscated everything."

They haggled for half an hour before reaching an arrangement on price—a rather high one, for there were to be several parties to this transaction. "It has been a pleasure to be of service to you, ya Anissa," Mr. Mish Mish said. "You will have the passport in a few days." Then he left by the servants' staircase, for he was a cautious man.

"Did you hear that, Michel?" Solafa cried out when Mr. Mish Mish had gone. "My passport! At last! Rome! Paris! My villa at St.-Jean-Cap-Ferrat! My bank account in Switzerland!"

"Nous voulons voyager," Michel intoned from behind the potted palms,

"sans vapeur et sans voile!
"Faites, pour égayer l'ennui de nos prisons . . ."

The Ambassador's message was an airmail-express letter which a duty Marine delivered to him at the Residence just before he retired. It was postmarked Tangier. He opened it eagerly, hoping. Yes. It was from Winifred, his wife.

Shawnie

I received your letter just now and I'm answering at once otherwise I might never. To answer your questions no I don't like Tangier, no I don't go over to Tetuan, yes I took the boat over to Gibraltar once but not to Algeciras yes I hope things would have been different if we had had a child. You say you've taught the houseboy how to mix a decent martini and do I want to pay a visit. At the moment I can't think of a better reason. The martini I mean.

Things have gone rather badly for me here, yes its another man (I suppose you heard you always do) but you spared me your details so I'll spare you mine. I'll make my arrangements and contact you in a few days. I'm tired Shawnie. The way I feel at this moment I'd follow you to the ends of the earth.

Winifred

The Ambassador sat down at the Chippendale desk in his bedroom and wrote a warm reply. He added a postscript: "Lately, I've been thinking a great deal about my youth. Perhaps—if you decide to stay and we can make a go of it—we can have our marriage sanctified by a priest. It wouldn't make any difference to you, would it?"

"Now," he said half aloud as he sealed the envelope, "if I can just manage to hold on here . . ."

The Prime Minister's message was a telephone call on his secret line.

"Yes, I'm alone," he said. "What happened today? I see. Yes. I see. I thought it might be him, though I must admit he had me fooled till yesterday. How much did he give him? Well, did you get a look at the map? Did he mention any names? No, not of Americans, of army officers. All right, I'll work on that myself. Hassan Walahadan or Taj Pasha, eh? They'll be sorry! Give me those again. Prime Minister's palace, army headquarters, radio station, telephone exchange, Ministry of Interior. Good work. Tomorrow night at midnight! I had a *feeling* it would be sometime this week. I'll be waiting for them. By God, that was a brilliant precaution—giving you to Mohammed as a birthday present! Look, has the King gone to bed yet? Well, as soon as he does, you'd better come down here and give me a full report. Yes, I realize that Mohammed has nothing to do with the plot. No, I'm not going to tell him about it. He'd find the whole thing much too confusing. Besides, I shall crush the traitors before they get anywhere near him. Look, I told you not to worry. I love Mohammed as much as you do. His safety will be assured—that's a promise. By the way, when this business is over I'm changing your assignment. You deserve a raise in wages, too. You've been a deaf-mute long enough . . ."

17

The next morning, exactly on schedule, the Arab East erupted in a series of spontaneous demonstrations against American imperialism. Shouting *Hambshire to the Hangman!,* churlish mobs marched on the American Embassies of Beirut, Baghdad, and Damascus. In all three capitals, the offices of the Mutual Understanding Commission were put to the torch. Trams and automobiles were overturned; American nationals were hastily advised by their consulates to keep off the streets; Western commercial enterprises closed down for the day amid a clanging of steel shutters. In Beirut, for good measure, the British Council was burned to the ground.

A similar, though less robust, exercise was repeated in Al Asima itself. The outrages which transpired in other countries could not, technically at least, be blamed on Mustafa ibn Mabrouk—and in his own capital it remained his strategy to deny Calvin Hampshire a pretext for severing diplomatic relations. Accordingly, he ordered that the spontaneous demonstrations in Al Asima were to be noisy but not convulsive. At nine o'clock in the morning, the police began to corral vagrants and passing pedestrians into the courtyard of the Ministry of the Interior. When they had impressed perhaps seven hundred persons, a little man in steel-rimmed spectacles and a red fez wove his way mechanically through the crowd distributing five-piastre notes to each spontaneous demonstrator. Then the cheerleaders arrived on scene, and the sound trucks, and unkempt young men bearing bright green and crimson banners and great placards painted with patriotic slogans—some of them familiar, others composed especially for the occasion. *Long Live Mustafa, Warrior of Islam, Torch of Arabism! . . . Death to Hampshire, Imperialist, Epileptic, Dope Fiend!* (The standard stipend for placard and banner bearers was ten piastres; for cheerleaders, fifteen.) As usual, an immense portrait of the Prime Minister was borne aloft beside an equally large likeness of Gary Cooper. At about ten o'clock the spontaneous demonstrators were turned out into the street and instructed to march on the American Embassy, a mile distant on the other side of the broad Mabrouk.

From past experience the police estimated that the size of the mob would quadruple by the time it reached its destination. But it was another of those particularly hot days, and the spontaneous demonstrators who actually persevered as far as the Embassy barely exceeded a hundred in number. They found waiting for them a phalanx of two hundred riot police, brandishing night sticks, tear-gas bombs and fire hoses at the ready, in keeping with the Prime Minister's wish that the rage of the population be contained within civilized limits.

The ensuing demonstration was as obstreperous as its depleted numbers allowed. The zealots beat on their drums, sang patriotic songs, and shouted an assortment of deplorable epithets against the Secretary of State, the Queen of England, and the poor showing of the Al Asima Football Club. Otherwise it was a gay, almost friendly affair. One of the demonstrators recognized an acquaintance—a gardener—on the opposite side of the compound gate, and protracted greetings were exchanged over the steel-helmeted heads of the riot police. The windows of the enormous Embassy were open and alive now with attachés and stenographers, curious, laughing and pointing. The Potable Water Attaché came out of the building with his candid camera, walked down to the gate, and began taking snapshots. In the competition to be photographed, a fist fight broke out between two of the demonstrators and a policeman.

High above them, on the terrace of the Tower, stood Ambassador Fitzgibbon, watchful and amused. His wife's letter last night had put him in extremely good spirits, and he wondered whether Eminence Grise might not enjoy this spectacle as much as he. He extracted the little creature from his air-conditioned cage and carried him to the balustrade. Now the policemen were fighting each other.

"Voilà, chéri. Les bêtises du Moyen Orient! C'est drôle, n'est-ce pas?"

Unlike most of his subordinates, Dr. Pantry was not watching the demonstration. At the moment he was alone in the auditorium of the Mutual Understanding Building across the street from the Embassy, impatiently awaiting the arrival of his guests.

This was a day of great personal satisfaction for the Director of Mutual Understanding, for finally his vision and tenacity had prevailed over the frugality and skepticism of his superiors in Washington. At long last the printed pamphlets, elaborate visual aids, didactic comic books and gramophone records were compactly housed within a cheerful, portable, plastic case: the perfected model of Dr. Pantry's Do-It-Yourself Anti-Communist Kit.

He had invited a number of high Khadrian officials and many of the more glittering names of Al Asima society to witness the ceremony of unveiling, and also to hear a scholarly paper which he intended to deliver on Soviet atrocities in Estonia. Unhappily, every government official on his invitation list was under strict instructions to stay away from Americans. Even the society Arabs, those *ancien régime* Christians and vicarious Europeans who normally gave a local dash to his cocktail parties, sensed the unusual precariousness of the political climate and dared not accept his hospitality today. In his zeal Dr. Pantry had neglected to take recent developments into account; a full half-hour after the appointed time, he was still hopeful of an audience. Finally a black man in shirtsleeves appeared in the rear of the auditorium. Dr. Pantry hopefully identified him as a minor official from the Ministry of National Enlightenment; in fact, he was one of the new janitors, looking for a quiet place to say his prayers. Dr. Pantry decided not to delay the ceremony any longer. Better to light one candle, he reasoned, than to curse the darkness. He walked to the podium and called out to the black man. "Come up front, sir," he said, "and make yourself comfortable!" The janitor advanced with great uncertainty toward the Director of Mutual Understanding.

"Now, if you'll just take a seat, sir, I'll get on with the unveiling," Dr. Pantry said.

"Shu bitriid, ya Basha?"

"Don't you speak English?"

"Ma btihki arabi?"

"I'm afraid I didn't quite catch that. Do you know YOUR COUNTRY'S IN DANGER?"

"Mit asif, ya hawaja, bas ma bifhamak."

"Oh dear. What I'm trying to tell you is COMMUNISM IS AGAINST YOUR RELIGION."

They were interrupted by a loud shattering of glass; the spontaneous demonstrators were throwing rocks through the windows of the auditorium. They threw three, and no more. Three was the limit imposed by the Prime Minister.

Matters more urgent than street demonstrations occupied the Prime Minister at that moment. He was in his office on the other side of the city, having a heated discussion with Captain Anwar A'war. At issue was the strategy for crushing the Pullmotor plot. Captain A'war favored immediate action, but Mustafa had overruled him.

". . . Don't you see, Anwar? First, we only know that four of the seven Bedouin battalions camped around the city are involved in the conspiracy. We don't know for sure which four, or which officers. If we start making wholesale arrests now, we risk alienating every Bedouin soldier in the army. Then we'd *really* have an insurrection on our hands. Secondly, Yahutha did not actually see the map showing where the arms for the Bedouin irregulars—"

"I could have a search party scouring those mountains in an hour."

"If we did that, we would only tip our hand again. No, the only sensible course is to let the conspirators collect the arms for us. Then we will draw all the traitors into our net, and *pounce*. Trust in me, ya Anwar! Besides, I want to keep Pullmotor thinking right up till midnight that he's won this little game. I'd give anything to see the look on his face when he discovers he's been outplotted."

"Aren't you gambling a great deal just to keep Pullmotor in suspense?" Captain A'war asked.

Late that afternoon, a band of perhaps two hundred Bedouin tribesmen mounted camels in Wadi Mafish and marched out for their rendezvous in the capital city. They visualized the impending struggle in epic images: they saw it as the great battle, not only for bread, but for their way of life. They had made themselves magnificent for this adventure. Their costume was a panoply of scarlets and blues and checkered head-cloths, wooden switches and leathern whips, a few flintlocks slung over shoulders, torsos criss-crossed with ammunition belts, silver daggers glinting in the sun. They had caparisoned their camels with wooly sheepskins, red and turquoise tassels and jigging talismans to guard against the Evil Eye. Flapping in front were two or three tattered blue flags, and the green standard of the House of Hamad. On the barren hill crests above, carved like black gargoyles across the cloister of cloud and sky, crouched the tribal women, whooping their farewells. They knew nothing of the secret business which had snatched their men away from them that day; but they surmised that something great and terrible was about to happen, and the sounds they sent from one side of the valley to the other were as full of lamentation as of godspeed. The men galloped onward and upward out of the wadi; the women lingered on the hills until at last the dust of the departure, mingling with the ululation, dissolved in malignant sunshine.

Shortly after dark, the men reached the mountains which divided the great depressed plain from the valley of the broad Mabrouk. Chuckles Vespucci's map made their treasure hunt an easy one; they had no trouble recovering the arms which Pullmotor's helicopters had left for them the night before. They concealed the weapons beneath their baggage, and then rode down toward the city, singing songs in praise of the Prophet and King Mohammed. They had not quite reached the capital when the full moon began to rise.

. . .

Shortly before midnight the Bedouin military units roared in trucks and armored cars out of their desert encampments and into the city. They had carefully synchronized their wrist watches. At exactly one minute before midnight they took up positions in front of the broadcasting station, the telephone exchange and the Ministry of the Interior. At the two most strategic points—the Prime Minister's palace and army headquarters—they joined forces with the irregulars from Wadi Mafish. It was all splendidly coordinated, the Pullmotor plan having been observed to the letter. But other timepieces, not of their party, had also been synchronized. At precisely fifteen seconds before twelve, in all five of the strategic places, a chorus of concealed loudspeakers began booming out, over and over again, a terse, recorded announcement: *This is the Prime Minister speaking. You are surrounded on all sides by troops loyal to the Government and to me. Lay down your arms, and Mustafa will be merciful.*

Then the windows and doors of buildings were thrown open, revealing machine-gun nests amid sandbags piled high, and the roofs came alive with loyalist soldiers aiming automatic weapons and bazookas. Suddenly several squadrons of Mustafa's Hawker Hunters swooped low and menacingly overhead—they were deafening.

The Bedu were brave men, but they knew a hopeless cause when they saw one. There was—in the name of honor, perhaps—some scattered resistance. Several of the rebels were wounded, and a loyalist lieutenant colonel was shot in the foot. Otherwise the uprising was disposed of quickly, cleanly, and without bloodshed. It was all over in less than ten minutes. The insurgents were stripped of their arms and marched off, under guard, to barracks; their officers were clamped behind bars.

Mustafa's strategy for crushing the plot had been a masterpiece of planning and execution, flawless in every detail.

Except one.

The Prime Minister had made his own office the command post, and he was at his steel desk receiving final reports from various sections of the city when, at about twelve forty-five, one of his colonels telephoned with unexpected news. Some hundred or so

Beni Talal diehards, detained in one of the smaller camps on the periphery of the city, had gone amuck, overcome their captors and broken out of barracks. They had hijacked some weapons and armored cars and were believed headed for the Royal Palace, high on the Jebel al Malouk, overlooking the capital. Apparently they still hoped to prevail upon the King to dismiss the Prime Minister —as if he could.

Mustafa immediately ordered a strong mobile detachment in hot pursuit, hoping it would intercept the Bedouins before they reached the Palace. Though the insurgents had no chance of success, this unexpected twist of events disturbed Mustafa. He had wanted to keep the King out of this.

He picked up his private line to the Palace. It was dead. Pullmotor's work. He slammed down the receiver in a fit of anger, and turned to Captain A'war.

"Anwar," he said, "if there's going to be trouble at the Palace we've got to get Mohammed out of there. Take the helicopter and go up and get him. Bring him down to the Sheraton-Zahra for the night. I'd do it myself, but I can't risk leaving here so soon. Hurry, and guard him well."

His Majesty was alone in his library, pasting pictures in his scrapbook.

He had been sleeping badly of late. His nightmares had been getting worse, and now not even his amulets, talismans, and charms could tempt him into bed before the first glimmerings of dawn. He had felt strangely all day. After supper he had put on his Field Marshal's uniform—it always made him feel better—and gone down in his red Ferrari to the city to see Christopher Grundoon. Christopher was out. Then up one flight to the flat above Christopher's to say hello to Solafa. Solafa was out. Then to the Sheraton-Zahra to find Chuckles Vespucci. Chuckles was out. So he had come home at about eleven-thirty, alone and in low spirits, to his Palace. Never had it loomed so large and hollow in the ashen light of a full moon. His guards had gone to bed; only a sentry or two struggled somnolently to attention as he hastened past them down the dark, interminable corridors to his private apartments in the rear of the Royal compound.

Yahutha, however, was still up—scarcely able, on this eventful night, to conceal his anxiety for the King's safety. Now he hovered outside the royal library, puttering every few minutes in and out of the room, emptying ash trays, opening and shutting windows, bringing Pepsi and potato chips that His Majesty did not want.

"What's the matter with you tonight, ya habibi?" Mohammed asked. "I know you can't hear me, but you can tell I don't need you. No, I've got plenty of glue—leave it alone. There's a blessing! There's a kiss! Now go to bed!" He waved him away.

Yahutha retreated out of sight into the gloomy antechambers; the King went back to his scrapbook. He had collected all the snapshots from his year at Harvard and was attempting to arrange them in sequence; before pasting them onto the page, he carefully composed little commentaries in Arabic and English across the corners. His eyes glazed with the memory of his American happiness. There they were again, all the treasured scenes and places: the Charles, the arched footbridge of the four obelisks, Adams House, St. Paul's, George Washington on horseback and Mrs. Webster's Bavarian bird castle in the Public Gardens. Then the scores of snapshots of Miss Finnegan, and of himself at her side, both of them serene on the Swan Boat. As he attached these to the black pages, he sang their song to himself. *Does your Mother know you're out, Cecil-ia?* cha cha cha . . . He came upon two copies of the same photograph, and decided he would give the extra one to Christopher Grundoon. On the bottom he inscribed, *To Christopher a memory of my Boston. Cecilia isn't so ugly, is she? Yrs, Moh. vii, Rex.* Christopher should be home by now, he thought; he decided to call him. He lifted the telephone receiver on his desk, and found it dead. This puzzled him.

Then a strange, whirring, chopping sound outside, rather like the one he had been hearing in his bad dreams. He went to the window and leaned out. In the moonlight he saw an army helicopter, lowering clumsily into the large courtyard beneath him, the tips of the propellor blades just skimming the fringes of an orange tree, slicing away a leaf or two. Beside the pilot in the cabin sat an army officer, and from the eye patch the King recognized him at once. The officer leaped from the machine before it had touched the ground.

"Is that you, Captain Anwar A'war?" the King called out.

"Your Majesty? Could you come down here, please?"

"The stairway is by the door there, Captain. I shall wait for you up here." He turned away from the window.

As a rule the King liked everybody, but he did not particularly care for Captain A'war. For one thing, it was usually the Captain who intercepted his telephone calls to Mustapha. The King had not been able to see or speak to the Prime Minister for several weeks—and for this he blamed not the Prime Minister, but Captain A'war. Moreover he had heard unpleasant stories from the Bedouins about the Captain's cruelty; above all he could not understand why a man with perfect vision should want to wear such a large and horrid black eye patch.

The King decided he was not going to take any nonsense from Captain A'war. He buttoned up his splendid tan military tunic, put on his Field Marshal's cap—the one with the gold braid and all the scrambled eggs—and sat down stiffly at his cluttered desk. Captain A'war came quickly and rather breathlessly into the royal library.

"Your Majesty, will you please come with me at once?"

"What's going on, Captain?"

"We think you would be more comfortable tonight at the Sheraton-Zahra."

"I'm quite comfortable right here in the Royal Palace, thank you."

"You don't understand, Your Majesty. This is an emergency."

"Emergency?"

"There has been an uprising in the city. Mustafa has crushed it. Some of the traitors have escaped. They are headed here now."

"Who are the traitors?"

"Your Majesty, there is little time."

"There is certainly time for you to identify the traitors."

"Bedouins."

The King leaped to his feet. "Which tribes?"

"Your Majesty, we must hurry."

"Captain, I will not step a foot outside this Palace until you tell me which tribes."

"Beni Talal, mostly."

"Beni Talal? *Traitors?* You must be mistaken, Captain. The

Beni Talal are my brothers. I go out every week to Wadi Mafish and bring them cigarettes and tinned vegetables. They are my brothers. I am their King. They fought beside my father, and my father's fathers, and my ancestors in the time of the Prophet. They rode up from Mecca and Wasta and Wadi Yenbo, holding high the green standard of the House of Hamad, proclaiming from Mesopotamia to Tunis the glorious gospel of Islam! I remember my father telling me, when I was a child, 'Trust always in the Beni Talal—they are your only real friends.' There must be some misunderstanding. I must remain here in my Palace until they come, and speak to my brothers about this misunderstanding."

From beyond the courtyards and battlements came the cries of men and the cha-cha-cha of machine guns exchanging fire. In the doorway of the royal library appeared the wretched Yahutha.

"I beg you, my lord," he blurted out, "go with the Captain!"

"You *spoke!*"

The Government column had caught up with the insurgents just as they reached the royal compound. The Bedouins took cover at once among the outer battlements, but they were sparsely armed, and soon they fell back among the orchards and neglected gardens to the Palace proper. The Royal Guards, stumbling half naked from their beds to investigate the disturbance, gave immediate relief—and more arms—to the insurgents. Since the guards themselves were Bedu and Beni Talal, no national government could ever have compelled them to fire on their fellow tribesmen. Thus it was that the battle began to rage in the corridors and courtyards and gardens of the Royal Palace, among the molding mosaics and vagrant bougainvillaea and unkempt sycamore, by the crumbling statuary and chipped marble fountains where water no longer flowed, beneath the arabesque aches and perforated plaster windows, delicate with stained glass and ingenious geometric traceries . . .

Less than an hour later, Captain A'war, his hair disheveled, eye patch askew, brought the Prime Minister the dreadful tidings.

"When Yahutha started to talk the King went out of his mind," he began, his eyes not daring to meet Mustafa's. "He cried out that all his nightmares of treachery and betrayal had come true. He went on and on about his father and grandfather and the caravan of martyrs and his direct descent from the Prophet in the line of Khadijah—"

"Come to the point, Anwar!" the Prime Minister exclaimed. "What happened? Where is he?"

"Finally Yahutha—he had gone wild, too, weeping, kissing the King's hand, begging forgiveness—finally Yahutha and I seized the King and dragged him downstairs to the helicopter. We were about to push him inside and take off when he grabbed my revolver and broke away from us—you know how strong he is, ya Mustafa! —when he broke away from us and ran away toward the firing. The guns were making a terrible racket all over the place. We chased him down all those dark, twisted corridors, and he kept crying 'Stop! Stop killing my brothers!' We saw him dash into a courtyard. It was dark . . . they didn't see him . . . he was in his uniform . . . maybe the Bedouins mistook him for a Government officer . . . it happened so quickly . . ."

The Prime Minister remained very calm. "Is he dead?" he asked.

"No. But he is badly wounded. When the men in the courtyard saw what they had done, they stopped shooting. There was so much confusion. They helped us carry him to the helicopter. I brought him down to Liberation Hospital."

"Anwar," the Prime Minister said, "you have failed me. If the King lives I shall make you the meanest corporal in my army and banish you to the loneliest outpost in the Eastern Desert. If he dies, I shall have you shot. Now get out of my way. I am going in the helicopter to see Mohammed."

"You cannot go in the helicopter, ya Mustafa."

"And why not?"

"When we flew away the insurgents on the other side of the Palace fired at us. They damaged the fuel line, I think. I was lucky to get back—"

"I've changed my mind, Anwar. I think I'll have you shot anyway."

At Liberation Hospital, the resident British surgeon and a dozen Arab doctors and nurses were battling for the King's life. Two bullets had entered his body, one passing through his right lung, the other lodging in his lower intestine. All the expedients of modern medical science—transfusions, antibiotics, coagulants, oxygen, adrenalin, morphine—were used to assure the success of the operation. Mohammed did his part; though unconscious, his young body struggled visibly to remain alive. When they were done, the British surgeon said, "He's lost a great deal of blood and he's still terribly weak, but I think he's going to make it. We'll know before dawn."

The Prime Minister's palace and Liberation Hospital were on opposite sides of the city. Mustafa decided against the delay of requisitioning another helicopter, and embarked at once for the hospital in his official Rolls, under motorcycle escort. By his own previous order, the main streets were still congested with loyalist troops, tanks and armored cars. Lights had gone on in houses and public places all over the city as the news had leaped by radio bulletin and word-of-mouth of the abortive Bedouin *putsch*. Bands of young men and proletarians in their pajamas had poured into the streets—now with genuine spontaneity—shouting patriotic slogans, pounding on pots and pans, and snake-dancing. Mustafa realized at once that if he were recognized in his progress through the old city he would be engulfed in demonstrations. By avoiding the thoroughfares, the official convoy made haste quickly until it reached the Red Mosque quarter. There, in the attempt to avoid the traffic and tumult of the Bab el Mandeb, it became entangled in the gnarled, cobblestoned side streets. Through one labyrinth into another raced the Prime Minister on his mission, careening, braking, reversing all over again in the ambages and blind alleys: no man on earth could decipher those streets. In exasperation, Mustafa leaped from the Rolls, rebuking his escort for their stupidity and dismissing them; he and his driver would go on alone. No matter: a band of patriotic youths, their hands on one another's hips, came snake-dancing wildly in and out of the alleyways. The departure of the motorcycles caught their notice, and it was then, in a squeezed lane, that they came upon Mustafa in his limousine. They recognized him at once. He regarded them with horror. "No . . . let me through . . . important business . . . urgent appointment . . . put me down . . . please, put me down . . ."

. . .

Shortly after surgery, Mohammed began hemorrhaging. He was attended to instantly, and when they were finished the British surgeon said, "For a minute there I thought we had lost him. But he seems determined to live. I'm still convinced he will. We'll know before dawn."

The Prime Minister's protests had puzzled but not disheartened the youths. On their shoulders they bore him—writhing furiously at first, then exhausted, then resigned—in triumph to the Bab el Mandeb, which was teeming with citizens agog over the night's happening. When they saw Mustafa, the buildings literally rocked with their greeting. The youths deposited him atop a sound truck blaring patriotic songs outside the Red Mosque; the music was disconnected and some clutching, disembodied hands pressed a microphone to his lips. Helpless, Mustafa contemplated the multitude at his feet; never had he found the spectacle so intoxicating, or so strange. The mob was a potpourri of impoverished people in their bedclothes—mostly in striped pajamas, but in tattered bathrobes, nightgowns, and cotton underwear as well. With the vendors of licorice water and Pepsi, and children selling sugar cane and sweet cakes, it seemed a sort of sleepwalkers' carnival. He looked down the length of the street, until it twisted out of sight several hundred yards distant. All the trellised, jutting balconies and windows were thronged with his countrymen; the decaying corbels swayed beneath the burden as everyone clapped in cadence and called out to him his name. Mus-ta-fa! *Mus-ta-fa!* MUS-TA-FA!

The King regained consciousness for a moment, and raised his head from the pillow. He gazed blankly into the boiled, antiseptic face of the British surgeon, and spoke.

"Mustafa," he said.

"The Prime Minister has been informed, Your Majesty. We expect him at any moment. Now you must sleep."

The King smiled, put his head back on the pillow, and relapsed into a babbling coma.

The Prime Minister knew that he would never reach Liberation Hospital until he gave the mob the oration they demanded. Politics, he remembered telling Fitz Pasha, was a caravan of compromises: now he must make just one more compromise for the sake of seeing Mohammed that night. And yet as he heard the abandoned rhetoric gush out of the loudspeakers on the sound truck he could not believe that the words were coming from his own mouth. He seemed to stand aside while this stranger spoke; he felt disembodied, lifted aloft, as detached as the distant spectators on the turreted gates and mother-of-pearl minarets above. ". . . traitors . . . dogs . . . whores . . ." He marveled that one ignoble name before all others had not yet passed the speaker's lips. ". . . witchcraft . . . imperialism . . . plots hatched in the dark . . ." Wasn't there a limit to good sportsmanship? ". . . Arabism . . . Islam . . . Allah . . ." Not one word about Pullmotor! ". . . And now please please let me go."

It took him another half-hour to reach his limousine, and then—they still would not let him go—another twenty minutes to reach Liberation Hospital on the outskirts of the new city.

There it was at last, an enormous, modernistic structure in a pine forest not far from the river: he had built it: a monument to the living. He was out of his Rolls even before it had stopped, and up the cement steps three at a time. He saw the British surgeon waiting for him in the vestibule. *English doctor. Composure. Reserve. Queue in Threadneedle Street.* He halted, and walked slowly into the hospital.

"How is the King?" he asked quietly.

"What a pity, Prime Minister," the British surgeon answered antiseptically, "that you could not have come sooner. His Majesty died fifteen minutes ago. We did everything we could. We could not control the hemorrhaging. I was alone with him when he went. He asked for you—rather often, actually. I have taken the liberty of telephoning the British Ambassador. Sir Charles said he would inform the American Ambassador and the other chiefs of diplomatic missions at once. Now, as to arrangements for the body . . ."

18

Ambassador Fitzgibbon called Christopher immediately after hearing from Sir Charles Chetwynd-Pott.

"I'm afraid I have some rather distressing news, Christopher. There's been a shoot-up at the Royal Palace. The King is dead. Christopher? Have you seen the tanks in the streets? The Bedouins attempted a coup. Mustafa has crushed it. Now we know why Pullmotor came back! Christopher? Look, lad, I know Mohammed was your friend, but you've got to get a grip on yourself . . ."

Paul Pullmotor heard the news of the King's death over the radio in his suite at the Sheraton-Zahra. He had known for several hours that his plot had failed: at midnight exactly, a military brass band had appeared below his window and played, for thirty minutes without stopping, "Anything You Can Do, I Can Do Better." As he watched the abundant movement of Government troops and tanks in the streets, he realized how thoroughly he had miscalculated.

He remained very calm. He was alone. Since midnight he had been considering his next move. He was mildly concerned about his present position in Al Khadra, but knowing Mustafa, he was fairly confident that he would simply be expelled from the country without much fuss. His real worry was about the reaction in Washington: his mystique was predicated on the belief that "Pullmotor never makes a mistake." He realized that he must produce a plausible and persuasive reason for this rare misadventure.

The tune of the brass band kept coming back to him as he sat on his open terrace contemplating the silver pillar of moonlight reflected in the broad Mabrouk. *Anything you can do I can do better, I can do anything better than you. No you can't. Yes I can.* Now whistling, now singing the lyrics to himself, he went back inside the suite. *No you can't. Yes I can. No you c-a-a-n-t. Yes I c-a-a-n.* He switched on the lamp beside the white-oak desk, and unzippered his portable Olivetti. *I can shoot a partridge with a single cartridge.* He slipped a piece of hotel stationery into the machine. *I can get a sparrow with a bow and arrow.* With one finger he began pecking out a personal letter to the Secretary of State.

". . . and therefore still absolutely certain that my plan was flawless. However, in adhering to your numerous directives—not to mention the Congessional statute—to keep our Ambassadors-in-residence informed of all special operations, I did give advance notice in a general way to our friend Fitzgibbon. Fitzgibbon, I now have reason to believe, was in his libations last night when the Prime Minister called him on the telephone . . ."

Can you bake a pie? No! Neither can I. He was still whistling when he went downstairs to the gentlemen's room to exchange post mortems with Chuckles Vespucci.

At dawn, the Prime Minister despatched a special company of troops to occupy the Royal Palace. The fighting the previous evening had flickered out quickly as the combatants shouted to one another across the corridors and courtyards of what had happened to the King. Paralyzed with grief, the Bedouin insurgents all surrendered within an hour, and they mingled with the Government

Arabs asking confused questions and sobbing until vans and ambulances arrived to take them down to the city. About twenty men on either side had been wounded, some seriously, but incredibly the only fatality of the Bedouin uprising was King Mohammed.

Or so it was believed until the troops entered the royal library in the morning. There, in the King's chair, they found the body of Yahutha, his head thrown back, mouth agape. In his right hand he held a barber's razor, dripping with blood. Clutched in his other hand were his two ears, and his tongue.

IV

. . . Yes, I own I sometimes grieve and sigh
But not for the things they mourn: the dazzles die
Swiftly in ash. I mourn because they rue
Not what they should: the phantoms they pursue.

From a poem by Sri Gurugrantha Sahib
translated by Dilip Kumar Roy

19

In keeping with Moslem custom, the King was buried quickly—barely thirty hours after he died. Mustafa ordered a state funeral of a scale and splendor unprecedented in the modern history of Al Khadra. On the eve of the interment Mohammed's corpse was returned to the Royal Palace, where it was washed in rose water and an essence derived from the leaves of the Lote tree; sweet spices were inserted into his wounds, and he was wrapped in muslin and a rich silken garment of green, the color of the House of Hamad and the descendants of the Prophet. Then he was sealed in a teakwood coffin and carried into his Throne Room to be prayed over by the Grand Mufti of Al Khadra and an assemblage of venerable ecclesiastics. Throughout the night Mustafa watched with them.

In the morning the coffin was enshrouded in the magnificent green flag of Al Khadra embroidered with a golden crown, and placed on a black gun carriage drawn by a dozen black horses.

Surrounded by mounted lancers, the body was brought out of the Royal Palace and down the Jebel al Malouk. As Mohammed's mortal remains passed for the last time beneath the battlements of his ancestral home, the sky began to quake with the boom of distant cannon, thundering out their homage to the last in the line of the House of Hamad. Mohammed had no heirs, nor was any member of his family present in the city to mourn his passing. Those few relatives of his who had survived the slaughter of three years ago had long since elected safe exile in the spas of Europe.

On the outskirts of the new city, under the flame trees in front of the Gazooza Sporting Club, the cortege met the official procession which was to escort the gun carriage to the Red Mosque. It was a considerable gathering; a full half-hour elapsed before all the delicate rivalries of rank and precedence had been appeased and each dignitary was in his proper place. Further delays attended a fist fight which broke out between the Uniate and schismatic archbishops of the Armenians. Finally, at about nine o'clock, under a very warm sun, the procession was on its way. First came the flags and mounted police, and the army cavalry on white horses, then the armed infantry and high military officers, the drummers behind them. In order there followed the Grand Mufti and numerous sheikhs, ulemas, mullahs and imams in kaftans and turbans. Then came the Christian hierarchy: the Greek Orthodox Patriarch, white-bearded, weighted down with ikons and gold chains, leaning on his staff; the rival Armenian metropolitans in their goblinesque black hoods; the Maronite, Melchite, Chaldean and other Uniate metropolitans; the Latin bishops, in black soutanes and flowing purple *ferraioloni*. The Governor of Al Asima, Judges of the High Court, Mudirs of the provinces, special delegates of foreign states, recipients of the Grand Cordon of the Broad Mabrouk and other high officials in silken sashes and shining medallions marched behind the churchmen. Then came the diplomatic corps, led by the doyen, Sir Charles Chetwynd-Pott (emblazoned with feathers, gold braid, and various orders of chivalry), followed by Ambassador Fitzgibbon in morning clothes and top hat, the Soviet Ambassador in quasi-military garb, the Papal Internuncio in watered silk, and other envoys in sequence according to their longevity of service in Al Khadra. Then the gun carriage, encircled by the mounted lancers, red and yellow pennants and gold halyards fluttering from their staves. Immediately behind the bier marched Mustafa, in dress uniform, and his cabinet, all fifteen of them walking abreast, followed by hundreds of Bedouin soldiers—none of them armed—on foot, on horseback, and atop camels. Lining the route like inverted flower pots were the red fezzes of regular troops arrayed almost shoulder to shoulder on either side of the street, each man presenting arms as the coffin passed.

No trumpets heralded Mohammed's last journey. Only the clip-clop of hoof and the movement of so many feet shuffling to the slow rhythm of rolling drums disturbed the silence which had descended like a cerement over the city. When the procession reached Liberation Bridge the cannons began booming out again, and squadron after squadron of old propellor planes and Hawker Hunter jets flew in spear-shaped formation across the heavens. It seemed as if all the machinery of the state had been mobilized for the occasion. A miracle of extemporaneous planning and mastery of detail, of which the Arabs were—as yet—incapable in the things of life, they had achieved almost without trying in the things of death.

On the outskirts of the city the spectators were sparse, but as the cortege proceeded down the Corniche along the river, the mob was immense, thronging not only the pavements and balustrades but every window, terrace, tree and housetop in view. Hordes of impoverished peasants and Bedouins had flocked into the city to render homage to their King and to witness the death pageant. The demeanor of the population was curious. Along the first mile or so of the route they were uncharacteristically restrained and solemn; when the Royal remains passed by, a deep hush fell upon them, their stillness only the more unnatural for the tip-tap of the drums and the patter of horse hoofs. Occasionally from the men there would come the soft, sighing utterance of Islamic submission and acceptance, *"Allahu Akhbar!"* God is most great. Or an old woman would cast a handful of dust over her head, point a palsied finger at the coffin and cry *"La illaha illallah, wa Mohammedu rasulullah"* —I testify there is no God but God, and Mohammed is the Messenger of God. Otherwise an inscrutable, uncanny calm.

It did not endure. By degrees a multitude of schoolboys, female mourners and miscellaneous riffraff attached themselves to the rear of the procession, despite the exertions of the police to discourage them. Murmuring as they multiplied, then chattering, then shouting and shoving, they stalked the official party down the Corniche past Victory Bridge, past the pretentious, futuristic Sheraton-Zahra, then away from the river into the European quarter and past the immense cinemas and smart shops, past the Vespas and Balenciaga gowns beckoning from behind potted palms and plate glass, past the air-conditioned airline offices and the fashionable cafés. As the procession entered the knotted and much narrower ways of the old city the mob became unmanageable, their sheer numbers obstructing the progress of the mounted police and marching dignitaries alike. The death wail of the women grew extravagant and shrill. When at last the Royal remains were lifted from the gun carriage and borne on Bedouin shoulders into the Red Mosque, a pair of oxen were held down by the beautiful bronze doors and ceremonially slaughtered. Black blood spurted out from their severed neck veins and splattered the great green flag hanging limply from the teakwood coffin.

The interior of the mosque became almost as turbulent as the street outside, and even more stifling. Thousands of people, perspiring and lamenting, poured into this petrified forest of crooked pillars, dislodging many of the dignitaries from their places of honor and squeezing them against the mosaic murals.

Ambassador Fitzgibbon: Ooph! I understand Mustafa sat up all night with the body.

Sir Charles Chetwynd-Pott: So, to his long list of enormities he has—ooph!—added a taste for necrophilia. Now be a good chap and get off my foot.

The Bedouin bearers deposited Mohammed's coffin beneath the prayer niche, with his right side nearest Mecca; the imams chanted the prayers for the dead, the *Fat'hah,* the Testification, and the *Hashreeyah.*

> I extol the perfection of Him . . .
> The perfection of the Lord of the two Easts
> The perfection of the Lord of the two Wests
> The perfection of the Illuminator of the two lights
> The sun, to wit, and the moon.

His perfection: how bountiful is He!
His perfection: how clement is He! . . .

On and on they prayed—interminably it seemed, they and the great congregation now kneeling back on their heels, now plunging their brows to the tattered carpets. Finally the Grand Mufti mounted the domed pulpit to deliver the eulogy. The old man made an exquisite oration, rich in that extravagance of style and hyperbole of sentiment so intrinsic to the Arab tongue and so suitable to the occasion. ". . . and may God render his memory as fragrant as arum lilies, and may He confer upon him a myriad of mercies and a rainfall of honeyed graces . . ." A consistory of insects hovered about the mouth of the Mufti's microphone, chanting to the dead monarch a dirge all their own. When he had completed the eulogy the Mufti raised his open hands to either side of his turban, touched the lobes of his ears with the extremities of his thumbs, and cried out *"Allahu Akhbar!"*—God is most great.

"Allahu Akhbar!" thundered the congregation.

"Give your testimony of King Mohammed," he commanded them.

"He was of the virtuous!" they roared.

So congested was the old city that Christopher Grundoon had not been able to get near the Red Mosque. Instead he and Solafa had gone together to the City of the Dead, to await the arrival of the body and to witness the interment.

On the evening before last Christopher had returned home at midnight, from a tedious dinner party at Dr. Pantry's, to find a message under his door. It was on the back of a cigarette wrapper, written in pencil in an uneven, almost childish, hand. *Christopher I was not so busy and I came to say hello you were not here. Mabey I'll call you later tonight. Moh. vii, Rex.* So Christopher had stayed up until two, writing in his journal, reading a novel by Bernanos and waiting for the King's call. When it did not come he assumed that his friend had found diversion elsewhere, and he went to bed. He was awakened from a sound sleep by the ringing of the telephone in his study. He groped his way there in the dark, cursing the King for disturbing him at such an hour. But when he picked up the receiver it was the Ambassador at the other end, telling him that Mohammed was dead. Solafa was as inconsolable as Christopher; she had, after all, been Mohammed's lover, if only very briefly.

So, to the City of the Dead. It was a vast place in the desert just beyond the walls of the old quarter, crowded with common gravestones, heaps of rubbish, and, on its periphery, a necklace of tomb-mosques: the mausolea of departed grandees, princes and Kings. In their original condition these buildings had been glorious. Even today the pagoda-like minarets and bulbous, fretted domes retained intimations of an erstwhile enchantment. But just barely, for they were all in ruins; even the most beautiful of them had been badly neglected; now little more remained than their towers and domes and some fragments of outer walls persevering in confusion among parched aloe plants and mountains of debris. The entire necropolis had declined into chaos and desolation, possessed by wild dogs and ascensions of hoopoo birds who by day feasted on excrement and by night nested among the timbers of the tumbling tombs.

Thousands besides Christopher and Solafa had come to the City of the Dead, ardent not only for a glimpse of the royal coffin but for a speech by Mustafa himself. For it was the necropolis which the Prime Minister had chosen as the scene of his own oration. One of the finer mosques had been hastily tidied up, and a crypt prepared for the reception of the King's corpse. Next to the mosque a spacious, multicolored marquee had been erected and filled with chairs for the seating of the dignitaries; it opened out onto the vast graveyard where the population were expected to gather. And gather they did, kicking up choking clouds of ocher-colored dust as they streamed into the City of the Dead. Christopher and Solafa navigated themselves through the mob to within a few hundred feet of the official marquee; she had brought along her parasol, and the two of them huddled close together in its tiny shadow; otherwise, waiting for the cortege to come was a living death. The heat wave which had possessed the city for the past week was never worse than at this moment, in this desert. The sun blazed in a milk-white sky. The crowd was becoming restless, even short-tempered. Already men were dashing about dumping buckets of water on recumbent bodies. In former times, buffaloes and rams had been slaughtered at the gravesides of the great, and their flesh distributed to the poor. Today the government was giving away Pepsi-Cola to whomever wanted it; everyone did. In fact the heat wave had caused a run on Pepsi; the government's requisition for the necropolis had exhausted all reserves, and now in the city the Pepsi people could no longer keep up with the public thirst.

Squatting in the dust near Christopher and Solafa were a group of holy men called *fukaha,* some of them blind, chanting verses from the Koran and invoking divine mercy on the dead King. "O God, save him from the Stoned Devil! O Apostle of God, intercession! intercession!" They rocked rhythmically from side to side as they sang, cupping their jaws in the palms of their right hands. "Look there, Solafa," Christopher said, pointing at them. "That one in Bedouin dress. Doesn't he remind you of Chuckles Vespucci?" Actually, it *was* Chuckles. He too had returned from Dr. Pantry's dinner party to find a note from the King. *Chuckles I came to see you, you were gone. Can you come to luncheon tomorrow? Moh. vii, Rex.*

At last the official procession emerged from the walls of the old city and advanced with difficulty through the mob to Mohammed's tomb. In its backwash marched still more thousands of mourners, most of them women wailing hysterically. The royal sepulchre was a small building, minaretted, domed and in great disrepair; half its roof had fallen in; what were left of its walls were not long for this world. Still, it was fitting that Mohammed be laid to rest here, among his ancestors. Only Mustafa, his cabinet, a number of ecclesiastics and some guards were permitted to enter the mausoleum; the other dignitaries were directed to the marquee. The interment was accomplished quickly. A dozen Bedouin soldiers reverently deposited the teakwood coffin in a stone vault, which they sealed with masonry, embellished with blue hyacinth flowers and palm branches, and perfumed with frankincense. They wept quietly while they worked. Mustafa remained impassive. His mind was on that day in the desert, when Mohammed had stumbled on him herding goats; he meditated on their young manhood together in the Royal Palace; he remembered all the favors Mohammed had heaped on him, and that night of terror when he had rescued

Mohammed from the mob, and Mohammed asking him, *Would you like to be Prime Minister, Mustafa?* And he was sorry, in his way; but in death, just as in life, Mohammed bored him, to distraction though not to tears.

By the time the Prime Minister and his party emerged from the mausoleum, the wailing women had gone mad in their lamentations. In hundreds they had forced themselves to the front of the mob, and now at the very foot of the marquee they were transporting themselves into a delirium of sorrow. They had all smeared themselves with indigo dye; some were tearing their hair and ripping off their mourning necklaces of dark blue beads and rending their garments, exposing their bare arms and even their breasts. Others commenced a curious kind of death dance, at once immemorial, rhythmical and abandoned. They swayed backward and forward, revolved in circles, stamping the ground, some brandishing blue and green handkerchiefs, others tambourines, others palm branches, smiting their faces as they danced. *"Ya seedee Malik Mohammed!"* —O my master King Mohammed!—*"Ya jemali!"*—O my camel!—*"Ya seb'ee!"*—O my lion! "Still young, O my brother! Come and get up!" How melancholy and piteous was their howling; how it echoed and lingered in the cobwebs of the mind; how despairing, how wanton, how otherworldly, how eschatological it was. Like surf breaking against a great rock, the ecstasy of the women ascended in spasms, crashing against the official marquee until most of the Arab dignitaries and even some of the European ambassadors were openly sobbing.

But not Mustafa. He mounted the rostrum and into the battery of microphones shouted for silence. At that moment a hoopoo bird soared out of the ruined mausoleum, exalting on zebra wings above the shrieking women, its crest unfurling like a scarlet fan in the malignant sunshine. Its cry was swallowed in the keening. The women saw the bird and keened still louder. They believed that hoopoos were the souls of the dead—and that this creature ascending directly from the royal tomb was the soul of King Mohammed, winging its way to Paradise. The spectacle inspired the women to new prodigies of frenzy. They snatched buckets of water and bottles of Pepsi-Cola from the men, dumping them wildly into the dust, daubing themselves—even on their bosoms and bare feet—with lumps of mud, shrieking, waving their arms aloft, violently smiting themselves with sticks, scratching and clawing themselves until their arms and faces ran crimson with blood. *O my master! O my camel! O my lion!*

The Prime Minister contemplated this scene with a very different sort of anguish. All of yesterday and last night and through most of that morning he had been rehearsing in his mind the elegy he was waiting to deliver now. The microphones and loudspeakers were turned on; the great news corporations of the world were copiously represented; from the Atlas Mountains in the west to the lateen-sailed dhows of the Indian Ocean, Arabs everywhere were waiting for him to speak. Mustafa was a gifted orator, renowned for his ringing voice, his mastery of Moslem hyperbole, his genius for gazing into the very souls of the Arabs. He had planned an oration abounding in dithyrambic half-truths and lyrical fictions; he had intended to turn his elegy on the late Mohammed into a pitiless attack on imperialism in general and on the Americans (but not on Pullmotor!) in particular. He would begin slowly, depicting Mohammed as a martyr to imperialist plotting, and then scale a ladder of linked phrases in which dozens of sentences would end with the same obscene word—*istiamar-r-r-r* (rolling his *r*'s like that)—*imperialism!* And then—for he knew the innate needs of his people—he would flatter and fawn on them, and add to his own mystique. And he knew that he would detest himself as every word tripped off his tongue, just as he knew there was no other way—at the moment—to rule his Arabs.

But now as he stood before the microphones and watched the keening women in the death dance, rending their garments, caking themselves with mud, disfiguring their faces, he knew that he could not go through with it—he could not deliver the speech he had so carefully and cynically assembled in his mind. Wasn't this dreadful spectacle—in front of the photographers and the foreign press and the diplomatic corps and Sir Charles Chetwynd-Pott—enough vulgarity for one day? He could not bear to add to it; he was ashamed; he wanted to hide his face. He wondered what he had let happen to his vision of the queue in Threadneedle Street—common men and women in their caps and tweed coats, hatless messenger boys, a little girl holding a woman's hand, several gentlemen in bowlers, an old lady, a soldier in uniform, a pair of nuns, all waiting silently and shivering in the sleet, not pushing, persevering without word or grumble—and of his vow to remake the personality of his own people in that image, and to turn his Arabs into English gentlemen.

The women would not stop. Mustafa held up his arms. Soon the tens of thousands of his countrymen in the City of the Dead began to clap and to call out his name and to extinguish the screams of the women. Mus-ta-fa! *Mus-ta-fa!* MUS-TA-FA! To them, never had he seemed so handsome, so strong, so *Arab*. His fantasies persisted. He saw himself, as he had in so many dreams at night, in ermine and coronet, delivering his learned address in the House of Lords. He toyed with the temptation to begin his speech now with a quotation from Lord Byron—"Grief must be the instructor of the wise; sorrow is knowledge"—attributing it to Saladin. But no, he had ruled out lyrical fictions. He felt cleansed. Perhaps Mohammed's death had a meaning; perhaps he had died for a good purpose; perhaps this was a turning point.

Now the wailing women were exhausted, and there was silence in the City of the Dead. Now the truth. He spoke.

> "Where is my Chief of Police? That is what I said. Where is the Director of the Municipality Police Department? Does he dare show his face in my presence? When I find him I shall relieve him of his high office. I gave him strict instructions to prevent these wretched creatures from coming here and creating the spectacle we have just witnessed. I'm sure it made all these lovely gentlemen from *Life* and *Paris-Match* and *Picture Post* very, very happy. How the snapshots will amuse their subscribers in Westchester County and Neuilly and Mayfair! These gentlemen from the foreign press—they don't take snapshots of the schools and industries I have built. They don't write articles about my hospitals or how in three years I've cut the infant death rate in half and wiped out the hashish trade and closed down all the brothels in the Fish Market. But Bedouins on camels? Pathetic women clawing their faces and beating themselves with sticks? That will always sell magazines in Westchester County and Neuilly and Mayfair! Well, not this time, dear gentlemen. My troops will relieve you of your cam-

eras and destroy your film. Sergeant, you may proceed to enforce that order."

As the troops guarding the marquee advanced, pistols drawn, on the flabbergasted foreign press photographers, Mustafa translated the command into English for the benefit of its victims. "Hush, Mr. *Life* Magazine man!" he admonished. "You will get your camera back when the sergeant has disposed of your snapshots." Soon the dust in front of the marquee was strewn with streamers of ruined film.

"Why, the man is mad," mumbled Sir Charles Chetwynd-Pott.

". . . this degrading death dance will never be danced again. Not while I am President—Prime Minister—of Al Khadra. From now on anyone who makes a nuisance at a funeral will be seized by the police and put in prison. My enemies accuse me of trying to destroy Islam. I am not trying to destroy Islam but to restore it. The wailing of women at funerals was explicity forbidden by the Prophet. These horrid practices are not Islamic, but the dark residue of idolatry and paganism. The belief that a bird can be a human soul is especially ancient—and particularly pagan. Herodotus, the Father of History, when he visited this country more than two thousand years ago, recorded all these squalid convulsions in detail. Were he here today, he would not have had to change a word—and I would have confiscated his notebook. So help me God, if I have to do it with my bare hands I will destroy this past. This detestable spectacle will never be repeated. Mustafa believes in the living, not in the dead.

Now look around you. See the condition of this necropolis. See the heaps of rubbish and rubble everywhere about. See the decrepit mausolea and mosques of our departed Kings. See these tombs, and how their graceful stone inscriptions and mosaic pavements crumble before your eyes, and how their minarets lean and their domes tumble down! My enemies reproach me for neglecting these stately temples. And I say, let them decay into dust. Mustafa builds temples to the living, not to the dead."

. . .

Improvising variations on this theme, he continued talking for nearly an hour. By degrees he expanded his denunciation of the wailing women to include every man, woman, and child in Al Khadra. He scolded them for their superstitions, rebuked them for their backwardness, taunted them for their sloth. ". . . bad habits . . . improper attitude . . . building a nation . . . hard work . . . cleanliness . . . personal hygiene . . . and from now on one wife to a man . . . no more easy divorce . . . sexual laxity . . . immorality . . . obscene dancing . . . bribing is a sin . . . national income . . . Gross National Product . . . Five-Year Plan . . . Mustafa sings hymns to the living, not to the dead."

In his fervor, he failed even to mention the dead King. When he finished, the applause was perfunctory. A weird, unwonted silence prevailed among the mob as he descended the podium, got into a Land-Rover, and rode off to his palace. The dignitaries too were eager to be elsewhere; their limousines had come to collect them by the gates of the graveyard; soon they were away to their air-conditioned offices and chanceries. The rabble lingered, milled about, and dispersed slowly. Mustafa's speech had left them confused and frustrated. For the first time he had gone against his instinct and violated all his own rules. He had addressed his Arabs as if they were already Englishmen; with a little less hectoring he might have made the same speech, if not in the House of Lords, then at least to a political convention in Brighton or Blackpool. If he had spoken today as he first intended—if he had wept over Mohammed, if he had dispensed his habitual half-truths and lyrical fictions, if he had attacked imperialism or the Americans or the British, if he had flattered and fawned on his Arabs and told them what they wanted to hear—then most probably there would have been no trouble; the mob would have been satisfied and pleased and would have gone home quietly. But now Mustafa's alien, schoolmasterish oration had deranged the very rhythm of their mourning. They felt no real grief for the King—they had hardly known him—but they had welcomed the pageant of his last rites as a golden pretext to propitiate and purge collectively their own private sorrows. Mustafa had cheated them of their catharsis. He had left them confused and frustrated—and angry.

Most of the mob did in fact go home, though not very quietly. The legions of police and military retired to barracks. But a hard core of some several hundred youths, wailing women and miscellaneous rabble quit the necropolis only to continue their lamentations in the lanes of the old city. They wandered aimlessly up and down, in and out the cobblestoned ways, weeping, shouting, and smashing windows. Occasionally one of the youths would rip away a window shutter, break it into sticks and distribute the weapons to his companions. Many of the men were already armed with *naboots,* those long wooden staves commonly seen among the peasantry, some of them studded with nails. It was noon now. The aimless pilgrims were hot and thirsty. They invaded one of the more respectable cafés near the Fish Market, made a terrible racket, overturned and tore apart chairs and marble-topped tables, and abused everybody in sight. To save his premises from being totally dismantled the Greek proprietor offered free tea to the troublemakers.

"Bebsi! Bebsi!"

"But there is no more Bebsi. The heat wave—"

This news endowed the mob with a mission. They finished demolishing the café and then went elsewhere in their quest. In every public place, the cringing answer was the same: no more Bebsi. More destruction, more clubs torn from tables and chairs, more iron gratings ripped from walls.

"But there is *no more Bebsi."*

"Imperialist plot!"

The Pepsi-Cola plant was a paragon of the new epoch: a single-story building of chartreuse-colored concrete sprawling athwart the old city and the new. Its exterior was made even more glorious by a great bottle-cap billboard atop its roof and scores of Diesel trucks caparisoned with empty cartons in its asphalt parking lot. For the past week the plant had been operating at capacity, twenty-four hours a day. The American manager and his Lebanese lieutenant were on the verge of collapse; they had been deluged by telephone calls and even personal visits from high government officials, hotels, hospitals, schools, orphanages, embassies, prisons, the police, army quartermasters, factories, shops, department stores, merchants large and small, even the Prime Minister's office—all making thirsty representations for adequate quantities of the elixir. In his ardor to reconcile supply with demand the manager had taxed both his machinery and his labor force beyond their maximum capacities. First the electric eye in the automatic bottle inspector had gone blind, and the pre-rinse jets had broken down. Then they ran out of caps for the mechanical crowner, and the water-syrup syncrometer developed an erroneous feed ratio into the carbo-cooler. Finally the Arab laborers rebelled against the inhuman hours and staged a sit-down strike for half a day. Since yesterday the manager had refused to answer his telephone or to receive any more outraged delegations.

But there was nothing very much he could do when the mob of wailing women and wild-eyed roughs suddenly stormed out of the old city and invaded his plant—except to beat a hasty exit by the rear door, which he and his staff accomplished only in the nick of time. Beating on empty kerosene tins and brandishing all manner of makeshift clubs, the mob poured into the Pepsi plant through doors and windows, and in an ecstasy of vicarious self-destruction proceeded to tear the establishment to pieces. The very strangeness and complexity of the equipment taunted them to a new fury. With their crude weapons and bare hands they assaulted everything in sight—conveyor belts, gauges, pistons, automatic bottle washer, de-aerator tank, dumb waiters, lime and ferrous sulphate cylinders, air compressor, magnetic conveyor, alkali-solution vats, carbo-cooler, water-syrup syncrometer—everything. They advanced on the administrative offices, hurling desks and chairs, typewriters and adding machines through the clapboard partitions and out of windows; they demolished the canned-music console—though inexplicably the ubiquitous loudspeakers blithely continued to blare selections from a Cole Porter musical comedy.

The rabble ran wild in room after enormous room of empty bottles in wooden boxes heaped high to the cement ceiling, overturning them in an apocalypse of crashing glass. Finally they came upon a steel door inscribed, in large Roman and Arabic characters, SYRUP ROOM. With great difficulty they broke down this obstacle and emerged into the *sanctum sanctorum*. There they found the immense cylindrical stainless-steel tank, lying lengthwise on tubular pilasters. It was incandescently clean; the immaculate chamber smelled of chemical disinfectant; the loudspeaker continued to coo Cole

Porter. The mob chopped at the tank with their table-legs, knives, nail-studded staves, adzes, cast-iron gratings, tree props and lead pipes. Their exertions made no impression; the tabernacle was inviolable until a child accidentally discovered the hatch door in the belly beneath. The syrup gushed out, engulfing the rioters, and they made merry until the cobblestoned street outside ran red with the essence of Pepsi-Cola.

Then they marched on the American Embassy.

By this time the police had been alerted. They telephoned Ambassador Fitzgibbon and told him that although the demonstration was by now much too large to head off, they would do everything they could to prevent any damage to the Embassy.

The Ambassador took his own precautions. Into the squawk-box on his Regency desk he barked out a succession of terse commands. Within five minutes the steel shutters were down on nearly every window in the Embassy; white helmets were donned by the section wardens; fire extinguishers and water hoses were dislodged from the walls; the Marine guards were issued small arms and posted in strategic places about the compound, and all gates were bolted fast. The Embassy staff remained calmly at their desks and went on working; they had been through all this fuss before and nothing serious had ever happened. The Ambassador was as calm but not so serene; what concerned him was that the approaching demonstration, unlike most of the others, had not been organized by the government. It was too late to send everyone home, but he wondered whether it wouldn't be wise at least to spare Eminence Grise—a high-strung creature in any case—the noise and unpleasantness of a screaming mob. He sent for Fawzi, his chauffeur, and then went out onto the terrace of the Tower.

Amidst the profusion of potted palm he opened the air-conditioned cage to find his angwatibo in an already distracted state, as if he anticipated not only the disturbance but some sort of personal danger. *"N'inquiéte-toi pas, chéri,"* the Ambassador reassured him. *"Viens. Je vais t'envoyer dans la voiture à la Résidence. Tu seras sain et sauf là-bas. Allons."* The exotic beast gazed at his master with piteous, teddy-bear eyes, and clung tenaciously, with an almost human strength, to the bars of his cage. *"Allons, Eminence! Nous sommes pressés!"* The Ambassador grasped the furry bundle with both hands, attempting to pull him loose; the little lemuroid emitted a most curious and eerie hiss, and bit Fitz Pasha on the forefinger with his fine, fanglike teeth. "You little bastard!" the Ambassador exclaimed, darting the wounded finger to his mouth, tasting the blood. Fawzi came out onto the terrace, and together they extracted Eminence Grise from the cage. The Ambassador entrusted the beast to his driver's protection, and told him to hasten home with it to the Residence. "Okay Basha! Blenty quick!"

In the elevator, Eminence Grise clawed Fawzi on the face, wiggled out of the chauffeur's grasp and attached himself to the grille overhead; dislodging him caused further delays. The Ambassador meanwhile stood by the balustrade on the terrace waiting impatiently for Fawzi to emerge from the chancery entrance below. Just as he did, Fitz Pasha from his high vantage point sighted the mob turning into the street some several hundred yards from the compound. He leaned over the balustrade and shouted down in Arabic, "Never mind, ya Fawzi! It's too late! Come back!" A warm, gusty wind was blowing; Fawzi did not hear him; he hopped into the Cadillac clutching Eminence Grise, and zoomed down the drive to the wrought-iron gates, which the Marines were unbolting. The Ambassador beat the air with his arms and cried out to the Marines; they did not hear him; the Cadillac turned out of the compound.

Sean Sebastian Fitzgibbon stood on the terrace of the Tower and watched his Cadillac collide with the advancing mob. The encounter was not a happy one. With good reason had Fitz Pasha through half of his life loved these poor Arabs; when they were not rioting they were the most gregarious and good-hearted of beings, devoted to their religion, kind to their children and compassionate toward animals. But now the venom of their frustrations had transfigured them. They overturned the Cadillac and began chopping at the windows with their crude weapons. Wild with fear, Fawzi managed to get out of the machine, only to be beaten badly by the mob. They set the limousine on fire. Eminence Grise was still inside. Soon the Ambassador saw him, leaping from the conflagration, his body ablaze. The men were beating him against the asphalt and stabbing him with their long, pointed sticks when the riot police arrived, truncheons swinging, submachine guns spitting bullets above their heads. Past the gates of the Embassy around the corner of the compound the police stalked the rabble, giggling now and bearing the charred body of Eminence Grise impaled aloft on a wooden spear.

20

At eleven o'clock the next morning, Mustafa ibn Mabrouk proclaimed Al Khadra a Republic, and himself its first President—pending only a plebiscite whose results were not difficult to augur. At noon he rang up Paul Pullmotor at the Sheraton-Zahra.

"Oh hello, Mustafa, I'm glad you called. Listen, what's all this new crap requiring an exit visa to get out of the country? I've been having the most hellish time."

"How inconvenient for you."

"You have a bunch of half-wits working for you down in that department."

"So everyone says. I must get around to reorganizing it one of these days. By the way, do you remember that request for wheat I had pending with you people?"

"Vaguely," Pullmotor said.

"It was for half a million metric tons. I imagine now that you've discovered you can't get rid of me you'll want to come to some sort of understanding. I imagine I'll be getting that wheat after all, along with the medicines and a few other things. I'm making up a list, but we can deal with that in due course. At the moment I'm faced with a Bedouin uprising—I mean a real one, the whole desert this time, unless I can feed them. I need five thousand tons of wheat at once."

"Well, what do you expect me to do about it?"

"What do you expect me to do about your exit visa? Have you ever wintered in Al Khadra? The tourists tell me it beats Miami."

"Mustafa, you wouldn't dare."

"Wouldn't I? Listen, you haven't even got diplomatic immunity. And besides, you don't like publicity, do you?"

"All right, Mustafa, you win—this time. But this wheat deal is not going to be easy. There are ships to be chartered, for one thing, and—"

"Who said anything about ships? I want an airlift."

"Out of the question."

"By the way, Paul, beginning tomorrow you will not be allowed out of your hotel. The day after that—"

"All right. I'll see what I can do. It's not going to be easy."

"You'll manage. I expect you're tied up for dinner tonight."

"As a matter of fact," Pullmotor said, "I'm not."

"Do you want to take pot luck over here, at my place?"

"I suppose so."

"I'll send my Rolls round for you at seven. See you."

"Not so fast! When do I get my exit visa?"

"When I get my wheat."

In London the *Daily Sketch* was splashing a new exclusive, full of outrageous allegations that a Boston investment banker and a rock-and-roll singer had attempted to overthrow the legitimate government of Al Khadra. The Foreign Office declined to comment.

The Secretary of State had returned prematurely to Washington, having hastened home from his conferences in Bonn to cope with a new crisis in South America. Pullmotor's letter about the abortive Bedouin coup had been brought to Washington by special courier, and was among the first items of importance which the Secretary discovered in his *In* box. ". . . plan was flawless . . . our friend Fitzgibbon . . . libations last night. . ."

Calvin Hampshire grunted, and turned to his Undersecretary of State. "How many new African nations are we recognizing this week?" he asked.

"It's rather a job keeping track, Mr. Secretary."

"Get me the poop sheet, will you?"

The Undersecretary withdrew, and reappeared posthaste with the poop sheet. Calvin Hampshire perused it.

"I notice one here—Fernando *Poo*. Where is it?"

"I'm afraid you've got me, Mr. Secretary. I never heard of it."

"Neither have I. Would you mind finding out for me where Fernando Poo is?"

Two hours later, the Undersecretary returned. "Sorry for the delay, Mr. Secretary. No one on the African desk could tell me anything about Fernando Poo. The Reference Room wasn't a bit helpful. I went down to the pharmacy and bought a World Almanac. Fernando Poo is in the Bight of Biafra."

"Where's *that?*"

"Beats me, Mr. Secretary. Perhaps the Congressional Library—"

"Never mind. Fernando Poo, in the Bight of Biafra, eh? I hope Shawnie likes it. And Osgood."

"Mr. Secretary?"

"Cable Pullmotor to come home, will you? I need him to clean up this mess in South America."

Sean Sebastian Fitzgibbon's appointment as Ambassador Extraordinary and Plenipotentiary to the infant African Republic of Fernando Poo was leaked quickly to the newspapers. Fitz Pasha read about it on the Associated Press wire a full day before being advised by the Department. He received the news with uncharacteristic stoicism. The death of Eminence Grise had emptied him of passion. He was innocent. He knew there was nothing he could do. He knew Pullmotor was responsible. He knew Calvin Hampshire would not be Secretary of State forever. He hoped that, in a year or two perhaps, he might emerge, as others before him had done, from humiliation and exile. The prospect of reunion with Winifred—hadn't she written she'd follow him to the ends of the earth?—was the best incentive of all not to despair. So, no more vodka martinis to assuage his loss of face, nor fresh fish to satisfy his Eucharistic hunger. He sought out a priest, confessed his sins and—his eyes welling with tears, his mouth trembling—feasted on the Flesh he had craved for thirty years. Besides, even Fernando Poo was preferable to an efficiency flat in Chevy Chase and on weekends going up to Boston to visit his sister.

The King's death had enveloped Christopher Grundoon in a vague stupor, and the news of his patron's peremptory demotion and imminent departure had stunned him almost as much. Nonetheless he aspired to remain on indefinitely in the Embassy—and thus in his beloved Al Khadra—in some new capacity. He was in the Tower supervising the packing of the Ambassador's voluminous personal papers when Fitz Pasha called him into his office.

"Have you been writing a novel?" the Ambassador asked.

Christopher was surprised and puzzled. He did not remember ever having mentioned his clandestine opus to the Ambassador. "Well, sort of, sir," he answered now. "A silly little thing I poked at in my spare time."

"Was the title *Perfidious Albion?"*

"Well yes, as a matter of fact, it was. How did you know?"

"My God! Then it's true. They're not making it up."

"Not making what up? What's happened? It was all a joke—British soldiers bayoneting Arab babies and that sort of thing. My strategy for keeping in good odor with the Political Police. My servant, you see—"

"You kept in good odor all right. Have you seen the government newspaper this morning?"

"Newspaper?"

"They're *serializing* it. Sir Charles Chetwynd-Pott just called me, and he's livid. He's protesting to Washington."

Thus it was that barely forty-eight hours after Fitz Pasha's reassignment, Christopher Grundoon received his own curt greeting from the Department, terminating his dreamy sojourn in the Arab Orient and ordering him home with all possible despatch.

Chuckles Vespucci, torn by remorse for the part he played in the death of King Mohammed, had quarreled violently with Pullmotor on the day after the event and forthwith severed their association.

He disappeared. In fact the last person to see Chuckles had been Christopher, when unwittingly he observed him clad in Bedouin costume, squatting in the dust among the holy men in the City of the Dead, rocking rhythmically from side to side, crying "Intercession! Intercession!"

Telegram from Winifred Fitzgibbon to her husband: I SAID I WOULD FOLLOW YOU TO THE ENDS OF THE EARTH NOT TO FERNANDO POO.

Dr. Pantry was promoted.

On the day of Ambassador Fitzgibbon's departure, and on the eve of his own, Christopher Grundoon went to see Solafa for the last time.

She led him, by the hand, out onto her terrace. "Where's Michel?" he asked.

"They're trying to draft him into the army," Solafa said. "He's gone into hiding for a few months."

"Really? Where?"

"That's a secret."

"Not in his old seminary by any chance?"

"How did you guess?"

"Solafa, why didn't you tell me you only had love affairs with spoiled priests?"

"You never asked me."

"Is it our innocence which attracts you so?" Christopher asked. "Is it because chastity is the only thing worth conquering, worth envying, really worth having? Never mind. Fitz Pasha says it's your way of getting even with God."

"He's unkind. I like to think it's my way of getting close to God."

"Ah. In that case I forgive you everything."

He sat down in a deck chair and she stood behind him running her fingers through his golden hair. It was midday, and the sun was very nearly invisible in haze. The sky above and broad Mabrouk below were the color of dull silver; the heat wave had passed away; the wind was blowing from the west. Solafa leaned down and kissed Christopher on the ear. "You're sweet," she said. "I'm going to miss you terribly. I'll often think of you, way off on the other side of the world, in Washington."

"I'm not returning to Washington," Christopher said. "I've decided to leave the government. I have no future as a bureaucrat."

"What will you do?"

"I wish I knew. I'd stay here, if I thought I could make a living. But even if I could, it wouldn't be the same—without Fitz Pasha, without Mohammed. I don't have much money. I'll kick around in Europe for a while. Will I see you there? Meet me in Paris! We'll take a garret together and live on Metrecal and Graham crackers."

"I don't like Graham crackers."

"Onion soup, peanut-butter sandwiches, what does it matter? You're getting your passport. Meet me in Paris."

"I have my passport," Solafa said. She extracted the precious document from the pocket of her toreador trousers and showed it to Christopher. "I *have* it. That's the trouble."

"Trouble? Isn't it what you've been fighting for over a year to get? Come away with me tomorrow."

"I could," she said. "But if I do, do you know what will happen? It's a horrible business. I've never wanted anything as much as I wanted this passport. I moved heaven and earth, I bribed all sorts of people. Mustafa found out about the bribes. I don't know how, but he found out, and now everybody who had anything to do with the transaction is in jail. Mish Mish Effendi, the director of the passport office—everybody. Everybody but me. Mustafa sent an army officer here to my apartment. The officer returned to me every piastre I had paid out in baksheesh—and he gave me the passport too. He said, 'You understand of course that once you leave the country you cannot come back—ever.' I'm an undesirable, you see. *Ancien régime*. My father and grandfather were corrupt Pashas. I'm a decadent aristocrat, a stain on the new order. . . . 'you cannot come back—ever.' Exile! That's Mustafa for you. Oh, Christopher, how I *hate* him. Everywhere I look, there is Mustafa. His picture on every wall, in every cinema, in every newspaper, over every radio day and night, night and day, Mustafa, Mustafa, Mustafa. Whenever I met your Ambassador, all he ever talked about was Mustafa. When I was with Paul Pullmotor that evening at the Soviet Embassy, he couldn't keep still about Mustafa. And Mohammed—even when we were making love he talked about Mustafa. My own brother blew his brains out because of Mustafa. How I *hate* Mustafa. Well, I've done a great deal of thinking about this passport.

I've got a villa on the Riviera and a great deal of money in Switzerland. Here I have nothing—just this shabby flat and the tiny pension because of my father. Mustafa has taken everything else. If I knew I could come back in five years, or even in ten, then I'd go with you to Paris tomorrow. My first language is French—I'm more European than I am Arab. Perhaps I should do it, go away from here . . . forever. But never to return? Never to see this river again? Or this city, where I was born? Where is my country? Help me, Christopher. I don't know what to do."

Christopher hesitated. He knew that it was at least partly because of him that Ambassador Fitzgibbon had returned to the Eucharist. Now Solafa was placing her destiny in his hands.

"Give me the passport," he said.

She handed him the passport, its black exterior embossed in gold Arabic and English.

"You know what I'm going to do with it, don't you?" he asked.

"Yes. I'll help you."

Christopher ripped the passport in two, and gave one of the halves to Solafa. Together they tore the document into tiny pieces, and then cast them out onto the wind and watched them float languidly away, over the broad Mabrouk, like little sails, or confetti, or tears.

Solafa said, "If you're going to kiss me like that, we'd better go inside."

"God," Christopher lamented, "if I only had time! I've got to get to the airport and say good-by to the Ambassador."

In happier days, whenever Ambassador Fitzgibbon had departed from Al Asima airport, the entire senior staff of his enormous Embassy had been in attendance to bid him bon voyage, lined up like wooden ducks according to their seniority: the Minister-Counselor; the Political and Economic Counselors; the military attachés in their gold braid, scrambled eggs, and swagger sticks; the first and second secretaries; the Director of Mutual Understanding; and so on and on down the ranks to the Locust Control Attaché, the Potable Water Adviser and the Contraband Opium Control Officer. This afternoon the Ambassador dispensed with all of that. He had already eschewed established practice and had not even bothered to make the rounds of the Ministries and other Embassies to extend his diplomatic farewells. He could not have faced them: his humiliation was too great. He had forbidden any farewell parties. His senior staff had insisted nevertheless on giving him a well-intentioned and altogether too appropriate going-away present—an engraved silver platter.

And so today the only people permitted to say good-by to Fitz Pasha at the airport were Fawzi, his chauffeur, Abdel Kader, his footman, Gassem, his houseboy, the Three Stooges, his Bedouin bodyguard, and Christopher Grundoon. When the aircraft was ready to leave, they all followed him to the ramp, and before he went up the steps he had a word for each of them. The Arabs were sobbing shamelessly, like children. He had already given keepsakes to Fawzi and Abdel Kader and Gassem; impulsively now he removed his golden cufflinks, tie clasp and wedding ring and impressed them on the Three Stooges. They kissed his hands, and sobbed. He had first come to their country nearly three decades ago, before any one of them was born.

But it was to Christopher Grundoon that the Ambassador spoke last.

"Have you forgotten anything?" Christopher asked. "Is there anything else to do?"

"I guess not," the Ambassador said. "I would have appreciated a phone call from Mustafa."

The stewardess told him he must come aboard now. "Good-by, Christopher," he said. "Keep away from the Political Police, wherever you are. Why don't you write a real novel?"

"Perhaps I shall."

When he reached the top of the ramp, Fitz Pasha turned to wave. Christopher wanted to call up to him how much he cared, how deeply he loved him. "I heard Pullmotor and Mustafa have become quite chummy again," he blurted out.

No sooner were the words off his tongue than he loathed himself for having said them. But the Ambassador understood. "And why not, lad?" he called down. "Doesn't the earth belong to them—to the Borgians?"

21

The Borgians. Inheritors of the earth. Pullmotor and Mustafa were at that moment in a Land-Rover racing across the desert in the direction of Wadi Mafish. Their vehicle was in the vanguard of a great convoy of armored cars and military trucks filled to overflowing with American wheat.

"Jolly sporting of you to come along with me this afternoon, Paul," the President-designate said.

"We'll have to make it short and sweet. My plane leaves at ten."

"My driver here will bring you back in plenty of time. I'll probably have to pass the night in the Sheikh's dirty old tent."

"You're going to tell the Bedouins where all this wheat came from, of course," Pullmotor said.

"Am I?" Mustafa asked.

Five thousand tons of wheat airlifted to Al Khadra was, all

things considered, a reasonable enough ransom for Calvin Hampshire to pay for the sake of getting Pullmotor back in time to clean up the mess in South America. The wheat had arrived quickly—little more than a week after Mustafa demanded it. Moreover, the remainder of the half-million metric tons—and the medicines—were shortly to be sent along in ships. The nasty anti-American tirades over Radio Al Asima had already begun to subside; street riots against American imperialism in the other Arab capitals had sputtered out altogether. The serialization of Christopher Grundoon's horror novel in the newspapers had already set the stage for a new onslaught in another direction—a resumption of the sacred crusade against Great Britain. For the last two days, rumors had drifted through diplomatic receptions and dinner parties that Mustafa and Pullmotor had made some sort of deal. An immense amount of money was said to be involved—not quite as much as Mustafa had hoped for, but a generous sum even by American standards. In the *New York Times,* a front-page dispatch from that knowledgeable newspaper's State Department correspondent quoted a "high government official" as "categorically denying" that "anyone in the American Administration" had "ever intended to suggest" that the President-designate of Al Khadra was a communist.

"I do wish this desert weren't so *bumpy,"* Mustafa said.

"Well, this is hardly the place to be writing letters," Pullmotor observed.

"Not letters—this is the new Constitution."

"I should think you'd have your lawyers do that."

"I did. A dozen of them. Very sloppy job of work. So I'm writing it myself. Tell me, Paul, for the plebiscite, which would you consider a more convincing majority—ninety-seven point six per cent, or ninety-eight point eight per cent?"

"The first is more convincing, but the second might be more fashionable."

"In that case I'd better make it ninety-eight point two per cent. I wouldn't want anyone to call me a conformist. Dear me, I'm afraid this Constitution is going to be rather a hotch-potch. The lovely *Time* people won't like it at all, but it will just have to do until I can risk something more liberal. I was going to put in a bill of rights, habeas corpus, freedom of speech, assembly, bicameral legislature, independent judicature—the whole shooting match."

"Why don't you?" Pullmotor asked. "You know very well it would only be window-dressing."

"Because they don't deserve it! Not even as window-dressing! When they stop acting like children, I'll start treating them as grownups. That performance in the graveyard, that riot in the Pepsi-Cola plant, that attack on Fitz Pasha's limousine—disgraceful, disgusting. That reminds me. I meant to call Fitz Pasha to say good-by. Oh well."

"Now that he's gone, Mustafa, tell me—what did you really think of Fitzgibbon?"

"I liked him. Intelligent, well-informed, spoke beautiful Arabic. Perhaps a little too fond of the Arabs to represent his own country effectively. Whom is Hampshire sending to succeed him?"

"I doubt if that's been decided," Pullmotor said. "I suppose you'll want someone who speaks Arabic, like Fitzgibbon."

"I'd rather have someone who speaks only English—and whom Hampshire will listen to."

"I'll see what I can do."

"You know, Paul, I'm rather pleased that your country and mine have decided to be friends again. I don't know that I really much care for these Russians. They drink too much vodka, their English is atrocious, and they have even less sense of humor than you Americans. They bore me. Their first shipment of machinery arrived yesterday. It's pretty shoddy. I expect it will improve . . . otherwise I may have to mention the matter in some of my speeches."

The convoy of Land-Rovers, armored cars and military trucks were retracing the same route which Chuckles Vespucci had traveled on the day of his ill-fated expedition to Wadi Mafish. Soon they were away from the flat land of ebony gravel and volcanic clinker and the slightly fretted foothills, and navigating the gorges of those fantastic cliffs. On they went, underneath the cracked and fissured granite walls, below the boulders teetering on frail pedestals, the fantasy-formations of black lava, the malevolent pillars of bluish basalt, down and down those chasms so desolate, so timeless, so full of silence. Finally they emerged into the vast, endless valley far below the level of the sea, and they were at large on that glacial, crystalline plain. There again were the distant mountain peaks, veiled in a purplish, otherworldly vapor; there again were the wretched thorn and ashen stubble, garnished by the bare bones of ibex, and gazelle. And today on the lips of arid pools lay tangled heaps of snakes, dead of thirst, and the skeletons of jackal and jerboa and of a unicorn-profiled oryx, their bones picked clean by vultures who themselves, for want of water, littered the landscape in lifeless slumber. The plain was like a battlefield. The heat was less intense today, but still on all sides of the Land-Rover could be observed the glassy movement of mirages.

"A penny for your thoughts, Paul."

"I was just thinking, Mustafa—all this desolation, all this death—this is your country, this is where you came from."

"Look at that mirage there—olive trees, tamarisk, jacaranda. Such a variety of vegetation this afternoon! One day it's going to be within my power to make all these mirages come true. Someday this wilderness will be a network of canals interlaced with asphalt roads, housing developments and petrol stations. I will do it, Paul, you wait and see."

"I believe you will."

"We'll be making motorcars within five years, jet aircraft within ten. History is intoxicating. Didn't we own Spain once, and Sicily, and half of France? Is it too far-fetched to suppose that one day we will own them again? Great Britain a colony of Al Khadra—there's a thought. I can just see it now: Arab officers strutting down Piccadilly and the Charing Cross Road, poking diseased and servile Englishmen in the ribs with their swagger sticks. The brown man's burden! Tearing down the Nelson pillar in Trafalgar Square to make way for a mosque!"

"It will never happen, Mustafa, because in the meantime we intend to make you people into carbon copies of ourselves. My attempt to overthrow you last week was just a game of cowboys and Indians, but our real conspiracy will be vastly more difficult to resist. We have so many secret weapons, you see. We will pacify you with Pepsi, sweeten you with deodorant, and emasculate you with mouth wash. We will bury you—in dog biscuit, jiffy cake mix, and instant mashed potato. You're free now because you're poor, but we'll make you eager accomplices in your own enslavement. In fifty years everybody on earth will be identical. And they're not going to be English gentlemen, Mustafa—they're going to be Americans."

"We shall see. This heat makes me sleepy. Tell me that story again—about the time you dined at Windsor Castle."

"Mustafa, be reasonable. I've already repeated it twice."

"I want to hear it again."

"Well, when the Queen came down with Prince Philip, and we went in to eat—"

"No! Begin at the beginning. The part about the liveried footmen, and Lord Bertram-Bertram arriving a little bit tipsy."

And so once again Pullmotor told his tale of high life at Windsor Castle, until the President-designate, his alternate spells of enraptured listening and quiet laughter spent, was content to retreat into a world of his own making; he hummed a little as the Land-Rover winged over the trackless wasteland, his black eyes now luminous with the residue of vicarious pleasure, now heavy from the heat of day. He leaned his head against the window, and, still clutching the foolscap draft of his new Constitution, drowsed off. He was perspiring; the armpits of his khaki tunic were pooled with sweat; yet even in such awkward slumber the expression on his face was one of faint amusement.

The three men were in the front seat, Pullmotor sandwiched between the driver and Mustafa. Pullmotor turned his head and contemplated Mustafa for a few moments, wondering just what it was that made this erstwhile goatherd superior even to himself. He marveled that so handsome and masculine a man should cling so tenaciously, so jealously, to his virginity. Perhaps that was the secret—or rather, one of the secrets—of Mustafa's extraordinary strength: he was inaccessible. Mustafa began talking in his sleep. His mouth opened a little and out came a soft, intermittent stream of Arabic words, and a number of names, among which Pullmotor heard the uttering of his own. He turned to the driver, and saw the fellow's lips repeating silently to himself every word of Mustafa's, as if to enshrine them forever in his memory. "What is the President saying, corporal?" Pullmotor asked. *"Mit asif, ya*

Basha, bas ma bifham inglisi," the driver replied. For once Pullmotor keenly regretted that he spoke no language save his own. Ghandi had once told him, "When Nehru talks in his sleep, he talks in English." Why couldn't Mustafa do the same? Most inconsiderate of him.

Mustafa dreamed on. By barely perceptible degrees the Land-Rover ascended from the great depressed plain to higher land. Now they were in the midst of tiny individual valleys—wadis and watercourses where water never seemed to flow—bistrous and burnt umber in color; it was mid-afternoon. The Land-Rover lurched discourteously on a turn. Mustafa stirred.

"Paul," he asked sleepily, "wasn't it Bernard Shaw who said that Islam was the most enlightened form of Unitarianism?"

"That's right, Mustafa," Pullmotor laughed. "A Unitarian is a man who believes in one God—at most."

Mustafa giggled. "Now I know why you and I got along so well," he said. "We're both such upright Unitarians."

He dozed off again. Pullmotor thought he heard the cries of children from afar. He looked ahead and saw more umber hills and some incredible rock formations projecting at random from them, like great scoops of butterscotch pudding. The convoy came over the crest of a hill, and a tremendous roar reached for the heavens. Mustafa stirred, rubbed his eyes, and looked around him. The hills and ravines were filled with people—starving Bedouins, every one of them waiting to be fed. On every summit crouched hundreds of tribal women, like live gargoyles, whooping and ululating welcome. Through a great veil of dust in the distance charged dozens of camels, the men atop them stabbing the air with their flintlocks, firing haphazardly as they galloped forward to greet the convoy.

Within minutes the Land-Rover emerged into more open desert, bordered still by hills; this was Wadi Mafish. There, strewn before Pullmotor and the President-designate for almost as far as the eye could see, were scores of black, rectangular tents arranged anyhow on the desert floor, campfires blazing before them, exhaling clouds of white smoke drifting like djinns among the hundreds of camels and horses and fluttering pennants and the thousands of Bedouins who covered the face of the wilderness. A thousand flintlocks fired simultaneously, and then another roar was raised, and another and another without stopping, and the clapping of hands in cadence, all so deafening that Pullmotor had to put his palms to his ears. MUS-TA-FA! MUS-TA-FA! MUS-TA-FA! There were Bedouins in blue and saffron; Bedouins in crimson; Bedouins all in black; Bedouins in checkered head-cloths; Bedouins barefoot and sandaled; Bedouins in the trousers Mustafa had sent them three years ago peeping from beneath their skirts. There were camels —ashen, auburn and cream-colored, garlanded with woolly white and brown sheepskins and broad-striped purple and black blankets and green and yellow talismans and red and orange and turquoise tassels and tinkling bells; there were green flags, black pennants, blue banners. Pullmotor had never seen such a sight. In the center of the scene was pitched a great complex of tents encircled by bright carpets, upon them arrayed the great sheikhs of these many tribes which had come from near and far, from Wadi Zifer, Wadi Walashi and Wadi Walahaga; and at their head stood Hassan, patriarch of the Beni Talal, paramount sheikh of Al Khadra, his robes as white as his beard, leaning on his staff, a living Abraham, waiting paternally to receive the new Chief of State. MUS-TA-FA! MUS-TA-FA! MUS-TA-FA!

The President-designate observed the spectacle without speaking; his nap had given him a slight headache; and yet the same expression of faint amusement lingered on his lips, glimmered in his black gypsy eyes. In a glance he encompassed the saga of his birth, boyhood and circumcision; he saw the barren hills where less than twenty years before he had wandered half-starved, living on husks, an incipient consumptive in rags, tending goats with a stick. He had never returned here—until today, President of the Republic, a prodigal son come home to be reconciled with his people.

The convoy was halfway through the encampment and almost to Sheikh Hassan's tents when the hundreds of youths and multitudes of half-naked children, unable to contain their fervor any longer, stampeded toward the Land-Rover. On and on they came, so many of them sickly and consumptive, their bellies bloated with hunger, intent on snatching their redeemer out of the Land-Rover, enthroning him on their shoulders and transporting him in triumph to the pontiff of the desert. MUS-TA-FA! MUS-TA-

FA! MUS-TA-FA! It was at that moment that Pullmotor had his premonition.

Suddenly he knew with an uncanny certainty that when he left Wadi Mafish that afternoon he would never see Mustafa again. He did not know the reason; perhaps simple circumstance would intervene, or an assassin's bullet for Mustafa, or even his own death. Whatever, it was good-by. He would linger for a little while on the fringes of the ceremony and watch Mustafa—without a word of gratitude to America—distribute the sacks of grain; then the corporal would drive him back to the Sheraton-Zahra and at ten he would take the plane home to Washington to resume his insatiable pursuit of power without glory. Pullmotor had never felt deeply about anybody—not his wife, not Calvin Hampshire nor even his own sons. But as the sickly, pot-bellied children surrounded and arrested the Land-Rover and began to rock it from side to side, and he thought about never seeing Mustafa again, Pullmotor for possibly the first time in his life knew what it was to be sorry.

Now Mustafa's bodyguards had leaped from their armored cars and were struggling to beat back the children with rifle butts and truncheons. Mustafa motioned to them not to bother; Mustafa believed in the living, not in the dead. In a moment or two the hundreds of clutching hands would tear away the canvas topping from the Land-Rover, and at last they would possess their hero. MUS-TA-FA! MUS-TA-FA! MUS-TA-FA! And so it was good-by; Pullmotor was too touched to speak; he hoped his Arab friend would find the fitting words to seal such reciprocal esteem. Mustafa turned to the American and—in that last instant before the Bedouins snatched him away—uttered his farewell.

"Don't forget to send the medicines," he said.

About the Author

Born thirty-three years ago in Newton Centre, Massachusetts, Edward R. F. Sheehan still makes his permanent home there. Following graduation from Boston College and service in the U.S. Navy, he spent three years abroad as a foreign correspondent. Working for the *Boston Globe* and other New England newspapers in Europe, North Africa and the Middle East, he covered such events as the Hungarian uprising and the Suez crisis.

From 1957 until 1961 Mr. Sheehan served as press officer at the American embassies in Cairo and Beirut. Since then he has devoted his time to writing, and his articles have appeared in several American and English magazines, including *Harper's, The Saturday Evening Post* and *The Cornhill,* of London. *Kingdom of Illusion* is Mr. Sheehan's first novel, and he is already at work on a second.